THE MOON ON THE HILLS

BILL PAGE

THE MOON ON THE HILLS

Matador
9 De Montfort Mews
Leicester LE1 7FW, UK
Tel: (+44) 116 255 9311 / 9312
Email: books@troubador.co.uk
Web: www.troubador.co.uk/matador

ISBN 978-1906510-589

British Library Cataloguing in Publication Data.
A catalogue record for this book is available from the British Library.

Mixed Sources
Product group from well-managed
forests and other controlled sources
www.fsc.org Cert no. TT-COC-2082
© 1996 Forest Stewardship Council

Typeset in 11pt Stempel Garamond by Troubador Publishing Ltd, Leicester, UK
Printed in the UK by The Cromwell Press Ltd, Trowbridge, Wilts, UK

Matador is an imprint of Troubador Publishing Ltd

CHAPTER ONE

Late May, AD 367

Yesterday – and through all the other yesterdays of these three long, lonely years – I was so certain you were dead. They said the summer storm which hit the Zephyrus was the worst in living memory, that no ship ever built could have survived it. But in a secret country of my mind you never ceased to be warm and alive, sometimes even whispering to me in the quiet hours of the night as I drifted between waking and sleeping.

And when you whispered I saw your face – your small blue eyes and wide, expressive mouth, all framed in that tangled profusion of dark brown hair. Unruly, artless, never sleekly combed: sometimes you tied it back behind your ears with a ribbon, or sometimes the wind blew it back. It emphasised that protean quality of your face, those ever-changing expressions of light and shade, always animated, never still. Smiling, laughing, shaking your head to agree or disagree. Always that beguiling mixture of timidity and boldness, of vulnerability and confidence. Sometimes I'd turn and catch you looking at me shyly, as if thinking … what were you thinking? Or biting your lower lip when you were apprehensive, or happy, or excited – breathless to tell me some news or confidence or joke. You had a dozen faces, each one subtly different, and they could shade from one to another in the space of a heartbeat.

And your hands … sometimes gesturing animatedly, or with the spread fingers of one or both hands pressed against your throat and shoulders for emphasis as you talked. Sometimes, in your rare moments of seriousness, your head tilted slightly to one

1

side, you would sit on your hands, as though that were the only way you could keep them still ...

But now I think that nothing is certain, not even the past. Or those dreams that come out of the past.

It is shortly after sunrise in the little city of Corinium. Since well before dawn Saturninus has been sitting in his room, high in one of the semicircular bastion towers which flank the great Verulamium Gate, the chair reversed, his chin resting on his crossed wrists on the chair's high back as he gazes out through an unshuttered window, a blanket from the bed draped around his shoulders like a cloak. An awareness of distant footsteps begins to break into his restless thoughts.

Tense, he listens to the footsteps coming nearer, suddenly louder as they emerge from the staircase and onto the stone slabs of the passageway. They halt outside his door, then comes two quick raps on the oak. He relaxes and calls out, 'Come on in, Canio – it's not bolted.' A moment later the door is unlatched and opened, the hinge post creaking in its sockets, top and bottom.

'*Salve*, my Primicerius! Been awake long?'

'Since before first light.' Saturninus nods a welcome to his second in command, then turns back to the window. He notices, out of the corner of his eye, that Canio too is looking out of that window, as if trying to see what so interests him in the waking May countryside beyond the city walls.

You can't see them, Canio. The things I saw in the night are only pictures inside my head. I will tell you about them. But not just yet.

After forecasting the day's weather and mentioning that he had won three siliquae in a dice game the previous evening – using someone else's dice too – Canio enquires, with apparent casualness, 'Couldn't you sleep?'

'It happens,' Saturninus replies, trying to sound equally casual. 'Any particular reason for asking?' He does not turn again, aware that faces can sometimes betray more than words.

'Young Quintillus – he was on duty under here last night. Saw him in the barracks this morning and he told me he'd heard someone – or something – up here give a yell like a lost soul.'

Saturninus waits, wondering what else is coming.

'In the middle of the night it was, apparently. Quintillus said he thought you might have had a woman in here – that's why he didn't tell anyone, except me. That was his excuse, anyway. Did you …?'

'No.'

There's been no other woman in my life. Not since the first day we met in that stony vineyard beside the Moselle.

After a short silence, Saturninus adds softly, 'I could wish he'd said nothing.'

'Perhaps he was worried for you?'

'So why didn't he raise the alarm last night?'

Not that I would have wanted him to.

Canio shrugs. 'Scared of making a fool of himself, I suppose.'

Saturninus hesitates, as the competing urges to tell and not to tell struggle for mastery. 'I had a strange dream, that's all … Just a strange, strange, dream.'

How much – or how little – should I tell you, Canio?

He stares out at the great red disc of the rising sun, and at the long tree-shadows it casts across the distant hillsides. Then, impulsively, he cannot resist asking, 'But have you ever had a dream so vivid that it seemed more real than the world you woke to? Almost as if …' He stops, uncertain, the impulse regretted.

'As if what? Want to tell me about it?' Canio settles himself, uninvited, into the room's only other chair and scratches his chin through the close-cropped full beard that makes his long face so wonderfully wolf-like.

But Saturninus shakes his head. 'No, I'll tell you later. There are a few things I've got to do first.'

'Such as?'

'Oh, visit our old friend Clemens to retrieve a report that came in from Fonscolnis a little while back.'

'Which report – not that silly one?'

Right first time.

Saturninus watches Canio pull an exaggeratedly baffled face, but does not enlighten him further. Instead, he props against the wall the small lyre that had been resting on his lap, then pulls the chair around to face him. 'Meet me for breakfast at The Serpents. Maybe I'll tell you about the dream then.' Thinking it time to change the subject, he asks, 'Did anything else happen during the night – anything that I should know about?'

'No, not really; it was a fairly quiet night ... Oh, there was a little incident at Viventia's.'

'Serious?' Saturninus gets the impression that Canio hadn't really thought it worth mentioning.

'No, not what I'd call serious. It was the old story – two goat-brained rustics after the same girl, then one of them accidentally walked into a knife that the other just happened to be holding. He'll probably survive, if he keeps well away from the medics.'

'And the one who did it?'

Canio stretches and yawns. 'No name, and the description Viventia gave would fit half the male population of the hills. He was long gone by the time we arrived and we never got anything from the man he knifed, of course. He'll want to settle the score in his own way.'

'And probably will.' It is Saturninus's turn to yawn. 'Well, I'd better finish dressing ... see you at around the beginning of the third hour.'

Taking the hint, Canio gets up and starts towards the door.

But before he can reach it, Saturninus comes to a decision and asks, 'By the way, have you ever heard of a man called Caelofernus?'

'Caelofernus? No, I don't think so. Should I have?'

'Not necessarily; I just wondered, that's all. You've never

come across anyone of that name?'

'No: can't say that I've even heard the name before. Who is he?'

'Just someone I want to find.'

'Has this got something to do with your dream?' Canio asks suspiciously.

'Perhaps. I'll tell you at The Serpents, but in the meantime, while you're wandering around the city, could you …?'

'I'll ask around.' Canio sighs. 'What does this Caelofernus look like?'

'Oh, about my age – thirty or so. Tall too, at least as tall as me. Cruel eyes. Wild, rough hair and beard, both the colour of new oat straw. Good clothes though – the sort of clothes you wouldn't expect to see on a man worth less than two hundred gold solidi a year.'

'Not someone you'd forget in a hurry.'

Saturninus picks up the note of unease creeping into Canio's voice. 'No. And one more thing; make sure both our horses are ready for a long ride.'

'*Both* our horses, Primicerius, sir? I thought you'd been ordered to escort Old Laeto –'

'Sometimes known as His Perfection, Governor Laetinianus, I believe.'

'Escort him and our glorious leader, Aemilianus, all the way to Glevum today … Oh, *merda* – they don't want me to tag along as well, do they?'

'Don't worry yourself on that account, Canio. I don't think that either of us will be going to Glevum today. I have a feeling we'll be going north, up into the hills – Fonscolnis way, probably. Just wait and see.' Saturninus smiles: reassuringly, he hopes.

But Canio appears unconvinced. 'What makes you think that, my leader? Aemilianus will never let you off escort duty – especially if Laeto himself wants you along … Just why *does* he want you along, anyway?'

'To stop savage packs of barbarian dormice from leaping out of the hedges and molesting him. That's my theory anyway'

'Hill dormice are the size of badgers. You'll never wriggle out of it.'

'Want to bet?' Saturninus is aware that Canio is looking hard at him now, waiting for the explanation he is not yet ready to give.

'Bet? No, I don't think so,' Canio replies, uncharacteristically declining a wager. 'Saturninus ...'

'Yes?'

'Young Quintillus said it might have been a woman's name you called out last night.'

'Did he?' Saturninus hesitates, then can't stop himself from asking, 'And did he say what name?'

'Said it could have been Pascentia.'

Saturninus had known it was coming, but he still feels his heart miss a beat to hear that name spoken by someone else. 'Pascentia? I can't say I've ever come across a woman called Pascentia here in Corinium. Have you?'

In Burdigala, in Londinium, and beside the quiet waters of the Moselle. But not here. Never here.

'No, I can't say that I have. Must be one or two though.'

He sees that Canio is waiting for more, but time is passing too swiftly now. He smiles a farewell. 'Breakfast at The Serpents, remember?'

Canio looks disappointed. 'I'll be there.' He walks to the door and with droll formality lays his fist across his chest in salute before leaving.

Saturninus listens to his footsteps dying away, then turns back to the window. A heavy cart is trundling out of the city and across the stone bridge that spans the little River Churn, its iron-rimmed wheels crunching the packed limestone gravel of the road surface. He watches, with unseeing eyes, as it slowly dwindles into the distance, while into his mind there return drifting ghosts from the two great tragedies of his life.

As in the dream, he wanders again through the battlefield of Mursa Major, in the Danube-bordered province of Pannonia, where, as a fourteen-year-old boy who loved books and music, he had seen his father killed and his boyhood abruptly ended, to be replaced by the corrosive brutalities of a soldier's life. A life that had taken him further and further away from these hills he had once called home, and to which he had at last returned as a stranger.

And I can see your face again, Pascentia. As it was at Burdigala. Wistful, your lips redder, as they always were when pursed in worry. Fingers distractedly combing aside the wind-blown strands of long, dark hair. Your face so close I can almost smell the perfume of your skin.

Now growing ever smaller and indistinct.

Now dissolving into infinity as the Zephyrus sails down the Garonne with the morning tide on that July day.

The tip of his tongue moves unconsciously over his lips, seeking once again the faint salt of her tears. Tears begin to blur his own eyes and he brushes them roughly away.

Who are you, Caelofernus? And where are you? In the dream, that damned priest, Gulioepius, led me to you. So he must at least know where you are – or if he doesn't, then the dream makes no sense at all.

He quickly finishes dressing. To the dark green uniform of tunic and loose-fitting trousers he is already wearing, he adds a pair of soft leather calf-boots, a flexible cuirass of overlapping steel scales and a bronze helmet – both the latter made lustrous by polishing with fine sand. He straps around his waist a broad leather sword belt, then unsheathes and checks the sword from blade tip to the ivory hilt that terminates in the snarling head of a man-lion. The sword was given to him by his father sixteen years ago, just before they set off on the long road that led to Mursa. He stares at it, then abruptly sheathes the blade. He shakes his head angrily, but the unhappy awakened memories linger.

Emerging from the gloom of the gateway staircase, he returns the

7

salute of the guard and begins walking quickly along the wide
streets towards the already-bustling heart of Corinium. Passing
the rows of narrow-fronted shops, which shelter behind their
stone colonnaded and roofed verandas, he smells the aromas of
hot food that waft from bakeries and cookshops whose ovens
have been alight since before dawn.

*I've got to go north, but there's no point in telling Aemilianus
why. I once heard him say that warning dreams are nothing but
pagan nonsense. Which, for a man who believes in demons, was
a curious remark.*

*Perhaps I could plead sickness, then go north after he's left for
Glevum. But what will happen when he returns this afternoon
and finds me gone? He might be angry enough to send someone
after me to find out what I'm up to – someone who would make
a nuisance of himself.*

*No: this is the surest way. Why break down the gate when the
sentry will open it for me?*

He walks on, along the grid-iron of metalled streets that
carve the old city into insulae blocks, until he comes to the
archway which leads into the early morning shadows of the
forum piazza. To his left broods the great basilica. To his right,
beyond a low flight of steps, stands the *praetorium*, the official
residence of the governor. He turns and walks towards it,
noticing how the low morning sun has lit like a flame the great
bronze figure of Jupiter standing high on top of his limestone
column in the centre of the forum. Saturninus pauses, glances
around to make sure he is unobserved, then lets his fingertips
drag along the stone as he passes.

*If the old gods exist, and care about the fates of men, then in
these coming fateful days I need them to be on my side.*

He walks up the steps, nods to the guards and slips through
the large double gates into the outer court of the *praetorium*. A
hundred paces and several flights of stairs bring him to the door
of an office high up on the north-west side of the building. He
pauses, listening.

When I was a child, I was taught that it is wrong to deceive.

But to find Caelofernus I must go north – to Gulioepius.

And to go north today I must have a reason that even Aemilianus will accept.

And so, it seems, I must deceive.

CHAPTER TWO

He knocks softly and opens the door. There is no one inside.

Good morning to you, Clemens ... Mind if I help myself to a report that came in from Fonscolnis a little while ago? No, don't get up. I'm sure I can find it for myself.

Saturninus looks back to confirm that the corridor is deserted, then begins rifling quickly through the racks of tightly-rolled scrolls that line both sides of Clemens' office.

What he wants is not where he expected it to be. Time races. 'Clemens, how in the name of sweet Venus do you ever find anything in this chaos?' he murmurs. He glances out into the corridor again. It is still deserted, but soon ... Suddenly he finds the scroll he is seeking, unrolls it just far enough to confirm that it is indeed the correct one, then lets it re-curl and taps one end on the desk to straighten it.

Further down the corridor he reaches his own small office. Once there, he shuts the door carefully behind him and places the parchment on his desk, beside the inkwell and palimpsest scraper. Not long afterwards he quietly opens the door, looks both ways, then gently waves the partially unrolled scroll from side to side in the air currents that breathe along the corridor.

He scans through the document one last time, although now his thoughts are far away.

That last morning when we parted on the quayside at Burdigala, when you hugged me tearfully and whispered the dream that had come to you in the night.

You said that you had seen us walking, hand in hand, along a track that passed through a summer meadow; a place where the warm breeze sighed through the long grasses and the sun was bright in the blue sky. Then we came to a place where the track forked – and you went one way, and I the other, down the way that led towards a dark wood.

You said that you cried out to me – called me to come back to you. But I kept on walking, and you watched me until I had vanished into the wood and you were left quite alone.

You told me then that you feared the dream meant that something terrible was going to happen to me. On that quayside I laughed – said that the dream was nothing more than the product of the cheese you had eaten the previous evening. And promised that we would be together again in a few short weeks. And kissed you. And never saw you again. Except in dreams.

He finds Vitalinus, Prefect Aemilianus's clerk, in the Prefect's outer office. The clerk, a thin-faced, intense man in his early twenties, is re-cutting a quill with a small folding knife, the bone handle of which is carved into the outline of a hunting dog chasing a hare.

As Saturninus approaches, Vitalinus stands up. But before the clerk can move towards the great double doors of the inner office, Saturninus has smiled, knocked, and walked straight in, to find Aemilianus sitting behind his magnificent desk of carved and polished Purbeck marble.

A forbidding-looking man, Gaius Ulpius Aemilianus is Prefect in charge of all the units of the civil guard, or corps of *beneficiarii* as it is still officially known, in the central region of the province of Britannia Prima. When Saturninus enters he raises his head briefly, frowns, then continues studying one of several papers that litter the desk.

Aemilianus is the brother of Governor Laetinianus's wife. He is also a fervent Christian, no other religion offering such an explicit promise of protection against the powers of evil. It is a promise that Aemilianus clings to like a drowning man, for he has a morbid terror of magicians and sorcerers and, above all, of those mythical creatures called demons that such men are believed to control.

And Saturninus knows where this terror came from, knows that...

Long ago, on an idyllic summer day deep in the sunlit countryside of the south-eastern Gallic province of Narbonensis Secunda, the four year old Aemilianus chanced to notice a strange-looking crow perched on the weathered stone shrine of some obscure rustic godling. With a child's curiosity he had watched the bird, haloed by sunlight, until it appeared to catch sight of him. And in that instant the crow turned into a small, dark man, naked but for a cloak. This creature sprang up and seemed to come running slowly through the air straight towards him, growing ever larger, the cloak streaming out behind. What happened next, Aemilianus could never, ever, remember.

And this not-knowing is the worst part of it all, because nothing that his tortured imagination can now invent seems too bizarre or horrific to have actually happened.

Saturninus did not learn any of this from Aemilianus himself, but from those few people to whom the Prefect confided, a little here, a little there, when seeking escape in wine. He has never before exploited this knowledge, and has told no one that he possesses it, not even Canio. But today... For a moment he wavers, his conscience pricking.

But today I must go north, and what else will make you send me there, Aemilianus?

He closes the doors behind him, salutes, and says quietly, 'Sir, an odd report has come in from Fonscolnis – one I think you ought to see. I thought at first that it was just someone's idea of a joke, but now that I've re-read it I'm not so sure. Apparently a *paganus* went digging for buried treasure in a hillside somewhere up to the north of there – '

'As the rustics in this part of the world sometimes do, damn them,' Aemilianus mutters, not raising his eyes again from the closely-written document he is reading. 'So – deal with the matter yourself. Now, if that's all you wanted to see me about, I must continue with my preparations for the Glevum tax shortfall inquiry.' He looks up sharply. 'You haven't forgotten have you – that you are to accompany us there for the next five days?'

'No, sir, I haven't forgotten. However, it seems that the *paganus* didn't find any treasure.'

'Then why – ?'

'But what he does claim to have found and seen is somewhat ... disturbing.'

'Disturbing? How?'

'Well, if the man can be believed, then he just might have uncovered an entrance to what some call the Lower World.'

Aemilianus looks gratifyingly startled, so Saturninus adds, 'But perhaps you should read the report yourself and draw your own conclusions.' Unrolling the top of the scroll, he places it on the desk in front of the Prefect, pointing with his index finger to the beginning of the relevant passage.

Aemilianus stares at him and frowns instinctively, but then begins studying the document intently, quoting aloud with increasing frequency, until, '"... Dug around the rock for much of the night ... managed to dislodge it just before dawn, but could see nothing inside the hole because it was so dark." Well, there's a surprise!'

Saturninus smiles politely, and Aemilianus continues, '"Started digging with his hands, but couldn't find the bowl ..." What bowl?' He looks up, but Saturninus shrugs to profess ignorance. '"Then he heard the sound of marching feet, and out of the hole came an army of fierce men led by a giant who had no head ..."' Aemilianus stops abruptly, clearly horrified by what he has just read. 'Dear Father in Heaven,' he whispers, 'do you hear that – no head!'

'Yes, I must admit that is ridiculous, but – '

'No, you don't understand, do you? No ... head.' Aemilianus repeats slowly, and Saturninus observes that he seems more than a little agitated by the description of the giant. 'Have you really no idea of who – of what – that might have been?'

'Sir?'

'Surely you've heard of The Great Headless One?'

'Who?'

Let him draw his own conclusions: that way he'll believe them.

'Oh, the name may sound faintly amusing to the ignorant, but let me assure you that he is one of the most terrible demons in all the legions of Hell.' Aemilianus's voice drops to an awed whisper. 'I once read – in the course of my official duties, you understand – a forbidden book from Aegyptus, one of the so-called magical papyri. Not only did it describe the creature, but it even contained a picture of him, drawn by a man who had actually seen him with his own eyes. The picture was surrounded by what I was informed were spells – incantations by which the wicked might summon the demon up from the Infernal Regions to do their bidding. They were written in Greek, so mercifully I couldn't read them myself, but I have heard it said ...' Aemilianus's voice drops another register until it is barely audible ...'that whosoever can command him could, with his help, seize and rule the whole empire. Think of that – and of what our sacred Emperor Valentinian would do if an informer were to allege that we had seen this report and then ignored it. That we had not even attempted to suppress that ... that creature, to prevent some would-be usurper from seeking to control him. And there are spies and informers everywhere.'

Saturninus notes dispassionately that the Prefect has gone very pale, his forehead glistening with a thousand minute beads of sweat. 'But do you think it really was a demon that idiot rustic saw? You know as well as I do that stories like these tend to get exaggerated every time they're told. I mean, look at this.' He indicates a few lines below the point where Aemilianus stopped reading. 'It says here that the men who came out of the hole just walked off into the sky. Can you really believe that?'

'Believe it? Of course I can believe it! There's nothing that demons can't do, absolutely nothing – walk, run, fly – through air, through fire, through the very earth itself if they wish – it's all the same to them! And now some moronic rustic has ...' Aemilianus stops suddenly, and with a convulsive effort appears to control his anger. In silence he stares down at the parchment and breathes deeply and evenly, although the pulsing of a zigzag vein in his right temple betrays a continuing violence within. Then he says hoarsely, 'You must of course investigate this at once.'

'But I can't, sir, not with the Glevum enquiry about to – '

'Oh, damn that! Priorities man, priorities! This must be dealt with now, without delay. Don't worry about His Perfection. It's best that we don't inform him of this … this incident. But I'll think of a good reason to explain your absence to him.'

Yes, I'm sure you will. So necessity makes deceivers of us all.

'If those are your orders, then I'll go today.'

'Excellent. And if you leave this morning you should be at that hillside by, what, early afternoon? When you get there …' Aemilianus's voice trails away, seemingly undecided.

'Sir?'

'When you get there, block up that hole. Block it up so completely that nothing can ever, *ever* come out of it again.'

Saturninus thinks he sees Aemilianus actually shudder, as if the man's imagination is picturing what might have emerged into the daylight less than twenty miles away across the hills. And now might be much, much closer. His conscience pricks again.

Aemilianus pauses, then says, 'Now, is that quite clear?' which Saturninus recognises as being the Prefect's usual way of indicating that an interview is over.

'Completely, sir. I'll be ready to leave within the hour.' He salutes smartly and turns to go.

'Oh, and one more thing, Primicerius.'

'What's that?'

'Take Vitalinus with you. He can make a transcript of your interrogation of that damned *paganus*. Write down every word, on the spot.'

What!

'Is that entirely …' Saturninus stops himself before the word 'wise' can escape, seeing Aemilianus's face begin to take on the

15

affronted look it always does when one of his decisions is questioned. 'Very good. I'll brief him on my way out.'

'No need; I can do that myself. But I don't want either of you gadding about in the hills for too long – when the interrogation is concluded, make sure you return to Corinium without delay.'

'I certainly will, sir.' Saturninus opens both leaves of the tall doors, then closes them carefully behind him.

He smiles at Vitalinus, who gives him a resentful glare in return. Controlling access to Aemilianus is supposed to be his prerogative, a prerogative which Saturninus routinely ignores. Saturninus notes the glare, pauses, then whispers, 'A word of warning: if I were you, I wouldn't make any plans for the rest of the day. As a result of certain information which I've just brought to his attention, I think Aemilianus will be sending for you shortly.'

He deliberately does not explain, and watches impassively as a flicker of alarm crosses Vitalinus's face: Canio once hinted to him that the clerk occasionally conducts a little private business involving the unauthorised use of Aemilianus's official seal.

As he walks away through the echoing halls of the *praetorium*, Saturninus pictures Aemilianus, still sitting at his desk: first frowning again, then looking down, intending to re-read the scroll – only to find that it has vanished. In his mind's eye, he can even see the look of irritated bafflement on the Prefect's face. And the fear that follows it.

One thing at least is certain: neither you nor Clemens will ever see this particular scroll again.

And he touches the front of his cuirass to reassure himself that it is still there.

CHAPTER THREE

The Twin Serpents is a large bar and eating house situated one block north of the forum. When Saturninus arrives it is still busy, serving breakfast to a diverse crowd of the city's inhabitants – mostly men, but with a scatter of tough-looking women of various ages. Julia, wife of Reburrus the owner, is standing in her usual spot behind the bar as she watches – *like a greedy starling,* Saturninus thinks – the scurrying slave girl of about fourteen, whose face still retains a freshness that two or three more years of toil will destroy for ever.

Saturninus does not know her name: the girls here come and go so often – some sold on to new owners, others simply running away, desperate to escape Julia's cane and Reburrus's goatish appetites, despite the draconian penalties which the law imposes on captured runaways.

I remember that one girl, vanished now like smoke, declared this place was named long ago in anticipation of its current owners. Despite his dark thoughts, he smiles at the recollection.

Walking down the room he passes through zones of smells rising up from the steaming bowls on the bar top, or drifting in from the kitchen beyond. Smells of fresh-baked bread, and rissoles in liquamen – the pungent fish sauce used throughout the Roman world to disguise the taste of other foods, particularly meat that is less than fresh. Seeing Reburrus emerging from the kitchen carrying two large loaves, Saturninus points upwards. 'Is Canio here yet?'

'Yes, Primicerius, he's here all right. Been here a while,' Reburrus adds sourly.

And Canio never pays for anything he eats or drinks at The Serpents.

On one side of the room is an archway, closed off by a curtain of dark blue cloth. Saturninus eases it aside and walks up a flight of stone steps and into a chamber containing a table and four comfortable-looking wickerwork armchairs. The walls and ceiling are whitewashed and brightly painted in a pattern of octagons with exotic birds at their centres.

Canio glances up as Saturninus enters, spoon poised halfway between his mouth and a large bowl of stew. '*Salve* again, Primicerius. What are you having this morning?'

'I haven't ordered yet. What's that you've got?'

'Supposed to be mutton stew with beans. Try some?'

Saturninus sniffs the proffered spoon and grimaces. 'Smells like a Pict's armpit: sure you haven't got one of Reburrus's famous barking sheep in there?'

'Tastes all right to me.'

Saturninus shrugs. 'Well, whatever it is, it certainly didn't come out of Rosmerta's magic tub. What else has the old lecher got today?'

'Not much. Roast wood pigeon, perhaps – I remember someone saying he'd bought a dozen birds from the bailiff of a villa somewhere down south.'

'No, not pigeon. There's no flavour in them at this time of year.' Saturninus trots quickly back down the steps and seeks out Reburrus, then returns carrying a small loaf, still steaming hot from the oven, and a red pottery bowl containing a clutch of hard-boiled eggs. Behind him comes the girl, carrying a flagon of Celtic beer and two beakers of pale green Rhenish glass.

When the girl has gone, with a coin from him and a wink from Canio, Saturninus settles down in one of the armchairs and begins eating. Between eggs he remarks, 'Better make the most of that stew. We'll be setting out for Fonscolnis by the end of the third hour.'

Canio looks up and eyes him sardonically. 'So your intuition was right then. How did you manage it?'

'I didn't "manage" anything. Aemilianus wants us to

investigate that report about the odd things a *paganus* is supposed to have seen when he went a-treasure hunting.'

Canio appears more than a little sceptical. 'What? I thought we both agreed that report was nonsense.'

Which it was.

'Nonsense or not, it's got us both a ride out in the fresh air. Did you get the horses ready?'

'I did, my leader.'

'Good. But you'll have to saddle up a mule as well: we've got to take that little darling Vitalinus along with us – Aemilianus's orders,' Saturninus adds quickly, in an attempt to forestall the inevitable protest from Canio.

'Oh, *merda*,' Canio mutters. 'I can do without that. What *is* this all about, Saturninus?'

'I've just told you.'

'But that's not the real reason, is it? Come on – it's got something to do with that dream of yours, hasn't it?'

'Perhaps. What did you find out about Caelofernus?'

'Not a thing. Like me, nobody seems to have even heard of him.'

No. I somehow knew in my bones that we'd learn nothing here in Corinium. But I can't leave the city without trying.

'It might help if I knew why you want to find him?' Canio adds.

'Because I have to kill him.' Saturninus looks him directly in the face as he speaks, but if Canio is surprised he doesn't show it.

'Any particular reason?' he says slowly. 'Or shouldn't I ask?'

'To stop him killing me.'

'So … we're back to that dream again, aren't we? Look, you might as well tell me about it. I wasn't in it, was I?'

'No, you weren't in it.' Saturninus knows that telling is inevitable now. And besides, if Canio is coming with him on his search for Caelofernus then he has a right to know. 'All right, I'll tell you.' He takes a long, slow drink and begins.

'In the dream it was night and I was alone, wandering among

the dead on a great battlefield. It was in moonlight, brighter than it had ever been before – so bright that I could see the scattered bodies of men and horses stretching far away into the distance.'

And I was carrying the battered helmet that bore my then-new name scratched inside the neck guard. Over the years I've often wondered who he was, that other Saturninus – what he looked like, where he came from, whether he too survived the battle? The chances are he died at Mursa: just scattered bones now. I'll never know.

'I was walking from body to body, sometimes moving on immediately, sometimes crouching down to look more closely at the face.'

But none was my father's. I can never find his body.

For a moment Saturninus fears that Canio is about to ask who he had been searching for, so he says quickly, 'And I was still wandering when I saw the priest. Something made me look up, and there he was, standing a hundred paces away, his pure white robe almost glowing among all the shades of grey. With the tip of the long staff he carried he was pointing to the grassy hillside behind us.'

Even at that distance I thought I recognised him, and when I came closer I said, 'Gulioepius? … it is you, isn't it?' And Gulioepius bowed slightly in acknowledgement.

'He told me his name was Gulioepius. Then he turned and started walking away up the hillside. I said, "No, don't go." But Gulioepius kept walking, so I followed him. I followed for what seemed miles, until at last he halted on the steep scarp edge of the hill. And there he stood, looking down over the moonlit plain far below. And all over that plain fires were burning, like living things, forever changing shape as great orange tongues of flame leapt upwards and as quickly died.

'I asked, "What is this place?" And Gulioepius slowly swept out an arm as if to say, "Look around you." And so I turned, and saw the great stones for the first time. They stood in a circle, like those set up long ago by the old, vanished people. There were at least forty of them, most as tall as a man, and they looked so ancient and weathered that they might have been there since the beginning of time itself.

'Gulioepius went inside the circle, moving around the stones and peering at each one in turn. I watched, until at last he seemed to find the one he had been searching for and beckoned me to come and see. This stone was much like all the others, except that on it was carved a single word in deep-cut letters a finger high. That word was CAELOFERNUS.'

Saturninus pauses, half expecting Canio to say something when he hears that name. But Canio remains silent, waiting.

'I remember that Gulioepius's staff was tipped with a silver hand that held a pomegranate between the tips of its extended fingers.'

The pomegranate which is a symbol of eternal life. And resurrection.

'And there were spiral twists in its wooden shaft, like those made by honeysuckle bines as they wind around growing saplings.'

And the honeysuckle's fragrance evokes the sweetness of love.

'He touched the top of the Caelofernus stone with that silver pomegranate, and straightaway the stone shimmered and quivered in the moonlight … and turned into a living man. A man who wore an expensive tunic, brightly coloured and richly embroidered: a man with wild hair and beard, golden as the sun – even in the moonlight I knew that. And cruel eyes that were staring straight at me.'

Canio seems about to say something now, but Saturninus forestalls him with a raised palm and says, 'But now Gulioepius was searching again among the standing stones, searching until he found another that he seemed to recognise. This second stone bore no name, or none that I could see. But with the silver pomegranate Gulioepius turned it into another living man, one whose face was hidden by the hood of the long cloak he wore. I was still looking at this second man –'

Oh sweet Venus, it's just come to me – perhaps it wasn't a man! That first day I met you beside the Moselle you were wearing …

'When suddenly I felt a pull at my waist. I swung around and realised that my sword was gone and that the man who had been the Caelofernus stone now held it and was striding towards the man in the cloak.'

But if it was you, Pascentia, then what was it that the dream was telling me?

'I knew instinctively what he was going to do. I tried to shout a warning, but my tongue was paralysed and no sound would come. And then the man, Caelofernus, stabbed the sword – my sword – deep into the body of the cloaked man. His legs buckled, and he fell backwards onto the grass. I stared at Caelofernus, and Caelofernus stared back, smiling like an evil satyr.

'Then I started running towards him, but he just glided away like a moon-shadow, back to his place in the circle. And the moment he reached it, he simply melted back into the stone that he had been.

'I remember crying out, "Gulioepius! – what in the names of all the gods is happening here?" before I realised that Gulioepius had gone. I ran from stone to stone looking for him, but he'd vanished, and I was left alone with the dead man and that huge full moon, that floated pale gold and serene in the night sky above me, as the only witnesses to what had happened there.

'I thought I knew who the dead man was, but I had to be sure. So I walked over to him, knelt and eased back the hood. And there, staring up at me, as if in a hazy mirror, was my own dead face.'

But perhaps it wasn't my face? When I woke I was so sure, but now …

'And … the dream ended there.'

Except that, afterwards, I think I had another dream. I saw a beach, with the surf roaring in the distance and never-ending lines of wavelets rolling in to the shore. The beach was long and sandy, curving away into the distance on both sides, and enclosed by great dunes scattered with spiky grass. And crawling up that beach on her hands and knees was a woman in a blue dress. Her head was down and her long, wet hair half-covered her face – but I knew it was you.

Or perhaps it wasn't a real dream at all? It was so brief – more a momentary vision – and already my memories of both dream and vision are relentlessly fading, leaving only memories of memories.

Canio exhales a long breath. 'Was it a real place, this battlefield?' he asks. 'Somewhere you'd actually been? I know men often dream of battles they've fought in.'

Canio, I trust you as much as any man I know. But not enough to tell you that I fought at Mursa. Inevitably you'd ask which side I was on, and today there's probably no one left alive who knows that I was part of Magnentius's rebel army on that terrible day.

Saturninus refills his glass and says blandly, 'It was just a nameless battlefield, and all battlefields look the same, don't they? The way that all dead men look the same. All the same ... all different.'

He notices Canio's bushy eyebrows moving upwards slightly.

'That same dream had come to me before,' he volunteers. 'Only then it always ended with me still wandering lost among the dead. Last night was the first time the priest appeared ... and Caelofernus too.'

'So you believe the dream was a warning. You think this Caelofernus is going to kill you on the night of the full moon – unless, of course, you kill him first. And the full moon is, what ...?'

'Four days away, Canio.'

Only four days to find and kill a man I've never seen or even heard of. Except in a dream.

'As I see it, I have three alternatives: run away and hide, stay here and let Caelofernus come to me, or go after him – take the fight to the enemy. Which one would you choose?'

'Running seems safest.'

'I was taught never to run away.'

It was beaten into me.

'Besides, where would I run to? And instinct tells me that if I wait until the full moon, then Caelofernus will find me and kill me wherever I am. But if I can find him before that moon rises …'

Canio pulls a face. 'But what makes you think you'll find him at Fonscolnis? That place in your dream wasn't Fonscolnis, was it? There's no stone circle around those parts that I ever heard of.'

'Fonscolnis is just a staging post – somewhere on the way to somewhere else. That priest, Gulioepius – I think I know where he comes from. A dozen or so miles north of Fonscolnis, in a wood on the west-facing scarp edge of the hills, there's a temple dedicated to the goddess of a spring that rises there. Do you know the place?'

'I've heard of it. Never been there though.'

'No matter. The important thing is that in the dream it was Gulioepius who led me to Caelofernus – so he must know who Caelofernus is and where I can find him.'

'Yes, I suppose he must. Strange dream though,' Canio adds uneasily.

'Strange dream,' Saturninus agrees. He sees more questions forming on Canio's face, questions he doesn't want to answer – or perhaps cannot answer. He quickly drains his glass and stands up. 'So, now you know why we're going north today. Before we leave though, I want to make a few enquiries of my own, here in Corinium.'

'Then I'll see you at the stables at around the end of the third hour, my leader.' Canio stretches, belches vigorously and begins helping himself to the remaining eggs.

Saturninus snaps his fingers. 'That reminds me, would you call in at old Eutherius's place and buy me a flask of his best horse purge. Make sure it's well stoppered and leave it in one of my saddlebags.'

'There's nothing wrong with Antares, is there? He looked fine to me when Bupitus was saddling him.'

'No, he's in the best of health. But get it anyway,' Saturninus calls out over his shoulder as he hurries down the steps, 'you never know what might happen on the journey.'

Do you, Vitalinus?

CHAPTER FOUR

The small stone house of Eutherius the apothecary stands in a narrow street which cuts across one of the insula blocks in a poor quarter of the city. When Canio arrives he notices that the solitary ground floor window on the street side is shuttered. But aware that this isn't unusual, even in summer, he gives the door a cursory knock, lifts the latch and pushes it open. By the light of a small charcoal brazier which burns day and night, whatever the season, he makes out the figure of the old man sitting immobile in a high wicker armchair. The lurid light and the shadows cast by the fretted rim of the brazier accentuate the furrows and creases in his face and make him appear as old as Death itself.

'Aren't you awake yet, you old slug?' Canio asks amiably.

Eutherius peers into the strong daylight against which Canio stands silhouetted in the doorway. 'Who's there?' he demands irritably. 'Whoever you are, be so good as to come in and close the door – do you want me to catch my death of cold?'

'Cold? It's not cold – the swallows have come and summer's almost here. Don't you ever open your window?'

'When you're my age it's always winter. Oh, it's you, Ducenarius Canio. What do you want today?'

Canio thinks he sounds less than overjoyed by his arrival. 'That's a damned cheerful greeting. Aren't you pleased to see me?' he asks, stepping into the room and latching the door behind him. Wisely not waiting for a reply, he continues, 'What I want, Eutherius my ancient friend, if it's not too much trouble of course, is a bottle of your finest horse purge.'

'Do you indeed? Don't you trust the veterinary skills of the ostlers at the guards' stables any more? Not that I'd blame you if you didn't. From what I've heard of Bupitus and his crew, their only real talent in that line of work is for stealing large quantities of oats and getting away with it.'

'You shouldn't believe all you hear,' says Canio with ironic gravity. 'A more honest bunch of men never shovelled horseshit.'

Eutherius grunts his disbelief. 'So what is it for, may I ask?'

'For a horse, naturally. My primicerius Saturninus's horse, to be exact. He and I are setting out on a journey today and he seems to have a premonition that the beast will fall sick somewhere along the way.'

'So why doesn't he take another horse?'

'How in the names of the fornicating *Parcae* should I know? Why don't you go and ask him? I'm sure he'd welcome your interest in the matter.'

'Never take the names of the *Parcae* in vain, Canio. I merely asked the obvious question. Anyway, which one do you want – stallion's or mare's?'

'What's the difference?' asks Canio, without thinking.

The old man snickers. 'Now that's a question I never thought I'd live to hear you ask, Canio. Not you of all people!'

'Oh, very funny. You should have been on the stage – with your face you'd save a fortune on masks. You know damned well what I mean.'

'Well now, Master Canio, the difference is mainly that your stallion's is more powerful. It contains more of – well, everything. And a little bit of something else besides,' Eutherius adds with a benign smile.

'Then that's the one I want, Ancient One.'

With some difficulty, Eutherius levers his withered body up out of the chair and begins to peer along his shelves. He scans across dozens of small pottery bowls with lids bearing cryptic signs in thick black ink, and rows of glass vessels, each partially filled with liquids varying from the colourless to the smokily opaque. Bunches of dried and drying herbs hanging from the ceiling beams obstruct his search, their sharp, competing fragrances permeating the whole room. Rummaging between these bunches and between small, square-sectioned sticks of eye-salve, each bearing the impress of a tiny stamp that reads on one face EUTHERIUS'S SALVE FOR SORENESS AND REDNESS OF THE EYES, and on another DISSOLVE IN WHITE OF EGG, he at last appears to find what he is looking for.

It is a blue glass bottle with a globular body and a long, thin neck. The bottle bears no label, but Eutherius lifts it down, removes the stopper, sniffs cautiously at the contents and hums apparent approval. He pours half of the pale yellow contents into a small flask of dull orange pottery, the neck of which he then closes with a wooden bung. The bung he seals with molten wax from a taper softened in the heat above the brazier. Handing the flask to Canio he says, 'Just add it to a bucket of water and make sure that the horse drinks it all. It'll cure anything from colic to glanders.'

Canio weighs the flask up and down in his hand. 'Perhaps I should try some myself. I've been feeling a bit rough first thing in the morning these last few days.'

'I really wouldn't advise it, Canio. Or if you do, then please make sure that none of your bodily orifices are pointing in my direction.'

'Powerful stuff, eh?' whispers Canio with exaggerated respect.

'Powerful enough.'

'Right then, how much do I owe you for this wonderful elixir?'

'To you, half a siliqua.'

'What's the usual price?'

'Half a siliqua.'

Canio grunts with something close to amusement and counts out the copper coins, clinking them one by one into an empty pottery bowl on the table.

He is halfway through the door, on his way out, when the idea strikes him. 'Have you ever heard of a man called Caelofernus?'

'Who – Caelofernus? Cae-lo-fer-nus,' the old man repeats slowly, as if rolling the name over in his brain to examine it from all sides. 'No. Can't say that I have. Who is he?'

'Just someone a friend asked me to find.' Canio closes the door again. 'Perhaps you could look into your fire and see where he is?'

He sees a flicker of surprise cross Eutherius's face. 'I don't do that sort of thing any more,' the old man says sharply. 'You of all people should know that – it was your master the Prefect that banned it, remember? May Atropos cut his thread,' he mutters under his breath.

Canio smiles and leans across the table. 'I know that well enough, Ancient One. But you and I both know that it still goes on, and I've heard rumours that you are one of those who do it – for a small fee, of course. Now, a man in my position,' he continues reflectively, 'really ought to investigate rumours like that. But then, we're old friends. And friends do little favours for each other … don't they?'

For a long moment Canio watches Eutherius stare him straight in the face, as if trying to decide whether or not to brazen it out. But Canio out-stares him, and the old man's eyes drop.

He sighs. 'What do you want to know about this Caelofernus?'

'Where I can find him will do – for a start.'

Eutherius stands again and pulls aside the curtain that closes off the doorway to a back room. 'Wait – I won't be long.' He does not invite Canio to follow him.

Through the arched doorway Canio glimpses, in the light of a solitary oil lamp within, a room quite unlike the one in which he stands. There the walls are plastered and frescoed with scenes of satyrs and maenads and fauns, revelling and dancing in a leafy summer countryside to which winter never comes. Then the curtain is tugged closed and the vision vanishes.

Left alone, Canio begins looking idly along the shelves of glass bottles and flasks. No two are the same; all differ in shape or colour or size. He takes out a stopper here and there and sniffs the contents. He tastes a drop of brilliant green liquid from a colourless bottle with deep moulded ridges spiralling up its sides, and rapidly spits it out, scowling in disgust.

'Not pregnant, are you, Canio?' comes a quiet voice from behind him, and he swings round to see Eutherius standing by the brazier. 'Because if you are not, then there is very little point in drinking that.'

'If I drank that I'd probably abort,' Canio mutters.

'That is its purpose. Now, shall we begin?'

On the table have appeared two small silver bowls. 'Listen, Canio, and listen well,' Eutherius murmurs. 'You must look into the flames and think of nothing but this man, this Caelofernus. Look into the flames and think only of him. Let his image fill your mind, like wine pouring into a goblet. Picture it pouring in, red and bright – pouring in until the goblet is full to the brim, the surface quivering at the very moment of overflowing –'

'I can't. I've never seen the man,' Canio admits bluntly.

Eutherius gives an exaggerated sigh. 'Ah, then there is nothing I can do for your friend. You really should have said,' he adds testily.

Canio suspects that Eutherius is being less than frank. 'Damnation, what does it matter whether or not I've actually seen him? I've a pretty good description. I'll think of that and the name together – surely that'll be enough?'

'Oh, no, no, no! You must conjure up the real man inside your head; nothing less will do,' Eutherius scolds, as though he is speaking to an idiot child.

'Perhaps. Perhaps not.' Canio still doesn't believe Eutherius. 'Maybe the gods know a few more tricks than you do – they've certainly been around for a year or two longer. Sprinkle your dust, Ancient One, and let the flames show us what they will.'

Eutherius hesitates, but perhaps he is too tired to argue further. He shrugs in resignation. 'Oh, as you wish.'

Taking a pinch of powder from one of the bowls, he deftly scatters it over the glowing charcoal of the brazier. For a moment nothing happens. Then a sheet of apple-green flame springs up all over the incandescent surface.

Canio pulls up a stool and stares intently into it. 'I can't see anything,' he complains.

'Keep looking,' Eutherius murmurs. 'I dare say the gods will show you all they think you ought to know.' Canio thinks he also mutters something else, something he can't quite catch.

Time passes, and still Canio gazes into the winking, slowly rolling flames; and still he sees nothing. And then, suddenly … 'Hades, there *is* something there! I can see trees – scattered trees, and a stream running along a valley bottom. And there's a building of some sort too – a villa, I think. Yes … a villa. A nice one too, really big. Stone walls, and roofs covered with fired clay tiles and stone slates like a lizard's scales. Snug in winter. Good hunting, too, I'll bet, in that wooded country. If I had the money that's just the sort of place I'd want for myself.'

'Can you see your Caelofernus there?' Eutherius asks tonelessly.

'No, I can't see anyone. Too far away perhaps … *Merda*! The flames are dying. More powder, quickly! Quickly – before the vision fades!' Canio hisses.

Wordlessly, Eutherius obeys and the green flames spring up again, higher than before.

'That's better. I'm closer to the villa now.' But then Canio realises that the scene is not quite as it was before. 'Strange … it's as if the villa's got smaller.' A few moments later he murmurs, 'And the trees seem to have become thicker, and much closer to the villa than they were. And why are the flames turning from green to white?'

'The flames are still green, Canio. They always were.'

Puzzled, Canio glances up at the old man, then back to the brazier. 'They're definitely white now, can't you see? … Ah, no, it's snow falling on the villa. Surely you can see it too?'

'Not I, Canio. Only you can see it.'

Fascinated, Canio watches the snow steadily falling. 'It's thick over the woods and the villa now. Sweet Rosmerta ... the roof's sagging in and collapsing! I'm damned glad I'm not inside it now.'

'How can you be sure you aren't?' Eutherius asks softly.

Canio looks up to see the ghost of a smile gleaming out of the old man's eyes. He thinks it is a malicious smile and gives the old man a sharp look, but does not reply. His eyes return to the flames, and presently he whispers, 'It's just a shell now. An empty shell in the middle of the wildwood. There are even small trees and bushes growing up inside the walls.'

Then he notices something else. He rests both arms on the table as he peers closer. 'I *can* see somebody there now,' he says slowly. 'Up on the high ground, beyond the wood, there's someone standing, looking down at the ruined villa.' He waits until he is quite sure, then whispers, 'It's a woman – a woman in a long, pale dress. And there's something standing beside her too ... a big, black animal – a hound, I think. They're just standing, unmoving, in the snow ... Can't you really see them?'

Eutherius shakes his head. 'The flames are ebbing again, Canio. Shall I make them rise up one last time? Perhaps then you'll be able to see who that woman is?'

Canio hesitates. For several moments, before the flames had begun to sink, the woman had looked up and stared directly at him. Her eyes had seemed to seek his own, and he had felt himself being drawn into that wintry landscape, to feel its chill. 'No, don't bother,' he mutters, 'I haven't the time. But ... what did they mean, Eutherius?'

'They?'

'The villa, the snow, that woman – what did they all mean?'

'They meant nothing to me, Canio. Didn't they mean anything to you?'

'No, why should they?' Canio's voice is harsh. He suspects that the old man does know and is mocking him.

'Then it would seem that the gods have been wasting their time.'

'And not just their time.' Canio stands up and squeals the stool backwards over the stone flagged floor as his temper gets the better of him.

'Perhaps that villa is the place where your man Caelofernus will be found?' Eutherius suggests, and smiles enigmatically.

'What use is that to me? I've no idea where the place is, and even if I had, it's just an empty shell now. And he's not *my* Caelofernus.'

'Ah well, I dare say the meaning will become clear in time,' says the old man serenely.

'In time we'll all be dead.'

'Then it will no longer matter, will it? Nothing will matter.'

'What a comfort you are,' Canio mutters.

'I try to give satisfaction to all my clients.' The old man inclines his head in a slight bow.

'Well you didn't this time, you old bastard.'

Eutherius bows again, nothing ruffling his tranquillity, and Canio, more out of superstitious unease than a sense of obligation, tosses a few more coppers onto the table before he leaves.

When Canio has gone, Eutherius makes sure that the door is firmly latched and then sinks back into his armchair. From the other silver bowl he takes a pinch of powder and scatters it over the charcoal. The flames spring up again, yellow this time, and he gazes intently into them. Occasionally a slight hiss of breath or a whisper of half-formed words escapes his lips. Once he slowly shakes his head, as if not fully understanding what it is he is seeing. He gazes on, until the last flickers of the yellow flames are creeping low over the pulsing charcoal. Then he leans back, sighs, lets his eyelids close, and drifts into the shallow and unrefreshing sleep of the old.

CHAPTER FIVE

Cosconia, a mouse of a girl sitting behind a table near the wide staircase, replies that she is very sorry, but Viventia is still in bed and it's more than her life is worth to disturb her. Can she help?

Saturninus shakes his head. 'Thank you, but it's Viventia I have to see. Ring the bell and let her know she's got a visitor.'

'What bell would – ?'

'Ring the bell, Cosconia.' Saturninus leans over the table until his face is less than a foot from her own.

'Yes, Primicerius,' she squeaks. She reaches out to the wall and tilts forwards the bronze statuette of a naked Venus that stands inside a small alcove.

Listening intently, Saturninus can just make out the faint tinkling of a bell from somewhere on the floor above. He smiles at Cosconia and begins climbing the stairs.

The plastered walls of the first-floor corridor are painted with panels of erotic scenes from Greek mythology, set between pairs of grotesque theatrical masks which leer out at the beholder.

Standing in front of one mask, Saturninus says loudly, 'Put some clothes on, Narcissus: I want a word with Viventia. I'm sure she knows what it's about.'

He detects a slight movement behind the blank eyes of the mask. There comes the muffled sound of voices, then a bolt slides silkily back and a door opens.

Viventia is sitting up in bed, a fur mantle around her shoulders. She holds a silver mirror in one gold be-ringed hand as she teases a stray curl of her elaborate coiffure back into place with the other. A large, muscular youth in a well-cut tunic stands alongside the bed, looking at Saturninus with a faintly resentful expression. Viventia puts on her brightest smile and beams it at Saturninus.

'My dear Primicerius, it will never happen again, I swear it. We had no idea that man had a knife.'

'Didn't Narcissus check him for weapons? I thought it was routine?'

'Unfortunately, Narcissus was engaged in other duties at the time,' Viventia says smoothly.

'Oh, performing other duties, was he? I thought you looked tired, Narcissus.' Saturninus winks at the youth, who reddens.

'Narcissus was running a little errand for me, weren't you, dear?' Viventia explains. But before Narcissus can reply she turns to Saturninus and says, 'They say the stabbed man will almost certainly recover – apparently the wound wasn't very deep. So, there's no great harm done, is there? Have you caught the man who did it yet?'

Saturninus can't help admiring the way she deftly shifts the focus of responsibility. 'No, not yet. From what I've heard, your description was a little imprecise.'

'Yes, well to tell you the truth, I didn't actually see much of him myself; I was – '

'Engaged in other duties?' Saturninus suggests. 'Can you find some other duties for Narcissus here, just for a little while?'

Viventia looks surprised, but turns to Narcissus and says, 'Go and see how our breakfast is coming along, there's a good boy.'

Narcissus hesitates, but Viventia smiles encouragement and blows him a kiss. So he does as she asks, giving Saturninus a distinctly unfriendly look as he leaves.

Saturninus ignores him, closes the door and turns to Viventia.

'Whatever can you want with me all alone?' she says archly. 'Though whatever it is, please, I beg you, do take your sword and helmet off before you do it.' She eases the fur down off her shoulders, just far enough to let him see that she is not wearing a nightdress.

He smiles tolerantly: they have played this game before. 'Don't act the fool, Viventia. Tell me, have you ever heard of a man called Caelofernus? Tall man, bushy blond hair and beard, staring eyes. Colourful dresser.'

'Alas, do my charms mean nothing to you?' Viventia sighs theatrically, but Saturninus knows she is only buying time while her memory races.

'This is important, dammit.' He sits down none too gently on the edge of her large bed, the look on his face intended to convince her that he is in no mood for playing games this morning.

'Caelofernus you say? What, here in Corinium?'

'Here or anywhere.'

Viventia frowns for a few more moments, then shrugs apologetically. 'No; I can't say that I have. What's he done? I suppose it must be something serious if you're after him personally.'

'He hasn't done anything, yet – not that I'm aware of anyway. But I want to find him and I thought, if anyone in Corinium has heard of him then it'll be Viventia.' He draws the nettle of his disappointment gently across her skin.

'Sorry I couldn't help, Primicerius,' Viventia says humbly, and Saturninus is fairly sure she means it: remaining one of his best informants is sound business policy. 'Shall I ask the girls?'

Saturninus considers this offer. 'When they're up, perhaps. But don't tell them why you want to know. Keep that to yourself. But if you should hear ...'

'Then you will be the first to know, Primicerius. Oh, but there is one thing that might interest you though. I would have told you sooner, but you haven't been to see me for over a week now, have you?' She pouts. 'Do you know Rianora?'

'Yes, I think so. Blonde, with all the blessings of the gods?'

'Except a brain – yes, that's the one. Well, a couple of days ago she returned from a visit to Londinium. To see her father, she claimed.'

'So?'

'She said that while she was in the docks there, sharing a quiet drink with a sailor, as one does, she heard of a woman who'd been asking after you.'

'Asking after me? What, there in Londinium?'

'No, no – in Burdigala it was, apparently. That's where the sailor had just come from. I gather the man was fairly drunk – he told Rianora half his life story – but it seems that this woman in Burdigala had been asking people if they'd heard anything of a man called Saturninus, who had been there in Burdigala some three years before.'

Saturninus has become skilled at hiding his reactions to information, but this is ... 'So what in the names of all the *Cucullati* made Rianora think that *I* was the man this woman was after – Saturninus isn't exactly an uncommon name? Was she actually asking after *Flavius* Saturninus?'

'Well, to be honest, I don't really know. Saturninus is the only name Rianora mentioned.'

'Ah ... And I don't suppose Rianora was told the name of this mysterious woman?'

'It seems not. *But* the Saturninus she was after was a soldier, of about your age, a big man with dark hair and sun-darkened skin. Rianora was sure of that. It *could* have been you, couldn't it?'

Saturninus is aware that Viventia is regarding him through narrowed eyes. He cannot recall ever mentioning to her that he had visited Burdigala, but he might have done. He decides not to risk an outright denial. 'Me and a thousand others,' he replies easily. 'So what did she look like, this inquisitive woman?'

'Well, according to the sailor, she was in her mid-twenties, with dark brown, curly hair and wearing a blue dress. Quite pale and thin and exhausted-looking, Rianora was told – not the sort I thought you'd go for, I must admit ... You really haven't any idea who she could have been?'

Saturninus's heart is thumping so hard in his chest that he can hear it. He wonders if Viventia can too.

'No, why should I? That description doesn't mean a thing to me. Is that all the sailor told Rianora?'

'Yes, that's all. Oh, except that the woman was also asking if anything had been heard of some ship that was caught in a storm at around the same time that this other Saturninus was in Burdigala.'

'What ship – did he tell Rianora its name?' Viventia's eyes meet his own for a long moment and Saturninus realises that he'd asked just a shade too quickly.

She waves one hand apologetically. 'Rianora never enquired ... Shall I wake her and see if she remembers anything else?'

But Saturninus knows Viventia well enough to be sure that she has already extracted all the wine that enticing skin ever held. He stands up. 'No, don't bother the lady. Duty calls, and I have to be away ... This romantic meeting with the sailor happened, what – four, five days ago?'

Viventia looks disappointed. 'About that. When she does wake up, do you want me to ask her what else she remembers?'

'Oh, why not,' Saturninus replies carelessly. 'If there is anything else you can always tell me about it when I get back to Corinium.'

'Back from Glevum, you mean?'

'My, you are well informed. Enjoy your breakfast,' he adds slyly as he eases the door open.

Viventia smiles like a fireside cat and hoists the fur back up around her shoulders. 'I usually do,' she replies. 'While I eat I watch Narcissus count the takings.'

Outside in the corridor he pauses, and the memories come flowing back.

The docks beside the Tamesis – the same docks we walked along a week or so after we'd sailed into Londinium in the early June of 364. I can still see the uneven planking, the stacks of barrels and bales, the crates of red pottery amphorae ... and the greeny-brown waters of the Tamesis flowing slowly, endlessly, past. It must have been the best part of half a mile from one end of that wharf to the other, and all the way along there were ships riding at anchor, most of them bustling with loading or unloading, their crews from every corner of the empire.

Do you remember how, every few yards, you'd stop and point out the name of a merchant or a factor, painted in big red letters on the wall of his warehouse. You knew what every one of them dealt in – hides, fleeces, wine, olive oil, dried figs, coloured glassware from the East, liquamen fish sauce ... everything and anything that could turn a profit.

On that day you wore fancy openwork sandals of blue leather and a dress of dark blue wool. It clung softly to your body, smooth as your skin itself. We strolled across the long wooden bridge over to the south side of the river, then past the few buildings that stood there beyond the reedy marshes, and out into the fields beyond. The countryside seemed strangely deserted that day, as you slipped your hand into mine and we wandered down overgrown paths between high hedges, until at last we came to a hay meadow at the edge of a wood. The grasses were long there, with hundreds of tall ox-eye daisies growing up amongst them. The sun was hot and we seemed to be the only people in the world.

Perhaps mistaking the expression on his face for anger as he slowly descends the stairs, Cosconia asks nervously, 'Is anything the matter, Primicerius?'

He looks up and sees her standing beside the bottom step. 'No, nothing. I was just thinking about something, that's all. And don't look so worried – Viventia seems to be in a good mood this morning.'

CHAPTER SIX

With Saturninus leading, the two horsemen and one mule rider clatter out from under the arches of the Glevum Gateway on the north-west side of the city. It is, as near as he or anyone else can tell, about the end of the third hour after sunrise. A little way beyond the city walls they branch off the broad, metalled highway of the Via Erminus and onto the trackway known locally as the Via Alba, which leads north towards the small town of Fonscolnis, thirteen miles distant. The Via Alba is not metalled, but where it ascends the long and wearying gradient up onto the plateau of the hills the traffic of centuries has worn away the topsoil, exposing the pale limestone below.

I couldn't have been more than five years old when I first stood on top of the city walls and watched that narrow ribbon of cream winding upwards until it seemed to touch the sky.

As the three riders climb out of the shelter of the valley of the Churn, Saturninus glances back and sees the rising wind from the south-west sending great banks of white clouds scudding across the bright sky. Every time they cover the sun the temperature drops noticeably. It doesn't bother him: he and Canio are used to riding in all weathers. The clerk, Vitalinus, though, is not accustomed to the outdoor life.

After little more than a mile he calls out, 'For pity's sake, will you both slow down! You know this infernal mule of mine can't keep up with your horses.'

From the way Vitalinus is squirming uncomfortably in his saddle, Saturninus guesses that the leather is already beginning to rub the skin of his inner thighs raw with each jolting step of the mule. Though his tone is pleading, Saturninus sees the anger in the clerk's face, and it stifles sympathy.

'We're supposed to be hurrying, Vitalinus,' he shouts above the gusting wind. 'Aemilianus's orders, remember?'

'I can't carry out his orders if I never get there,' Vitalinus shouts back. 'At least let me ride in front and set the pace.'

Seeing Canio grinning at the prospect of the clerk's continuing discomfort, Saturninus hesitates then shrugs acceptance. And so they continue, with Vitalinus's mule trotting jerkily ahead of the two horses.

Soon afterwards they meet a man trudging towards Corinium with two large wicker baskets suspended from a yoke across his shoulders.

Before Saturninus can stop him, Canio has reined to a halt. 'Snails! I haven't tasted a single one so far this year. Do you fancy some, Primicerius?'

Saturninus is about to decline, before suddenly realising the opportunity which the situation presents. 'If they're yours to sell?' he asks the pedestrian – a swarthy *paganus* with arms as thick as twenty-year ash trunks and skin like tanned leather.

'That they are, soldier, that they are.'

'And well flushed out?' Saturninus recalls that it's always a wise question to ask.

'For three whole days, soldier; and fed on nothing but pure goats' milk for all that time as well.'

'Pure goats – what in the House of Hades are they?' asks Canio.

'Ones that have never made your acquaintance,' Vitalinus mutters.

Saturninus grins. 'How much?' he asks the rustic.

'A copper for four. You'll not find better if you search the hills for a month – just look at the beauties!' Picking a couple of snails at random he tosses them up to Saturninus, who drops his reins, deftly catches them with both hands and examines the glossy shells. They are over an inch-and-a-half across, the spiralling bands of orange-brown and greyish-white giving them the appearance of carved agate.

Like the ones I used to find when I went searching along the edges of the beech wood above our villa. And how many summers have come and gone since then?

He jiggles the shells up and down in his cupped palms. 'They certainly are a good weight.'

'So heavy I can barely carry them. And seeing as how it'll lighten my load, I'll let you have the pick of them at five for a copper – what do you say to that?'

'That sounds like a bargain to me. We'll take sixty ... here, this should hold them.' Saturninus reaches across and extracts a small sack from Canio's saddlebag.

'I just hope they really are well purged,' Canio murmurs as he helps the rustic transfer the snails to the sack.

When the sack is almost full, Saturninus delves into his belt pouch and pulls out a handful of the ubiquitous small copper coins that bear the diademed head of Valentinian, the reigning emperor in the West. He counts out twelve and hands them down to the rustic.

'Nice new 'uns,' the man observes appreciatively. Struck barely two months before at the imperial mint of Lugdunum on the River Rhone and received as part of salary, the still-untarnished copper sparkles with iridescent fire in the bright sunlight.

'They are that,' Saturninus agrees, as he flicks the reins and starts Antares into a trot.

Half a mile further on he notices dark clouds appearing among the white chariots racing across the high, windy sky. The black clouds rapidly increase in number, and by the time the three riders have covered another half mile the sky is uniformly dark, with only one small patch of brightness far off on the eastern horizon. The wind sighs on, all the while gaining in strength, and soon large drops of rain, the heralds of the coming storm, begin to splash irregularly down.

Vitalinus's mule stops and its rider turns and looks questioningly at Saturninus, who curses mildly, then scans the landscape for shelter. 'Over there looks best,' he calls out to the other two, pointing towards a clump of massive beech trees growing around a depression left by old quarry workings in the open, hawthorn-dotted grassland. Digging heels into the flanks of their mounts, they leave the trackway and hurry towards it.

They have only just reached the place when the full force of the storm strikes, the rain driven almost horizontally by the force of a wind that tosses and shakes the branches of the great trees, whose leaves have only weeks before expanded to full size in that high, cold place. Then, briefly, the silvery curtains become hailstones. Saturninus hears the staccato patter as the pellets of hard ice scythe into the young leaves, severing dozens, which the uncaring wind then whirls far away.

One leaf sticks, glistening wetly, to Antares' flank. Saturninus reached down, picks it off and studies it – its softness and beautiful light green, its edges still covered in silky hairs like those on the ears of a kitten.

'I wonder ... is that what they call predestination?' he murmurs.

The wind carries his words to Canio. 'Did you say something, Primicerius?' he asks loudly, turning and squinting against that wind.

Saturninus glances across to him. 'Some philosophers would say that, ever since the beginning of time, it was predestined that this leaf was fated to be destroyed by the hailstone that cut it down. And that not even the gods themselves could have prevented it. Can you believe that?'

Did you believe it, Pascentia?

Canio's horse is tossing its head and shifting its hooves restlessly as the great boughs groan and creak above them. 'No ... that's got to be nonsense. Maybe a man's death might be predestined, or maybe not. But never a leaf's.'

'If a man's extinction can be predestined, then in logic why not a leaf's?' Saturninus gazes dispassionately across to the rain-obscured horizon. 'They both live; and then, at a certain time, in a certain place, they both die. And sooner or later something is going to cut down each and every one of us. We know that. But we don't know when or where or how, not for sure. Is it that uncertainty that makes us think it's worth fighting Death when we see him coming?'

Canio appears puzzled how to reply, but Vitalinus saves him the trouble. 'The concept of predestination is rooted in Manichean fatalism, Primicerius. It denies the existence of free will and, as such, I was taught that it has no proper place in Christian doctrine.' His voice comes struggling out of the folds of his *cucullus*, the hooded cape in which he is now swathed, his back turned against the wind.

'The existence of free will, or the illusion of free will?' muses Saturninus, his eyes still on the horizon. Then, turning, 'So, neither of you believe in predestination?'

'You don't believe in it, do you Primicerius?' asks Canio, as if suddenly anxious that he might have disparaged one of Saturninus's most deeply held beliefs.

'I most certainly do not. Particularly if it is not part of proper Christian doctrine.' Saturninus keeps all trace of irony out of his voice. He flicks the severed leaf into the wind, which whirls it away and down into the sea of wet grass.

Canio laughs, but it is the uneasy laugh of a man who is not entirely sure that his companion is joking.

Some way off, on a branch of an isolated hawthorn tree, a magpie settles and attempts to keep its balance in the blustery wind by jerky movements of its long black tail. But the wind soon defeats it and it flaps off again, flying haphazardly before the storm.

And then, almost as quickly as it had started, the storm ends. First the wind eases, then the rain stops. Patches of blue sky open up among the dark clouds, which are themselves rapidly supplanted by a few fluffy white cumuli, blown in by the same south-west wind that brought the rain. The sun shines down, bright and hot, and soon the storm is only a memory, with nothing but the wet leaves and grass, already steaming faintly under the sun's heat, to mark its passing.

Conscious of the time lost – and disregarding Vitalinus's protests – Saturninus canters back to the Via Alba and sets off northwards at a smart trot, Canio and Vitalinus following close behind. He has gone barely two hundred yards along the Via Alba, and is almost level with an ancient solitary ash which stands, tall and gaunt, beside the trackway, when suddenly, without the slightest warning and out of a now near-cloudless sky, there comes a blinding flash of bluish light and a tremendous explosion. Antares rears and plunges in panic, and in these first moments after the lightning strike it is all that Saturninus can do to avoid being thrown. His nostrils catch a sulphurous smell of burning, and something else too, something curiously reminiscent of the wind from the sea. He hears a high-pitched creak from somewhere high above, followed immediately by a loud rending, splitting noise as a great branch falls from the ash. It crashes down right across the Via Alba, so close to him that Saturninus feels the earth shake and the extremity twigs whip against his leg as he struggles to calm the capering horse. But Antares, good cavalry mount that he is, soon quietens, and Saturninus looks up to see wisps of smoke and the long, pale scar on the trunk where the branch tore off a jagged strip of bark as it fell. He looks back and sees Canio swearing profanely as he struggles to bring his own horse under control. Astonishingly, Vitalinus's mule is standing calmly on the trackway with an almost-human expression of boredom on its face as if, for it, thunderbolts are an everyday occurrence. It even begins to crop the trackside grass. Its rider, however, is less sanguine. Vitalinus sits staring at the fallen branch as though it had dropped from the skies.

'It's an omen,' he whispers hoarsely. Then, louder, he cries out, 'It's an omen – they're warning us not to go to that hillside!'

Canio, whose horse is still jittering nervously, snarls, '"They?" Who in Hades' name are "they", Vitalinus? I thought you Christians only had one god? … And that you don't believe in omens?'

The clerk glares angrily at Canio. 'I mean the Father, the Son and the Holy Ghost, of course – and we don't believe in what you pagans call omens. But we're not stupid enough to ignore a sign from heaven when we see it, and that thunderbolt was sent as a warning to us not to go on.'

'It hit the tree, not us,' Canio reminds him. 'And it would have happened whether we were here or not. I've seen trees in the middle of woods that have been struck – blown apart – when there wasn't a soul around to see it happen. So tell me, who were those thunderbolts supposed to be warning, eh? The woodpeckers, perhaps? Or was it the squirrels?'

Who are you trying to convince, Canio? Vitalinus or yourself? But you're probably right: the lightning has no hidden meaning – no more than the rain and the hail and the wind and the passing clouds. But whatever its meaning, or none at all, I'm going to find Caelofernus, come what may.

For a few moments more Saturninus watches Canio and Vitalinus sniping at each other. Then, without a word, he knees Antares forward around the fallen branch and sets off again along the road to Fonscolnis. When he looks back he sees the other two following some way behind, Canio riding alongside Vitalinus's mule and urging the animal on with a leafy switch he must have snapped from the fallen branch as he passed.

CHAPTER SEVEN

It is well before noon when they arrive at the place, set deep in woodland, where the Via Alba forks. Saturninus chooses the right-hand track, the thin grass growing over much of its surface showing it to be the less travelled of the two.

'We'll eat those snails when we get to the Coln,' he calls back encouragingly to Vitalinus. 'Not far to go now.'

'Aren't you going to call in at the Villa of Censorinus today, Primicerius?' Canio asks. 'You never know; you might find your old friend Dagobitus there.'

Saturninus turns in his saddle and gives him a hard stare.

'No, perhaps that wouldn't be such a good idea,' Canio concedes.

Vitalinus looks puzzled, but neither of the soldiers enlightens him.

The hollow way that winds down through the woods to the River Coln is narrow and steep, the trees on both sides arching over to form a dark tunnel where occasional shafts of sunlight lance obliquely through the gloom. But eventually the gradient eases, the trees thin, and Saturninus trots Antares the last hundred yards to the ford through almost-level grassland, dotted with hawthorn trees smothered with blindingly white may blossom. As the three riders near the ford across the meandering little river, Canio points to a great blue-grey heron standing in the water. Seeing them approaching it flaps slowly up into the air, wheels, then settles in a hollow of the hillside on the other side of the Coln, where it stands, sentinel-like, as if patiently awaiting their passing.

At a dozen paces wide, the ford is over four times the general width of the Coln in those parts, but very shallow. It is paved with small limestone slabs, over which the cold, clear water races and bubbles. Standing in the ford, the two horses and the mule drink noisily; neighing, snorting and shaking their heads from side to side, their riders cursing as the resulting chill droplets spray over them.

Afterwards, Saturninus rides a little way upstream into the shade of a spinney of large hawthorns. Despite the bright blossom, he notices that the leaves are changing from light green to dark, their youth already vanishing, their mortality signalled.

Another spring almost gone.

The riders dismount and tether their animals, leaving them cropping the sweet, abundant grasses.

Vitalinus's relief is obvious. 'May Christus be praised!' he breathes as he levers himself slowly out of the saddle. Straightening his body, he begins to walk stiffly upstream.

Guessing his purpose, Saturninus calls after him, 'Hey! Downstream, Vitalinus, please. I don't fancy drinking water that you've just soaked your backside in.'

Canio grins and clutches his own buttocks, giving an exaggerated wince and howl as he does so, while Vitalinus, with obvious ill-grace, retraces his steps, stalks past them both and disappears from sight around the curve of the stream.

Saturninus watches him go, then walks quickly over to Canio's horse. Unhooking the sack with its cargo of snails, he lobs it over to Canio. 'You winkle them out of their shells and I'll get a fire going.'

By the time he has collected dry wood from the spinney, dead grass for tinder, and started a fire with flint and steel, Canio has all the snails bobbing up and down in the water with which he had half-filled his official-issue bronze cooking pot. Their buff-coloured skins are reticulated like those of reptiles.

'Hmm, like several ladies I've known, they don't look quite so tempting out of their clothes,' he remarks, more to himself than Saturninus. 'Too late now though.'

From a cluster of young ash trees Saturninus cuts three short sticks. Pushing one forked stick into the soft earth on either side of the fire, he hangs the blackened cooking pot from the crosspiece. By the time that Vitalinus returns, looking distinctly more contented with life, the pot is bubbling merrily, wisps of vapour curling from its rim and immediately vanishing into the warm air.

'Ah, the water nymph returns at last,' Canio remarks. 'I was beginning to think I'd have to come and lead you back like a lost sheep.'

'God forbid! But speaking of leading sheep,' Vitalinus adds coldly, 'do you know what Prefect Aemilianus once said to me? He said, "That man Canio has all the leadership qualities of a sheep with foot rot."'

Saturninus, who had been about to sample a snail impaled on the end of his dagger, stops and looks at them both.

'Oh, did he now?' Canio enquires silkily. 'And what are your own views on the matter, Vitalinus?'

'Oh, I think I agree wi – ' Saturninus sees Vitalinus freeze, suddenly aware that Canio is now standing no more than a yard away, his eyes hard, unsmiling. The clerk quickly retreats several paces and appears distinctly relieved when Saturninus calls over, 'Right, my heroes, they're about ready. Bring your mess tins and I'll dish them out.'

'I haven't got a mess tin,' Vitalinus says testily, his eyes still on Canio's fists.

'Of course you have – perhaps you civilians call it a skillet? It's part of the standard kit that Canio put in your saddlebag before we left Corinium – didn't you, Canio?'

'I certainly did, my leader. We wouldn't want little Vitalinus to go without a warm meal all the while he's away from the big city, would we now?'

The two soldiers' mess tins are already unpacked and lying on the grass. Vitalinus goes over to his mule's saddlebag, rummages and fetches his own, maintaining a good distance between himself and Canio as he does so. Meanwhile, Saturninus drains most of the boiling water from the pot and, when Vitalinus returns, divides the contents equally between the three mess tins by flicking out the snails with his dagger.

'Now, what they really need,' he remarks, 'is a dash of liquamen to bring out the flavour ... and by great good fortune, I just happen to have a little flagon in my saddlebags. Vitalinus – if you would be so kind?'

For a moment he thinks that the clerk is going to refuse, but then Vitalinus gives an exaggerated sigh and walks over to Antares. 'Which bag is it in?' he shouts.

'The nearest one!' While Vitalinus's back is turned, Saturninus takes from his belt pouch a small pottery flask which, until a short time before, had also nestled in one of his saddlebags. He swiftly unstoppers it and sprinkles a few drops of the contents over the snails in Vitalinus's mess tin. He is aware that Canio is watching him, but the ducenarius makes no comment.

Vitalinus returns and hands the liquamen to Saturninus, who thanks him and promptly pours a generous helping over the snails in all three mess tins, stirring them around with the dagger. He spears one of Vitalinus's snails and chews it. 'Mmm, quite good. Not the best I've ever tasted, but not bad for this early in the season. Better eat them while they're good and hot: nothing tastes worse than cold snail.'

'But what do I eat them *with*?' Vitalinus mutters. 'I haven't brought a spoon and you know I'm not allowed to carry a dagger.'

Saturninus stares at the clerk, then shoots a severe look at Canio. 'Ducenarius, you haven't forgotten to pack the silverware again, have you?'

'What? ... Oh, forgive me, Primicerius. I was that busy before we left Corinium that it went completely out of my head. Never mind, the Falernian wine will make up for it.' Canio springs up and rifles through his own saddlebags. He turns, his face a picture of dismay. 'Damn me, I've forgotten that too!'

'Very funny.' But Vitalinus's face does not register amusement. 'I see that I am among barbarians. So be it.' He picks up a snail between finger and thumb and pops it into his mouth. After a few hesitant moments his expression registers mild approval of the taste.

'You learn fast, Vitalinus. We'll make a soldier of you yet,' remarks Saturninus, and begins eating his own snails in the same way.

'I'd as soon play the flute in a brothel,' Vitalinus murmurs under his breath, but not quietly enough. Saturninus and Canio exchange quick, pointed looks.

Saturninus eats hurriedly, anxious to be off. To speed the time while he waits for the other two to finish, he leans back and begins watching a flock of twenty or so martins as they wheel and swoop overhead, hunting flying insects.

They were swallows, weren't they, endlessly circling low over the garden of the villa near Burdigala in the evening of that hot July day? We sat around a table in the sunlight-flickering leaf shade of a great tree and watched them while we ate sea bream and green peas and sweet wine cakes and drank the red wine from Metilius's vineyard. Near where we sat were several rustic arches over which great masses of honeysuckle had grown. The air was heavy with their perfume and the warm wind loosened several of their delicate yellow trumpets. They skittered across the table and we both tried to catch the same one. I brought my cupped palm down on it, and your hand came down on mine a moment later. I remember how your fingers began gently stroking mine.

You moved around to sit beside me and we talked into the night, just you and I, long after the swallows had gone and the sun had set and the little bats had begun flitting erratically backwards and forwards in the darkening sky. You wore a white, sleeveless dress, with your hair newly washed and drawn back and tied with a ribbon. And –

He feels Canio's boot kick gently against his own. Twisting round he sees, several hundred yards away to the north-east, two horsemen descending the hillside on the other side of the Coln. Perhaps attracted by the thin smoke of the dying campfire they advance rapidly at first, then slow to a trot before finally halting a hundred paces from where Saturninus is sitting. Out of the corner of his eye he notices the old heron at last abandon its vigil and launch itself into the air, flying downstream low over the Coln with slow beats of its wide wings. From the saddle of one of the two strangers hang loops of chains and manacles that clink with every movement of his horse.

'I do believe it's your old friend Dagobitus,' Canio whispers loudly. 'Aren't you going to invite him to lunch?'

Saturninus does not reply, trying to suppress the anger rising in his throat. Motionless as a cat within striking distance of a rat, he stares across at Dagobitus, a burly man who could be any age between twenty-five and thirty-five. Dagobitus stares back. His companion, a huge man astride a small, sturdy horse, says something to him, then urges the horse forward a step. Dagobitus shakes his head, clutching at his companion's sleeve as if to dissuade him from going further. Vitalinus says nothing, but his eyes flicker back and forth, as if sensing something fearful, as cattle sense an approaching thunderstorm.

Suddenly anger wins and Saturninus feels himself possessed by a fatalistic recklessness. He springs to his feet and races towards Antares, untethers the horse and swings up into the saddle, all in one fluid movement. Wheeling about, he drives Antares into and across the Coln, the splashing hooves throwing up a curtain of water droplets through which the bright sunlight is refracted into a transient rainbow. Then he is up on the opposite bank and urging the horse into a gallop.

But Dagobitus clearly has no wish to renew his acquaintance. Even before Saturninus enters the Coln he has wrenched the head of his own horse around and begins riding it hard back up the hillside, his heels flailing wildly against its flanks. Confused by the rapidity of his companion's flight, the huge man first looks back at Dagobitus, and then forwards at Saturninus, before he too decides that it is time to be somewhere else. He urges his horse into a trot, moving off to Saturninus's right, parallel with the little river.

Saturninus ignores him and continues after Dagobitus. But the hundred-pace start is too great and Dagobitus, his own panic seemingly communicating itself to his mount, manages to maintain the distance between them. Halfway up the hillside, Saturninus realises that he is not going to catch him: realises too that, even if he did, Vitalinus's presence makes it impossible to do what he had in mind in those first mad moments. He reins to a halt. Dagobitus, however, does not look back, and his lathered horse remains at a near gallop as it reaches the crest and disappears from view.

Saturninus, almost calm again now, watches him go. Then he turns and canters back to Canio and Vitalinus, re-crossing the Coln via the ford, beside the great clumps of mauve-flowered comfrey and yellow flag irises which grow on the banks there.

Canio is finishing the last of his snails, apparently unconcerned by what he has just witnessed. Looking up at Saturninus he simply asks, 'Conscience still bothering you, Primicerius?'

'That boy, Mettus, couldn't have been more than fourteen years old.'

'Ah, but his master didn't object, remember? He reckoned it was worth it to discourage other runaways. So it wasn't a crime, according to the law.'

'No, not a crime,' Saturninus replies, the anger rising again. 'I handed him over to Dagobitus. Dagobitus flogged him to death. But it wasn't a crime.' He glances towards Vitalinus to make sure the clerk is out of earshot, then leans over Antares' neck and says softly to Canio, 'And when, one day, I run across friend Dagobitus, all alone in a lonely place, then what I'll do to him won't be a crime either.'

'Would that be wise?'

'No, not wise at all.'

'Then why do it?'

'Why? To try and make my peace with the dead, that's why. And because I hate the bastard, and because he needs killing to stop him torturing anyone else to death. How many reasons do you need? … Or do you think I'm supposed to enjoy acting as a pimp for turds like him?'

'It's what we do.' Canio shrugs.

'So it is … And it's time we weren't here.'

Vitalinus is walking towards them now, a puzzled look on his face. His lips part, as if he is about to ask a question. Saturninus pauses, but before any word comes out an uncertain look appears on the clerk's face. One hand moves hesitantly up towards his mouth and he turns slowly away. Saturninus notices Canio catch his eye and give a quick, fierce grin.

The mess tins and the cooking pot are swilled in the Coln and the ashes of the fire, still hot enough to send up a hissing cloud of steam, are doused with water. When Canio and Vitalinus have remounted, they join Saturninus as he splashes back through the ford and together they follow the course of the little river, first west, then north, until it brings them to Fonscolnis an hour or so later.

CHAPTER EIGHT

By then, Vitalinus is slumped forwards over the ears of his mule, his face exhibiting an ashen pallor not often seen on the living. 'Christus, save me,' he whispers feebly. 'I think I'm dying.'

Saturninus is beginning to feel slightly worried: he had anticipated that the horse purge would bring on nothing worse than an acute bout of diarrhoea. 'No you're not,' he says encouragingly. It's only the riding – sometimes it can have that effect on a man who's not used to it.'

Even Canio is not wholly unsympathetic. 'Now we're at Fonscolnis you can have a lie-down. You'll soon feel better after that,' he remarks cheerfully.

'Yes, you'll soon recover once you're off that lousy mule,' Saturninus adds. 'A short rest, some wine to settle your stomach, and then you'll be galloping off to find that hole in the hill, leaving us two trailing behind.'

He has scarcely finished speaking when, in some mysterious way, the word 'galloping' seems to set off a violent muscular convulsion in Vitalinus's digestive system. With an explosive croak, the late meal of snails, and much else besides, bursts from his throat in a torrent of yellowish vomit and shoots horizontally through the air for at least three feet, before splashing to earth in a graceful arc.

Saturninus halts Antares, turns and waits for the eruption to cease.

'You'll soon feel better now you're rid of that,' says Canio, trying not to grin and almost succeeding. Catching Saturninus's cautioning glance he does not elaborate on the reasoning behind his prognosis.

Old Fonscolnis. Always different, always the same. When we shared our childhood memories, you still recalled so many things about this place – even though you only saw it the once, and that when you were scarcely eight years old.

From its southern outskirts, Saturninus scans across Fonscolnis. It lies near the east bank of the Coln, a little to the south of the cluster of springs which feed into the headwaters of that little river. When he was young he was told that, at some point in the long-ago, men came to believe that Fonscolnis was a place where beings from the Unseen World gathered. And perhaps still do.

He leads the way through the town until they come to the main temple, dedicated to Mercury and his Celtic consort, the Lady Rosmerta – she whose magic tub contains an inexhaustible supply of food and drink. It is a high, square building, with mellow limestone walls and a roof covered with riven slates of the same material. Saturninus notices the resident priest loitering outside the long entrance portico, warily scrutinising them as they pass.

He lets his eyes roam over the dozen or more stone and wooden shrines in the temenos enclosure that surrounds Mercury's temple, murmuring as he does so the old, remembered names. The names of the Roman deities, of Mars, of Silvanus, god of wild places and hunting, and of Fortuna, her hand resting on the ship's rudder with which she might guide a man's fate through the unquiet seas of life. Outnumbering them are the native Celtic gods and goddesses, foremost amongst them the three Mother Goddesses, whose stone faces gaze out at Saturninus, sometimes benign, sometimes stern, as he rides by; infants, bread and fruit resting on their ample laps.

And here and there, sometimes in attendance upon the Mothers, sometimes alone, he sees the three *Genii Cucullati*. They stand, watchful, in their long, hooded capes, the spirits of the earth and of the deep, dark powers of the earth; of the cycle of the seasons, of birth, of healing, of death and rebirth. Saturninus had been born into a world inhabited by people to whom such beings were as real as the hills themselves. And sometimes, in the still of the night, or in the wild, high places of the hills, they are real to him too.

He is well aware that there are no Christian shrines at Fonscolnis – that for any trace of what has been the official religion of the empire for the past fifty years, a traveller will search in vain. Aware too that, among the *pagani*, the native peasant population of the countryside, the old gods still retain their dark, compelling powers.

All around the sacred enclosure are dozens of shops and stalls, ranging in quality and permanence from substantial, stone-built structures, through timber huts, down to makeshift tables protected from the weather by no more than a sailcloth awning.

Riding up the widest street at a slow walking pace, Saturninus lets Antares find his own way between the noisy, jostling crowds. Fonscolnis – the old Fonscolnis – is part of his past. During lonely nights camped near the Persian frontier he walked through the market so many times that the memory of how it once had been is now fixed forever in his mind:

Past Mocuxsomus's cheese and butter stall, on your right ... what?

Tetrintus's herbs.

Name ten ... count them off on your fingers.

Mint, garlic, sage, parsley, thyme, coriander, dill, borage, chives, fennel ...

And then?

The salt woman ... Curmissa.

Past her, past the man who made horse and plough-oxen harnesses, (Saturninus could never remember his name, and now he is long gone), left hand side, who?

Old Pacatus, the ironsmith, and his brother Feliculus.

Name fifteen things on his stall.

Kitchen knives, pruning knives, folding knives, meat cleavers, sickles, scythe blades, axes, adzes, mattocks, spade irons, plough coulters, kitchen griddles, pothooks and chains and nails ... hundreds of crude, large-headed, square-sectioned nails of all lengths from one to six inches ...

Over the intervening years the stalls and their contents have changed remarkably little, but of all those stallholders Saturninus remembers from his childhood, not one now remains. Mocuxsomus, Tetrintus, Curmissa, Pacatus, Feliculus and the rest have all been scattered by the winds of time, their fates unknown. He wonders if some lie in the shallow graves of the unkempt little burial ground on the northern edge of the town, where only mounds in the coarse grass mark their long homes. Some of the present stallholders may be the time-changed sons and daughters of those people: he does not know, and for reasons of his own he has never asked.

The civil guard post stands on rising ground a little to the east of Fonscolnis, a weathered stone building with a roof of orange-red clay tiles and a watchtower, from the high window of which a man can look out over the entire settlement.

Tranquillus, the biarchus in charge of the little garrison, is a florid man with a pronounced paunch. When Saturninus arrives he finds him eating his mid-day meal in the company of one of his two troopers – a man, dark as a crow, who goes by the name of Delfinus. The meal, Saturninus cannot help noticing, is a sumptuous one: roast mutton and a brace of chickens, with a large flagon of wine to wash them all down. Tranquillus lives well for a man on a junior NCO's pay. Perhaps too well.

Saturninus's unexpected appearance – he had not been due on his regular inspection tour for at least another week – proves so disconcerting that Tranquillus chokes violently as he attempts to swallow a mouthful of mutton too quickly. Flanked by Canio, and with the hapless Vitalinus trailing behind with half-closed eyes like a dying bird, Saturninus waits patiently as the biarchus gasps, 'Primicerius, sir ... this is an unexpected pleasure ... may I offer you ... such hospitality as my humble table affords?' before doubling over with another furious attack of coughing.

'Thank you for the invitation, Tranquillus, but today we really can't spare the time. On my next scheduled inspection, perhaps?... Although,' he can't stop himself from adding, as he catches sight of a small barrel of live oysters in brine beneath the table, 'as I recall, you never seem to have food of this quality on such occasions, do you?'

Tranquillus's face is already far too red to register any embarrassment, but Trooper Delfinus starts easing noiselessly towards the door. Saturninus becomes aware of the stealthy movement. 'No, don't go, Delfinus. I may need you to help the Biarchus remember a few things.'

Canio, grinning wickedly, positions himself so as to effectively block the doorway. Delfinus flicks his tongue nervously across his upper lip, halts, and slowly turns around.

Saturninus seats himself at the table opposite Tranquillus. 'The reason why I'm here is that, a little while ago, I received a report from you. It was about a *paganus* who dug a hole in the side of a hill some miles north of here. You wrote that he heard strange noises and then saw men – soldiers, of sorts – come marching out of the hole. Remember that?'

He thinks the relief that appears on Tranquillus's face would make a dog laugh. 'Oh that! That was just a bit of nonsense I heard from a packman. A travelling coppersmith he was – you know the sort: wanders around the countryside buying and mending old pots and skillets, selling cheap new ones, and hearing all the gossip as he goes. I only put it in the report because I thought you'd be amused by the witlessness of the rustics up there. Anyway, I sent that report in, what – nearly two weeks ago? So why, if I may ask, Primicerius, are you interested in it now?'

Saturninus turns for a moment and looks for Vitalinus, but the clerk seems to have disappeared. 'Your report came to the attention of *Dominus Noster* Prefect Aemilianus. Need I say more?'

Tranquillus mutters an obscene curse. 'I didn't think he ever read my damned reports.'

'Well, he read that one, and here I am to prove it. So, what I want to know is this: was what you wrote a complete wagonload of horseapples, or was it a fair approximation to what you were told by that packman? And did he tell you anything else – anything that even you weren't donkey enough to put in the report?'

Tranquillus appears worried again now. He scratches the hairless crown of his head. 'No, Primicerius, every word I put into that report was just as the packman told it to me. Every word. Nothing added, nothing left out. You can back me up on that, can't you, Delfinus?'

Both Saturninus and Canio look towards Delfinus, and Delfinus, after a momentary pause, replies dutifully, 'Yes, Biarchus. Every word was just as he told it.'

'So how did the packman come to know about it?' Saturninus asks.

'Oh, he heard it at the Villa of Julius Martinus. Apparently they were all talking about it up there.'

'Is that where the rustic who dug the hole came from?'

'Why, yes. Didn't I put that in the report?'

'Not that I can recall. Did your packman tell you the digger's name?'

'No, Primicerius – and I'm afraid I didn't think to ask: it didn't seem of much consequence at the time.'

'And I suppose you don't happen to recall the name of the packman, or where I can find him?'

'Ah, his name's Candidus. That's what he calls himself, anyway – though he's brown as a turd and slippery as a dozen eels. He passes through here two or three times a year, but where he goes to in the months between, only the *Cucullati* themselves know. Perhaps he went on to Corinium?'

Saturninus half turns to Canio, who shakes his head. 'I can't say that I've ever heard of the man, Primicerius.'

Good. And I certainly won't be asking the Cucullati.

'Well, I don't suppose it really matters. Exactly where is this wondrous hillside?'

'From what I could make out, Primicerius, it's a mile or two west, or maybe south-west, of the villa.'

'Not far from Maglocrouco?'

'The big long barrow? Yes, that's right, Primicerius.'

'It's wild and lonely country up there.' Saturninus remembers.

'It is that. Do you know it well?'

'Well enough. I make it my business to know my own territory. And what goes on in it,' Saturninus adds, looking directly at Tranquillus. 'Until next inspection then.' He turns to leave.

'And when will that be, Primicerius, if I may ask?' Tranquillus tries to sound casual. Catching Saturninus's ironic stare, he adds, 'I only ask so that –'

'You can hide any unsolicited gifts? Where's Vitalinus gone?'

Canio points downwards to a spot just outside the door. Saturninus looks, and sees the clerk sitting slumped against the wall, his chin on his chest. 'Time to go, Vitalinus,' he says quietly. 'We've got that hillside to find.'

Vitalinus makes a half-hearted attempt to rise, then flops down again as if his legs have turned to grass stalks under him. 'Can't do it. Everything's spinning round inside my head.' He speaks slowly and emphatically, like a child.

Saturninus sighs, then squats down in front of Vitalinus and looks him full in the face. 'Well, you're certainly in no fit state to travel yet,' he concedes. 'I'll tell you what though: to give you a chance to recover, Canio and I will make a few enquiries here in Fonscolnis. You never know – maybe someone in the market knows the name of the hole-digger. But we can't wait long. In the meantime Tranquillus will look after you – won't you, Tranquillus? First thing to do is get you into a comfortable bed. Lend him a hand, Canio.'

Between them, Tranquillus and Canio carry the moaning Vitalinus to one of the troopers' bunks at the back of the guard post and tenderly drop him onto it.

'Chances are he won't be much better by the time we return – but I don't think he's seriously ill. In fact, I'll lay odds that he's better by nightfall,' Saturninus adds reassuringly, seeing the expression of something less than enchantment on Tranquillus's face at the prospect of playing nursemaid to a man who will almost certainly inform Aemilianus of everything he sees and overhears.

'I dare say it was something he ate before leaving Corinium,' Canio remarks confidently. 'A couple more good pukes and he'll be back on his feet again.'

The words have barely passed his lips when the sound of retching floats from the back room. With a smothered oath Delfinus hurries towards it, guessing, correctly, on whose bunk Vitalinus is lying.

CHAPTER NINE

Leaving the guard post, Saturninus and Canio part and go their separate ways through the bustling market crowds. At the temple of Mercury and Rosmerta, Saturninus spots the priest again, this time standing outside in the temenos enclosure, deep in conversation with a man in a blue tunic and cloak. From the concealing shelter of a stall awning Saturninus watches impatiently, but the blue man shows no sign of leaving. He hesitates, then, to kill time, begins walking slowly through the market. When he meets nodding acquaintances he asks if they know the identity of the hole digger. All deny any knowledge of the incident. Saturninus is sceptical, but doesn't question them further: he has other things on his mind.

As he approaches the salt stall, the woman behind the trestle table has her back to him. But when he draws level she turns abruptly, and her eyes seem to seek and find his own, though he is half-hidden in the crowd. She smiles. It is Curmissa. Startled, he pretends he hasn't seen her, and walks on. It is only several dozen paces later that he realises that she looked exactly as he remembers her from twenty years ago. He stops abruptly, turns and walks uncertainly back. There is no woman at the stall now, only the middle-aged man he saw when he rode through the settlement half an hour before. The man looks baffled when he asks who the woman was.

Returning to the temple, he is just in time to see the blue man waving farewell to the priest and disappearing into the crowds. Seizing the moment, Saturninus hurries across the roadway and enters the temenos. The priest is a man of about thirty-five with a blank, impassive face. He wears a long robe, embroidered with the symbols of Mercury: the caduceus, winged petasus hat and money bag, alternating with the ram, the cock and the tortoise – the god's attendant beasts. At the sight of Saturninus he stiffens into total immobility.

'Decenorix ... it is Decenorix, isn't it?'

The priest inclines his head to Saturninus in guarded acknowledgement.

'Can we go inside? – there's something I want done.' Saturninus ushers Decenorix back into the long entrance portico and through into the cella, the heart of the temple, where a solitary oil lamp burns in the cavernous gloom. It radiates just enough light to darkly illuminate the great cult statues of Mercury and Rosmerta set up on a high plinth in the middle of the cella, and to reflect softly off the numerous wafer-thin feather and leaf-shaped dedicatory plaques of silver and copper which decorate the walls.

'I want a curse tablet made,' Saturninus begins. 'A *defixio* – written backwards in the old style. Can you do it?'

Decenorix hesitates for a moment, then appears to realise that, with a group of some twenty such tablets nailed to the wall behind the altar, it is pointless to deny he makes them. 'Yes, it can be done, Primicerius,' he replies. If you have the desired wording written out it can be ready by sunset.'

'No, it must be done now – I want to see it done.' Saturninus lets the urgency show in his voice. 'You have lead and a graving tool here?'

'Yes, but – '

'Three siliquae if you do it now – twice your usual fee, I think?'

Decenorix bows his head again in acknowledgement. 'You have the text?'

'In here.' Saturninus taps his forehead.

From a small chest hidden in the shadows, Decenorix selects a thin sheet of lead about four inches square, a burin with a triangular steel blade and polished wood handle, a bronze pen, ink and parchment. He unstoppers the inkwell and dips the nib into it, then looks up at Saturninus and says, 'Right, Primicerius, I am ready. What wording do you require?'

Saturninus pauses, suddenly uneasy.

Why am I doing this, Pascentia? – once we laughed at such things, and now …?

But Saturninus could not have explained why, not even to himself. All he knows is that instinct, powerful and unignorable, is whispering insistently that what he is about to do must be done. He breathes deeply, then dictates, slowly and deliberately, looking not at the priest but into the lazily swaying flame of the lamp.

'To the god Mercury … to the man whom I know as Caelofernus let there never again come sleep, either by day or by night, until Atropos and I both find him and drive him into the eternal night from which there can be no return … May the hunting dogs of despair pursue him through his mind and his memory, through his veins and through the marrow of his bones. Let their cruel teeth seize him and devour him utterly, so that not one atom of his body or his spirit remains on the earth …

'And so it ends. Do you wish me to repeat any part of it?'

'No, I think I've got it all, Primicerius,' Decenorix answers calmly. Saturninus guesses that he has heard worse.

He looks over the priest's shoulder and scans the words written on the parchment, in the cursive script of seemingly careless strokes that bear little resemblance to the formal capitals of monumental inscriptions. 'Good,' he says quietly. 'Now copy it onto the lead. Mirror writing, remember, so that only the god himself can read it at a glance.'

While Saturninus waits, silent and watchful in the shadows, Decenorix spreads the thin sheet out in front of him and begins carefully incising the letters in the same cursive script, but reversed. When it is done, the priest holds it up for his inspection in a small mirror of polished pewter, the new-ploughed letters glinting silver through the dull surface of the lead.

Saturninus murmurs his approval.

'Shall I nail it up, Primicerius, or would you perhaps prefer to do that yourself? You may pick any spot, although I assure you that the god will see it wherever it might be.'

Saturninus briefly considers the offer, then shakes his head. 'No, I'll carry it with me. As you say, Mercury may read it wherever it is.'

And wherever I am.

He takes the defixio from Decenorix and rolls it into a neat cylinder, lettering inwards, before placing it carefully into his belt pouch. He thanks the priest, pays him his three siliquae, then goes to find Canio.

'The blessings of Our Lady Rosmerta be upon you, Primicerius,' Decenorix calls after him. It means nothing: Saturninus knows he gives the blessing to all who pay him.

Guessing where Canio will be, Saturninus makes his way over to the refreshment stalls on the outskirts of the market. Sure enough, he finds him there, drinking barley beer among a throng of people watching a pair of seated men playing a game of mercenaries. The battlefield is a large red tile, furrowed with a knife point into sixty-four squares before firing, resting on a small folding table set between them.

Black appears to be winning, with nine of his fifteen pieces still on the battlefield. But as he approaches, Saturninus hears Canio urge one of the onlookers to put his money on white, who still has two tribunes left to black's one. Catching sight of Saturninus he raises a hand in greeting, gulps down the last of his beer and, with exaggerated expressions of regret to his companions, extricates himself from the crowd.

Back at the guard post they find, to Canio's ill-concealed satisfaction, that Vitalinus, although looking slightly better, still feels too ill to travel.

'Not that I expect he will be,' Saturninus tells Tranquillus, 'but if he is still sick at first light tomorrow then get a message to

Aemilianus. Maybe *Dominus Noster* will want to send one of the medics on the Governor's staff out to him.'

And with that, he and Canio untether their horses, mount and trot off at a smart pace towards the tree-scattered, sharply rising ground that lies to the north. He avoids the little cemetery.

And the dead who might once have known me.

CHAPTER TEN

Saturninus is fairly certain that he knows where to find the hillside which Tranquillus described. If it is the place he remembers, then it does indeed lie in a stretch of wild and lonely country. A place where the high sheep pastures end and the thickets of gorse and bracken begin. By mid-afternoon he and Canio, riding northwards along the high ground, have reached a point no more than a mile from this wilderness, and there they halt, several hundred yards from a big long barrow. It lies before them like a great, green whale beached in the grasslands, on the edge of a steep, wooded hillside. Scattered around it, and far away into the distance on three sides, a flock of several hundred sheep is grazing peacefully.

'Maglocrouco,' Canio remarks.

'Maglocrouco,' Saturninus confirms. 'Where we turn west.'

'There's someone sitting up on top of it,' Canio points out.

Where I used to sit on hot July days, watching the little brown lizards sunbathing on the scattered fragments of limestone. Slim and quick they were, with tiny black eyes and hair-thin toes splayed wide, vanishing into the surrounding grass in the blink of an eye at every sudden gust of wind.

'I see him ... I suppose we ought to ask if he knows anything about our hole-digger.'

As they ride closer, Saturninus begins to hear the thin, haunting notes of the simple wooden flute the man is playing.

Sweet Venus – can that really be who I think it is?

But it is too late now for him to turn aside. When they are almost at the foot of the barrow the shepherd stops playing and eyes them cautiously. He is an oldish man with dark hair and beard, streaked grey, sitting with legs outstretched amid the thin, lengthening grasses and rich yellow flowers of rock roses that grow on the barrow.

'Afternoon, masters,' he calls down to them. 'Nice day for a ride.'

It is you, Etternus ... after all these years. Or are you a ghost too?

'Nice enough,' Saturninus replies neutrally. 'Tell me, we've heard a rumour that someone – not you, I'm sure – dug a hole in a hillside somewhere near here, looking for buried treasure. Would you happen to have heard anything about it?'

'Treasure you say? Buried treasure?' Etternus slowly shakes his head. 'No, I don't know about anyone finding any treasure.'

So he doesn't recognise me. Saturninus's first instinct is relief. *To him, I suppose I would be the ghost now.*

'Ah, but I didn't say he found treasure.'

'No? What did he find then?'

'You tell me.' Noticing a haze of minute, mauve-purple flowers growing between the grasses on the side of the barrow, Saturninus leans from the saddle and picks a few of their tiny leaves. Crushing them between thumb and forefinger, he breathes in the faint scent of wild thyme.

Memories of passing clouds ... And the long summer days when I watched them, lying up there on top of the barrow, almost hidden among the grasses. Those white clouds that drifted by, endlessly changing shape as they slowly dissolved into the great emptiness of the sky.

He thinks again of Pascentia.

Riding around to the north end he sees the remembered stones of the false entrance – the two uprights, the lintel, and the big closure slab below – set between twin horns of neat, curved drystone walling. Canio follows. Just in front of the false entrance, sheltered from the wind, the dying embers of a small fire are sending up a faint spiral of blue smoke.

'I wouldn't know what he found …Whoever he was.'

Saturninus looks up and sees that Etternus has walked along the top of the mound and now stands above the false entrance. 'Or tell me even if you did.' Before Etternus can protest, Saturninus asks, 'So, what do you know, shepherd?'

'I know lots of things. I saw the Dark Lady, at dusk on the night of the last new moon. Far away she was, but I knew it was her.'

So you don't want to talk about the treasure hunter. Which probably means you do know who he is.

'The Dark Lady – you mean Hecate?' Saturninus does not try to hide the scepticism in his voice. He has heard tales like this before: some of them from Etternus himself, in the long ago.

'The very same. The Queen of the Night – she who passes freely between this world and the Lower World.'

And is the goddess of wildernesses and wild places, and crossroads where three ways meet … And is the Queen of Ghosts.

Saturninus remembers the tales to frighten the children.

'Are you sure it wasn't just a big bush swaying in the night breeze? Twilight can play strange tricks on the eyes.'

'It *was* her! As sure as I'm standing here, it was her.' Etternus declares indignantly. 'And she had her great black hound with her – I saw them both.'

Saturninus is not convinced: he doesn't want to be convinced. 'A big bush and a little bush – or maybe a big bush and a big sheep. What do you think, Canio?'

'Who knows what he thought he saw?' Canio replies brusquely, almost angrily. 'Whatever it was, it's got nothing to do with why we're here. Let's be away and find that hillside.' He flicks the reins and starts his horse into a trot, around the barrow and off towards the west.

Puzzled, Saturninus looks towards his retreating back, then wishes Etternus long life and happiness, and rides after his ducenarius. When he has gone no more than twenty yards he hears Etternus's flute again. Now he is playing the tune of the *Pervigilium Veneris* – the Vigil of Venus – the same tune he taught

Saturninus to play one summer evening more than twenty years ago. Saturninus turns in the saddle, half-expecting Etternus to be looking directly at him as he plays. But the shepherd is still gazing across the grasslands to the north, seemingly oblivious to his presence now. Saturninus tells himself that it is best this way, to be known only as a stranger here.

But still it hurts to be forgotten.

He soon catches up with Canio. He has already decided that it is no business of his why the mention of Hecate seemed to trouble him. But wonders anyway. They ride on together for another mile, through the buttercup-studded grasslands, past lone, wind-bent hawthorns white as snow with may blossom, until they arrive at the gorse and bracken lands at the edge of the hills. Here they halt briefly at the head of a narrow coombe that winds slowly down to the plain below. Saturninus whispers a caution to Canio, then they ease their horses forwards again along the grassy track, the hooves making scarcely any sound audible above the gentle singing of the wind.

As they continue downwards, the wooded slopes on both sides of the coombe gradually become higher, until the track curves and the relatively gentle slope on their left changes abruptly into a massive flank of hillside – so steep that nothing grows on it but short grasses between which shards of pale, weathered limestone poke out through the thin soil.

At the foot of this hillside, on the floor of the coombe, lying on and surrounded by a mass of earth and brash, is a huge lump of limestone, honey-coloured and unweathered. For a few moments Saturninus stares at it, and at the three figures who stand beside it, their heads bowed, their voices united in a muttered chant. Their backs are turned, allowing the horsemen to come within thirty paces before a hoof clipping against an outcropping rock gives them away. Then comes a nervous glance over the shoulder, a hoarse shout of alarm, and suddenly two of the figures are running wildly away.

Hemmed in on both sides by the slopes, they stand no chance of escape. Like hunting dogs unleashed, Saturninus and Canio spring their startled mounts into a canter, easily overtake the fleeing pair, turn them, and herd them back to the rock like errant sheep. The two panting runners are men, one oldish, one fairly young; the one who did not bolt is a young woman.

All three are dressed in coarse, undyed woollen tunics, the woman's distinguishable from the men's only by its greater length. The effects of toil and hard living are etched on their faces, every inch of visible skin tanned by the action of sun and wind. Saturninus notices their fingers and palms are deeply stained by the usual mixture of soil-water, plant juices and lanolin from sheep fleeces, so that every natural crease and line is highlighted with the clarity of a skeleton leaf.

'Will you look at that!'

Saturninus glances up sharply and follows Canio's pointing arm towards a dark hole in the hillside, some fifteen feet above the fallen rock. It is roughly the size and shape of a large doorway, although from below he cannot see how far it extends back into the hill. 'You sound surprised, Canio. Don't tell me you didn't believe the report?'

Canio looks at him sideways. 'I certainly wasn't expecting a hole that big! You don't really think ...?'

'Who knows? Perhaps these good citizens can enlighten us?'

The men stare up at their captors, sullen and scared, but the woman gazes at them with the wide eyes of a child. She stretches out an arm to stroke the nose of Canio's horse, then snatches it away with a high-pitched little laugh as it tosses its head and snorts softly. All three cluster around the rock.

As if they believe it will somehow protect them.

Saturninus remembers back down the years to the other curiously-shaped rocks and vast ancient trees that were pointed out to him in wild, lonely places of the hills – by Etternus and others – as being where the guardian spirits of those places dwelt.

Set out on the rock's irregular surface is a bowl of cloudy

liquid (barley beer, Saturninus guesses), two small loaves and several bunches of wild flowers – yellow archangel, buttercups and the delicate pink of herb Robert, all fresh and unwilted. He notices that the simple woman still clutches a bunch of similar flowers in one hand.

At last Saturninus breaks the silence, speaking quietly and slowly in the British Celtic which is as much his mother tongue as Latin. 'Do you know who I am? … No? My name is Flavius Saturninus, and I command all the civil guards in Corinium and the Long Limestone Hills.' He lets the words sink in, then says, 'I've received a report of the things that happened here – strange and unlawful things … Do you know what the penalty is for those who conjure up creatures from the Lower World?' Slowly he unsheathes the sword with the snarling man-lion pommel, then turns the blade so that it catches the sunlight and glitters fire. He pauses to study their faces.

He can see the fear in the men's eyes; smell, or thinks he can smell, the pungent sweat that fear produces. Only on the woman do his words seem to have no effect. He gazes grimly at her and she smiles serenely back. Is she simply stupid, he wonders, or does she somehow sense, with an animal's instinct for survival, that he will not harm her?

Her smile slightly disconcerts him. 'So, what are your names?' he demands sternly.

The two men look one to the other, as if uncertain who should speak first. Saturninus puts on an expression of fierce exasperation and points his sword towards the older man. 'You?'

'Ind …' he swallows hard, 'Indutius, master.'

'And …?'

'This is my daughter, Ferna – and Lopsicallus, her husband.'

'And where do you come from – where do you live?'

Indutius appears uneasy. Saturninus repeats the question, and the man turns and points vaguely eastwards. 'Over there, master.'

'Does "over there" have a name?'

'Yes, master.' Saturninus frowns, Canio grins and Indutius adds quickly, 'The Villa of Julius Martinus, master.'

Saturninus gives him his most sceptical look. 'At the farm buildings, you mean? Nobody lives in the villa itself. It hasn't been lived in since the days of the Magnentian rebellion ... isn't that so?'

'Lucco the bailiff lives in it now, sirs,' Ferna breaks in earnestly. 'Ever since early spring. When he got married, our master let him and his pretty wife live there.'

'Your master? Would that be Aurelius Charax?' Saturninus sheathes his sword.

'Do you know him?' asks Ferna, awed.

'Of course,' Saturninus lies. 'But you say that Lucco the bailiff lives in the little villa now?'

'He does, sir, and now him and pretty Dulcitia sit in a beautiful room with pictures of strange birds perched in long trails of brambles all around the walls. The brambles go like this ...' and she traces their coils in the air.

I remember watching that fresco of vines being painted.

'What colour are the birds, Ferna?'

'Red and orange and blue ... and the brambles are green.'

'And why did you come here today?'

'To give the spirit of this place – and the dark gods too – food and drink and flowers so that they'll ... be nice to us and do things for us.'

'What sort of things, Ferna?'

Ferna's face clouds, and she appears puzzled. 'Not sure. Ask Loppi; he knows. He knows everything – he saw the strange men himself, just as plain as I see you now.'

Saturninus gives Lopsicallus a shrewd look. 'Is that so, Loppi, is that so? Then you'd better tell us all about them, hadn't you. Start at the beginning – and don't leave anything out.'

Lopsicallus flashes an angry, despairing glance at Ferna. As if realising that she has said the wrong thing, she looks down at the ground, away from them all, for the first time furtive and unhappy.

Now Canio joins in the act. 'Come on, Loppi, how did all this nonsense start? If you won't tell us, then we'll have to beat it out of you – and who knows what other undetected sins will come out as well, eh?'

Lopsicallus glances at Indutius, licks his lips and begins. 'It started two weeks and more ago, masters, at the time of the waning moon. I had this dream, the like of which I'd never had before. So vivid it was – as if I was wide awake and it was all really happening … Have you ever had a dream like that?'

'Perhaps.' Saturninus is aware that Canio is watching him, but he keeps his face expressionless.

'Well, in this dream I saw the edge of a rock sticking out of the hill up there. Over the years I must have seen it for real a hundred times. But in the dream it came to me that there was something special about it. So I climbed up and grabbed hold of it, and it felt loose. And I pulled, and out it came, light as a feather. Then I dreamed that strange men came out of the hole that the rock had left in the hill … and that was all there was to it really – just a weird sort of dream.' Lopsicallus shrugs apologetically.

'So why come along and dig the real thing out?' Canio enquires silkily. 'Yes, we know you did it, so don't try to tell us that you were just as surprised as everyone else to find it where it is now.'

'And what about the gold, Loppi?' Saturninus looks him straight in the eye. 'Oh yes, we know about that too – that and a lot more besides. You try to play us for fools and it'll earn you a one-way trip to Corinium. Now, tell us the whole story – every last bit of it. And if I believe you, then you can go free. But if I suspect that you've left anything out …' He taps the hilt of his sword.

CHAPTER ELEVEN

Lopsicallus has nowhere left to hide. He looks down at his feet and says quietly, 'It was like this, masters: in the dream, when I looked into the hole where the rock had been, I saw something shining. It was a big red bowl of fancy-patterned pottery, like one I once saw in the big villa, but this one was piled high with gold coins. So I reached in and took a handful – and I knew they were real, though I'd never seen a gold coin before in all my life. Then I took another handful, and then another, but no matter how many I took, the bowl always remained full.'

'Just like Rosmerta's magic tub, you mean?' Canio enquires sardonically.

Saturninus stifles a grin. 'So then what happened?'

'I woke up, masters.'

'And?'

'And what, masters?'

Canio gives an exasperated grunt. 'Don't pretend you're as daft as your wife, Loppi. What did you do? Who did you tell about the dream?'

'Nobody, masters, I told nobody at all,' Lopsicallus answers quickly.

'So, the very next night ...?' Saturninus prompts.

Lopsicallus hesitates, but he is trapped and Saturninus knows it. 'The very next night,' he mutters, 'I came up here, all alone, with a mattock, and I levered out the rock – '

'This rock? You expect us to believe that you came to prise out this damned great thing all by yourself?' Canio interrupts, incredulous.

'How was I to know it would turn out to be so big, master?' Lopsicallus sounds indignant, as if life had played yet another dirty trick on him. 'The bit that was sticking out of the grass was no bigger than my head.'

'And about as dense,' breathes Canio.

'It must have taken you all night to dig it out,' Saturninus observes, injecting a note of admiration into his voice.

'That it did, master, that it did. All of the blessed night. You can see the size of it, and a mattock's a poor tool for that sort of digging. But just before dawn, when I was thinking it would never come, I gave one last great heave on that mattock and out it came – bang! Right down to where you see it now. Nearly took me with it too,' he adds plaintively.

'And then all the little men, bless them, came dancing out of the hole – didn't they, Loppi?' says Canio.

'No, not at first they didn't, masters – or else I'd never have stuck my head into the hole to look for the gold. But when I did, all I could see was loose, brashy rock and earth.'

'What! – no gold at all? That must have come as a terrible shock,' Canio sympathises.

'It did, masters – and after all that work too!'

'It's a hard world,' Saturninus observes. 'So then what did you do?'

'I started to dig around inside the hole with the mattock. I dug deeper and deeper into the hill, and scraped out all the loose rock and earth with my hands, but I still couldn't find the gold.'

'How strange – I wonder where it could have all gone?' Canio shakes his head, baffled.

Saturninus shoots him an impatient glance and tells Lopsicallus to pay him no mind.

'It must have been about then that I first heard the noises.'

'What noises?'

'Like distant thunder it was … first off I thought it *was* thunder and didn't take much notice. Afterwards though, thinking back, it was more like the sound of a great door slowly grinding open, deep under the hill.' Lopsicallus half turns and glances nervously at the hole above him. 'Then I heard the sound of marching feet – and voices too, only all muffled so I couldn't make out a single word they were saying. I thought they were coming from the top of the hill above me, so I stopped digging and waited, still as a mouse. But the noises grew louder and then, all of a sudden, I realised that they weren't *outside* at all. They were coming from *inside* the hill, right towards me there in the hole! Pity me, masters! My heart near stopped beating and for a few moments I couldn't move a muscle, my arms and legs were that frozen with fear. But somehow I managed to scramble out of the hole, near-fell down the slope and crawled on all fours to behind those bushes over there. Then my legs gave out completely and I flopped down behind them like a dead man.'

'And what was it that you saw, Loppi? Tell me – I won't mock, I just want to know.' Saturninus speaks soothingly, aware that Lopsicallus is becoming increasingly agitated by his telling of the story.

'I saw wild men ... soldiers of sorts, though not wearing regular uniforms like you. They came a-marching out of the hole, two by two. Laughing and shouting they were, their voices all harsh and fierce-like. And they weren't little men either, they were as big as you. And they had helmets and swords and spears ... some of them with chopped-off heads stuck on the ends, and they waved them around in the air like they were flags.'

'How many of them were there, these wild soldiers?' Saturninus asks.

'Hundreds, master – hundreds and hundreds. They just kept on a-coming out of the hill, till I was thinking they never would stop; and all of them with the same sort of cruel, burnt-up faces.'

'And which way did they go ... up or down the coombe?'

'Why, they never came down here, master – praise be to the Mothers of the Hills! They just walked out into the air, for all the world as if it were solid ground. And then they kept on going

78

upwards, like they were marching up another hillside that I couldn't see. Up and up they went, and by the time they disappeared over there' – Saturninus follows his pointing finger to the wooded bank on the other side of the coombe – 'they must have been a good ten feet above the tree tops.'

'Sure you weren't walking on air yourself, Loppi? In a happy cloud of fermented barley, perhaps?'

'Canio, will you shut up and let the man finish. Is that it, Loppi? The wild soldiers went over the hill and you never saw them again?'

Lopsicallus looks shifty. 'I can't rightly say that, master.'

'Meaning what?'

'Well, after they'd gone I waited a long time, and then I walked up the coombe as best I could. And from the top, I thought I saw them again, high up in the sky over Fonscolnis way, in a long column marching south ... But maybe it was only a dark cloud – it was that far away I couldn't rightly tell,' Lopsicallus concludes lamely, aware of the look of amused disbelief on Canio's face.

'So you went back to the Villa of Julius Martinus and told your friends and relations what had happened. And then, you all came back here to ... just what did you come back for, Loppi?' Saturninus asks.

Lopsicallus stares dumbly at the ground, but then Indutius takes up the story.

'It was me who said we ought to come here, masters. I reckoned – we all reckoned – that doing what he did, Loppi had offended the guardian spirit of this place, and maybe even the dark gods of the Lower World as well. So I says we'd better come and make our peace with them all, and that's why we've been back here every day since.'

'Have you been up there too?' Saturninus points to the hole above them.

'No, master!' Indutius appears horrified. 'This rock's as near as ever we get, and we wouldn't even come this close if we didn't feel we had to.'

'Right, then I'd better have a look myself.' Saturninus turns to Canio: 'Make sure our little flock doesn't stray.' He dismounts and scrambles up the steep hillside, grasping the small outcropping rocks to steady himself, until he is standing in the hole. It is about six feet high, just wide enough for two men to emerge side by side, and extends between five and six feet back into the side of the hill, ending in a wall of broken and fissured limestone. He gives this wall several lusty kicks, but it feels solid and unyielding, and after studying it for a few moments he climbs back down.

'Nothing there, Canio. Just rock and empty space ... and friend Loppi's empty dreams.'

Canio eyes him curiously. 'You sound disappointed, Primicerius. You weren't really expecting to find a few funny little men still in there, were you?'

'No, Canio; no funny little men.'

'Or even a headless giant?'

Saturninus hesitates. 'What?'

'Vitalinus mentioned him when I was saddling his mule – said Aemilianus had told him. I don't remember reading about him in the report?' Canio rather overdoes the perplexity, furrowing his brow and shaking his head.

'He must have been there though – unless you think he appeared by magic after you'd read it?'

'Magic? Yes – that's the only possible explanation,' Canio replies, nodding sagely.

Saturninus just looks at him.

He remounts, then says quietly, so that only Canio can hear, 'You're right about one thing though: even if that rock was loose to start with, one man alone could never have levered it out by himself. Take these three back to the Villa of Julius Martinus and find out just who it was that helped Loppi with his spot of nocturnal digging. And make sure you question bailiff Lucco too. I'll lay long odds that he knows something about this business.'

'What makes you think that?'

'Because they couldn't have come wandering up here every day without him knowing about it.'

'True. Right, I'll sweat him. But what about the hole – didn't you say that Aemilianus wanted it filled in?'

Saturninus is impatient to be off. 'If you want to fill it in, go ahead.'

Canio appears mildly horrified by the prospect of manual labour. 'Me? I thought we'd get Loppi the hero and his relatives to do it.'

Saturninus grins. 'We'd never get him back into that hole again.'

'Not even if I threatened to chop off his most valuable possession – and I don't mean his head?'

'Not even that. Anyway,' Saturninus continues, 'we filled it in solid before we left – don't you remember?'

'So we did, Primicerius, so we did. Damned hard work it was too. Ah, but what if Aemilianus wants to come here and see for himself?'

'Aemilianus? Our Aemilianus? He won't come within five miles of this place ever again. A legion of elephants couldn't drag him here.'

'And if someone should tell him that the hole's still open?'

'Then they can also tell him that there's nothing but solid rock at the end of it. Besides, who knows what might have happened after we'd gone? – the powers of darkness move in mysterious ways.'

'That's a fact .... but ...?'

'Yes?'

'Do *you* think that jackass Loppi really did see men come out of the hill? I mean, he must have seen something, mustn't he? He's not bright enough to have made it all up.'

'Oh, he saw them right enough. But whether they were really

there is another matter entirely. That's something you can debate with Loppi and family on your way back to the Villa of Julius Martinus. And with bailiff Lucco too, remember.'

Myself, I don't want to believe that anything came out of that hole: the world is complicated enough at the moment. I think that what Loppi didn't dream, his imagination must have invented. It was past dawn and time was running out. Maybe he was terrified of Lucco. Then he heard distant thunder –

'And in the meanwhile you'll be at the temple of Leucesca, asking Gulioepius about your dream?'

'I will ... Shouldn't take long.' And before Canio can ask any more questions, Saturninus adds quickly, 'Just south of the road between Fonscolnis and Vadumleucara, about halfway between the two, there's another of those barrows built by the old, vanished people. Like Maglocrouco, only smaller – do you know it?'

'Corvusida?'

'That's the one. I'll meet you there at around noon tomorrow. Then we'll join the Fosse Way at Vadumleucara – and maybe you'll be back in Corinium in time for supper.'

'But what if Gulioepius tells you where Caelo – ?' Canio begins to ask, but Saturninus has already urged Antares into a trot and is moving off down the coombe. Ferna waves hesitantly. He waves back and she smiles, happy again.

CHAPTER TWELVE

Further on down the coombe the track enters a belt of woodland, but after a few hundred yards the trees end as abruptly as they began and Saturninus finds himself in open grassland again, still quite high above the plain. Leaving the track he canters north-eastwards, all the while slowly descending, until he comes to a babbling stream of bright water in the bottom of another small valley. There he pauses to let Antares drink, then splashes across and begins climbing up the valley side.

Two miles of steady riding up a long, steepening gradient bring him back onto the high scarp edge of the hills, at a point some four miles from where he left Canio. Halting to rest the horse, he looks back and sees the lowland plain spread out before him – its green patchwork of woods and small fields stretching to the far horizon, slowly becoming bluer and hazier, until at last the land seems to merge almost indivisibly with the sky.

Is it possible that you really are out there somewhere, Pascentia? Still alive, but still lost to me. Lost in the lonely vastness of the world.

He nudges Antares forwards and begins trotting north along the undulating rim of the hills, occasionally glimpsing the slowly-changing plain over the canopy of woodland which covers much of the slopes below.

As the miles pass there comes the uneasy feeling that the present and the past are converging: that the present is becoming the past.

It was sixteen years ago, almost to the day, when I last rode along this track. And nothing that I remember has changed. The sky, the trees – even the flowers – they look just the same. It's as though time itself has paused, waiting for me to return.

But the observation brings him no comfort, only a vague disquiet.

He had been with his father then, but the destination was the same – the temple of Leucesca, goddess of the never-failing spring that rises inside her temple in a wood on the edge of the hills.

That had been two days before they set out together to join the army of the usurper emperor Magnentius, an adventure which, for them, ended at the horrific battle of Mursa in the late September of that same year, 351.

They say that over fifty thousand men died in that terrible battle, Pascentia. Fifty thousand and my father. I had to leave him there, unburied. I was big for my age. Strong too. But there were many times that day when the cruel blade of a sword, or a wickedly sharp spear point, missed me by inches. Strange to reflect on this bright spring day that by now I could be nearly sixteen years dead – all that's left of me a few dirty bones scattered deep among the grasses in a place a thousand miles from here.

They gave me a choice: either join the army of Constantius II – the so-called victor of that butcher's shop – or be executed there on the battlefield. I was fourteen years and five months old. And you were still almost thirteen years away.

Unbidden and unwanted, other memories of the battle begin to return. He tries to drive them away: they are not wanted, not today of all days. But they will not go.

Stories about Leucesca were part of Saturninus's childhood. The goddess of the spring was well known throughout the northern parts of the hills, and in the flatlands far beyond, for the visions that she sometimes revealed to those who gazed into her waters. Visions that held the answers to the questions that troubled men and women and cast shadows across their lives. Questions about mundane matters, like the whereabouts of a lost or stolen beast, or a cloak, or a ring. Or of deeper things: of a lost child, or a lost love, or of a frail life that might soon slip away and be lost forever.

As he rides, Saturninus tries to ignore the suspicion which has haunted him down the years: that his father foresaw his own death in the waters of Leucesca's spring. He had made Saturninus wait outside while he went into the temple with Gulioepius, and when the priest came back out into the night, he had been left alone inside. Later – much later – he had emerged looking shaken and grim, but he never spoke of what he had seen. And whatever it was had died with him at Mursa.

But if he had seen himself die in battle, then why did he still join the Magnentian army? And why did he take me with him?

Saturninus does not know, will never know, and the not-knowing torments him as much today as it did all those years ago.

The south-west wind, warm now, blows boisterously up from the plain. It shakes the leaves of the trees and bushes … and it brings back memories of Pascentia that at last drive away the horrors of Mursa.

Wherever you are, Pascentia, in this world or another, do you still remember that hot, windy day in the vineyard near Burdigala? When we strolled between two of those endless rows of vines that flowed over the rolling land? From the high spots we gazed across the seas of green vines, and down in the hollows we were in a secret world where no one could see us, hidden behind thick walls of leaves that danced in the wind.

The hot sun of early July shone down as we sat on the cracked, baked earth and talked of the future – the future that for us never came. I noticed then, more than ever I had before, that your face had that subtle quality of changing like a spring landscape changes on a day of sun and flying clouds. Yet beneath that protean surface was always the same gentle soul that was you.
That is you.

It is already late afternoon when he arrives at the point on the scarp directly above the temple. Leaning forward in the saddle he gazes westwards at the land as it sinks irregularly down to the faraway plain, now bathed in mellow sunlight. Immediately in front of him is tussocky grassland, scattered with darker clumps of young nettles and thistles, through which a narrow path winds down the slope until it disappears into a sea of woodland. His eyes prolong the line of the path and there, just visible below the swaying tree tops, nestles a conical roof of lichen-stained orange tiles. For a few moments he stares at that roof, then urges Antares down the slope towards it.

When he reaches the trees he dismounts and leads the horse into the wood, where the air is cool and still, the wind muted to a whisper in the tree tops high above. At the woodland margin yellow archangels grow, their mysterious, convoluted flowers the bright heralds of summer. Inside the wood are expanses of bluebells, fast-fading now, and clumps of newly uncurled ferns. The path continues downwards, threading its way between great beeches, their ancient, gnarled buttress roots contrasting strangely with the exuberant spreading fronds of the new season's growth on the younger trees. Other roots spread half-exposed across the path, like veins on the back of an old man's hand; and hidden in the branches, high above, a pigeon croons the same three notes over and over again, as if in a self-induced trance. As the wood encloses him he feels a womb-like sense of peace and tranquillity.

Like I felt deep among the vines at Burdigala, when you were beside me. Sweet Venus, are you here – is that what the dream …?

He walks faster, and after a hundred paces sees the path open out into a large, sunlit clearing. His eyes rake the clearing, seeing on one side the circular temple whose roof he glimpsed from the plateau above. Built of honey-coloured stone, its central tower is some thirty feet high and surrounded on all sides, like a collar, by an enclosed ambulatory. The only windows he can see are beneath the eaves of the tower, little more than a ring of vertical slits, their arched heads formed of flat red tiles set on edge. On the far side of the clearing is what he remembers as being the priest's house, a two-storey building constructed of the same materials as the temple.

And midway between temple and house, seated in a wicker chair with solid arms and a high back, he recognises Gulioepius. But only just. In his dream the priest had been as he remembered him from sixteen years before, and those years have withered him into an old man. Pale robed, he sits in the sunlight, his gaunt face framed by a mass of white hair and beard. Still leading Antares, Saturninus walks towards him, out of the shadow cast by the temple. As he comes closer he realises that the old man is not looking directly at him but is turning his head away slightly to one side, listening like a wary animal. And then Saturninus notices the dull blankness of his eyes: the man is blind.

CHAPTER THIRTEEN

'I bid you welcome, soldier.' The voice sounds querulous and thin. Perhaps slightly nervous too. 'And what has brought you to the temple of Leucesca on this fine, sunny day?'

Saturninus tenses for a moment, uncertain, then relaxes as he realises that the old priest's sightless eyes are directed towards a point at least a yard away from where he stands. It is the rustle of his scale cuirass and the soft clink of the little medallions on Antares' harness that have announced his trade. 'My horse has brought me here, Gulioepius – my horse, Antares.'

A flicker of amusement crosses the old man's face. 'Indeed, soldier? And has the sagacious beast informed you why he has done so – or would he prefer to tell me in his own words?'

'Oh, we have no secrets from each other, do Antares and I. He's looking for a man called Caelofernus, and he's taken it into his head that you know who he is and where we might find him.'

'Caelofernus, you say? Caelofernus?' Gulioepius's face distorts in a strange look that could be puzzlement or pain. 'I seem to know that name, and yet I can't recall from where.'

So he has heard of him!

Saturninus feels his pulse quicken. 'Would a silver siliqua help to clear the mists from your memory?'

Gulioepius ignores the cynicism, perhaps because he is too deep in his own thoughts. 'Was it in a dream?' he wonders aloud. There is a long pause, and then he adds, 'I remember that once I dreamed I was in a great, darkened hall. So vast it was that I could barely make out the roof high above me. Torches, smoky torches which lit up little but themselves, burned all along the far-away walls.'

Surely that can't be where Caelofernus is?

But Saturninus has to ask. 'Where was this great hall?'

Gulioepius slowly shakes his head. 'I have no idea. I had never seen it before, or seen it since, not even in dreams.'

'But Caelofernus was there, wasn't he – what did he look like?'

'Caelofernus? No, there was no other man there, soldier; only myself and the three women.'

'What three women?' Saturninus begins to feel the frustration of the hunter who has glimpsed his quarry on the far side of a river which he has no means of crossing.

Gulioepius appears to be struggling to remember. 'In the middle of the hall there was a high platform, and on that platform were three great chairs, like thrones, and in each chair sat a strange woman. They had the faces and bodies of young women, but I knew that they were old – far older than myself. Then one of the women spoke to me, and her voice was like the winter wind sighing through dead grasses.'

Saturninus waits, but Gulioepius shows no sign of continuing. 'So what did the woman say, Gulioepius? Did she talk of Caelofernus? Is that where you heard the name?'

'I cannot remember what she said. I have tried many times to recall her words, but now I think they are gone forever.' There is an infinite sadness in the old man's voice.

'But you are sure it was in this dream that you heard the name Caelofernus, aren't you?' Saturninus persists. He feels desperation now. To have come so close, and then …

'Soldier, in these days of darkness I am sure of nothing, nothing at all.'

'So where *did* you hear the name Caelofernus?' Saturninus tries not to let the exasperation show in his voice, knowing it will achieve nothing.

'Perhaps it was Bodicca who told me? We used to talk so much in the old days.'

'Bodicca? Who's Bodicca?'

There is another long silence, and then Gulioepius says, 'I remember that she had a handful of wool and a spindle, and even as she spoke to me she was teasing out the wool and spinning it into thread – '

'Who, Bodicca?'

'Bodicca? … No, it was one of the women in the dream …' Gulioepius's voice fades away, and the silence that follows is like the final dying of a long-smouldering fire.

Saturninus's patience dies with it. He drops Antares' reins, stoops down and grasps Gulioepius's thin wrists. 'Think, old man, think!' He is aware that his voice is harsh and urgent now, but he cannot soften it. 'When and where did you hear the name Caelofernus? You *must* have heard it somewhere. Think – was it in another dream, perhaps – a dream of a battlefield, a circle of standing stones and a bright, full moon? Was Caelofernus once a stone that you turned into a man?'

But Gulioepius's dead eyes stare up at him without comprehension, and Saturninus at last realises that the old priest knows nothing of his dream.

'Don't you dare hurt him! If you harm her priest in this holy place, then the vengeance of Leucesca will pursue you to your death and beyond!'

It is a female voice. Saturninus drops Gulioepius's wrists and swings around to see a slim young woman standing beside the temple and glaring angrily at him. She is, he guesses, no more than fifteen, with a pale, intelligent face and abundant dark red hair swept up into a tightly coiled bun. She puts him in mind of a young kestrel, fierce and beautiful.

Before he can reply, while he is still considering whether to play indignant or conciliatory, Gulioepius calls out in his high, rusty voice, 'It's all right, Vilbia – don't distress yourself. The soldier wasn't hurting me.' He turns his head slightly and adds, 'You mustn't mind Vilbia, soldier; these days she worries over me like a mother with her firstborn child.'

'Your daughter?'

The old man sighs. 'No: I had no wife. The goddess would not have wished it.'

While Gulioepius was speaking, the young woman had circled around Saturninus in a wide arc and now stands beside the old priest. Taking his hand she gently rubs the backs of his long, thin fingers.

'Vilbia, the soldier wants to know where he can find a man called Caelofernus, and I'm sure I've heard that name somewhere before ... Somewhere. But now I can't recall where, or when. I simply can't ...'

Still looking anxiously down at Gulioepius, Vilbia says coldly, 'I'm sure he has told you everything he possibly can, soldier. Please go now, and leave him in peace.'

Saturninus shakes his head. 'No, I can't do that. He must know where I can find Caelofernus – or if he doesn't, then nothing makes sense.'

'I don't understand – surely you must have other and better sources of information than a blind old man who hasn't left this place in years?'

Saturninus hesitates, considering how much he will have to tell her. 'At dusk yesterday,' he begins cautiously, 'I had never even heard the name Caelofernus. But last night ...'

'Yes?'

She is looking directly at him now and he knows there is no way back. 'I had a dream. A strange dream. In that dream Gulioepius led me to Caelofernus, and so brought about my death.'

'I still don't understand?'

'I dreamed that Gulioepius showed me a tall stone which had the name Caelofernus carved on it. Then he turned that stone into a living man, and that man then killed me with my own sword – all under the full moon which is now little more than three days away. And that is why I believe – why I believed – that he must know where I can find Caelofernus. Now do you understand?'

Vilbia regards him curiously, then nods. Placing Gulioepius's hand back on his lap, she walks quickly over to Saturninus and whispers, 'There is perhaps another way to find your Caelofernus ... I could ask Leucesca.' As if anticipating his scepticism she adds, 'If Gulioepius ever knew, then she must know too.'

'*You* ask her?'

'Why not? I am her priestess. Before his illness, Gulioepius taught me all that he knew, all that he had learnt in her service over more than forty years. So now I am the one who looks into the waters of her spring to see what she chooses to show. I am the finder of the lost and the interpreter of dreams.'

But can you really find Caelofernus for me?

To give himself time to think, Saturninus asks, 'So how did Gulioepius come to choose you as his successor?'

'Gulioepius did not choose me,' Vilbia replies simply. 'It was Leucesca who chose me.'

'Have you ever seen her, your goddess of the spring?'

Vilbia appears surprised by the question. 'Nobody has ever seen her, at least not that I've heard tell.'

'And yet you believe that she exists?' It is as much a statement as a question.

'Of course she exists. Don't you believe in the old gods?'

'I believe ... that in such matters people often believe what they want to believe – what they think is in their best interests to believe,' Saturninus replies coolly.

'And sometimes they disbelieve because they don't want to believe. And sometimes they even believe against their will – as you believe in your dream, perhaps?'

And sometimes they're impressed against their will.

'Well, whatever I believe or don't believe, I've come a long way to get here. So, I might as well find out what your goddess knows. Let's go and ask her, shall we?'

'It's not so very far from Corinium, is it? Not on a fine horse like yours, Primicerius Saturninus.' He sees an impish amusement in her face as she scans his own, watching his reaction to the revelation that she knows his name. But he lets the ice in his grey-blue eyes freeze her in the still-warm sunlight, so that she continues quickly, 'I saw you in Corinium, on that day around the ides of October last, when you escorted that poor man Frontinus through the streets and out into the amphitheatre. I think I'll remember the look of terror on his face for as long as I live.'

Perhaps she wants to stop there, but he stares into her eyes, forcing her to go on, to tell him all she knows.

'I heard the roar of the crowd when at last they set the dogs on him – I heard it from a mile away. Nobody deserves to die like that, not even a brigand and murderer like Frontinus. And he didn't die quickly, did he? The shouts went on for too long ... and I can still see his face.' Her eyes shut, as if to blot out the memory, and the spell is broken.

Why, of all things, did she chance to witness that? Saturninus wonders bitterly. 'No, the good people of Corinium had their money's worth that day. You can't blame them of course, executions being the only entertainment they're allowed to see in the amphitheatre these days.'

'And did *you* enjoy the show too?' Vilbia asks, almost inaudibly. Her head is turned away from him now, but he thinks her eyes are still closed.

'Well of course I did: I'm a soldier and we soldiers all like killing.' He is fatalistically aware that she must already think him a brute.

Vilbia opens her eyes then. He sees her looking into his face, as if trying to judge how much truth is mixed with the irony. But he keeps his face as expressionless as his voice. He will not seek understanding; not hers, not anyone's.

Except Pascentia's, if ...

'You don't really mean that, do – ?'

'Oh, enough of this!' Time and the bitter memories of this place sixteen years ago are crowding in on him now. 'Frontinus is

93

dead and gone. Forget him. But Caelofernus is alive and out there somewhere. So go and ask your goddess where he is. Go on, ask her now and have done with it!'

His sudden anger flusters her. 'I can't – not now. We must wait until nightfall before I can ask.'

He gives an exaggerated sigh. 'Oh yes, I forgot – your goddess is a creature of the night, isn't she? Just like a … what do they call them, those ladies in Corinium who wear yellow – ?'

'No, please, I beg you – do not speak of Leucesca so!' Saturninus hears Gulioepius's voice, animated with distress. He turns, to see the old man half risen from his chair, his thin arms, corded with blue veins, shaking with the strain.

'Ah, so you've decided to return to the world of the wicked. Don't fret – I was only joking. A brutal soldier's joke. Vilbia understands that, don't you Vilbia?' He turns and smiles bleakly at her.

But Vilbia is looking up at the sky. 'Soon now the unconquered sun will sleep in the west. You should go now, Primicerius Saturninus, and await that sunset. Then wait as long again. Please eat and drink nothing while you are away, and when you return go straight to the temple. In the doorway you will see a single candle burning, and in a niche below it, a bowl. Place five silver siliquae in the bowl and then go inside. Wait for me there. I will not be long … But Primicerius Saturninus, please, please, on no account look into the waters of the spring alone.'

'And what would happen if I did – accidentally, of course?'

'Her waters are where the spirit of Leucesca dwells,' Vilbia says carefully. 'Those whose eyes trespass into them without invitation will never find what they seek there.'

'I wonder if my father found what he sought there?' Saturninus murmurs. Vilbia looks at him questioningly, but before she can ask, he says, 'Then I shall restrain my natural curiosity until the proper time – which, it would seem, will be after star-rise.' As he gathers up Antares' reins, he asks, 'By the way, who is Bodicca? Gulioepius mentioned her. Said he might have heard the name Caelofernus from her.'

'Bodicca? She's a wise woman – or a mad woman: people call her both. She lives down on the plain, about three miles from here.'

'Does she now? But where, exactly?'

'Just follow Leucesca's stream downhill. Bodicca's house is near the bank – you can't miss it.'

CHAPTER FOURTEEN

And so Saturninus leads Antares through the wood and follows the little stream as it splashes and sings its way down between the trees and out onto the plain. In the evening sunshine he walks along its meandering bank, among the white clouds of cow parsley and the deeply-veined leaves of the meadowsweet which will rise up tall and flower in the high summer that he wonders if he will live to see.

Not long before sunset he comes to a circular, stone-walled dwelling with a thatched roof. It stands at the side of a small wood which grows right down to the water's edge. He knocks, and calls Bodicca's name, but there is no reply, so he pushes the door open. There is no one inside. Gambling that she is not far away, he starts walking again, intending to circle the perimeter of the wood.

And soon he sees, some fifty paces ahead, a woman carrying a large wicker basket. She appears to be searching for something among the dense vegetation. Antares neighs softly and the woman turns. She is, Saturninus guesses, in her mid-thirties, with thick auburn hair and a strong, expressive face. As he approaches, she swiftly pulls a cloth over the contents of the basket, her eyes narrowing in suspicion.

'Bodicca? ... Don't be afraid; Vilbia told me where to find you.'

'Did she now? And why did she do that?' Bodicca asks, still wary.

'Because Gulioepius remembered the name of a man I'm looking for, and thought he might have heard it from you.'

'From me? He can't have heard it from me: I haven't seen old

Gulioepius for ages now. Besides, I'm sure I wouldn't know anyone that the civil guard is chasing.'

'The civil guard isn't chasing him: I am. It's a personal matter.'

'So what's his name, this man you're after?'

'His name is Caelofernus. Have you heard of him?'

'Caelofernus? Let me see now … walk with me back to my house while I try to remember.'

So they walk together in silence through the lengthening shadows, while the great cherry-red disc of the sun begins to slide below a rim of cloud on the north-western horizon. Bodicca sits on the edge of the stream and Saturninus settles down beside her, setting Antares free to graze the lush grass. To re-start the conversation, he asks her what is in the basket that she doesn't want him to see.

'Oh, just leaves and flowers,' she answers vaguely. 'For medicines and ointments, you understand.'

'And spells?' Saturninus cannot resist asking.

She gives him a sideways look. 'How is Gulioepius these days?'

'Old and blind and rambling in his thoughts,' Saturninus replies, thinking that she must surely know that already.

'I should have been priestess after him, you know. But the goddess chose her, when she was no more than a child. Or so Gulioepius said.' Saturninus says nothing, and Bodicca muses on. 'It must be terrible to be blind, never to see the beauty of the world again … Do you know what I saw at dawn yesterday, as I stood at this very spot?'

'No, what did you see?'

'I saw one of the hooded spirits, a *Cucullatus*.'

'Did you indeed? And what was he doing?'

Bodicca seems not to notice the amusement in his voice. 'Just drifting a little way above the ground, he was. Over there, against the lower slopes of the hills, travelling north. Only the one, mind; I didn't see the other two.'

'Have you ever seen all three?'

'Once I saw them all – saw them as plain as I see you now. Many years ago that was though ...' Bodicca seems herself to be drifting, away into her memories.

'But what about Caelofernus?' Saturninus reminds her. 'Do you remember if you've ever heard that name before?'

Bodicca raises her left index finger. 'Yes! – it's just come to me. I saw him several times when I was a little girl, down towards the south country.'

Nearly thirty years ago?

'That can't be the Caelofernus I'm looking for. What did he look like?'

'Look like? Why, much like all the others, as I recall.'

'What others?' Saturninus is beginning to suspect that she has never heard of Caelofernus, but cannot bring herself to admit it. 'Who was he with?'

'With?' Bodicca repeats. 'Why, his own people, or so I was told.'

'And where exactly was this?'

'I told you, down towards the south – '

'But exactly where? Don't you remember?'

'Yes, of course I remember,' Bodicca replies dreamily. 'They said it was a terrible place and I shouldn't go anywhere near. But I went anyway, because I didn't believe them; and besides, it was so lovely and peaceful there, where the dog roses flowered early in the warm summer winds that blew across from the estuary.'

Saturninus shakes his head in resignation. 'Bodicca, I don't think you'd ever heard of Caelofernus before I spoke the name. And besides, it's time I started back.' He gets to his feet and strolls over to collect Antares.

Bodicca lies back on the grass, fingers interlaced beneath her head, radiant as she basks in the last golden rays of sunlight. 'Goodbye ... Saturninus.'

He halts abruptly. 'How in the name of Hades ...?'

She giggles. 'Oh, I know lots of things. I'm not nearly as mad as some people say.'

'Maybe not … but you don't really know where I can find Caelofernus, do you?'

'Oh, but I do, Saturninus. And so do the *Parcae* – and if they've decided that you're to meet, then they'll guide you to him, never fear. All you have to do is follow wherever they may lead, and I promise you'll find him waiting there. Old Caelofernus has been waiting a long, long time.'

CHAPTER FIFTEEN

The first stars are already winking coldly when Saturninus reaches the edge of Leucesca's wood again. The thin night breeze is shivering the leaves of the tall beeches and he pauses for a moment and looks up at them, silhouetted black against the pale clouds drifting across the darker sky. Then, leading Antares, he hurries on into the Stygian darkness of the wood, where leafy twigs whip his face, hidden roots trip him, and only the constant plashing of the stream to his left reassures him that he is still on the correct path. At last he glimpses hazy moonlight, and a few moments later stands at the edge of the temple clearing. Taking off his helmet he hangs it from the saddle, then ties Antares' reins to a low branch and walks across to the temple. There is no sign of either Gulioepius or Vilbia.

Inside the arched entrance porch a single candle burns in a niche cut into the thickness of the stone wall. Below it, in a larger niche carved to resemble a scallop shell, he notices a small bowl of the cherry-red Samian pottery that, long ago, had been imported from Gaul by the shipload. From his belt pouch he pulls out a handful of coins and selects five of the small silver pieces called siliquae, no bigger than a man's fingernail. On the obverse they all bear an emperor's diademed head – three of Constantius II, the "victor" of Mursa; and two of Julian, who had been mortally wounded in battle against the Persians four years ago. Saturninus looks down at their tiny silver faces as they gleam softly in the candlelight, arranged on his open palm like a five of dice.

Not even you, who once ruled the whole world, could escape Death. But was it the Parcae or only blind chance that decided when you should die?

He sighs, and slides all five coins into the Samian bowl.

The door stands slightly ajar. He pushes, and it swings open almost noiselessly. He steps inside, pauses for a moment, listening, then eases the door closed behind him, hearing a sharp metallic click as it latches. On his right is a blank wall; to his left the corridor of the ambulatory curves around before him. It is lit quite brightly by candles that burn in iron sconces projecting from the outer wall at regular intervals, and by their light he sees that this outer wall is plastered and painted with vivid frescoes – three long paintings, each separated by a narrow panel depicting the whirling, dancing figures of a nymph and a satyr.

All this is new to him, for he has never before set foot inside the temple. Even after his return to the hills the old sad memories made him shun the place. There was a ghost here that he could not face: not his father's but his own.

But last night's dream has changed everything. It's as if this place is calling me back: as if there is something here that it wishes me to learn.

He looks more closely at the long frescoes.

In the first he sees a fantasy landscape, loosely based on the surrounding hill country. Here and there, on crags and in deep valleys, stand small temples and magnificent villas. In the foreground, a shepherd in a wide-brimmed hat leans on his staff as he watches his sheep graze the lush grass. From the rocky hillsides behind, several springs of azure water cascade down into the valleys.

A length of freshwater stream flows through the second panel. Above the waterline is dense vegetation – reeds and bulrushes and yellow flag irises – between which moorhens, herons, ducks and curlews watchfully stalk. Below the surface dart shoals of silvery-bellied fish. And on the surface itself, reclining on the leaf of a great yellow-flowered water lily, is a water nymph. Saturninus notices that her serene and lovely face, framed in long, auburn hair, is not unlike Vilbia's.

He moves on to the final panel, in the centre of which floats a giant clam shell. On it lies a sea god, trident in one hand, strands of seaweed woven into his hair and beard. The god clasps the hand of another water nymph *(or perhaps the same one?)* who lies beside him, her slim body naked to the waist. At her side, a large amphora empties its contents of blue fresh water into the surrounding sea. And around them both circle winged cupids, riding the waves on the backs of dolphins.

Is that what they claim you are, Leucesca, goddess of this spring: the child of a sea god and a naiad from a freshwater stream? Are these pictures telling me that your knowledge, and perhaps your powers too, are as far-reaching as the rain which falls on these hills – the rain which soaks down through the earth and limestone, until at last it is reborn from this spring? And from the spring it travels on, through the maze of tiny streams that wind their way to the rivers, and along the rivers out into the great salt ocean, which is your father's kingdom?

That same salt ocean where you died, Pascentia ... or did not die?

In the dim light filtering past the columns that separate the ambulatory from the cella, Saturninus glimpses a low circular font of carved yellow limestone set into the middle of the cella floor. The width of his outstretched arm, it rises some six inches above that floor. He moves towards it, easing between the columns. Inside the cella he glances up and sees tiny shafts of night sky through the high windows of the cella tower, lesser darknesses in the inky blackness of the roof.

Beneath his feet is a mosaic floor, a series of concentric rings of guilloche and wave-crest patterns with the font as their centre. He looks across at the solid wall of the room occupying the last quarter of the ambulatory and here, as he anticipated, is a door. At head height someone has drilled an intricate pattern of small holes in the wood, through which they can observe unseen.

Was it all just like this, that night sixteen years ago when my father stood here, on this same floor of little coloured stones, staring into ...?

He notices that the feeble light from the candles in the ambulatory is shimmering faintly off the waters of the spring. Insidiously there comes the temptation to look down into those waters. He takes one step back towards the font, but the moment he does so the soft clack of a latch makes him stop and turn sharply towards the sound.

Standing in the open doorway of the small room he sees Vilbia, no longer a child. She wears a flowing, long-sleeved dress of pure white, gathered high at the midriff by a belt or cord hidden beneath the folds of the cloth. Her dark red hair is still swept up and coiled into a cylindrical bun, but around her temples is now a broad circlet of yellow gold. She seems completely self-possessed. For a long moment he looks at her and she at him.

'Welcome to the temple of Leucesca, Primicerius Saturninus.' She smiles at him, as if noticing a tenseness which he is sure he does not show.

'Amazing – that dress puts years on you. Makes you look at least fifteen.'

She smiles again, the same calm smile. 'Don't fight me, Primicerius. You say your enemy is Caelofernus: so, shall I ask the goddess to show us where he may be found – if you are still quite sure that you wish to know?'

'It's what I've come here for.'

'Quite so ... Did you find Bodicca?'

'I found her, but ...'

'She didn't recall the name?'

'She claimed she did, but nothing she said made sense.'

'No; she is a strange one ... Tell me, if you find Caelofernus, do you intend to kill him?'

'Yes.' Saturninus sees no point in lying. 'What else can I do but see my dream as a warning? Either I kill Caelofernus or he'll kill me. Do you think my motive matters to your goddess?'

'I don't know – not for sure. Leucesca seems to reveal or withhold for reasons that are hers alone – reasons which sometimes I don't even begin to understand.'

'That's unusually candid for a priest, even a junior one. Perhaps we should start now, before the fit of honesty passes?'

Vilbia gazes down into the spring. 'Gulioepius says that those who despise others often despise themselves more.' Saturninus sees the flicker of insight cross her face as she suddenly looks up and adds, 'Do you despise yourself for fearing what you may learn here tonight?'

He ignores the question. 'Yes, I'm sure Gulioepius is full of wise-sounding sayings. Priests usually are; they're one of the tools of their trade.'

'And what is your trade, Primicerius? Brave defender of the empire against the barbarian hordes, perhaps?'

He hears the restrained anger in her voice and realises that his cynicism is beginning to destroy the air of unruffled calm that she appears to have determined shall be her armour. 'Why, I'm a butcher by trade, madam – emperors and other riff-raff come and go, but the butcher's trade is always required. Surely you knew that already?' He gives her a wan smile. 'So, now that we've established our respective functions in this world, can we please proceed?'

Their eyes meet again. Vilbia says nothing. She turns and unhooks a thin chain from a cleat on the shadowed wall behind her. There is a metallic slithering sound from above and Saturninus looks up to see a triple-spouted bronze lamp descending from out of the darkness. When it has reached chest height, she re-secures the chain to the cleat and returns to her room. From the doorway she wordlessly hands him a long taper. He lights the taper from one of the candles in the ambulatory, and with it lights each spout in turn, holding the taper's flame just above the olive oil until it vaporises and ignites with a splutter. In the lamplight he notices the wide, lead-lined opening in the side of the font, just below floor level, through which the silently-upwelling waters of the spring disappear on their way to the stream in the wood.

Vilbia comes back into the cella carrying a tray, on which stands a silver flagon, two cups and a ladle. All are skilfully moulded and decorated with dancing satyrs and maenads: the satyrs goat-eared and naked; the maenads, their ethereal female companions, wearing loose, diaphanous dresses which swirl about them as they dance.

She kneels gracefully and sets the tray down on the floor beside the font. From the flagon she pours a bright liquid, reddish in the lamplight, into both cups, three-quarters filling them. Taking the ladle, she reverently dips it into the font and tops up the cups with spring water. She hands one to Saturninus as he sits on the other side of the font. He accepts it, but seeing him hesitate she drinks from the other. So he takes a sip from his: it is wine, but he tastes just a hint of something else. His brows furrow and he looks over the rim, directly into her eyes. Wordlessly, she gives him her own cup, takes his, drinks the contents and then inverts the cup, so he can see that none remains. With a fatalistic shrug he does the same.

'An interesting taste. Would there be any point in asking what's in it? … A distillation of little toadstools, perhaps?'

Vilbia gives what she probably intends to be an enigmatic smile, but which emerges as a mischievous grin. She settles herself on the floor. Her hands, large for a girl's with their long fingers, lightly grip the edge of the font as she peers into the spring. Saturninus does the same, but can see nothing except the hazy reflection of the lamp's triple flames. Lifting the flagon, Vilbia pours the remaining wine smoothly and steadily into the water as a libation. The dark stain sinks deep, but the upwelling waters swirl and dilute it, and moments later it has all but vanished. He watches her face tauten with concentration as she stares down and begins to call softly.

CHAPTER SIXTEEN

'Leucesca, Leucesca, goddess of this spring. It is I, your servant Vilbia. I – and Saturninus here – wish to find a man called Caelofernus. If you will, Leucesca, if you will, show us where Caelofernus may be found?' Vilbia repeats this last sentence, then gazes intently into the spring.

Her belief is so obviously genuine that Saturninus too finds himself staring down into the clear water. Time passes, but he can see nothing, and remarks as much to Vilbia. She whispers to him to be patient, to keep watching.

Slowly, ever so slowly, it seems to Saturninus that it is becoming darker inside the temple. The lamp is still burning above them, and the candles in the ambulatory are still lit, but they shed no light: they appear to have shrunk to tiny points of flame in the outer darkness. But in the spring, the water is as bright and transparent as a hill stream in sunshine. He can see right down to the bottom now, see the shining gravel pebbles there; but nothing more.

Tense and restless, he whispers, 'Those are very pretty pebbles, but they're not what I came here to see. Please ask your goddess to try a little harder.'

Vilbia winces, but says nothing; and suddenly he sees the crystal waters turn milky and opaque. She sighs and relaxes her grip on the font edge. 'Ah, it's no use. That's Leucesca's way of saying that she won't show us where Caelofernus can be found.'

'Won't or can't?'

'Oh, won't. If the goddess didn't know, then the water would have remained clear. She simply does not wish to tell us – or perhaps to tell you – where Caelofernus is.'

'Why?' He tries to keep the anger out of his voice.

'I don't know – I honestly don't. But, whatever her reason, we can do nothing but accept it.'

'I'll be damned if I will! Ask her again.'

'No, I cannot. Leucesca would be angry.'

'Ask her again, Vilbia,' Saturninus repeats coldly.

'I dare not. Accept her judgement, Primicerius.'

Saturninus hesitates, but now a terrible certainty is driving him on ...

That the secret of who and where Caelofernus is – or whatever else it may be that I've been drawn back here to learn – is hidden somewhere in the waters of this spring. And only you, Vilbia, can make it come to me.

He steels himself, then says softly, 'Vilbia, there are in Corinium certain Christians – my immediate superior, the Prefect Aemilianus, among them – who would derive considerable satisfaction from destroying this temple and driving you and Gulioepius away from this place forever. All it would require is a word from me. One word. And where would you go then? Where would Gulioepius go – an old, blind man stumbling through the icy rain on a lonely road far from here? Think of that, Vilbia. Think of that, and ask Leucesca again.'

He is ready to stare her out, but she does not raise her eyes to meet his own and he knows that he had won. But the winning brings only guilt. He realises that she must think him a swine. He is a swine. And he likes the girl, which makes it so much worse.

'Leucesca, Leucesca, forgive your humble servant. But please, I beg you, show me – show us both – where this man, Caelofernus, may be found. I do not ask this for myself, but for Gulioepius, who served you so faithfully for so many years before me. Let him end his days here, in peace, not as a homeless blind beggar.'

Saturninus looks into her face as she speaks and sees that her eyes are wet with tears. *Don't feel pity!* he hears the old, hard voice of self-preservation snarl. He stares back down into the water: it is still cloudy. He glances up at Vilbia again. Her head is turned away now, her eyes tightly closed. 'Look into the water, Vilbia,' he whispers.

She shakes her head, her eyes still closed, and the conviction, illogical but absolute, comes to him that it is only her refusal to look that prevents the waters from clearing and revealing Caelofernus.

Impulsively he cups his left hand around the back of her neck and, gently but irresistibly, forces her head down to within inches of the surface. Her eyes open wide and she gives a small, startled cry because, at that very moment, the white cloudiness begins to darken and the water churns like black, billowing smoke. Saturninus releases her and grasps the edge of the font with both hands.

Out of the corner of his eye he notices that Vilbia is not attempting to look away now. She is staring wide-eyed down into the font, with the horrified fascination of a vole cornered by a stoat. For slowly, deep down in the spring, the water is clearing to reveal a strange, sunless landscape. It is barren and rock-strewn, like a desert, but unlike any desert that Saturninus has ever seen. Now he can see it clearly – see the dark pools of evil-looking, stagnant water and the weird rock formations that rise like great anthills, thin curls of smoke trailing lazily from their tops. And in the midst of this awful land is a man. He sits on a rock, dressed like a beggar in the rags of what once must have been a fine tunic.

'Is it him – is it Caelofernus?' Vilbia whispers.

'I don't know. I can't see his face properly. Look up, man, look up!' And, as if he has heard Saturninus, the man does look up. He gazes about him, and Saturninus sees a sad, emaciated face with fever-bright eyes. But it is not the face of the man he saw in his dream. 'No – it's not him, it's not him! Oh damn you, Caelofernus! – where are you?'

Slithering down from the rock, the man in the desert clasps

both hands over his ears and utters a silent wail of anguish. He breaks into a shambling run, and Saturninus watches him begin to dwindle into the forlorn distance, before the black smoke billows back and hides everything.

'If that man wasn't Caelofernus, then who was he?' Vilbia is very pale, but composed. Only a slight tremor in her voice betrays fear. 'And where was he? Leucesca has never shown me that terrible land before. Surely it's nowhere in Britannia? It was like – '

'Like what?' But Saturninus thinks he knows what she is about to say.

'It was like a region of the Lower World – or how it was once described to me.' Then, as if fearing that he is about to do so, she says quickly, 'Please don't ask me to try to find him again.'

Saturninus looks up at her and forces a smile. 'No, I won't ask you ... Or bully you.' He wants to say something gentle and reassuring to her, to make some atonement for his roughness. But the years have leached so much of the gentleness out of his soul that the right words will not come – and then the moment is past and gone forever. 'But we'll keep watching, just in case Leucesca chooses to show us something else. Agreed?'

Vilbia hesitates, then nods her assent, and so they settle down to a wordless vigil.

Time passes, ever more slowly, until a point comes when, for Saturninus at least, it seems to have stopped altogether. He is possessed by a strange, light-headed sensation of being outside time, as if all the world beyond the walls of the temple has vanished away. As if the sun will never rise again and they will drift forever inside this globe of subdued lamplight and overlapping shadows, adrift on a great, black sea of endless night.

'What makes you so sure that what you dreamed will actually happen ... unless, of course, you find and kill Caelofernus first?'

Vilbia's voice, soft, but startlingly loud in the stillness of the temple, jolts Saturninus out of his semi-trance. For a few moments his wits are scattered and he answers evasively. 'That's a strange question, coming from the interpreter of dreams herself. Surely you, of all people, must believe that my dream was sent by a god – or perhaps even a goddess – to warn me of a coming danger?' In an attempt at humour, he smiles and adds, 'You really shouldn't ask questions like that, or you'll be out of business in no time and ...' He stops as he catches the intense gaze of her young eyes. She deserves better than a cheap witticism. He sighs. 'The truth is, Vilbia, that I'm not really sure at all.'

'But you said – '

'I know what I said. Certainty comes and goes, but the doubts never go away.' He hesitates, then realises that he wants to tell her. 'Years ago, and a world away, I sat beside a dying campfire in a desert, under a great dome of night sky that glittered with a hundred thousand stars. In Mesopotamia such skies are not uncommon, but you rarely see their like here, except on some bitter-cold nights in deep winter. On the other side of the fire sat a half-Persian trader who called himself Tamsomeres. We got talking, as strangers do at night when they're both a long way from anywhere that they can call home, and by and by the conversation drifted around to dreams and their meanings. He reckoned that those dreams which seem to warn of coming danger can have at least three origins.'

'And they are ...?'

'Well, there are those dreams whose roots lie in the bitter memories of things a man has experienced at some time in his past.'

'So they're just nightmares, nothing more?' Half statement, half question from Vilbia, as she sits cross-legged on the cool mosaic floor, clasping her foremost shin with both hands through the fabric of her dress.

'Just nightmares,' Saturninus confirms. 'The children of the mind's own fears.'

Was that the origin of your dream at Burdigala, Pascentia: the fear that you'd never see me again after we'd parted? Just as you never saw your parents again after they sold you to Metilius?

'So what are the other sorts of warning dream – according to Tamsomeres?' She seems eager to learn.

'The second and third types of dream are, so he believed, the ones sent by the Unseen – by a god or a goddess … or whatever.'

Vilbia inclines her head, the lamp's triple flames casting highlights into the tarnished copper of her hair. 'As you believe your dream was sent?'

'Perhaps … The problem is that we never really know *why* such dreams are sent – at least, not until it's too late.'

Vilbia makes no comment, but Saturninus reads the uncertainty in her face. 'You see, Tamsomeres said that a dream sent by Ahuramazda, his god of light, might be a simple, uncomplicated warning of approaching danger – that's the second type. But the very same dream, if sent by Ahriman, the evil one, the god of darkness, might be a trap – an attempt to frighten a man into doing something fatal that he would never otherwise have done.'

'But how could – ?'

'In the same way that a hunter sets one of his hounds at the spot where a path branches in the forest. That hunter's intention is to frighten a deer into going down the path he's chosen, the one that leads to the place where his nets are stretched and he and his other hounds are waiting. And so, trying to avoid the visible danger, the deer runs into a greater, hidden one. It doesn't see the raised spear, or the cruel teeth. Not until it's too late. Not until there's no going back. So, who sent my dream, Vilbia: Ahuramazda or Ahriman …?' He gazes at one of the haloed candles in the ambulatory, a small point of fire in the darkness.

'You really don't know which of those three types your dream might be?'

He shakes his head. 'It might be meaningless, but I don't think it is. It might be a genuine warning to beware of a real person called Caelofernus. Or it might be that the Caelofernus I saw in my dream was only a mask – and behind that mask there hides another danger, one which my mind has somehow sensed but can't identify. Like a dog barking in the night at something hiding out there in the darkness – something that it hears but cannot see.'

He realises that Vilbia is looking curiously at him. Then she glances down at the font, and a moment later gives a little cry of surprise. 'Oh, look! Look!'

Deep in the water, deep and yet so close, there has appeared the figure of a woman in a pale blue dress. She is quite young, lithe and alert, with long dark curly hair. She stands on a seashore, her back to the water. Behind her small wavelets lap the beach, and further out the sea merges into a wall of mist, tinted blue by the sunlight reflected off the water. The woman is looking about her, shielding her eyes against the invisible sun, as if searching for someone or something.

At the first sight of her, even before he can see her face clearly, Saturninus feels his whole body tense. His hands grip the font edges more tightly and he stares intently down. Then the woman looks up at the sky which only she can see.

'Pascentia! Pascentia!'

But the woman in the blue dress shows no sign of having heard him. She begins walking along the shore, still shielding her eyes and peering into the distance. 'Pascentia!' Saturninus calls again. He turns to Vilbia, now kneeling beside him, and asks hoarsely, 'Why can't she hear me? The man could hear me, so why can't she?'

Vilbia shrugs helplessly. 'I don't know. Perhaps it's because Leucesca – '

'Pascentia – look at me! Where are you?' he cries, desperate now.

But the woman continues her slow walk along the shoreline, and soon the mist out on the water starts to advance. It doesn't stop at the water's edge, but rolls inexorably up the beach until it has engulfed her and everything else in the vision. He stares at the swirling mist, until presently it dissolves away, leaving nothing but the clear water of the spring. He becomes aware that Vilbia is speaking.

'Shall I ask Leucesca to show you more, if she's willing? ... More of that woman, I mean, not of the man before her,' she adds quickly.

But he knows, knows with a leaden certainty, that it would be futile, and yet ... There is a long pause, then he whispers, 'No: I think that Leucesca has shown me all that she's willing to let me see.'

Pushing himself upright, Saturninus murmurs that he needs air. He walks slowly out into the ambulatory and Vilbia hears the double click of the door latch, then silence. After a little while she herself stands, smoothes her dress and methodically replaces the cups, flagon and ladle onto the tray and carries them all back into her room. She extinguishes the oil lamp's triple flames, then pads noiselessly around the ambulatory, softly blowing out all the candles until she arrives at the door. There she pauses for a moment and looks back into the darkness, before she too lifts the latch and slips outside into the cool night to join Saturninus.

CHAPTER SEVENTEEN

Saturninus is sitting in Gulioepius's chair, in a pool of the moonlight that comes flooding in over the black tree tops. Vilbia approaches, keeping in the moon shadows. Quiet though she is, he hears her coming. 'Why, Vilbia? Why did your Leucesca choose to show me her, after what I …?'

'I don't know,' she replies gently. 'But Leucesca must have her reasons. Perhaps if I knew more about Pascentia …'

Saturninus is trying to fix a fleeting image in his mind. For those few moments she had seemed so close, but already the fine details of that vision in the spring are slipping away, as those of the dream slipped away.

Perhaps talking would …

'I first met her almost exactly three years ago, in the mid-May of 364, on the banks of the river Moselle, a few miles downstream from the city of Treveri, in eastern Gaul – you've heard of Treveri?' He takes her silence as confirmation.

'At that time I was on my way back from Syria. I was sick of soldiering, and that last campaign into Persia was one too many for me. I'd taken an arrow in the shoulder towards the end of the retreat, and back in Antioch I let the legionary surgeon convince himself that my right arm would never be much use again. And so they kicked me out of the army, *missio causaria* – honourable discharge due to wounds – '

'Were you in Persia with the Emperor Julian – were you actually there when he was killed?' Vilbia sounds astonished.

'Yes, I was there. Right to the bitter end.'

There is an edge to Saturninus's voice: a warning.

Nevertheless, it seems that Vilbia cannot resist asking, 'Could you tell me about it ... not now perhaps, but before you go?'

'What do you want to hear? About Julian's glorious victories? Well, there weren't many of those, not in Persia. About the women and children slaughtered when he let his army – the army of which I was part – sack the city of Maozamalcha? Of how he burnt alive the Persian commander of that city's garrison? Of how he seemed to lose his nerve outside the walls of the Persian capital, Ctesiphon, and began a headlong retreat?

'Or would you prefer to hear about the final days of that retreat – when we marched across a near-desert, harried by Persian skirmishers and with scarcely any food or water left? When men dropped, exhausted, in their tracks and were left to die where they fell. I still see them in dreams.'

Sometimes, far away, one of them raises an arm, begging me to go back and help him. But I can't. I can never go back. In both dreams and life, I can never go back into the past and change it.

'Was it that terrible?' she whispers.

'It was worse than you could ever imagine.'

He notices her looking away, over the tree tops to the starry sky beyond. 'Then tell me about Pascentia.'

He sighs. 'Pascentia: I was riding north towards Treveri. Thirty miles from that city I had a disagreement with three German auxiliary cavalrymen from one of the units on the Rhine frontier. They'd apparently taken it into their heads that I was a deserter. I never knew why. One of them went for his sword, and it was him or me.

'The other two came after me, but night was falling and I managed to escape into the darkness. Even so, I thought it unwise to stay on the road, so I rode across country for much of the night. At dawn I stopped and got a few hours sleep before setting off again, all the while heading north.'

'Until you came to the River Moselle?'

'At around mid-morning. I came over a rise and there it was

below me, flowing east towards the Rhine in great, meandering loops. The slope immediately below me was covered with hundreds of rows of vines running down to the water. On the bank, a little way off to my right, was a long, low building, roofed with slate that gleamed like silver when the sun caught it. Behind it was a landing stage, and moored there was a sea-going ship, its single sail furled up and hanging in great swags from the cross-spar. And on the gangplank was this solitary figure in a long, leather *cucullus*, rolling a barrel slowly up towards the deck.'

'And that was her?'

'Patience, child.' He wonders if she can see his smile in the moonlight. 'To this day I can't give a logical reason why I went down to the river. The impulse came and I simply urged my horse forward. Next moment it was picking its way down the slope, slipping and slithering on what looked more like the debris from a stonemason's yard than soil. After I'd started down I didn't have time to look around, or think of anything but avoiding a broken neck, and when I reached the landing stage and dismounted I found it deserted.'

I remember how its warped planks creaked as I walked across them, and the musty smell of damp, sun-warmed timber that hung in the air all around.

'By then the barrel was standing alone up on the deserted deck of the ship, which had the name *Zephyrus* painted on its bow – '

'The kind west wind.'

'The west wind,' Saturninus confirms.

But not always kind.

'I guessed that the man who had been loading the barrel was either below deck or in the warehouse. I tried the warehouse first. As I stood in the entrance, staring into the dimness, I heard the squeak of a hinge from the back of the building and saw a tiny flash of sunlight as a small door opened and closed in a moment. I groped my way between the stacked barrels and found the door, just in time to see the man in the *cucullus* crouch down behind a row of vines. Realising that I'd seen him, he sprang up and started off again up that damned slaty scree like a mountain goat. But, agile though he was, he was more or less trapped between the rows. He heard me scrabbling up behind him and swung around with a wicked little dagger in his hand. The movement made the hood of the *cucullus* fall back, and I saw that "he" was a woman.'

'So it *was* her, that figure on the gangplank.'

Saturninus hears the faint note of triumph in her voice. He smiles again. 'Did I ever say it wasn't? She looked to be in her mid-twenties, slender, with dark brown hair, rich and glossy in the sunshine as it curled on her shoulders. I couldn't in truth describe her as beautiful, or even ordinarily pretty. Her mouth was a shade too wide and her eyes a shade too small for that. But there was an energy, an animal vitality and intelligence about her face that beguiled me from that first moment I saw her.

'I told her not to be afraid, that I wasn't going to hurt her. When she asked me who I was, she spoke with an accent that I hadn't heard for many a year – an accent I'd long lost myself. So I asked her from what part of these Long Limestone Hills she came. She smiled then and said that she was from the south; that she'd been born near the temple of Mercury at Alaunarraco.'

'Near Ovilregis? That can't be more than thirty miles south of here. How strange.'

'And stranger to think that, when we were children, we lived little more than a day's walk apart, and never once chanced to meet. And then, hundreds of miles away, in a foreign land on the other side of the Oceanus Germanicus, in a place where I'd never intended to be ... there she was.'

'Perhaps the gods had destined you to meet that way?'

'Or perhaps such things just happen as part of the random chaos of the universe: who knows?' He glances up at the moon. 'She told me her name was Pascentia, and that she was the wife of a wine merchant from Londinium, who was lying sick on board the ship. Metilius – that was her husband's name – had bought a consignment of wine from a Treveri vintner, and they were there to take delivery of it.

'But they'd scarcely set foot on the landing stage before the vintner's bailiff had come running up, sweating with fear and shouting a rumour that several hundred Franks had crossed the Rhine and were heading that way. Duty done, he'd jumped on his horse and galloped off upriver, back towards Treveri. But the crew had overheard the warning and promptly panicked and ran away. So, with the towing gang already long gone, she and Metilius were left quite alone ... On the Moselle they either carry wine barrels in big rowing barges, or else they use seagoing ships which they tow upstream, against the current, by a great rope attached to a dwarf mast near the prow.'

'I've heard they do the same on the Sabrina, from the point where the tide can't carry them any further.'

'So they do, Vilbia. So they do. Anyway, Metilius was not a well man. He was some twenty-five years older than Pascentia and had bought her from her parents when she was little more than a child.'

'Pascentia's a name the Christians often give to their girl children, isn't it? Was she ...?'

'No. Metilius's first wife was a Christian, and it was she who gave her that name when they bought her. But Pascentia and Metilius – no.'

'How old was she when they bought her?'

'Ten, she told me. Just ten years old.'

'So young,' Vilbia murmurs.

'And at first she was little more than a slave. But she was quick-witted and hard working, and as the years passed, Metilius – a widower by then – came to rely on her more and more in business matters. In the end he married her to give her his name so that she could legally act on his behalf. Oh, I don't think it was as cold-blooded as it sounds. He had treated her well from the first and she was grateful to him, but by the time I met them they were more like father and daughter than husband and wife.

'Metilius had been ailing for years, off and on. But Pascentia was a fighter. Metilius had paid good money for the wine stacked in that warehouse, and she wasn't going to leave it to be looted by a bunch of thieving barbarians. That's why she was trying to load it all by herself. And when she'd done that, she planned to cast off and let the current carry them down to the Rhine.'

'But wasn't that the way the Franks were coming from?'

'Oh, she wasn't afraid of meeting them when the ship was out in mid-stream – Metilius had told her that most Franks can't swim.'

'That's not true, is it?'

'No, of course not – some are even born with webbed feet.' That makes Vilbia giggle. It is the first time Saturninus has heard her laugh.

So like …

'But those barrels were big and heavy, and the gangplank was steep because the river level was high. Pascentia had been toiling for hours, but she'd only managed to load a dozen. So, she needed help, and I needed transport back to Britannia. At that moment it seemed a simple and uncomplicated arrangement.

Or perhaps it wasn't, not even then.

'Anyway, I loaded the barrels and she showed me how to lower them down another ramp into the hold, steadying them with a rope, and then how to lash them to the posts down there, to stop them shifting during the voyage. Sometimes I can close my eyes and I'm back in the warm half-light of that hold. Hearing the soft lap and swirl of the current against the hull, smelling the scent of the wine barrels and feeling my hands hot and prickly from the coarse-fibred rope.

'And I can see her face and her slim brown hands as she shows me how to tie a carter's knot to tighten the ropes that held the barrels down.

Actually, I already knew how. But I pretended I didn't, just to hear your voice and have you standing close beside me.

'There was a barely repressed hint of playfulness in her eyes, a sort of childlike quality that all the troubles of her life hadn't managed to destroy.'

'I think ... '

'What?'

'I think that you'd already fallen in love with her.'

'Perhaps I had.'

'Even though she was married?'

Saturninus thinks she sounds more puzzled than judgemental. He says quietly, 'Do you really think we choose who we fall in love with? Perhaps when you're older ...' He shrugs and leaves the rest unsaid.

'When all the wine was loaded, I unsaddled my horse and sent it trotting away upriver, because I thought it wouldn't be possible to take it all the way to Britannia on a ship that wasn't equipped for transporting horses. And then we cast off the mooring ropes and began to drift downstream. Most of the time I operated the great steering oar in the stern, but when the current carried us too close to the bank Pascentia took over, while I tried to push the ship back into mid-stream with a long pole.

'Shortly after we'd set off she called to me and pointed to my horse, which was following along the bank in fits and starts. It kept this up for a while, dropping behind now and then as it munched at clumps of the sweet new grass, then cantering to catch up again. Then it stood on the bank and neighed loudly, as if it didn't want me to abandon it there. Pascentia must have seen the indecision on my face. It was she who begged me to take the horse with us back to Britannia.

You had the gentlest soul of anyone I've ever known. You hated cruelty and the causing of pain. And although you never said so, I think you had your own fears of being left alone and friendless, a stranger in a strange land.

'So I steered into the bank, tied the *Zephyrus* to a couple of vine stakes, dropped the gangplank and somehow managed to bring it aboard.'

'Was that the same horse you rode here today?'

'The very same. Antares has seen almost as much of the world as I have. We had to stop from time to time to gather grass, but otherwise he was no trouble at all on the entire voyage. And that Moselle was the twistiest river I've ever seen. It turned and looped and doubled back on itself, as it wound between slaty hills that seemed to have a darkness in them, even at that brightest time of the year.

'In the evening of the second day we reached the town of Confluentes, where the Moselle flows into the Rhine. By then I'd guessed that there weren't really any Franks about, not west of the Rhine anyway. And once we'd joined that great river things became easier. We bought hay for Antares and hired a couple of sailors at Confluentes, and a few more at Colonia Agrippina, fifty miles downstream. By then Metilius had perked up considerably. He came on deck and sat with Pascentia and myself, and together we watched the flat lands beside the Rhine pass slowly by. We talked a lot in the hours and days it took to reach the Oceanus Germanicus. They told me their stories and I told them mine.'

'Did they have any children – Metilius and Pascentia?'

'No. Metilius wasn't a young man, and then he became sick ...'

Would we have a child now, you and I?

Saturninus realises that Vilbia is looking at him, so he says quickly, 'He'd been a wine trader all his life, based in Londinium and trading mostly with Treveri on the Moselle and with Burdigala on the Garonne, down on the south-west coast of Gaul. He owned a vineyard near Burdigala, and that's where they were going on their next wine-buying voyage, once they'd got those barrels of Moselle wine safely back to Londinium and sold. So we sailed on down the Rhine, until at last we came into the reedy delta lands that lead out into the Ocean.'

'I've never seen the Ocean,' Vilbia remarks wistfully. 'Gulioepius has described it to me, but I've never actually seen it.'

'Ah, you have to see it to realise how vast it is, and how beautiful it can sometimes be.

And how fearsome, too.

'It was beautiful that day. The weather was calm and fine as the sailors unfurled the big sail and we set off westwards along the coast of northern Gaul. I can still see the sunlight dancing on the blue-green water and smell the clean salt air.'

And I can smell the scent of your skin as I used my teeth to pull out that splinter you picked up when you brushed your arm against the deck rail.

He hesitates, then murmurs, 'Towards the end of the voyage, I'd come to realise that the attraction I felt towards Pascentia was mutual. She only showed it by a smile or a shared joke – or by a lingering as she brought me a bowl of soup that she'd made in the little galley right up at the stern, with its red-tiled roof that seemed so oddly out of place on a ship. Or by the way she looked at me as I played some of the tunes that I'd picked up over the years.'

'Played on what?'

'A lyre. A battered old lyre. I've still got it, back in Corinium.'

'Whenever did you learn to play that?' Vilbia asks, the surprise showing in her voice.

'Oh, years ago, when I was young ... I wasn't always the brutal soldier you see before you now.' Before Vilbia can reply, Saturninus adds, 'She loved music, did Pascentia. She'd sit on the deck with her back against the mast and listen with her eyes half-closed.

'For two days and two nights we sailed down the coast of Gaul. Then, as soon as the lookout shouted that he could see a smudge of white on the northern horizon across the Fretum Gallicum, we turned towards it. Several hours later we saw the great pharos of Dubris. That was the first sight I'd had of this country for nearly thirteen years.'

'But ... that means you must have been only a boy when you left Britannia. You couldn't have joined the army so young – could you?'

'Couldn't I?' Saturninus replies drily. 'Perhaps I was a child prodigy.'

'Like Hercules, you mean?' She giggles.

'Not quite. Anyway, when we came to the Flumen Tamesis the *Zephyrus* sailed upriver with the tides until we reached Londinium, and there we docked at a wharf built of vast baulks of squared timber. And then, over dinner on that first night, they asked me to go into partnership with them. My lack of knowledge was apparently no problem: they would soon teach me. What they really needed, they said, was someone strong that they could trust. So how, I asked Metilius, did he know that he could trust me? He said that Pascentia's intuition told her so, and he had never known it to fail.

'He also said that he would make me his heir, or rather co-heir with Pascentia, and the two of us would support him in his old age. And Pascentia and I would ... you understand?'

Vilbia moves sideways, towards the edge of the moon shadows. 'I'm not a child, Primicerius. I understand how it can be between men and women.'

'Yes, of course.' But he wonders if she really does.

There is a long pause, then she asks, 'How long did you stay in Londinium with Pascentia?'

But there is no reply, for Saturninus's thoughts and memories have floated free and far away – back to Londinium and those days in late May and early June three years gone.

CHAPTER EIGHTEEN

The voices wake Ferna. Straining her ears she listens in the darkness, Lopsicallus still sleeping heavily beside her. Then, silent as a shadow, she slips out of bed and tiptoes across the barn to the small window. The crude shutter stands half-open, and across the yard she sees three figures about to enter the building that was once the villa of Julius Martinus, but is now the home of Lucco the bailiff. Poor though the light is, she recognises Lucco, and Dulcitia his pretty wife, and the soldier whose name she heard but cannot now remember. Puzzled, she watches all three go into the villa.

Shortly afterwards stray gleams of light radiate out from around the edges of the window shutters of the room she knows to be Lucco and Dulcitia's bedroom. Ferna envies Dulcitia the soft feather mattress on their bed; sighs when she thinks of the straw-stuffed sacking on which she and Lopsicallus have to sleep.

A door opens and closes, and a single figure comes out of the villa: the soldier, Ferna assumes, before realising it is Lucco. She observes him pause, then creep stealthily around to the shuttered window of the lighted room. He seems to be peering and listening, although Ferna is too far away to hear anything herself. Now thoroughly mystified, she waits and watches as time passes and feathery wracks of pale cloud float across the waxing moon. Drowsily she kneels down and rests against the sill, her head cradled in her arms. And although she tries to keep her eyes open and fixed on the villa, soon she drifts back into sleep.

Suddenly she is wide awake, woken by the sound of running feet. Flustered, she stares across to the villa, but Lucco is gone. There is an almighty crash, the door of the barn flies open and for an instant she sees Lucco, whip in hand, framed in the moonlit doorway. He plunges into the darkness of the interior, stumbles over the water jar and falls heavily to the floor. Cursing like a man possessed by demons, he scrambles to his feet and begins lashing out at Lopsicallus, just beginning to wake from his heavy sleep, laying into him with demented fury.

'You cretin, you cretin, you *cretin*!' he screams. 'If you hadn't told me that pack of stupid lies about buried gold, none of this would ever have happened. None of it – none of it, do you hear? Do! – You! – Hear!' he bawls, bringing the whip down with all his strength to emphasise each word.

Lopsicallus howls with pain and shock and scrabbles grotesquely away on all fours in the darkness like a great insect, trying to avoid the lash that cuts like a sword. Flailing about, trying to locate her cowering husband, Lucco blunders into Ferna, who screams, and in the confusion Lopsicallus jumps up and runs through the open door, out into the night and freedom.

'Come back, you bastard!' Lucco yells after him. 'I haven't finished with you yet, not by a mile I haven't!'

Terrified and utterly bewildered, Ferna too begins edging towards the doorway, but Lucco grabs her by one arm and jerks her back. 'Oh no you don't, you silly bitch!' For a few moments he stands in front of her, his breath clotted and heavy, then he drops the whip and with his freed hand snatches at the neckline of her dress and pulls savagely. It rips to the waist, the force of the pull bringing her flying headlong onto the ground in front of him.

She screams again, screams for Lopsicallus, who can't hear her, and even if he could would do nothing.

'Howl as loud as you like, damn you. It won't do you any good. Thanks to your turd-brained husband that bastard soldier's with my wife now. Yes, that's right – with Dulcitia,' Lucco hisses. 'And you know what he's doing to her, don't you? Well, don't you? Even you can't be that stupid! Or doesn't that fool Lopsicallus ever ...?'

He begins to laugh, although Ferna, whimpering on the ground, has no idea why. He is still laughing as she hears him stripping off his clothes. And then he falls on her, taking her like an animal on the beaten earth of the barn floor.

*

'How long did you stay in Londinium with Pascentia, Primicerius?'

'How long?' Saturninus repeats, startled, suddenly aware that Vilbia is speaking. 'Oh, four weeks ... Four short weeks. Selling the wine they'd brought from the Moselle and hiring a new crew.'

'And then ...?' She prompts.

'And then we sailed for Burdigala.' He doesn't really want to tell her the rest, but cannot stop now. 'The weather was fine and the voyage took some two weeks. We sailed down the Gironde estuary, into the Garonne and docked at a berth in the port of Burdigala. It was high summer, a busy time, the harbour crowded with ships. Metilius and Pascentia selected the wine – a mixed cargo of barrels from their own vineyard, and others they'd bought in from neighbouring estates. I supervised the loading, which wasn't exactly an arduous job.

'Then, on the seventh day, when all the barrels were aboard and we were ready to sail, a couple of tax assessors arrived. They swooped down on us like a pair of thieving magpies. It turned out that they'd been going around all the local vineyards, claiming that the quantity of wine produced the previous year was double what it really was – and of course demanding tax on the higher amount. Which threw Metilius into a panic, because he couldn't delay sailing.'

'Why not?'

'Because he'd signed a contract to deliver that wine to a Londinium vintner on the nones of August. At what he reckoned was a good price, too. If he'd sailed from Burdigala that day, as planned, he would have had plenty of time to get back by the nones. But the contract stipulated a penalty of three solidi for every day he was late in delivering, and if he'd had to hang around in Burdigala disputing the tax claim, then the gods alone knew when he'd get back to Londinium. He became so agitated that Pascentia feared he'd make himself ill.'

'I wonder if those assessors knew about that contract?'

'I wondered that too.'

'So great minds do think alike – '

'As Gulioepius no doubt says. I'd dealt with men like them in my army days and I convinced Metilius that, given a little time, I could handle them. That calmed him, but with the uncertain state of his health Pascentia didn't dare let him make the voyage home alone. I didn't want to stay behind, not without Pascentia, but it seemed the only logical thing to do. And so I told them to go.'

'They sailed for Londinium without you?'

'On the morning tide of a calm July day. Pascentia's eyes were wet with tears when we kissed goodbye. Neither of us wanted that parting, so soon after we'd found each other – but what else could I do?' From the tilt of her head, Saturninus realises that Vilbia is gazing intently at him. Realises too that what he has just said must sound like an appeal for understanding. 'But then …'

'But then, what?' Vilbia asks uncertainly.

'It took only two days, and a comparatively small bribe, to convince those assessors that they'd got their figures wrong. And there, in the harbour, was another wine ship about to leave for Londinium, so I begged a passage on it. The south wind, light when Pascentia and Metilius sailed, was growing stronger. By the time we were level with the mouth of the Loire, I reckoned that we might be only a day behind them. I even began to picture the look on Pascentia's face if we were to pass them in the night, and she were to find me waiting on the dock at Londinium when she and Metilius arrived.

'Sometimes, in the dark stillness of the night, I allow myself to believe that it really did happen that way. I see her standing in the prow of the *Zephyrus* as it drifts up the Tamesis with the tide, her face coming slowly nearer all the time, until she catches sight of me and smiles ... But, of course, that isn't what really happened.'

'So what did ...?' Vilbia begins asking, and Saturninus hears the anxiety in her voice.

'As we turned westwards, along the southern coast of Brittany, the wind changed and a storm, black as night, came howling out of the west. We were sheltered by a headland, but ... There were moments when I thought the violence of the wind and the foam-flying waves would overwhelm the ship, as if it were no more than an acorn cup.

'But the storm passed, and a few hours later the sun was shining, the sky was blue and the sea was calm again. And so we sailed on. Next day we put in to a small port on the western tip of Brittany to make minor repairs. It was there we heard that what we had encountered was only the edge of the worst summer storm in living memory. They said it had come screaming out of the wilderness of the Western Ocean, destroying everything in its path.'

'You say that Pascentia's ship was a day ahead of you? Does that mean that when the storm struck she was – ?'

'Right in its path.'

'What happened to her and Metilius?' Vilbia asks quietly.

'I think you've already guessed.'

Vilbia does not reply.

So he says, so quietly that she has to move closer to hear him, 'We rounded the tip of Brittany and crept along the northern coast of Gaul, all the way to Bononia, but we never found the *Zephyrus*. Then we crossed the Fretum Gallicum and made our way to Londinium. Pascentia wasn't there. She never returned. I waited for months, but she never returned. And in all that time, of all the merchants who sailed to and from Gaul, not a one saw any trace of the *Zephyrus,* or heard what had become of her. That ship, and every living soul aboard her, had vanished as though they had never existed.'

'But if only they'd waited those two more days at Burdigala ...'

'Then she'd still be alive?' Saturninus whispers.

'I'm sorry – I didn't mean …'

'It's no more than the truth.' Then, quickly, to distance himself from the memory, Saturninus says, 'After that, there was nothing to keep me in Londinium. My first thought was to go back to Gaul and re-enlist in one of the army units there, but that idea barely survived a day. So I took this coin – ' He reaches down the front of his tunic and draws out a large coin, suspended by a thin cord looped through a hole drilled near its edge. On one side it bears the diademed head of the Emperor Julian, and on the other a great bull standing beneath two stars. He gazes at the coin, rocking it gripped between thumb and forefinger to catch the moonlight. 'Have you seen one of these before?' He holds it out for her inspection, as far as the cord around his neck will permit.

Vilbia draws the tips of her long fingers across the surface of the coin, feeling the crisp contours of the stamped copper. 'No, never. It's very beautiful. But if you had so little love for Julian, why do you keep his coin?'

He shrugs. 'The bull is my birth sign. Birth and re-birth, perhaps? I came across it on my last day in Antioch and thought it might bring me luck – guide me to a new life. It almost did. Almost. Anyway, I spun the coin three times for each direction, and west emerged the winner. So I travelled west, until I reached Corinium and these hills.'

'But it wasn't just chance that brought you here, was it?' Vilbia says, in her best wise-priestess voice.

'Wasn't it? What else did then?' He knows she is right, but he is curious to hear her say why.

'When I was a child, every summer the swallows built their nests under the eaves of my mother's house. One year, one of the fledglings was almost entirely white, like no other I've ever seen. In the autumn it flew away with the rest, but next summer it returned and made a nest of its own. It came the following year too, but never again. It must have died, far away.'

'And so …?'

129

'And so I learnt that it is the instinct of all creatures to return to the places they knew when they were young.'

Saturninus gazes at her face, inscrutable alabaster in the moonlight. 'Perhaps. When I arrived in Corinium I had only a dozen siliquae of my army gratuity left. But, by what seemed at the time to be curious good fortune, I heard that the post of primicerius of the civil guard had suddenly become vacant. They say my predecessor, a man called Novanticus, was something of a Goth –'

'He was a savage pig!' declares Vilbia with quiet passion.

'So I heard. But no one who mattered seemed to care, and he'd still be grunting around today if he hadn't tried to seduce the then-governor Septimius's daughter. As it was, Novanticus got a one-way pass to the Great North Wall and I got his job.' Saturninus rubs his eyes. 'Sweet Venus, I'm tired – you really shouldn't have put so many of those little toadstools in that wine ...' Trapped between hope and fear as to what the answer might be, there is a question he has not yet dared to ask. But sleep is fast overtaking him, and he knows that he must ask it now. He stares straight into Vilbia's face, now no more than two feet from his own, and says slowly, 'Tell me ... when people appear in Leucesca's spring – appear in places that are apparently somewhere in this world – does it mean that they are still alive?'

Vilbia seems reluctant to reply, so he adds, 'You see, yesterday I think I had another dream – a dream very like that vision of Pascentia we saw in the water. But in the dream I saw her crawling up the beach, away from lines of waves breaking behind her, as if she'd just emerged from the sea. As if she'd survived the sinking of the *Zephyrus*.'

Vilbia looks away, trying to remember the name of a bright star she can see high in the western sky. Gulioepius had taught her the names of all the bright stars, but now ...

Oh Saturninus, how I wish I could say yes.

But she will not lie to him. 'No, not necessarily ... I'm sorry.'

She is painfully aware that it is not what he wants to hear. Then, weakening, she adds, 'But Pascentia might still be alive – Leucesca *must* have had a reason for showing her to you.'

'I wonder?' he murmurs. 'They said that nothing could have survived in the black heart of that storm – that it was madness to go looking for her. But *did* she survive, Vilbia, did she? Is that what your goddess is telling me? I swear that if I thought she were still alive, then I'd search for the rest of my days to find her.'

Again, Vilbia does not know what to say. The romantic heart of a fifteen-year-old girl longs to tell him, yes: that the vision he saw in the waters of the spring – and in the dream – does indeed foretell an ecstatic reunion to come. But if he has offended Leucesca, then the goddess might have a darker, crueller motive. Vilbia edges away, back into the moonshadows, so that she does not have to reply, and is thankful when sleep overcomes him before he can ask again.

CHAPTER NINETEEN

Canio wakes just as the first rays of the new sun are filtering through the shuttered window of Lucco's bedroom. Still half asleep, he reaches out a lazy hand to caress the smooth stomach of Lucco's young wife. His hand encounters nothing but the soft wool blanket. She is gone – as are the dress and other items of clothing that, with his assistance, she had slipped off the previous night. He closes his eyes and sees her again, standing naked in the light of a single oil lamp whose soft radiance could transform almost any woman into a goddess. Not that she had needed its magic: she possessed her own.

Irritably he gets up, scratches, and, putting on only his helmet (and that for no obvious reason), unlatches and pushes open the window shutters before urinating copiously onto the yard outside. There is nobody about, but it would have made no difference if Governor Laetinianus himself had happened to be passing by. He is in that sort of mood.

When he has just about finished and is shaking off the last drops, Indutius seems to materialise out of nowhere and trudges past, a hoe over one shoulder. 'Morning, master,' he mutters.

'Morning. Hey – where in the names of all three *Cucullati* is Dulcitia?'

'Gone, master.'

'Gone? What do you mean, "Gone"? Gone where?'

'Gone with Lucco to the villa of our master, Aurelius Charax. Said he had to see him early this morning about something or other. Didn't say what.'

'Do you know when he's coming back?'

132

'Didn't say. Never, for all I care. After what he did to my daughter last night, I hope Jupiter-Taranis blasts the swine into little pieces with one of his lightning bolts,' Indutius declares venomously as he walks away.

Canio doesn't ask what Lucco has done to Ferna. He is shrewd enough to guess. 'Don't go far,' he shouts to Indutius's retreating back. 'I've got a few more questions for you, once I've put some clothes on.' Catching sight of two women standing together on the far side of the villa farmyard, pointing at him and giggling, he salutes them in a way not found in any drill manual.

He closes the shutters, dresses, and wanders out through Lucco's private rooms. In the kitchen he discovers a cold joint of cooked mutton, from which he carves and eats several slices. Then he goes out to find Indutius again, still carrying the joint and gnawing desultorily from it as he walks. He finds him in one of the barns, plucking a brace of dead chickens.

'These are for you,' Indutius mutters as the feathers fly. 'Lucco said you was to have them – them and that skin of barley beer over there.' He pokes a horny finger towards a bulging goatskin propped up against the barn wall.

'Very grateful I'm sure.' Canio pulls out the stopper and sniffs suspiciously. 'Smells all right.'

'Course it's all right. He hasn't the balls to try to do *you* any harm.'

'That's a comfort to know. Yesterday, if I remember rightly, Lucco said something about one of his shepherds seeing a big man in a fine set of clothes prowling around somewhere on the estate. I didn't take much notice at the time: had other things on my mind.'

Indutius gives a contemptuous snort, which Canio ignores.

'Besides, I thought Lucco was just trying to steer the conversation away from his part in your illustrious son-in-law's hole-digging antics. Now I'll be damned if I can remember the half of what he did say. What do you know about it?'

Indutius does not look up or stop pulling out the feathers. He seems to have hated those chickens. 'Not much,' he replies. 'A week or so back, shepherd Briccus came here for a sack of barley meal. Said that when he was out a-minding his sheep – somewhere away over to the east, as I recall – he saw two or three men prowling around as if they were looking for something.'

'And one of them was a big man in expensive-looking clothes?' Canio prompts.

'That's what Briccus said.'

'And?'

'And what, master?' Indutius asks wearily.

'And what else did this Briccus say?' Canio growls, before taking another bite out of the mutton joint.

'Didn't say anything else that I know of, but it was Lucco he told, not me.'

Canio yawns and stretches. 'So where can I find shepherd Briccus?'

'He lives about a mile and a half that way.' And Indutius points towards the south-east.

'Near Aurelius Charax's place?'

'No, no – the big villa's over that way more.' Indutius waves eastwards down towards the broad valley that lies beyond the barn walls. 'Chances are that Briccus won't be at home though, particularly if the shearing's started – which I dare say it has by now. But his wife will be there, and she'll know where he is. Why are you so interested, if you'll pardon me for asking, master?'

Canio rubs his beard. 'That man Briccus saw just might be someone that my primicerius is looking for. Did Briccus say what colour his hair and beard were?'

'Not that I heard, master. There, that's the last of the feathers off them. Now all I've got to do is gut them, swill them out, and put them and the beer in a sack. Then you can carry the lot away with you.'

'You do that.' Canio gets the distinct impression that Indutius will not be heartbroken to see him go.

By the time he has saddled his horse and led it around to the barn, Indutius is waiting with the sack, tied at the neck. Taking it from him, Canio hangs it on one of his saddle horns.

Still gnawing the mutton joint, he belches his thanks, then asks Indutius for more precise directions to Briccus's house. He has the whole morning to waste before he is due to meet Saturninus at Corvusida long barrow, and, in the absence of Dulcitia, a gentle ride through the countryside seems as good a way as any to do it.

Indutius trudges beside him until they stand on a rough trackway that runs along the rising ground behind the villa. 'Follow this track for a good mile or more, then start looking to your left, down into the valley. It's only a small place, but you shouldn't miss it. Give my regards to Matugena.'

'That his wife's name?'

'That it is master, that it is. And she'll make a big man like you very welcome, I'm sure.'

There is something in the way Indutius says it that makes Canio give him a sidelong glance. But Indutius's walnut face gives nothing away.

With the new sun in his eyes, Canio rides steadily along the twisting, undulating track. Eventually he spots, halfway down the valley side, two small stone buildings with thatched roofs. As he jogs closer he sees several circular lambing pens, built of the same drystone walling. When he is closer still he notices a woman sitting in a chair beside the doorway of the larger building.

She appears to be of about his own age, wearing a simple dress of pale, undyed wool, which contrasts with her sun-and-weather-tanned skin. Canio thinks she looks comfortable in that skin, that it fits her curves well. The supple fingers of her right hand are twirling a vertical spindle rod, weighted with a limestone whorl at its bottom end. Wedged into a crack in the wall above her shoulder is a much-branched distaff stick holding a cloud of raw wool. Between distaff and spindle a thread is constantly being teased out of the wool and winding around the upper end of the spindle. She works smoothly, the action seemingly as instinctive as breathing, as all the while her large brown eyes observe his approach, apparently missing nothing.

Canio too misses nothing, and what he sees interests him. He smiles at the woman. 'Is this where Briccus the shepherd lives?'

'This is where he lives when he's at home. But he's not here now; he's off at the shearing.'

'You're his daughter?'

'I'm Matugena, his wife.'

'His wife? From what Indutius said I was expecting an older woman. He told me you and Briccus have been living here for years.'

'I'm a good bit younger than Briccus,' Matugena replies, her eyes narrowing like a stroked cat's. 'What did you want him for?'

Canio picks up the trace of anxiety in her voice. 'Oh, nothing serious. I was talking to bailiff Lucco last night and he mentioned that Briccus had seen some suspicious characters prowling around. Said that one of them was a big man, dressed very fine – Briccus told you about them, I suppose?'

Unhurriedly, Matugena continues spinning her wool. 'Yes, he told me. It was, oh, let me see now … about a week ago, miles away, over to the east. He said it happened at first light one morning, as he and young Nundinus and a few others from Camboderna were driving one of the outlier flocks to new grass.'

'And?'

'And all of a sudden, out of the cover of some trees, came these three men. Briccus didn't recognise them – or much like the look of them either. Said two of them had the look of wandering men – *bacaudae* – about them. Apparently, they saw him at the same time and started walking towards him. But then Nundinus – who's a big lad – comes up, and the men stared at him, talked among themselves for a few moments, then just turned around and went away.'

'These men who looked like *bacaudae* – they didn't say anything to Briccus?'

'Not a single word. Whoever they were though, they're probably far away by now.'

'The other man – the big one in the fine clothes – did Briccus say anything else about him?'

'Such as?'

'What colour his hair was?'

'Is he the one you want?'

'Could be.'

'Well, Briccus said he had yellowish hair and beard, all tangled and rough like a magpie's nest. And he had fierce eyes too – eyes that looked as though they wanted to skewer him.'

'What about the other two – apart from them looking like *bacaudae*?'

'Briccus said nothing else about them, not that I can recall. It was the one dressed like a *honestus* – a gentleman – that he remembered most. By the way, have you eaten this morning?'

'Breakfasted on Lucco's finest mutton before I left his place. I'd welcome a drink though – my throat's as dry as dust.'

'I've only water, but it's sweet and fresh. I carried it from the spring at first light this morning. Come in and I'll pour you a cup.'

Canio dismounts and clamps the reins under a big loose slab on top of one of the lambing pen walls. He slips the sack that Indutius gave him off his saddle horn and follows Matugena into the house. Inside, by the subdued light that filters in through window slits in the thick drystone walls, he sees a large table and a couple of wooden chairs standing on the limestone-slabbed floor. A wall with a curtained doorway partitions off another room which, he guesses, is the bedroom. In the centre of the main room stands a raised stone hearth, the limestone reddened by fire, but ashless and cool now. On the walls hang several shepherd's crooks cut from branched saplings, their bare wood and remaining bark darkened and polished by the lanolin in the fleeces of the hundreds of recalcitrant sheep they have hooked over the years.

From a tall cupboard Matugena takes a pair of orange pottery beakers with patterns of crude wheels rouletted into the clay before firing. A wooden-staved bucket with iron banding sits on the floor nearby and she stoops to fill the beakers from it, seemingly unaware that as she does so the loose neckline of her dress dips to momentarily expose her breasts.

'Don't bother with that water – I've got something a bit more cheerful in here.' Canio opens the sack and pulls out the goatskin of beer. He extracts the stopper with his teeth and fills both beakers to the brim as she holds them out, then draws one of the chairs up to the table.

Matugena sniffs the heady brew. 'Isn't it a little early in the day to be drinking this stuff?'

Her disapproval sounds less than genuine to Canio. 'Nonsense. A cup or two of this first thing in the morning sets a man up for the day.'

'Or puts a woman flat on her back.' Nevertheless, Matugena pulls a chair over to the table and sits down beside Canio. She raises her beaker to her lips, wishes him health, then matches him swallow for swallow until both beakers stand empty on the table. 'Good beer,' she comments approvingly.

'Lucco's own.'

'No! How did you persuade the old duck-arse to part with it?'

'Ways and means,' Canio grins as he refills the beakers. 'When are you expecting Briccus back?' he enquires casually.

Not casually enough: Matugena's thick, dark eyebrows lift slightly. 'Oh, he'll be in no hurry to come home; not when he's at the shearing.' She sighs. 'There are times when I wonder if he doesn't prefer the company of his sheep to mine. Still, the longer he's away, the sweeter the reunion always is, bless him.'

'No hurry to come home? – the man must be mad,' Canio remarks smoothly. 'It must get lonely, here on your own all day. Haven't you and Briccus got any children? – most of these little places I come across have two or three running around.'

Matugena stares down at the table and runs her index finger around the smooth lip of her beaker. 'No, we've never had children, Briccus and me. Not for want of trying though,' she adds, glancing quickly up into Canio's eyes.

'Well, if a ewe doesn't get pregnant with one ram you try another, don't you?' Canio replies easily. Beneath the table he slides his hand under the hem of her dress and begins stroking one smooth thigh. He feels her tense momentarily, then relax.

'I've tried several rams, over the years,' she murmurs. 'None of them ever worked the trick though.'

'Perhaps those rams didn't know how to treat a ewe properly.' Canio works his fingers ever higher, easing between her thighs with light, circular movements. 'There's more to making one happy than just jumping on top of her and going baa.'

Matugena does not reply; her eyes slowly close and her soft breathing quickens. Then, without a word, she rises, graceful as a cat, and beckons Canio towards the curtained-off inner room.

CHAPTER TWENTY

The low morning sun blinds Saturninus. Shielding his eyes with one hand he squints and tries to make out the identity of the approaching horsemen, shimmering in the heat haze that is already turning rocks and men and horses into amorphous blurs in the vast emptiness of the desert. Perhaps they are Roman, but there is something about those unfocussed shapes that make him uneasy. He stares harder, then curses as with heart-stopping abruptness three Persian *clibanarii* heavy cavalrymen burst out of the haze. They are armoured from head to mid-calf in steel, their conical helmets and close-fitting coats of mail sparkling in the fierce sunlight. One of them holds a small bow with sharply curved horns, an arrow nocked on the bowstring which he is already pulling back.

Saturninus, the image of the fiery sun still in his eyes, is a moment too late. He jerks Antares' head violently around and has half turned when the arrow strikes him in the right shoulder, jarring against the bone. With a shout of pain and anger he drops his head low over Antares' neck and claps his heels into the horse's flanks, springing him into a gallop. He struggles to see the way ahead, but the whole sky is burning with a savage brightness that sears his eyes. Twisting and turning his head he seeks to escape that cruel light, and as he does so becomes vaguely aware that something is tapping against his arm. At first he ignores it, but it is persistent, and as he tries to push it away his fingers touch the fingers of another hand.

Suddenly he is wide awake and staring into the morning sun, which has already climbed high enough in the north-eastern sky to have cleared the tree tops and be shining full into his face. His mouth feels as arid as the desert of his dream. He turns his head and sees Vilbia gazing down at him. He wonders how long she has been standing there, watching him.

'Drink some water, Primicerius – it's the best tasting in all the hills.'

Saturninus accepts the proffered beaker, breathes his thanks to her, and swallows the winter-cold water. He requests more, but, while she is fetching it, memories of the night's events begin to return, some of them as sharp as swords. There comes the disconcerting realisation that he has told Vilbia things that he has never told another soul since his return to these hills. He damns himself for a fool; damns too the wine and whatever was mixed with it.

Vilbia is returning. As if she has guessed his thoughts, she startles him by saying, 'Incidentally, Primicerius, I never disclose whatever secrets I may learn while wearing Leucesca's crown. Not to anyone, ever.'

He thinks he detects a coolness in her voice, a moving away.

As if the harsh daylight is estranging us again.

'Not even to Gulioepius?'

'Not even to him.'

As he sips the water, Saturninus wonders if he can believe her.

Perhaps she's afraid of me? Of what I might do if I remember telling her things I now regret?

He recalls, with an uneasy conscience, that in the temple he had been less than gentle with her. But then fatalism takes over.

What else can I do but trust her?

'I believe you. And ... I'm sorry if what I made you see in the spring last night frightened you.'

'Are you really sorry, Primicerius? Wouldn't you do it all over again if you thought that, this time, it would find your Caelofernus?'

'Yes – I truly am sorry that I did it. And yes, I'd probably do it again if I thought it would find Caelofernus. Is that what you were waiting to hear?' He smiles, but she does not, and he adds, 'But you have my word that I'd never do what I threatened and denounce you or Gulioepius to the Prefect.'

'Wouldn't you, Primicerius? Do you really know yourself so well that you can promise that?'

He studies her face, wondering why she now seems so determined to distance herself from him. There is a long silence between them, broken only by birdsong from the depths of the surrounding wood and the babble of the little stream as it hurries on its way down to the flatlands below.

Then Saturninus looks up at the sky. 'The sun's getting higher and I have to be far away by noon.' He stands, stretches, hesitates, then quickly dips his fingers into his purse. 'Take another five siliquae. Double fee – you earned it.' He holds out the little silver coins on his palm, but she makes no attempt to take them. Gently seizing her hand he attempts to tip the siliquae into it, but she curls her fingers up tightly.

'I don't need to be bribed, Primicerius,' she declares with quiet anger. 'I told you that what I saw and heard will go no further. And you have *my* word on that.'

'It's not a bribe, child, it's a peace offering. I don't want us to part with you thinking I'm an even bigger brute than Novanticus.'

'My friendship can't be bought, Primicerius – did you really think that it could?

'If it could, then I wouldn't want it,' he shoots back. But his anger dies as quickly as it had flared, instantly regretted. He sighs and releases her hand. 'Goodbye, Vilbia.'

He doesn't wait for a reply, but drops the siliquae back into his purse and walks towards Antares, still tethered at the edge of the clearing. Untying the reins, he begins leading the horse towards the path that leads back up to the plateau.

But just before he reaches the trees he hears Vilbia call softly, 'Long life and happiness, Saturninus.' There seems no hint of mockery in her voice. Turning, he sees her standing only a few paces behind him. He looks at her curiously as she says, almost shyly now,

'I shall ask Leucesca to watch over you and guard you. And when you cheat the death you saw in your dream – as with her protection I know you shall – will you come back to this place and tell me how you did it? … And tell me too if you discovered the meaning of your other dream, the dream in which you saw Pascentia?'

Why …? Saturninus wonders. But he replies, 'Long life and happiness to you too, Vilbia. Yes, I'll come back and tell you. But until then, will you keep this safe for me?' Slipping the Julian medallion over his head, he holds it out to her by its cord. She stretches out her hand, opens her fingers and allows him to drop it into her palm. 'It never brought me much luck. Perhaps it will be kinder to you?'

He walks on, and she stands quite still, listening until all sounds of man and horse have vanished amid the myriad woodland noises. Then her long, pale brown fingers close tightly around the still-warm copper.

Once up on the plateau, Saturninus canters towards the south-east. The sun shines hot, and the faint, remembered tang of sheep droppings wafts on the warm breeze. In his childhood memories those droppings are almost as much a part of the hills as the limestone itself: dark and glossy when fresh, then drying grey, before finally shredding and fragmenting in the wind. He rides on, across the great open sheep pastures, where the turf is cropped short and splashed with buttercups and blue speedwell, and where small clumps of thistles and nettles form dark islands in the nibbled turf.

From the ewes comes an occasional languid, throaty baa, as they lie with their lambs in the shade of wind-and-sheep-teeth sculptured hawthorn bushes. As he approaches one small flock several crows take off into the wind, rising effortlessly, their broad black wings scarcely moving. Far away, where there are no sheep and the grass is lengthening, the sighing wind and the sunlight combine to send ripples of light and shade flowing like snakes across the open hillside.

Saturninus rides on until, half a mile ahead, he notices a wood spreading right across the route he is travelling. Coming closer, he sees a path leading into the trees and decides to follow it. Inside the wood the path grows rapidly less distinct and soon disappears altogether. Mindful of his rendezvous with Canio, he decides to press on, through the tangle of ancient woodland. Seldom glimpsing the sky, and never the sun, his sense of direction soon falters in that wilderness where dense trees and tangled hanging ropes of wild clematis, some thick as a man's wrist, make steering a straight course impossible.

Cresting a ridge he sees the downslope before him transformed into a sea of the pure white stars of wild garlic flowers. Riding slowly through them, between the trees, his nostrils fill with the oniony aroma of their moist, fleshy leaves. Suddenly he feels Antares tense nervously beneath him, as if something seen or scented has alarmed him. He reins to a halt and peers ahead, listening intently, but can detect no obvious danger. Nevertheless, before moving off again he pulls the short-hafted hunting spear out of the leather case strapped to his saddle.

He urges the increasingly restive horse slowly forwards until, no more than a dozen paces ahead, a vast wild boar sow, almost as long as a man and considerably heavier, erupts out of her nest of moss and dead grass. From all around her a litter of ten or so tiny piglets, striped lengthways light brown and yellowish-cream, scatter in all directions, squealing their panic. The old sow, her dense coat of brownish-black bristles standing on end, angrily turns to face Saturninus head-on. He sees the jaw beneath her long, mobile snout working convulsively, and a froth of foam begin oozing from both sides as she gives vent to several furious snorts. Although the tusks in her lower jaw are smaller than a full-grown male's, he is well aware of their wicked sharpness, perfectly capable of ripping open a man or horse. And all the while her small, red-rimmed eyes are glaring balefully at him.

Strangely, actually seeing the sow, knowing exactly where she is, appears to calm Antares. Slowly, ever so slowly, Saturninus grips the reins tightly in his left hand and raises the spear with his right. When his arm is drawn fully back to the throwing position both man and sow hesitate, staring into each other's eyes. Suddenly the sow's instinct for survival triumphs over her rage. In an instant she turns and trots off into the undergrowth with astonishing speed for so bulky a beast, her piglets tumbling after her in a shrill cacophony. Saturninus lowers the spear and lets her go.

Shortly afterwards he at last breaks clear of the wood. Stretching up in the saddle he squints against the hard sunlight to survey the undulating grasslands ahead. Then, urging Antares into a trot, he rides on until, from the top of a ridge, he finds himself looking down at a place where three trackways meet. He is about to ride on when he becomes aware of a woman in a pale, ankle-length dress standing at this little crossroads. At her side, sitting on its haunches, is a large black hound. The woman's head is turned directly towards the point where he came over the ridge, giving the impression, fleeting but disconcerting, that she had been waiting for him. She is too far away for Saturninus to see her face clearly, but he can make out that her hair is dark, though swept up and coiled on top of her head, as Pascentia's never was.

And yet …

Suddenly the woman turns and points towards the north. Saturninus looks, but can see nothing out of the ordinary there, neither immediately in front of her, nor all the way to the horizon and up into the sky. Intrigued, he starts Antares down the slope towards her. But as he descends, scattered bushes and the subtle undulations of the ground combine to briefly hide the crossroads, and when it comes back into view both woman and hound have vanished. His elation dying within him, Saturninus canters down to where they had been. All three trackways stretch stark and empty into the distances. There is nowhere that they could have gone or hidden in so short a time, and no footprints show on the exposed limestone bedrock and hard, dried mud of the trackways.

He shakes his head and tells himself that they must have been hallucinations – nothing more than the lingering effects of whatever had been in Vilbia's wine. But the longer he remains at that place, the stronger grows the feeling that he is being watched, of unseen eyes studying him. He shivers, despite the warmth of the late morning sun, and rides quickly away.

CHAPTER TWENTY-ONE

From fully half a mile away Canio hears the restless, random baaing of penned sheep. He follows the sounds, down one hillside scattered with trees and up another, until at last he spots a couple of hundred of the great woolly beasts. They are milling slowly around inside an enclosure formed by hurdles of woven split hazel rods, driven into the earth on the lee side of a wood. On the grass in front of the enclosure a dozen or so men, and a few women, are working busily in the bright sunlight. Most of the men are in pairs – one holding a sheep on its back by a crooked arm around its throat, the other clipping off its heavy, dirty-white fleece with a pair of one-handed shears forged from a single strip of spring steel.

In the shade of the wood is a large wagon, a solitary long-horned ox standing patiently between its shafts. One of the women briskly bundles up a fleece and tosses it over the side of the wagon, to join a steadily growing pile. All this Canio takes in as he slowly rides up to the shearers. And one by one, as they become aware of his presence, they all stop and stare at him.

'Which one of you is Briccus?' he asks nobody in particular.

Nobody replies.

'Come on, don't be shy. He's not wanted for any sins. I just want to ask him a few questions about some suspicious characters he's supposed to have seen wandering around these parts.'

'Briccus isn't here, master,' answers a tall youth, grimy – as they all are – from the greasy dirt of the fleeces. 'He should be here, but he's not. He's probably at home, a couple of miles back along the way you've just come.'

'No, he's not at home,' Canio replies, swiping at an early wasp buzzing around his head. 'I've just been there and his wife said he was here. Are you Nundinus?'

The youth hesitates. 'I am, master, but whatever Briccus has done, I had no part in it.' It seems that Nundinus does not believe Canio's reason for wanting to find Briccus.

'So you're the one who saw the wandering men, are you – the man in the fine clothes and the other two? Tell me about them.' Canio smiles at Nundinus in an attempt to reassure him, although he is not unaware that even his smile has a wolfish quality better suited to intimidation than encouragement.

'There's not much to tell, master,' Nundinus begins cautiously. 'There was a big man, dressed like a *honestus* but with hair and beard that didn't look as if they'd seen a comb for months. He was walking towards Briccus when I first saw him. The other two were a few paces behind, just ordinary-looking men. I don't remember much about them.'

'So what did they do after they'd seen you?'

'Well, they just talked among themselves for a bit – I was too far away to hear what was said – and then they all walked back the way they'd come, until the trees hid them.'

'Back in the direction of the Via Ricnild?'

'That's the way they were heading. But that was a week ago, so I expect they're all of a hundred miles away by now. It was nothing, really,' Nundinus adds casually.

'So why did Briccus think it was worth telling all and sundry?'

Nundinus shrugs. 'Who knows? – when you see nothing but your sheep for days on end, then anything's an event. Sometimes he's even been known to sneak off to a place miles away, well beyond the boundary of our master's land, a place where he can see a long stretch of the Via Ricnild. And do you know why?'

'Amaze me.'

'Just to watch the people passing along it, that's why. All those strangers with different lives to us. Then he'd tell Matugena about them.'

'Do you reckon that's where he is now – watching the Via Ricnild?'

Nundinus rubs the darkening fluff of his incipient beard. 'Well, he could be, I suppose. Or he could be at a little bothy over in that direction that he sometimes uses, especially at lambing time – or in the winter, when the snows are bad. It's not easy to find though.'

Canio grunts irritably. 'So how would I find it?'

'Well, from here you'd best head north-east for about two miles all told. Cross over one stream and keep on going until you reach another. Look around and you should see the bothy cut into the hillside on the far side of that second stream. And if you do come across Briccus, then tell him from me that if Lucco finds out that he's not been here, helping us with the shearing, then he'll do more than fleece him – he'll skin the old bugger alive.'

'I'll do that,' Canio promises. As he rides away he is conscious of them all still craning their necks to look at him, as if seeing a stranger on horseback is a rare happening in their lives.

He unstoppers the goatskin and takes a swallow of the strong beer, then eases his horse on down the long, gentle slope towards the second stream – the headwaters of the little Flumen Leucara – that runs babbling along the bottom of a valley in that never-flat land. Away to the south he notices a scattered flock of grazing sheep. He hunts along the stream for a few hundred yards until he comes across a pedestrian bridge formed of a single tree trunk, several slabs of beetle-galleried bark hanging off it, as though frozen in the act of falling into the water. And there, scanning among the gorse bushes and small hawthorn trees on the steeply rising land opposite, he spots the bothy. Given a short run at the stream, his horse jumps it easily, then picks its way up the slope.

If he hadn't been looking for it, he might have mistaken the bothy for the face of a small, abandoned quarry. Cut into the hillside, sheltered from the east wind, with all three walls and the slates of its lean-to roof constructed of weathered limestone, it appears a snug, if lonely, retreat from which a shepherd can look out across the Leucara and keep watch on his flock grazing on the west side of the stream.

As he nears the bothy Canio becomes aware of an odd noise, like voices heard from far away. The closer he gets, the louder it becomes – a high-pitched, restless hum. His horse catches the smell before he does, whinnying and snorting as if to blow it out of its nostrils. Dismounting, he draws his sword and paces slowly and warily up to the door of rough, weather-bleached planks. It stands slightly ajar on its nailed ox-hide hinges. He takes a deep breath and pulls it fully open.

A vast cloud of blowflies explodes off the thing that lies sprawled on the trodden earth floor, the thing that had once been a man. The cloud whines insanely around the small room for a few moments. Then individual flies begin to settle again. Several land on Canio's face and he claws them off, cursing. He backs out of the bothy, snatches a lungful of reasonably fresh air, sheathes his sword, then strides in, grabs the body by its ankles and drags it outside. The horse shies at the sight and smell and begins trotting away, down towards the Leucara.

'Come back here, Hades damn you!' Canio roars. The horse slows and Canio, muttering furiously, stalks after it. He catches up and ties its dangling reins to a stunted hawthorn.

Swatting away the ever-eager flies, Canio stares down at Briccus's face. It is difficult to believe that the shepherd had been alive only a few days ago. His throat has been slashed, the entire front of his tunic crusted with dark brown blood. There might be other wounds: Canio doesn't look too closely. Walking back to the bothy, he gazes around inside. There is a rough bed covered with sheepskins, a chair, and a table with a few plain orange-red pottery vessels and a small lead candlestick base standing on its uneven surface. A couple of coils of rope hang from large nails driven between the stones of the walls. It seems that whoever killed Briccus did not have robbery as a motive.

On the floor, a little to one side of where the body had lain, he notices a tiny limestone altar, no more than four inches high. He picks it up and turns it over in his hands. On one face is incised the standing figure of a man, crude as a picture a child might scratch in the dust. Beneath it is a meaningless jumble of letters. Canio reflects sardonically that Briccus's god, whose name had died with him, had not been his earthly salvation – although the altar, carved from the stone of the hills, does itself possess a sort of immortality.

From upwind he debates with himself what to do with the body. His instinct is to leave it where it lies: he is not unaware of the superstition that association with dead bodies brings bad luck. But into his mind has come a nagging suspicion which he cannot persuade to go away, however hard he tries.

Untethering his horse he jumps the stream again, then rides along it to a spinney growing beside the bank. There he cuts several ash saplings, from which he fashions a rough stretcher of two long poles and several cross-pieces, all lashed together with rope from the bothy. Recrossing the Leucara on foot, he holds his breath while he drags Briccus's bloated dead weight across the log bridge and onto the stretcher, then secures the body with more of the rope.

In the swiftly-flowing water he tries to wash the stench of death off his hands, but, like all evil, it is tenacious and lingers on. Later, passing a wood, he dismounts, snatches up some leaves of wild garlic and scrubs their pungent odour into his palms, the juice staining them yellowish-green. Then, with the fresh wind from the south-west blowing into his face, he continues riding slowly back to the shearing area.

When he gets there he makes straight for Nundinus, the metallic perfume of corruption trailing in his wake. 'Is that your friend Briccus?' he demands grimly, turning and pointing behind him.

Nundinus stares at the blackening skin and the claw-like hands clutching the air, then turns suddenly and vomits until his stomach is empty.

Canio waits until he has finished. 'Is it him?' he asks again. Nundinus nods.

'Why did they come back and kill him? Why, Nundinus? He had nothing worth stealing, so they must have had another reason. Do you know what that reason could have been?'

Nundinus appears struck dumb, so Canio continues, 'At first I thought they'd killed him because he'd recognised them. But if he had, he would have told you, or Matugena, or Lucco, or somebody – wouldn't he? But what if they thought that someone else had told him who they were ... So who were they, Nundinus? Who were they?' Canio stares straight at him as he repeats the question.

'They had no reason to do it!' Nundinus's voice shakes with anger. 'I never told Briccus ... he never knew.'

'And what he didn't know couldn't hurt him?' Canio sneers. 'For the last time, Nundinus – who were they? ... Did the fancy-dresser go by the name of Caelofernus?'

'I don't know what that bastard's name was. Or care,' Nundinus adds defiantly. 'The man I recognised was called Armiger. I'd met him two years back at the auction where I was sold to Aurelius Charax. Armiger was sold to an estate down south – I can't remember the name of the owner. He was kind to me, was Armiger, when everyone else was treating me like a dog ... But why did he kill Briccus? Briccus wouldn't have told anyone, even if he had known who he was.'

'Sweet Rosmerta! – why do you think? Because he was a runaway with a price on his head, of course. Because he knew that if he was caught he'd be flogged half to death – or maybe the whole way. Did you ever see this Armiger again, after that time with Briccus?'

'No, just that once. I swear it.'

'Just as well. Given the chance, the bastard would have cut your throat as well.'

'I still can't believe the man I knew two years ago would have harmed me.' Nundinus shakes his head. He carefully avoids looking at the body, on which a new swarm of flies is already gathering. The other shearers crowd around in a semi-circle, silent, staring at what Briccus has become: at what they will one day become.

'Believe what you want,' Canio replies indifferently. Noticing a medallion bearing the chi-rho monogram hanging from Nundinus's neck, he adds, 'The Christians think they're going to live forever, somewhere up on a cloud; but they still seem to end up just as dead and smelly as friend Briccus here.'

'We believe that, on the Day of Judgement, Christ will raise up all those who believed in him and bore witness, whether they've been dead for a day or a thousand years,' Nundinus declares with quiet conviction.

Canio looks at him, remembers some of the dead he has seen, then decides he can't be bothered to argue. He glances up at the sun. 'It's time I was somewhere else, so you can have the pleasure of burying him. Good and deep mind, so no one will disturb him until he's ready to pop up again, all fresh and lovely, on your Day of Judgement. Always provided he believed, of course.'

He dismounts and slashes the ropes that bind the stretcher to his saddle. It crashes down onto the grass, bounces ever so slightly and then is still. The cloud of flies is dislodged for an instant, then settles again.

Nundinus gazes down at Briccus, and Canio finds himself wondering what thoughts are passing through the youth's head.

'I'll bury him here,' Nundinus says softly. 'There's a spade in the wagon ... If you're going back that way, could you tell Matugena what's happened? It's best she doesn't see him like he is now.'

'No; I'm going another way,' Canio replies, pointing south. 'You'll have to tell her yourself.' He pauses, then on impulse asks, 'Did she love Briccus?'

Nundinus nods in unhappy confirmation. 'In their own strange way I think they were as close as a man and a woman ever were: it was as if they were their own children.'

Canio does not look back as he rides away. It is part of his simple philosophy of life never to look back.

CHAPTER TWENTY-TWO

Passing a steep hillside, Saturninus notices a thin stream of water tumbling down from the point where a small spring emerges from the outcropping rocks. He dismounts and stretches out both arms, letting the cool water splash onto his hands and bounce upwards for a moment before pattering down and snaking away through a narrow channel in the grass.

It was a week or so into the voyage down to Burdigala when we put into that little port for fresh water. And then we found we'd have to wait for the tide to turn before the Zephyrus could safely float out of the harbour again. So we walked together, just you and I, along that long, sandy beach until the headland curved and hid us.

We came across a great rock pool, full of sea water that had been warmed by the sun. We looked at each other and then, without a word, we undressed and bathed and swam in that pool, splashing each other like children in the greeny, almost-tepid water. It was the first time I'd seen you naked. I felt strangely shy, as if you were the first naked woman that I'd ever seen.

You stood up, the water lapping around your waist, and I drew you to me. Then I kissed you and felt your breasts, tautened and firmed by the seawater, pressing against me, below my ribs. You moved your body against mine, and I felt desire then – but with it an overwhelming tenderness that I thought I'd long lost the capacity to feel.

I think we would have made love there, on the warm sand between the rocks, but the tide had already turned and the rows of sly little waves were hurrying up the beach. And neither of us wanted it to be furtive or hurried. Not that first time. Or ever. So we gathered our clothes and walked to the bottom of the cliffs to dress. And there we discovered the little stream of fresh water – so like this one – that cascaded over the cliff and splashed down onto the beach below.

I stood beneath it and washed the salt water out of my hair and beard. You asked how cold it was, and I lied and said it was amazingly warm. So you trotted under – then shrieked because it felt icy cold, and chased me between the pools. And then we lay side by side on a great sun-warmed, wave-smoothed rock for a little while, and let the hot sun dry our bodies as the surf rolled in.

You stared up at the passing clouds, suddenly wistful, and said, 'I wonder if, when we're old, we'll remember this brief hour we spent together on a summer's day beside the sea?'

At least, that's what I used to think you said. But now I'm haunted by the suspicion that what you really said was, 'I wonder if, when you're old, you'll remember …?'

At Corvusida long barrow he finds Canio roasting the brace of chickens over a campfire which burns, almost smokelessly, close to its leeward side. Corvusida lies just south of the ancient trackway that winds across the rolling plateau between the little towns of Fonscolnis and Vadumleucara. Long grasses, just coming into flower, cover the mound, and between them peep out scores of buttercups and cowslips and the whitey-grey globes of dandelion seed heads.

'Well, my Primicerius, what did you find out about Caelofernus?'

'Nothing,' Saturninus admits. 'Nothing useful anyway. I still don't know who he is, or where he is, or why he should want to kill me.' Saying it out loud seems to make the disappointment so much worse.

Canio grins. 'You should have come with me to the Villa of Julius Martinus. I heard something interesting there.'

'Like what?'

So Canio tells him what he has heard and seen since they parted at the hole in the hillside. And when he has finished, Saturninus observes, 'But nobody actually heard the name of the man in the fine clothes?'

'No, only that one name, Armiger. But Straw-beard fits your description of Caelofernus, doesn't he?'

'He does. And this was a week or so ago?'

'That's what they said.'

'Over towards the Via Ricnild ... And the Via Ricnild joins the Fosse Way just north of Vadumleucara.' Saturninus realises that he is clutching at straws, but they are all he has.

'They won't be there now though – anywhere but there after what they did to that shepherd.'

'No, I don't suppose he will be at Vadumleucara.' Saturninus climbs to the top of the barrow and slowly turns through a full circle, gazing at the horizons. He halts facing north. 'But he's out there somewhere, isn't he?'

Canio prods one of the chickens with the point of his dagger. 'The further away the better as far as I'm concerned. These are almost done. Are we still going on to Vadumleucara?'

'Might as well: it's as quick a way as any to get back to Corinium from here. And while we're in the town we'll call in at the guard post – it's just possible that Magnillus has heard something about those three *bacaudae*.'

'Maybe – but I wouldn't bet on it.'

'No. Anyway, where did you get those?' Saturninus asks, nodding towards the chickens browning on their makeshift spits of green ash.

'They're two of Lucco's finest. And this barley beer comes with his compliments too.' Canio picks the now less-than-bulging goatskin out of the long grass and holds it up for Saturninus's inspection.

'Interesting. So how did you persuade Lucco to part with them? As I recall, he's not exactly renowned for his generosity.'

'I didn't have to persuade him. He couldn't do enough for me

when he realised why I was there. By the way, you were right –
Lucco was the one who helped our friend Lopsicallus to dig out
that rock.'

'He admitted it?'

'As good as.'

'And did he confirm the story about the wild men coming out
of the hill?'

Canio gives a non-committal shrug. 'Said he was down in the
coombe when dear old Loppi came tumbling out of the hole,
squawking about voices coming from inside. And our Lucco's no
hero either – apparently he didn't hang around to see the rest of
the show. Ran as if old Hades himself were after him – and by the
time he got back to the villa he was blowing so hard he sounded
like a rutting donkey ... that's what I was told, anyway.' Canio
sniggers at the recollection.

'But he must have believed that something nasty did come out
of that hillside: why else would he allow the Indutius family to go
back there and make their offerings?'

Canio's face takes on an uncharacteristically thoughtful look.
'Back there, I got the distinct impression that you believed
Lopsicallus about as much as I did.'

'Ah, but that was a long time ago, wasn't it? Almost a day.
Anyway, where's the rest of your plunder?'

'The rest of it, Primicerius?'

'Two chickens and a goatskin of beer aren't much of a price to
pay for keeping Lucco's name out of the official report ... I
assume that was the arrangement?'

'But I don't write official reports.'

'Lucco didn't know that. Come on, where's the rest of it?'

For the first time since Saturninus has known him, Canio
appears embarrassed. Almost. 'Ah, that. Well the truth is, there
was something else, but it wasn't something that I could bring
with me.'

'Like what?'

'I'm not sure you'd want to know,' Canio replies carefully.

And then Saturninus recalls what Ferna said about pretty Dulcitia. 'Not his wife? Not even Lucco would ...'

Canio's silence is eloquent.

'You're right; I don't want to know. Those chickens look ready to me.'

Canio draws his sword, skewers one of the birds with a deft thrust and draws it off its spit. Saturninus does likewise, and sinking onto the cowslip-studded grass of the barrow he steadily carves the bird with upward slices of his dagger, conveying each slice to his mouth between blade and thumb. 'Hades,' he mutters, 'I hope Lucco's wife was tastier than his chickens ... Or maybe the chickens were fine and you're just a lousy cook.'

Wisely, Saturninus thinks, Canio doesn't answer directly. Instead, he reaches over and hands him the goatskin. 'Here, this'll take the taste away. It's good stuff – I've forced one or two drops past my own lips, just to make sure you'd like it.'

'That was good of you.' Saturninus sways the flaccid goatskin from side to side, looking Canio in the eye all the while. He takes a long, slow drink.

'So, next stop Vadumleucara then?' Canio enquires, as if anxious to change the subject.

Saturninus stoppers the goatskin and touches his mouth with his fingers. 'That's right. We'll see if the sweet-tempered Magnillus knows anything about Caelofernus and his friends.' He licks his fingertips. 'This beer isn't at all bad ... Better than the chicken, anyway.'

The goatskin passes backwards and forwards between the two men; Canio relaxed, Saturninus brooding over the events of the last day and a half. At last it lies empty on the grass between them, while its contents, lack of sleep, and the warm breeze whispering through the fresh green leaves of a nearby clump of ash trees, all combine to lull them into sleep. The last thing Saturninus remembers seeing, before oblivion comes, is a solitary lark rising up into the sky. Higher and higher it climbs, its fluttering wings spread wide, until it is only a black speck against the bright blue, as all the while its liquid song ripples down to the barrow on which he lies. The drowsy thought comes to him that it is the same song that they must have heard – those people whose fragile brown bones now lie huddled in stone-lined chambers deep within the mound – when they too walked these hills, long, long ago.

Turn around, Pascentia! ... Turn, please! Why won't you turn and look this way?
I'm over here – standing a little way above that same shore I saw in Leucesca's spring – and I can see you clearly, no more than a hundred yards away, still shielding your eyes against that low sun.

But without so much as glancing towards me you begin to walk away along the shore ... And now that accursed mist on the water is creeping up to the shoreline again, coming ever closer to you. Desperate now, I'm shouting your name again and again, and running towards the shore.

But still you don't turn – seem completely unaware both of myself and the encroaching mist. I can't be more than thirty yards away from you now – but in another moment the mist has swallowed you. And now I'm plunging into the white vapour, hearing myself howl, Pascentia! – Pascentia! ... Wait! – where are you?

And now, at last, out of the mist comes a soft voice ... 'I'm here, Saturninus. Not far away.'

It is your voice, the voice I remember. But in the mist it seems to be coming from all directions and none. I'm crying frantically, Where?... Where – I can't see you?

'I'm not far away.' But even now your voice is fading, though I'm sure I hear it say, 'The gods will guide you to me ... Just follow wherever the roads may lead.'

I'm calling again, despairing now. But this time there is no reply, and I stumble blindly deeper and deeper into the mist.

CHAPTER TWENTY-THREE

Saturninus is still desperately searching when he feels something lightly touch his forehead. It pauses for a moment, then begins scuttling down his face. His eyes flicker open and he has a momentary image of metallic-green wing cases spread wide as the beetle whirrs up and vanishes into the vastness of the sky. And now he is wide awake and looking up at a line of high, white clouds sailing slowly by. Briefly he lies back among the grasses, remembering, then jerks upright and stares towards the west. Sunset can be no more than two hours away. He stifles a curse and struggles to his feet, then prods Canio none too gently on the shoulder with the toe of his boot.

Moments later Canio himself is lurching upright. 'By The Mothers, that beer was damned good stuff,' he remarks as he goes through the ritual of stamping on the ashes of the fire.

Saturninus, thinking feverishly, says nothing. He takes a long drink from his water bottle, then another, which he first swills around his mouth and then squirts out in a silvery stream as his contribution to killing the long-dead fire. 'I dare say we both needed the sleep,' he concedes philosophically as he pulls himself up into Antares' saddle. Then he sets off eastwards along the grassy trackway at a canter so brisk that it takes Canio half a mile to catch up.

At the beginning of the mile-long, curving descent into Vadumleucara they pass a little wayside shrine to Mars, there in his rustic role as protector of crops and livestock. Sheltered inside a horseshoe of drystone walling, roofed with thatch, sits a waist-high limestone altar. On its front face, carved in bold relief, stands the god in helmet and breastplate, a spear in his right hand, a shield in his left: eternally on guard against the unseen enemy. The thatch appears new, no more than a few months old. Both Saturninus and Canio salute the shrine as they pass by. It is the custom of the country: Saturninus remembers his father doing the same.

At the foot of the long hill, the trackway joins the great Fosse Way as it enters the sprawling old town. The two riders splash through the paved ford across the little Flumen Leucara, then trot on northwards through the town, past taverns, a cookshop and a row of small, open-fronted shops.

Glancing between the workshops of a blacksmith-cum-farrier and a wheelwright, Saturninus makes momentary eye contact with a priest of an obscure local cult. Dressed in a flowing green robe, the man wears a copper diadem with three circular medallions brazed onto the front. For an instant, as the low evening sun slanting into the alley catches them, Saturninus sees that all three depict strange winged beasts. A heartbeat later he is past the alley and the priest has vanished

The Vadumleucara civil guard post stands not far from the point where the Via Ricnild branches off the Fosse Way. It is a high-roofed, single-storey building with attached watchtower and stables, all strongly built of great squared blocks of the local limestone, now weathered grey and blotched with orange and sulphur-yellow lichens. Neat rows of dull orange *imbrices* and *tegulae* tiles alternate up the roof slopes. And running all around the eaves, closing off the open ends of the semi-circular *imbrices*, is a row of fired-clay triangular antefixes, mould-stamped with grotesque Medusa masks to ward off the evil eye. Saturninus has never noticed them before, and as his eyes scan along them the small, grim faces seem to stare malevolently down at him.

Are you my enemies too – like time and Caelofernus?

They dismount. Canio takes the reins of both horses and leads them around to the stable block, which occupies one side of the walled and gated courtyard at the rear of the building. Saturninus climbs the short flight of steps, finds the front door bolted and gives three hard thumps on the iron-studded wood with the side of his clenched fist. He waits impatiently, but there is no response and he is about to call out when a bearded face appears momentarily at one of the small, unglazed windows. The face vanishes. He hears hobnailed boots clatter harshly on the stone floor, then a heavy iron bolt is rasped back and the door swings open.

'You took your time, Vernatius.'

Somewhat flustered, Trooper Vernatius hurriedly salutes. 'My apologies, Primicerius ... We weren't expecting you for another week or so.'

'You should always expect the enemy to do the unexpected,' Saturninus replies drily. 'That's what I was taught – although I can't say it did me much good when it mattered. Where's Centenarius Magnillus?'

'With the prisoner, sir.'

'What prisoner?

'We've got a suspected highway robber, sir. Arrested him myself, right here in Vadumleucara not an hour ago.'

'Did you now ... He wouldn't by any chance be a big man by the name of Armiger, would he?'

'No, sir. Name's Gemellus. Little fellow. Have you ever run across him?'

Hope dies as swiftly as it was born. 'No, I can't say that I recall the name. Better let the Centenarius know I'm here.'

Vernatius salutes again and disappears behind a curtained-off doorway in the bare stone wall of the anteroom.

Saturninus hears the clack of his hobnails recede, then comes an indistinct murmur of voices, followed abruptly by, 'What! Why in Ahrimans's name didn't you tell me immediately? No, you donkey, stay here with the prisoner.'

Saturninus looks up impassively at the massive roof timbers. Once again there is the ring of iron on flagstones, then the curtain is pulled aside and a tall, hawk-like man in his mid thirties emerges into the anteroom, buckling his sword belt as he comes.

'Good evening, sir.' The man brings his clenched fist across his chest in salute. 'I'm sorry I wasn't here to greet you personally, but I was interrogating a prisoner.' There is, as always when they meet, a stiff formality about the man.

Saturninus returns the salute. '*Salve*, Magnillus. No need to look worried. I've been over to the western edge of the hills on a little job for Aemilianus, so I decided to call in here on my way back and get the inspection over and done with.'

Magnillus appears to relax. It seems that Saturninus's unexpected visit is not the result of any sins of his being discovered.

'Tell me, have you received any reports of three big men – strangers – seen wandering around in these parts? One of them with straw-coloured hair and beard and dressed in fine, brightly-coloured clothes? Perhaps trying to keep out of sight, only moving after dark or in the early mornings?'

Magnillus slowly shakes his head. 'No, Primicerius, I can't say that I have. Any particular reason for asking?'

'They're suspected of killing a shepherd from the Villa of Julius Martinus.'

'When? I hadn't heard.'

'It happened several days ago, but the body was only discovered this morning. So they're probably long gone by now.'

Perhaps it had only been a slim chance. But that didn't stop me from hoping ... Or now feeling a disappointment painful as a hornet's sting.

'Anyway, Vernatius tells me you've got a suspected robber in the cells. What do you know about him?'

'Not very much, so far,' Magnillus answers cagily. 'He's a shifty-looking bastard. Says his name's Gemellus – Gaius Aurelius Gemellus. Full *tria nomina*, would you believe. Claims that he's a poor but honest coppersmith on his way to Corinium to look for work.'

'So what makes you think he isn't?'

'Vernatius was tipped off about him by a man called Placidius. Corn merchant from Glevum. I've known the man for years, and he swears this Gemellus was part of a gang that robbed him and some other merchants last year.'

'Where?'

'Down south, on the road between Cunetio and Venta, so Placidius said – and he's got no reason to lie that I know of. Another thing, did you ever see a coppersmith whose hands weren't as black as charcoal?'

'And Gemellus's aren't, I suppose? Right, I'd better take a look at him.' Saturninus walks to the doorway that separates the anteroom from the living quarters and motions Magnillus to lead the way.

From the living quarters, a short corridor leads into a small, bare guardroom, where Vernatius now sits on a wooden bench set against one wall. Opposite him is a row of three grim cells, their iron bars black and pitted. Through the room's high windows streams in the golden light of late evening, bathing the upper halves of the cells with a warm glow that softens their natural bleakness. In the centre cell, standing grasping the bars with both hands as if for support, Saturninus sees a slight, alert-looking man in his early twenties.

As they enter, Vernatius springs to his feet and the prisoner stares intently at them. Saturninus, standing at Magnillus's shoulder, stares back. He sees puzzlement, recognition and then alarm register on the prisoner's face with the rapidity of cloud shadows chasing across a March hillside. He is the first to break the silence.

'Hullo, Bonosus,' he says quietly. 'Taken to highway robbery now, have we? That's quite a step up from chicken stealing.'

'You know this man, sir?' Magnillus asks.

'Oh yes, we've met before, haven't we, Bonosus? Two years ago come autumn it was, at the big October livestock fair in Corinium. Had his own stall did this young man, selling chickens. Trouble was though, they weren't his own chickens, were they, Bonosus?'

'Bonosus? My name's not Bonosus, Centurion. My name's Aurelius Gemellus, and always has been.' He might have been trying to sound bold and confident, but the words come out ragged and high pitched.

Fear does that, Saturninus remembers. *Dries the mouth, numbs the tongue.*

'Perhaps it was his twin brother, the other *gemellus*, who stole them, Primicerius?' suggests Magnillus, grinning at his own pun.

'No, there's only one of you, isn't there, Bonosus? And there must be a good few people back in Corinium who still remember you. Face it – you're caught in the net and there's no way out … Unless you can show us a scar-free back to prove you weren't the man who was whipped for that particular misdemeanour?'

Bonosus flinches, and Saturninus has too much imagination not to realise that the little man is already hearing the insane baying of the hunting dogs as they leap for his throat, feeling those terrible teeth …

'That whipping half-killed me, Primicerius,' he murmurs.

'Yes, that bastard Crotilio does enjoy his work.'

'How did he get caught last time, Primicerius?' Magnillus asks.

'A big, feathered informer tipped us off. Among all those hens was a rooster. Just the one, but he was an enormous bird, very distinctive. "Know him anywhere," his owner said, and I swear you could have heard his crowing at the first milestone beyond the city walls in any direction.'

Bonosus sighs. 'Ah, but he would have made a magnificent fighting cock. I could have made a fortune with him.'

Saturninus waits, but Bonosus says nothing more. He turns to Magnillus. 'Right, you'd better get a sworn deposition from that merchant, Placidius. Is he still in Vadumleucara?'

'Yes, sir. Staying at The Vine Leaf,' Vernatius chips in.

'Good. When you've got it, you'd better take our friend here to Corinium. He's your capture, so you can have any reward that's going.'

'And you know what's going to happen to you there, don't you, Bonosus?' With a humourless smile, Magnillus draws his right index finger slowly across his own throat, emitting as he does so a high-pitched squeal intended to be reminiscent of a dying pig.

Saturninus turns to go. He tells himself that Bonosus is probably a murderer by now and deserves his fate. Sometimes the tactic works, sometimes it doesn't. Today it doesn't.

CHAPTER TWENTY-FOUR

But before Saturninus has even reached the corridor, Bonosus cries out, 'Wait, Primicerius, wait! Oh, sweet Isis help me! You've heard of Carausius, haven't you? … Carausius? … You must have?' Not waiting for a reply, he gabbles on, 'I can tell you where he is – now, at this very moment. If you move fast, you can have him and all his gang in chains by dawn. Picture it, Primicerius – the whole pack of them. And it'll be you – and the Centenarius here – who'll get the credit for it. And the reward too. There must be quite a price on his head by now. Perhaps as much as ten gold solidi – maybe even more.'

Carausius? For moment I thought he said …

Saturninus turns. 'Yes, I've heard of Carausius … I take it you'd want your freedom in return for this information – always assuming that you really have it, of course?'

'That's all I ask, Primicerius. Just promise that you'll set me free and I'll tell you exactly where he is. But you must hurry – if I'm not back in his camp by one hour after sunrise tomorrow, Carausius will know that I've been captured and move on – fast. Believe me, he's as cunning as a fox – that's why he's never been caught.'

'Ah, but speaking of foxes, isn't there an old saying,' Magnillus asks reflectively, 'that if you let the fox go you must hunt him again? So why don't we simply loosen your little foxy tongue, here and now? That way, we won't have to promise you anything – or have the trouble of hunting you again.' He slowly draws his sword, all the while staring at Bonosus's hands, as if choosing which finger to remove first.

167

'Oh no, not that – for pity's sake, Primicerius!' Bonosus snatches his hands away from the bars as if they have suddenly become red hot. 'I'm not a strong man – I never have been. I'd die under torture, and then you'd never find Carausius.'

Magnillus, sword half out of its scabbard, looks to Saturninus for his cue. Saturninus hesitates, then gives a slight shake of his head. Magnillus lets the sword sink slowly back into the scabbard. Then he drives it home the last inch with a snap of brass hilt against copper mount which makes it clear that he would have much preferred a positive response.

But before the centenarius can voice his displeasure, Vernatius asks Saturninus, 'But who is this Carausius, sir?'

'Who, I don't know. As to what … army deserter, brigand, murderer several times over – and barking madman, from what I've heard. Take your pick. Carausius almost certainly isn't his real name, but apparently he likes to claim that he's the great-grandson of *the* Carausius.'

'And who was he, sir?'

'May the gods preserve us! Don't you know anything, man?' Magnillus snorts contemptuously. 'He was the great usurper. Made himself emperor of all Britannia and Northern Gaul, eighty-odd years ago.'

'You mean, like … Magnentius?' Vernatius whispers the proscribed name.

'Much the same – although Carausius at least had the sense not to try and grab the whole empire. I've never heard of our so-called Carausius coming this far north before though.' Saturninus looks hard at Bonosus.

'Perhaps the dirty little fox crapped in his own earth down south?' Magnillus suggests.

'That's it exactly, Centenarius!' Bonosus breaks in, as if anxious to feed his audience's growing interest in the man he is trying to betray. 'After three missions in as many weeks – missions was what he called them – they sent a whole squadron of cavalry after us. So Carausius decided to move up north for a few months.'

And suddenly – like a man who stands on a high hill watching the rising sun peep above the horizon and light up the dark plain below – understanding comes to Saturninus. 'What does Carausius look like?' he asks quietly. 'I've heard he's a little man, no bigger than yourself. Is that true?'

'Carausius? No – he's a great big man, Primicerius … maybe even taller than you.' Bonosus looks confused.

'Big man? No! Small, and with short-cropped hair and beard, to make his head look like the Carausius on the old coins my grandfather kept as souvenirs.' Before Bonosus can reply, Saturninus turns to Vernatius and explains, 'He was in Constantius Chlorus's army that took Britannia back from Allectus in 296 … and to save you asking, Allectus was the man who'd murdered Carausius and grabbed his little empire three years before.'

'But Carausius *is* a big man, Primicerius, I swear he is,' Bonosus pleads. 'And more fearsome than any man you've ever seen. When he stares at me, it feels as if Sol Invictus himself is frowning.'

'How do you mean, "Sol Invictus"?' Saturninus tries to sound sceptical.

'Because his hair and beard are all wild and rough and golden as the sun.'

'Oh, really … and I suppose you're going to tell me next that he dresses like the king of Persia – all the colours of the rainbow and gold rings on every finger?'

'That's him, Primicerius! You *must* have seen him yourself.'

Magnillus starts to snigger. 'And you must think – '

'Where is he?' Saturninus interrupts.

'If I tell you, you will let me go, won't you?' Bonosus wheedles.

'Where is he, Bonosus! Vernatius, have you got the key?'

'Yes, Primicerius.'

'Open the cell,' Saturninus orders, drawing his sword.

'Oh merciful Isis, protect me!' Bonosus shrieks. 'I'll tell you, I'll tell you!'

'Where is he?' Saturninus demands again, his voice cold as ice-water.

Vernatius pushes the plunger key into the end of the cylindrical padlock and pulls the two halves apart. The chain rattles shrilly around the bars and he yanks the cell door open.

'He's in a wood – Duboceto Wood they call it – not more than twenty miles north of here – him and all his gang!' The words tumble out of Bonosus as if he'd been turned upside down and shaken.

'North? Did you say north?' Saturninus asks.

The woman at the crossroads pointed to the north.

Then, sword in hand, he walks slowly into the cell. 'If you're lying to me, Bonosus ...' He lets the sword point, an inch away from Bonosus's throat, say the rest.

'It's the truth, Primicerius, I swear it! I'll guide you there ... I'll show you where the sentry hides ... Anything ... Just promise you'll let me go afterwards?'

'What's his real name?'

'Who, Primicerius?'

'Carausius of course – what's his real name?'

'I don't know, Primicerius. I've never heard it. Everyone calls him Carausius.'

'I think you do know. It's Caelofernus, isn't it?' Saturninus whispers the name.

'Yes ... perhaps ... I truly don't know! ... I've heard he used other names in the past, before he started calling himself Carausius, but that was long before I knew him.'

'I wonder, Bonosus ... I wonder if you really are telling the truth?' But the question is rhetorical: Saturninus is sure that he is, and the certainty calms him.

And Bonosus seems to sense that he is believed. Eagerly he confides, 'And Primicerius, I swear that robbery near Cunetio was the only one I ever took part in. Carausius ordered me to come with him on the mission because he had two men down with fever. Believe me, if I'd refused he would have killed me on the spot: he's more vicious than a mad dog. And I swear too, by the great goddess Isis herself, that I never hurt anyone in that robbery – or at any other time.'

Saturninus glances at Magnillus and reads the disbelief written on his face.

Bonosus must have read it too, because he quickly adds, 'Just think of it, Primicerius: Carausius and all his gang in exchange for nothing more than my freedom ... it's so pitifully little to ask. Do we have an understanding?'

Saturninus looks at him and sees the sweat glistening on his wax-pale face. 'Yes, Bonosus,' he murmurs, his thoughts far away. 'We have an understanding.'

CHAPTER TWENTY-FIVE

The last spectral light of dusk is rapidly fading when Canio at last wanders into the guard post. Since his arrival at Vadumleucara he has been in desultory conversation with Nitalis the ostler, catching up on the gossip and happenings of the district. Now, as he enters the anteroom, the indistinct murmur of voices he heard coming from the living quarters beyond ceases abruptly. Cautiously he eases back the rough curtain and peers inside.

A pottery lamp burns smokily on a large table in the centre of the room. Seated around the table, their faces lit from below, lurid, every irregularity and crease shadowed and accentuated, are Saturninus, Magnillus and Vernatius.

'Welcome back, Canio, you're just in time.'

'For what, Primicerius?'

'We're planning a little hunting expedition.'

Surprise, then pleasure register on Canio's mobile face. 'A boar hunt?'

Saturninus grins, well aware that Canio enjoys hunting – aware too that he usually leaves the actual pig-sticking to others, preferring to concentrate on the pleasures of drinking and gambling that frequently accompany it. He shakes his head. 'No, not boar. Highway robbers. Did you ever hear of a man who calls himself Carausius?'

Canio rubs his bristly chin. 'Yes, I've heard of him. A real charmer, isn't he – kills for the fun of it? But he never comes this far north … or does he?'

'Apparently he does. If what we've been told by a prisoner

172

back there in the cells is true, then the charming Carausius is camped in a wood no more than twenty miles north of here.'

'And we're going after him?'

'We are.'

'How many men has he got?'

'Bonosus, that's the prisoner – '

'I thought Nitalis said his name was Gemellus.'

'That's what he was calling himself. Real name's Bonosus – remember him?'

'Vaguely … chickens?'

'That's the one. He's been playing the spy for Carausius – spotting likely victims on the Fosse Way and Via Ricnild. He says that Carausius has only got four men with him at the moment.'

'Anyone I know?'

'You tell me. His second in command is a fellow army deserter called Igillus; only one eye and as mean as they come. Then there's a man called Bano; small, tough and wiry – origin unknown, but from Bonosus's description I'll lay odds that at least one of his parents came from east of the Danube.'

'Hun?'

'Or Sarmatian, or Quadi. Also, there's a couple of runaway slaves called Lemnus and Armiger –'

'Armiger?'

'The very same. And Carausius is a big man with yellow hair and a taste for fine clothes: remind you of anyone?'

Canio gives him a curious look 'So, you've found him then?'

'Yes … Or has he found me? Strange how it's working out, isn't it?' But before either Canio or Magnillus can ask questions, Saturninus adds, 'Oh, and there are two women as well. Carausius's woman is called Melania, and the other is … ?' He turns to Magnillus, but the centenarius shakes his head.

'Honorata,' Saturninus reminds him.

And if I can believe Bonosus's descriptions, then either one of those women just might be you, Pascentia.

'Four against five. That's not bad odds,' Canio reflects.

'No … but good or bad, they can't be improved. Old Himilico's patrolling in Vadumleucara now, but we'll have to leave him here to man the guard post while we're away. Oh, and to save you asking, there's no time to send to Corinium for reinforcements. Bonosus says that if he's not back in Duboceto Wood by one hour after sunrise, then Carausius will assume he's been caught and his gang will scatter to the four winds. So, it's dawn tomorrow or never.'

Saturninus sees a frown appear on Canio's face. 'Why wait until dawn? Why not hit them tonight, when they're least expecting it?'

'No … There's a sentry,' Magnillus growls, scratching progressively up his left side from waist to armpit, as if following the course of a wandering flea.

'So?' Canio's eyes flick from face to face.

'Near the entrance to the only path into the wood,' Saturninus explains, 'is a big tree, and in that tree Carausius has a sentry posted. Always. He's quite high up, inside a shelter made of oxhide. Bonosus says we haven't a hope of sneaking past him, day or night. Sometimes they set trip-ropes, or scatter rotten sticks across the path – sticks that crack when you tread on them.'

'And in any case, a good general never leaves enemy troops behind him when he advances,' Magnillus points out.

'Quite … especially when, at the first sign of trouble, that sentry's supposed to give a long warning blast on a hunting horn. And there's no use trying to blunder our way through a pitch-black wood in the hope we might stumble across Carausius before he hears us coming.'

'There's an almost-full moon tonight, Primicerius,' Vernatius points out.

'But it won't be shining in the middle of a wood,' Canio reminds him. A sudden thought appears to strike him. 'What if there's a guard dog as well?' – this to Saturninus.

Saturninus shakes his head. 'I asked Bonosus – apparently Carausius doesn't trust dogs: they can bark at the wrong times.'

Canio still seems unconvinced. 'So why don't we just creep up to the tree and tell the sentry to come down. He won't blow his horn once he realises we know he's there – it would be suicidal.'

'Bonosus says he will – says his men fear Carausius more than us. Maybe he's right, maybe he's wrong, but it's too great a chance to take.'

'Hmm ... so we've got to kill him? Yes?' Canio looks across to the three seated figures as if seeking confirmation.

Saturninus nods.

Surrounded by a darkness made darker by the feeble light of the lamp that casts their monstrous shadows onto the bare stone walls behind them, they resemble deities from the Infernal Regions as they decide the fate of a man whom none of them has ever seen.

'But how?' Canio asks. 'If that sentry's invisible in his hide, then there's not much point shooting arrows at him. And anyway, at the sort of range you'd have to be to avoid him spotting you, the chances are that an arrow wouldn't even penetrate oxhide.'

'Ah well, that depends on what sort of bow you're using, doesn't it?' replies Magnillus, with the air of one who knows a secret.

Saturninus watches Canio affect an air of mystification, the quicker to learn the answer. 'Did you know there's a bolt-firing ballista in the weapons store here?' he explains. 'An old one, said to be left over from the invasion scare of 'forty-three. The time when our late, illustrious Emperor Constans – '

'Of blessed memory,' intone Canio and Magnillus together, and erupt with derisive laughter, to the perceptible embarrassment of Vernatius.

' – Came over the stormy winter seas to save us all,' continues Saturninus, himself unable to suppress a grin.

Then Canio appears to realise the full implications of what Saturninus has just said. 'A ballista! You're joking?'

'Can you think of anything better? Especially when the entrance to the wood faces north-east.'

Canio appears not to understand the significance of this last remark. 'When was that ballista last fired in anger?'

'At a guess, quite some time ago,' Saturninus admits. 'It's one of the old type – a scorpio.'

'A scorpio! – one of those with a wooden front end built like a brothel's front door? They must have stopped making those things two hundred years ago.'

'At least that,' Saturninus concedes. 'The copper shield plate fixed across the front of ours has a dedication to Emperor Domitian and Legio II Augusta. But they built them to last in those days,' he adds, deadpan.

Canio shakes his head in exaggerated amazement. 'Atys wept!'

Magnillus gives him a stony look. 'But I know for a fact that the sinew rope-springs, the bowstring and the draw-rope were all renewed and tested no more than four years ago, just after I came to Vadumleucara. And it's all still in first-class working order – I'd stake my life on that,' he asserts, as if anxious to dispel any slur on his stewardship.

'And maybe not just your life, my hero. If that sentry does manage to sound the alarm then we'll have to rush them ... Just how far into this wood is their camp?'

'That ratbag Bonosus says about four hundred paces. Not scared of a fight, are you, Canio?' Magnillus gives a fierce grin that displays his strong, yellow teeth.

Canio ignores the jibe. 'So they'd have plenty of time to grab their swords and be waiting for us.'

'Very likely.' Saturninus isn't going to argue the point. 'But the *Parcae* seem to have cast the dice, and come dawn tomorrow we'll see what numbers they show ... Dawn tomorrow,' he muses. 'Time is not on our side.'

'No,' Magnillus agrees, gazing into the lamp's wan flame, 'time will always be the enemy of mortal men. But although Ahriman, lord of darkness, commands this aeon of boundless time, yet it is the duty of a strong man to fight alongside the God Mithras and great Ahuramazda in their endless battle against the enemies of the light.'

Saturninus glances across at Canio, who looks up at the ceiling.

The plan is talked around, honed and agreed. Then Saturninus sends Vernatius into the town to bring back Trooper Himilico. Canio goes back to the stables to rouse Nitalis, break the bad news that the ostler will have to accompany them to within a mile of Duboceto Wood, and help him to ready the horses. Magnillus fetches the iron latch-lifter key to the weapons store, unlocks the door, and then he and Saturninus drag out and inspect the great wood and iron crossbow mounted on a tripod base that is the scorpio.

And so, less than an hour after the little council of war has ended, six riders set off northwards into the night along the Fosse Way. Bonosus's hands are tied behind his back, Vernatius leading the little man's horse by the reins. Nitalis has charge of a packhorse carrying the scorpio, broken down into body and tripod base. In the doorway of the guard post, watching them go, stands Trooper Himilico, veteran of the frontier army of the Rhineland and a grizzled survivor of nearly fifty winters.

The soft light of the almost-full moon shines down, startlingly bright, from between ragged feathers of cloud drifting across the heavens. It makes the shadows of men and horses stand out black and sharp on the pale highway. Motionless as a rock, Himilico waits and watches as first the sounds of hooves die away, and then the silent shapes and their shadows slowly dwindle into invisibility. He shakes his head in apparent foreboding, then urinates onto the road before going back into the guard post and bolting the door behind him.

CHAPTER TWENTY-SIX

The sea, the Oceanus Hibernicus, is calm this night. Calm enough to mirror the great waxing moon and cast its glow shimmering across the tiny dancing wavelets. The faces of the nine men in the long, narrow boat built of hides stretched across a framework of woven willow, are grim and dark. Dark as the Cambrian coastline along which they are rowing, keeping sight of that coast without ever coming too close to it, as if anxious not to be seen by anyone on the shore.

During the day the boy had been collecting gulls' eggs from the ledges of the stack of barren rock that juts out into the sea. Now, waiting for the turning of the tide that cuts off his path back to the mainland, and with the incessant cries of seabirds preventing him from sleeping, he gazes out over the water and sees them. At first he notices only that one curragh. But, as his eyes learn to distinguish their matt black shapes against the subtly sparkling sea, he makes out another, then another, and eventually counts well over a hundred before the last of them disappears into the night. But how many passed before he first became aware of their presence, and how many more are too far out to sea to be visible, he will never know.

*

Night has submerged and estranged the land, but even when the moon is behind clouds Saturninus can still make out the shapes of trees and the crests of hill ridges outlined against the sky. There is almost no artificial light to destroy his night vision, only the glow from the dying embers of a hearth fire as the riders pass some small farmstead. Or the lamps of a great villa, miles away, blazing out across the rolling grasslands as some rich man entertains his guests far into the night. Bats flit swiftly and erratically overhead as they hunt nocturnal insects; and large dark birds, solitary or in twos or threes, occasionally fly across the road, low and slow and as silently as the bats.

Behind him he hears the constant clop of horses' hooves on the compacted stone of the highway, the soft jangle of harness, and the creak of leather as someone eases himself in the saddle. Whirring moths blunder into his face and the thin night wind sighs through the leaves of woods where owls hoot back and forth to each other in the cavernous darkness.

Vernatius is the first to speak. 'Centenarius, sir, when did you last fire that scorpio?'

'What? I've never fired it! Or any other sort of ballista. Those six arrows are all there were when I arrived. I once put in a request to Novanticus for more, but nothing ever came of it – which was typical of the man.' Magnillus's tone is brusque. It does not invite further questioning.

'Yes, of course, sir. How about you, Ducenarius; did you ever use one?'

'Not me, young Vernatius. In Germania I saw them used several times, but I never fired one myself. So that leaves you, Primicerius. If you don't know, then we'd all better turn around and go back to Vadumleucara.'

Saturninus, riding a few yards out in front of the others and setting the pace, turns in his saddle and frowns at Canio. 'House of Hades, of course I know how to use a ballista! I was taught years ago … by a legionary *ballistarius*.'

'Where?' Canio asks.

Saturninus is silent for several moments, then replies quietly, 'In the East … at Amida. They had dozens of ballistae there.'

'Amida?' says Canio, 'That was somewhere out Persia way, wasn't it?'

'How did you come to be there?' Magnillus asks.

Saturninus ignores both questions, but Magnillus persists, 'Come on, Primicerius, tell us all about it. It'll help the journey to pass – and convince us that you really know how to handle a ballista.'

Saturninus is about to give Magnillus an angry reply. Then he realises that they are all looking at him. Waiting. Wondering.

'Right – if you really feel you ought to know, then I'll tell you.' He hears the harshness in his voice; he is tenser than he had realised. 'Amida was – is – a walled city on the headwaters of the River Tigris in Upper Mesopotamia, near what was then the border with Persia. About eight years ago, in the July of 'fifty-nine, I was in command of a small unit of frontier scouts. They were bringing back rumours that Shapur, the Persian Great King, was preparing to invade our province of Mesopotamia. My orders were to shadow the Persian army as it moved northwards along the Tigris, and send reports of its progress every day to the Comes who commanded the garrison at Amida, a man called Aelianus.

'On the last day, the day before the Persians reached the city, I reported to Aelianus myself. But after I'd given him all the information I could, he ordered me not to leave. Said I'd be more use there in Amida, advising him on Persian weapons and tactics.'

'You mean that you were actually there, in the siege?' Magnillus sounds incredulous.

'Trapped like a rat by a hundred thousand Persians – including several legions of Shapur's finest armoured cavalry.'

'The ones with the pointy helmets and long coats of steel scales?'

'The same, Canio.'

'I saw some of that armour once,' Canio continues. 'Hanging in a legionary shrine in Colonia Agrippina it was. Supposed to have been captured by Emperor Galerius in one of his Persian campaigns, some seventy-odd years ago.'

'Yes, we could beat the Persians in those days – before our masters decided to spit in the faces of the gods!' Magnillus declares bitterly.

Saturninus doesn't rise to the fly. 'And some of those cavalrymen even had metal masks, moulded like faces – a metal which dazzled when the sun caught them. The proper name for those men is *cataphracti,* but we called them *clibanarii* ... You know what a *clibanus* is?'

'Some sort of oven, isn't it?' Vernatius sounds unsure.

'A bread oven – and that's what it must have felt like being inside all that metal with the Mesopotamian sun burning down on your head. The Persians had tens of thousands of foot soldiers too, of course – spearmen, bowmen, slingers, swordsmen – all in billowing tunics and trousers of every colour in the rainbow. And elephants – lines of the great, grey beasts, three times as big as a horse and every one with three or four bowmen on their backs in miniature forts made of wickerwork.

'And all we had in Amida were between seven and eight thousand infantry – some of them from Magnentius's old Gallic legions that Constantius sent to the East when Magnentius killed himself after losing his last battle at Mons Seleucus in 'fifty-three.

'On the first day, Shapur himself with an escort of his satraps – that's what they call their generals – rode up to within hailing distance of the walls and demanded our surrender. Both his helmet – which was shaped like a ram's head, horns and all – and his cuirass, were made of beaten gold. And his cloak and robes had so much gold thread woven into them that, when the sun's rays caught him, it was as if he were made entirely of bright gold.'

I remember that he looked like a god riding serenely across the earth.

'You actually saw him – you saw the king of Persia?' Nitalis asks, amazed.

'I did – though at the time I wasn't sorry he didn't see me.'

'And why was that, Primicerius?'

'Because Aelianus had no intention of surrendering. He gave Shapur a shower of arrows and ballista bolts for an answer, and one of them tore a great hole in his fine cloak. That sent him galloping back to his tents a damned sight faster than he'd come.'

This prompts a derisive cheer from them all – except Bonosus. Saturninus, looking back and seeing his taut face in the moonlight, guesses that the little man's terrors are increasing with every mile that brings him closer to Carausius.

'Anyway, after that insult to their Great King we expected the Persians to attack immediately, but they didn't. And the next day, just after dawn, a strange thing happened. Two satraps came riding up to the walls. One was a tall young man, the other much older and sitting awkwardly in his saddle. They were probably going to demand our surrender again, but they never did.'

'Why not?' It is Canio who asks.

'Because, before they could say a word, a *ballistarius* from one of our artillery units fired at the young man. The bolt hit him right in the centre of his breastplate, and he went crashing down off his horse.

When his body hit the ground it raised little rills of dust. In my mind's eye I can still see them, hovering motionless in the still air.

'We learnt later that he was the old man's son. After that, there were no more attempts at talking us into surrender.

'Later that day, up on the ramparts, I chanced to meet the man who'd fired that fatal bolt. His name was Atticus and he was a *duplicarius* in the fifty-five-strong ballista unit of Legio V Parthica, the original garrison of the city. In the hours that followed, Atticus himself taught me how to load, aim and fire – which I did a hundred times in the attacks that followed. So you can all relax: I know how to use a ballista.'

'Were they *scorpios* at Amida, Primicerius?'

'No, Vernatius. As it happens, they were *cheiroballistras* – the later type, with all-metal spring frames at the front. But the way of working them is just the same.'

More or less.

They ride on in silence for a little while, and then Vernatius enquires hesitantly, 'You say Amida was, what – eight years ago, Primicerius? You'll pardon me for asking, but have you used a ballista of any sort since then?'

'Hades, Vernatius!' … Saturninus breathes deeply. 'No, I've not used one since Amida. But there are some things you never forget.'

Another quarter mile passes, and then Magnillus asks, 'What happened in the end at Amida?'

Saturninus had been hoping that nobody would ask that question.

'After a siege of seventy-three days, the Persians built a great ramp of earth against the walls and stormed the city.'

'So how did you survive when the city fell, Primicerius? I seem to recall hearing that no one got out alive?'

You know more than you're telling, don't you, Magnillus?

'Some did. The Persians made slaves of what was left of the civilian population and the few soldiers they didn't butcher.' He wants to stop there, but Magnillus seems about to repeat his question, so he says, 'Myself, I survived by not being in Amida when it fell.' And before anyone can ask, he quickly adds, 'And why I wasn't in the city on that last day is a story that will have to wait for another time and place.'

The near-full moon glows down, bathing the monochrome countryside in its cool, wan light. Saturninus gazes ahead at the ribbon of limestone-metalled road that stretches away into the distance, startlingly pale against the greys and blacks of the grass and trees.

Are they out there somewhere, the dead of Amida? Watching me? Waiting for me to join them?

Being reminded of the fall of Amida seems to have jabbed a raw nerve in Magnillus's brooding soul. 'The gods have turned against us!' he suddenly declares. 'That's why disasters like Amida happened – that and the shameful end to the Persian war in 'sixty-three. And do you know why they've turned against us? One of you does – don't you, Trooper Vernatius?'

Vernatius, a Christian, says nothing, but that doesn't stop Magnillus.

'It's because, fifty and more years ago, that Emperor Constantine who called himself "The Great" – him and his three degenerate sons after him – decided to turn their backs on the gods who had made Rome truly great. Instead, they decreed that we all had to worship a crucified Jew!' Magnillus hawks and spits ferociously onto the highway. '"Those whom the gods wish to destroy they first make mad" – isn't that what somebody once said?'

'Euripedes, I think it was.' Saturninus knows where Magnillus is leading; guesses that the others do too, particularly Vernatius.

'Who was he?' Nitalis enquires.

'A fat Greek who ran a whorehouse in Moguntiacum. Any girl in the place for only half a siliqua,' Canio replies, his voice deadpan.

'That was cheap.' Saturninus thinks he might as well keep the conversation going, if only to interrupt Magnillus's flow of invective.

'You wouldn't have thought so if you'd seen the girls.'

'Not very pretty?'

'I heard that one of them was Euripedes' own sister.'

'So it was a family business. Besides, Greek women are renowned for their beauty.'

'Not in Moguntiacum they aren't. She was even fatter than Euripedes.'

Magnillus seems less than amused by the interruption. 'Do you really think it's a joking matter – even now, when Constantine's madness has spread throughout the whole empire like rot through a store of winter apples? Do you think it's funny that the gods have finally despaired of us ever recovering from that madness – because they have, you know? That's why they no longer march beside us into battle, as they did in Galerius's day – and why the whole empire's sinking ever deeper into the Pit of Tartarus. As even you can see, can't you, Trooper Vernatius?'

'Yes, Centenarius,' Vernatius replies tonelessly.

Magnillus looks as if he is about to continue his attack, but before he can do so Saturninus says quietly, 'Julian believed in the old gods, and loved them too, and thought they loved him. But they seemed to desert him in Persia. Myself, I wonder if the gods have ever been on anyone's side – if they do what they do for reasons that are all their own?' He gazes around at the moonlit landscape and adds, 'Perhaps they're like the hills – they were here long before we came, and they'll still be here long after we've gone. For most of us, I suspect that they have no feelings whatsoever. Nothing so human as love, or pity, or even contempt. They watch us for a little, and then we're gone; and only rarely do they mourn our passing.'

'*Merda*, but you're a cheerful bunch to travel with!' Canio breaks in irritably. 'Forget Amida – who wants to hear the story of the Burgundian at Moguntiacum barracks?'

Saturninus shakes his head. 'No thanks, Canio. I've heard it several times already – both the drunk and the sober versions.'

'Is that the one where the Burgundian forces a boy down into the sewer under the latrine seats to look for his dropped helmet, and the boy half-fills it with the brown stuff before handing it back?' Vernatius asks.

'Ah, I remember now,' says Magnillus. 'And as the shit is running down his face and dripping all over his nice clean uniform, the great and illustrious Emperor Constans – who just happens to be taking the parade that day – says to the Burgundian, "You may only be a private soldier, but I can see you have the brains of a centurion."'

'I don't remember telling you two that story.'

'As I recall, you had drunk a fair amount of wine that night, Ducenarius,' Vernatius cautiously reminds Canio.

Magnillus gives a grunt of something close to amusement. 'Enough to float a coracle in – isn't that what you said at the time, Vernatius?'

Vernatius busies himself in changing over Bonosus's reins from his left to his right hand and mumbles an incoherent reply.

Some ten miles north of Vadumleucara, at around the halfway point of their journey, they are challenged by a solitary civil guard trooper standing in the highway where it passes the little town of Dornolana. In the late autumn, when the *annona* grain tax is collected there, it is garrisoned by three or four troopers, but for the rest of the year it has but two.

The moon is behind clouds as they approach. In the feeble yellow glow cast by the trooper's lantern, Saturninus sees the man peering nervously ahead as he tries to identify the cloaked horsemen coming towards him out of the night. Then, recognising Magnillus as much by voice as sight when he responds to his challenge, the sentry salutes and lets them pass.

Magnillus growls at him as they trot by, demanding to know why he hadn't been carrying a weapon of some sort as they approached.

The trooper protests that he can unsheathe his sword as quick as lightning, should danger threaten.

'I bet you say that to all the girls,' Canio shouts back.

Later, they pass a pair of benighted travellers sitting around a campfire at the side of the road, the orange firelight giving their bearded faces a sinister glow under their cloak hoods, while the pungent smell of wood smoke drifts into the nostrils of horses and men. And once, a solitary horseman riding fast on a foam-flecked horse comes thundering out of the moonlight, passes them, and vanishes back into the night, his identity and purpose alike unknown.

These apart, they see no one else on their twenty-mile journey northwards. Saturninus is not surprised: in an age when most men still believe in the existence of a multiplicity of supernatural powers, many prefer not to travel through the countryside at night, fearing what they might encounter walking, flying or hovering there.

CHAPTER TWENTY-SEVEN

Avoiding the pools of moonlight, Vilbia slips noiselessly across the clearing. Reaching the temple she pauses and glances behind her, then eases open the door and steps inside. Slowly, so as to make no sound, she latches the door and slides the iron bolt along into its keep, then stands with her back pressed against the hard wood, listening. The only sounds she can hear are the whisper of the spring water overflowing from the font and the rapid beating of her own heart. She relaxes, takes the solitary burning candle from its sconce in the ambulatory and steps calmly into the cella.

By the candle's wavering light she fetches a blanket from her robing room and spreads it out on the cool mosaic floor. Setting the candle on the edge of the font she lies on the blanket and begins gazing down into the shimmering water, her hands and forearms resting on the smooth limestone rim. She does not attempt to invoke the goddess of the spring: Leucesca must surely be aware of what it is that she wants to know.

And so she waits, statue-still, while the candle burns steadily lower into the depths of the night, until suddenly she realises that the dim reflection she sees in the water is no longer her own.

'Who are …?' she whispers, wonder in her voice.

'Don't you know?' comes the quiet reply. The face is smiling.

Vilbia smiles back, and a strange sensation of weightlessness seems to flow into her. She feels herself floating upwards above the spring, up and up until she ripples effortlessly through one of the small windows beneath the eaves of the cella tower and out into the night and its mysteries.

Light as thistledown she glides over the moonlit land, drifting wherever the thin night breeze chooses to carry her. On a hilltop far away she sees a great fire burning, its orange tongues of flame leaping up into the darkened sky. Nearer, she feels the heat lancing through the cool air and catches the smell of wood smoke, mixed with something sweet and sickly, as the flames roar and crackle.

She dozes and wakes to find that dawn has risen over a barren, mountainous land. On the flat summit of one high peak she sees three seated figures. As the wind blows her towards them she sees that they have the bodies of young and beautiful women, but their faces are sharp and avian, with a look about them as old as time itself. And as cruel. One of the women sits a little apart from the others, spinning wool. The other two women are playing dice. One holds the shaker cup, and even as Vilbia watches she throws three dice onto the flat surface of the rock on which they sit. Nearby lies a pair of shears.

The first dice player glances up at Vilbia and smiles, but there is no emotion in the smile, not even contempt. 'Look, sisters, look who's come to see us.'

'And why have you come, Vilbia?' the second dice player asks. 'Oh yes – I know your name.'

'We know everyone's name,' says the first dice player.

'To learn how long the thread of your life will be – or to discover when I intend to cut it?' The second dice player's voice is as cold as the wind off melting snow.

'Perhaps you never will cut it, sister,' the first dice player murmurs. 'Remember, we do not always act alone in determining these things.'

'But she can always cut her own thread, at any time she chooses. Remember that, Vilbia – remember that through all the long years to come. It is the one real power that mortals possess.' And saying that, the second dice player picks up the shears and waves them slowly in front of Vilbia's face. She laughs softly, and Vilbia feels the winter in that laugh.

And the spinner spins on unheedingly, wholly absorbed in her endless task.

Then the merciful wind freshens and hurries Vilbia on, and she never once looks back until she is sure that the mountain and those three terrible women are far away.

As she drifts in and out of consciousness she sees the long day slowly darken into night and a full moon rise in the south-eastern sky. Below her, at the edge of a sprawling town, she notices a tall soldier standing motionless in the moonlight. Suddenly she hears him call out a single, hesitant word – 'Pascentia?' And even as she stares down, wide eyed, a dark-haired woman emerges from out of the long moon-shadow cast by a tree and begins walking slowly towards him.

She sees them come together and embrace. Listening intently, she detects the murmur of voices, but cannot make out the words. And then the couple are hurrying, hand in hand, through the moonlit streets until, to her anguish and disappointment, she loses sight of them as the night breeze wafts her away from the town and back over the open countryside.

She floats on across time and distance, waking and sleeping, until suddenly it is bright day. And looking down she sees a strange, exotic land spread out before her. It distantly resembles her own green hill country, but the valleys are deeper, the slopes more precipitous, and the trees tall and graceful, with feathery heads like the clumps of ferns that grow in the shady places of her own wood. Suddenly she realises, with a thrill of recognition, that it is the country pictured in the first fresco on the outer wall of the ambulatory.

Here and there, on the tops of hills or on terraces cut into the hillsides, stand small temples with red-tiled roofs and fluted columns carved from honey-coloured stone. In one valley, where a flock of sheep with long, twisting horns grazes peacefully, sits the god Pan, his shaggy goat legs stretched out before him as he plays a simple, haunting melody on his syrinx pipes. Around him, almost-human satyrs, naked but for their short, brightly-coloured cloaks, dance with beautiful young maenads whose filmy dresses swirl about them as they circle their partners.

And everywhere she hears the muted sound of running water. Small springs gush out of the hillsides and cascade down the rocks, their fine spray forming tiny rainbows in the sunlight. Streams wind through the valleys, their crystal waters singing merrily as they race and eddy over pebbles and yellow sand. The warm breeze carries her along one of these streams, in a valley starred with flowers. At the end of the valley stands a tall building, with the headwaters of the stream chattering out from beneath its walls. As she draws nearer Vilbia sees, curiously without surprise, that it is her own temple. Soon she is floating above it, and looking down through one of the high windows she sees a slim woman in a pure white robe standing in the cella below. Vilbia cannot see the woman's face, only its image, pale as the dawn moon, reflected in the waters of the font into which she is gazing. Slowly the woman looks up, and as she does so Vilbia recognises a face that is both her own and yet not her own. The woman smiles, and in that moment there comes to Vilbia, like the dawn sun rising above the hills, a glow of happiness that suffuses her whole body.

And when she wakes in the cool air of dawn, surrounded by a chorus of birdsong from the wood, that happiness is still with her. Lying back on the blanket, her eyes closed, she basks in the conviction that, both for herself and for those whose fates concern and trouble her, her goddess Leucesca will ensure that their diverse journeys will at last end in the reunions which they seek.

CHAPTER TWENTY-EIGHT

'Primicerius!'

The near-full moon is still some way above the south-western horizon when Bonosus twists around in his saddle, as well as his bound hands will allow. 'Primicerius ... Primicerius!' he whispers hoarsely, 'We should stop here: Duboceto Wood is only two miles away over there.' And he bobs his head towards the west.

Suddenly even Nitalis is wide awake and tense. Saturninus orders Vernatius to untie Bonosus, then stares westwards, trying to make out their destination. In the moonlight he sees a rising land of low, rounded hills and shallow valleys where, a mile or so away, a wood partially covers a hillside. And beyond that wood, on the skyline, he can just make out the edge of another wood, almost hidden behind the first.

It is to this latter that Bonosus points, once he has massaged life back into his numbed hands. 'That's it, Primicerius, that's Duboceto. Carausius and his gang will all be there, sleeping like babies. Just waiting for you to take them.'

Magnillus strokes the coiled rope hanging from his saddle. 'They'd better be, vermin – or your journey back to Corinium will be very, very painful.'

Bonosus looks pleadingly towards Saturninus, who ignores them both.

Is Caelofernus really there, only two short miles away? And are you there too, Pascentia? Weird feeling – to both want you to be there, and to hope that you're not.

'The plan – one last time. We ride for the first mile, then dismount, unship the scorpio and leave the horses with Nitalis.

Then we carry the scorpio to within firing range of the lookout tree and assemble it, all before first light. And then we wait for sunrise. Simple, isn't it?'

'It is if you say it fast enough,' Canio mutters, perhaps unsure whether or not Saturninus is being ironic.

'That moon is still very bright, Primicerius,' Vernatius observes. 'Very bright,' he repeats uneasily.

'It'll be gone before dawn. We should have a period of real darkness soon – long enough to hide us while we get close to the wood.' Saturninus pauses and looks to each face in turn. But there are no questions. 'Right then – here we go.'

He leads them off the highway and across a spectral landscape that bears no signs of human habitation. After a mile they cross a stream meandering through the bottom of a small valley. Here they dismount, turn the horses over to Nitalis, offload the scorpio and tie the tripod base to Bonosus by a rope knotted around his waist.

Canio nods towards Bonosus. 'Shouldn't we gag him?' he whispers to Saturninus.

'No need. If he calls out he's dead. If we don't get him then Carausius will: he'll know who led us here.'

'It could all be a trap.'

'No.'

'How can you be so certain? That moon over there is almost full, and in that dream of yours Caelofernus …' Canio leaves the rest unsaid.

Saturninus shrugs. 'I'm not certain. In the end, there are no certainties.'

'Except death.'

'Except death,' Saturninus agrees.

Or perhaps not even death, Pascentia?

Holding the case containing the six precious arrows, he begins leading the way up the hillside. Behind him follow Magnillus and Vernatius, carrying between them the heavy body of the scorpio.

Canio, coils of rope slung around his shoulders, and occasionally helping Bonosus with the tripod base, brings up the rear.

Cautiously they climb the hill, and as they near the crest the moon at last sets. To Saturninus it seems that one moment it is there, large and luminous and low in the south-western sky, and the next it has vanished. Instinctively he keeps well clear of the edge of the first wood and the threat of ambush that its Stygian darkness holds. When he reaches the flattened top of the hill he sees that it is just as Bonosus had described – between four and five hundred paces wide and thickly studded with gorse bushes. Here and there he can distinguish small trees rising up out of the gorse, like petrified plumes of smoke. And on the far side, just as the hill begins to dip away to the west, he sees Duboceto Wood itself, ink-black against the skyline. When Bonosus catches up he asks, 'So where's this lookout tree?'

Bonosus, his breath still rasping from the exertion of carrying the ballista base, stares at the wood, then indicates with outstretched arm a point some way off to the right of where they stand.

Saturninus gazes towards it, then turns to Magnillus and Vernatius and says quietly, 'You two stay here for the moment. Canio, you come with me.' With his sword he slices through the rope that ties Bonosus to the scorpio base, retaining sufficient to hold as a leash. 'Now show me *exactly* where. Understand?'

Bonosus nods, his face a pale blur in the darkness.

Saturninus increases the tension on the rope, easing him upright. 'And remember, Bonosus, the slightest hint of treachery and you're dead.'

Swords in hands, and with Bonosus out in front like a tracker dog, Saturninus and Canio begin picking their way forward through the spiny gorse. Bonosus attempts to steer a straight path, but the darkness and the shoulder-high bushes defeat him and their way forwards is a tortuous one.

At last, when they are no more than fifty paces from the wood, almost at the edge of the gorse, Bonosus turns and points directly ahead. There Saturninus makes out the silhouette of a great tree which rises at least ten feet above its neighbours. He scans around and sees, no more than a dozen paces away, a small hawthorn, and around it what appears to be a gorse-free patch of rough grass. He considers for a moment, then motions to Canio and Bonosus, and together they creep back along the way they came.

'We've found the lookout tree, and a place to set up the ballista,' Saturninus whispers to the Vadumleucara men. 'Follow me, and walk carefully ... and try not to trip, but if you do, then for all our sakes shut your teeth and don't utter a sound. Canio, help Bonosus to carry the base – and I mean *really* help him this time: if you drop it I'll have both your skins for tent leather.'

The five men have only just reached the little hawthorn tree when Saturninus notices the first pale orange heralds of the dawn beginning to streak the eastern sky. Magnillus and Vernatius are sweating, the rank sweat of exertion and nervous tension. They writhe in silent torment as they straighten backs that had locked bent as they carried the heavy body of the scorpio.

The two men rest briefly and then, so carefully as to make no sound at all, they lift the scorpio body onto the swivel coupling at the top of the tripod base. Then Saturninus eases the trigger block and sliding arrow-channel forwards, before hooking the twin prongs of the pivoted iron trigger claw over the leather-bound central section of the bowstring. To prevent the claw from rising – and so releasing the bowstring – he locks it down with the rotating iron trigger bar, known as the snake. Finally, he slots the lever poles into their sockets in the winch wheels, ready to wind back the trigger block. Hidden by the gorse, there is now nothing he can do but wait and watch patiently, and listen to the whisper of the thin dawn breeze and the ecstatic songs of the earliest-rising birds coming out of the fading darkness.

'Listen ... there's someone coming!'

It was Bonosus who hissed the warning. Saturninus,

crouching, spins around to see the man cowering back and staring wildly into the wilderness of gorse behind them. Straining his ears he catches the sound of stealthy movements. Pulse racing, he snatches his sword from its sheath, noticing out of the corner of his eye that the other three soldiers are doing the same. There is a brief silence, then the sounds begin again, louder and closer now. But still Saturninus can see nothing. He risks a glance at the others. Canio shakes his head.

Saturninus – everyone – had assumed that Carausius and his gang were inside the wood. But if they had been elsewhere during the night ... He sees shadowy movement in the gorse and tenses, ready to spring forwards the moment that the first member of the gang detects his presence. Almost without thinking he extends his left arm as a warning to the others not to move until he does. There is another soft rustle ... and Saturninus finds himself looking into the eyes of a heavily pregnant roe deer. The doe swerves aside in an instant and begins moving rapidly away, back into the gorse, utterly silent now. Saturninus watches her white, heart-shaped rump patch swiftly vanishing, then turns to the others. Magnillus is breathing a curse and sheathing his sword, his face, like all their faces, streaked with sweat. Slowly they relax and settle back again to wait.

With agonising slowness the sky continues to brighten, and Saturninus notices the world all around him changing from monochrome night to the coloured world of day, where the grey dots on the gorse become smothers of rich yellow flowers. Soon five pairs of eyes are scanning the immense beech which is the lookout tree, and each makes out, through the dense curtain of leaves, the broken outline of a small hide. Saturninus estimates it to be some thirty feet up, at a point where the great trunk forks. As the leaves ripple gently in the breeze he notices several eye-slits a little below the top of the hide. Instinctively he hunches lower, but neither sound nor movement come from behind the leather.

Twisting sideways, Saturninus sees that each man's face is now taut and anxious as he waits for their longed-for comrade, *Sol Oriens*, the rising sun, to join them. And at last he comes, rising majestically above the north-eastern horizon behind them. He illuminates every leaf on the face of the wood with a brilliant, jewel-like clarity – and he shines, blindingly, through the slits in the hide and into the eyes of the unseen sentry.

And this is what Saturninus has been waiting for. He points towards the wood and mouths the word, "Now!"

Not a single word is spoken, but the two Vadumleucara men immediately stoop down and shoulder the scorpio out from behind the concealing hawthorn tree. They set it down at the edge of the gorse, in a position that gives a clear field of fire towards the hide. Canio slides the six leather-flighted arrows out of their case, while Saturninus quickly begins winching back the trigger block, and with it the bowstring. Moments later the two rigid bow arms are at maximum tension, their free ends drawn back to within inches of the scorpio's stock.

Canio, who had been squatting beside the machine, now uncoils like a cat. He drops one of the eighteen-inch long arrows into the sliding channel in front of the trigger block, then deftly nocks it into the bowstring at the point where it is held between the twin prongs of the claw. He signals to Saturninus, who immediately takes aim along the line of the arrow, sighting the hide through the vertical slot in the central stanchion of the spring frame as he tilts up the front of the scorpio.

'Ready to fire!' Saturninus's voice is a harsh whisper.

I'm trying to kill a man I've never even seen. A man who's never done me any harm.

Necessity stifles conscience: he rubs the fingers of his right hand on his sleeve, grasps the cool iron of the snake and pulls it backwards in a smooth arc.

Faster than his eyes can register, the prongs of the claw jerk upwards to release the bowstring and the arrow flashes towards the hide. The line is good, but the elevation a shade too high, and with a muted thud it strikes one fork of the beech, about two feet above the target.

'Too high!' Canio hisses fiercely.

But scarcely are the words past his lips before Saturninus has smashed the trigger block forwards with the palm of his left hand, hooked the claw over the bowstring, locked it firm with the snake and is beginning to winch back the block. He is so fast that Canio barely has time to snatch up another arrow from the five lying on the grass before he is taking aim again.

Even as he does so, he hears Magnillus whisper urgently, 'Quickly, Primicerius! He's moving!'

Squinting along the arrow, Saturninus glimpses one side of the hide twitch and the trumpet end of a copper tuba horn come poking through the overlap between two sheets of leather. He pulls the snake, the bow arms crash back against the spring frame and the second arrow blurs on its way. To Saturninus, staring along its flightpath, it seems to hover in the air for a long moment before suddenly disappearing among the leaves. There comes a faint thud, subtly different from that made by the first arrow, but he cannot see what it has struck. Feverishly he starts to reload again.

'Look!'

He glances up sharply, his eyes following Vernatius's pointing arm towards the hide. A knotted rope has been flung out and, scarcely before its end has touched the ground, a large man in a greenish-grey tunic comes scrambling out and begins swarming down it.

'Get him!'

But Saturninus's command is superfluous: at the first sight of their prey, Canio, Magnillus and Vernatius have all started racing towards the sentry like hunting dogs unleashed.

CHAPTER TWENTY-NINE

Canio is the quickest, and by the time the sentry has reached the ground he is already halfway to the tree. The man spins around to face his pursuers, giving Saturninus a glimpse of a strong, weather-beaten face framed in a shock of dark hair and beard. For a moment the man stares wildly about him, as if uncertain whether to run back into the wood or along the relatively open ground at its edge. The sight of Canio rapidly bearing down on him with drawn sword decides him: he turns and starts running like a stag along the edge of the wood.

He rapidly disappears from sight, as do his three pursuers, leaving Saturninus silently cursing this unexpected turn of events. Fear of alerting the other members of the gang who, he can only hope, are still sleeping peacefully somewhere inside the wood, stops him from calling his dogs back. He turns to Bonosus. 'Which one was that?'

'Armiger ... I don't think your men will catch him though. I once saw him outrun a two-horse carriage trying to get away from an ambush Carausius set up on the road outside Durnovaria.'

'I thought you said you only took part in the one robbery,' Saturninus quietly reminds him. 'Near Cunetio, wasn't it?'

Bonosus bites his lip and looks down at the grass. 'Once, twice – does it really matter, Primicerius? I never did kill anyone, and that's a truth I'd swear to on the altar of any god you care to name ... Say you believe me?'

Saturninus gazes restlessly towards the point where Armiger disappeared. 'Perhaps you're right,' he murmurs. 'It doesn't really matter. Not now.' To stifle the impulse to go after Canio, he employs an old trick from his army days: he begins reciting the *Pervigilium Veneris* in his head, including the refrain after each verse – *"And the lover shall find love tomorrow."* As a child, he had learnt the poem by heart.

Do you remember, Pascentia, how I sang it to you on those June nights in Londinium? And how we then sang alternate verses, after I'd I taught you the words? Do you remember the soft notes of the lyre, and the lamplight, and the wine and the talk of the places we had been and the things we'd seen. On those June nights, if you had a dozen faces in daylight then you had twice that number in the shimmering lamplight.

There are ninety-two lines in the *Pervigilium*. When he has reached the end, he tells himself, then he will have to go after Canio.

With mounting restlessness he has got as far as line sixty when he sees all three men coming trotting back. Before he can ask, Canio declares starkly, 'Magnillus and Vernatius got him.'

Magnillus grins fiercely and holds up his sword to show the bright blood still glistening on the steel.

'The bastard was so scared that he ran straight into a maze of gorse bushes back there,' Canio explains. 'I went one way, they went another, and before he could find his way out again … they had him.'

'First one through the guts, second one across the throat before he fell. Hits no bones to blunt the blade that way. It's the first sword drill they teach recruits,' Magnillus adds.

Saturninus thinks he has never seen the man look so happy. 'So it is. Well done,' he replies softly. 'The gentleman whose close acquaintance you've just made was Armiger, or so friend Bonosus tells me.' He feels a strange, unfocussed anger, but …

What right have I to be angry with them? I was trying to kill him too.

'Armiger? Then it was a damned good job we got him. He was the one who – '

199

'I know, Canio: you told me. Now, if you're all quite ready, shall we go and get Carausius – always supposing he hasn't already died of old age?'

At the mention of Carausius's name, Bonosus starts edging away. For a moment Saturninus fears that he is about to follow Armiger's example and make a run for it. He tightens his grip on the little man's rope halter.

'No, Bonosus: don't even think of leaving us. Whatever fate awaits us inside that wood is going to be your fate too. Canio, unload the scorpio and hide the spare arrows. Quickly – and disable it too: slip the bowstring off and carry it with you.'

'Won't he be more hindrance than help now, Primicerius?' Magnillus mutters, inclining his head towards Bonosus.

'He comes with us – exactly as we planned. Understood?'

Magnillus hesitates, then nods.

Saturninus turns to where Canio had been only a few moments before, only to find that the man has vanished. Wheeling around, he is just in time to see him reach the top of the knotted rope, haul himself around the smooth, grey trunk of the beech and clamber into the hide. Moments later he sees him emerge, waving the tuba on the end of what appears to be a short stick. Transferring the stick to his teeth, Canio drops hand-over-hand down the rope and lopes back to Saturninus and the others, brandishing his prize. The tuba is a straight horn, two feet long and tapering gently from the funnel-like end to the simple mouthpiece. At little more than a finger's length from that mouthpiece Saturninus sees that the copper has been transfixed by the scorpio's arrow.

'Canio, what in Hades' name are you – ?' he begins whispering fiercely.

'It went straight through the hide and nailed it to the trunk!' Canio interrupts, keeping his voice low. 'No wonder that bastard Armiger took off like a chicken with its tail feathers on fire – this arrow must have missed his head by the length of Aemilianus's own tail, and that's no length at all, as half the whores in

Corinium could tell you. That's the half who are too old to run, just in case you were wondering, Vernatius.'

'It was a damned lucky shot,' Magnillus remarks.

But Saturninus is now looking anxiously towards the wood. 'It was indeed. If I tried for a hundred years I could never repeat it.'

'Then Christ must surely be with us,' Vernatius solemnly observes.

Magnillus rolls his eyes upwards and Canio gazes exaggeratedly around him, shielding his eyes against the sun. 'Where? I don't see him. Do you see him, Magnillus?'

'Christ is everywhere and sees everything we do ...' Vernatius stops abruptly, and Saturninus wonders if he is remembering Armiger, whose body will rot in the sun and rain and whose bones scavenging animals will gnaw and scatter.

Like my father's at Mursa.

'Everywhere or nowhere, it doesn't matter now. Nothing matters, except getting to Carausius before he realises we're here. And remember, once inside that wood nobody talks, except to me, and then only in a whisper. Understand?'

They all nod, and with sword in one hand and the rope tethering Bonosus in the other, Saturninus walks quickly across the open ground to the edge of the wood and plunges into the tunnel-like path, which he believes will lead him to Caelofernus, who is Death. And perhaps to her.

The interior of the wood is a subdued, subterranean land where the silence is broken only by unseen birds singing their rapturous territorial songs to the new day. But Saturninus, walking the narrow, winding path that leads ever deeper towards its centre, is acutely aware that the same birdsong that masks his own stealthy footsteps could also be drowning other sounds – sounds that might warn of an ambush. Despite the cool of the wood, he feels sweat, prickly and pungent, begin to break through the skin of his armpits and trickle, icy cold, down over his ribs.

As he cautiously rounds a bend in the path, a swarm of great black flies seems to materialise out of the very air itself. With deceptive slowness, interspersed with sudden, erratic changes of direction, the flies whine maddeningly around the men, darting in to settle on the bare, sweating skin of a face or arm, vicious probosces needling into flesh. Lightning quick though the flies are at avoiding retribution, Saturninus notices Canio succeed in smashing one with his open palm, instantly transforming the tormentor into a mess of dark red blood, legs and transparent, black-veined wings.

Give my compliments to Charon – and tell him that I too may be needing his ferry soon.

Three hundred paces gone. Bonosus had said four hundred from the edge of the wood to Carausius's camp. But Bonosus is a small man, almost a head shorter than Saturninus, so they must be almost there. Saturninus can hear his heart pounding in his ears, feel the sweat oozing between the fingers curled around the hilt of his sword. By instinct as much as by conscious intent he starts to walk more slowly, feeling the ground under each footfall before easing the full weight of his body onto it.

Three hundred and sixty – and now at last Bonosus turns, his face a strained white mask of fear. He first raises a finger to his lips to implore absolute silence and then, with the same finger, jabs the air in front of him. Gripping the end of the rope tightly, Saturninus motions him on. Reluctantly, Bonosus inches forwards, then halts again at a curve in the path, where forward vision is blocked by the decaying stump of a once-vast tree. Crouching low, Saturninus peers around the stump and sees, twenty paces ahead, a clearing, and in it the corner of a crudely built structure of hides draped over a framework of poles: nothing more. He turns and waves the other three on.

Bonosus is still peering anxiously forward when Saturninus drops the rope and chops him across the back of the neck with the edge of his left hand. The little man collapses without so much as a groan. Catching him as he falls, Saturninus leaves him lying unconscious beside the path, then creeps to the edge of the clearing. It is about thirty paces across, created by the falling of a great oak, the trunk and branches of which still bisect its centre. Saturninus guesses it came down in one of the gales of the previous autumn, still in full leaf, the leaves now brown and shrivelled. In front of the fallen tree stands the pole and hides shelter. The leather stops a foot short of the ground. Crouching down, he makes out the prostrate forms of at least three men, still sprawled in sleep on a mixture of furs and blankets. One big man and two smaller; no one else.

Saturninus straightens up and takes a step forwards, urgently beckoning the others to follow. But at that very same moment the oppressive silence is suddenly ripped apart by three piercing screams, like the cries of a snared animal. Looking wildly around he glimpses a youngish woman in a dark blue dress – *but not Pascentia* – emerging from behind the tangled mass of roots and dried clay at the base of the fallen tree. For a moment all four soldiers halt as if turned to stone, a fleeting calm before the storm.

An instant later and the men in the shelter have come manically alive, throwing off their blankets, cursing and calling on their gods. One lithe ferret of a man – Bano, from Bonosus's description – is already scrambling out of the shelter on all fours. Saturninus sees the woman drop the goatskin she had been carrying, sending the water it contains shooting upwards in a short-lived fountain. With her wild, streaming hair she is an unnerving sight, like one of the very Furies themselves, and it occurs to Saturninus that if she should start running towards them ... But, at that pivotal moment, she turns and bolts back into the wood, still screaming hysterically.

Her flight is like the smell of blood to hungry wolves, and with courage-raising howls the soldiers fall on their prey. Swiftly overtaking Bano just as he is stumbling to his feet, Saturninus smacks the flat of his sword down on the man's bare head, pitching him forwards onto the ground, where he lies motionless, his arms by his sides.

Igillus, Carausius's one-eyed lieutenant, manages to snatch up the sword that he, like a good soldier, had kept by his side as he slept. But before he can unsheathe it, Canio pushes the point of his own sword against the man's throat, stiffening him into immobility. He grins at Igillus, forces him up onto tiptoe, then knees him viciously between the legs.

Following Saturninus's example, Magnillus whacks Lemnus on the head with the flat of his sword while the big runaway slave is still looking wildly around. But unlike Bano, Lemnus does not collapse. Instead, he utters a roar like a maddened bull, grabs one of the vertical poles which support the shelter, and pulls half the structure down on top of Magnillus.

Still reeling and bellowing obscene curses, several rivulets of bright blood trickling down his face and half-blinding him, Lemnus catches sight of Saturninus and rushes towards him, fists flailing wildly. Saturninus sidesteps his charge, stumbling over a small stack of firewood as he does so. But before Lemnus can turn, Saturninus snatches up one of the lichen-studded branchlets and brings it down on the man's head as hard as he can. Lemnus comes to a dead stop, but does not fall, and for a few astonished moments Saturninus thinks he really is going to continue fighting. Then the whites of his eyes roll upwards, his knees buckle and he collapses like a felled tree, with arms spread wide as if embracing the earth. His face red with fury, Magnillus, who has just succeeded in disentangling himself from the ruins of the shelter, runs up and gives Lemnus's prone body a savage kick.

But where, sweet Venus, is Caelofernus? And –

'Primicerius, sir!' Saturninus hears Vernatius shout from behind the fallen oak. 'I think there's another one of them hiding here.'

He races around the great trunk and finds the trooper prodding cautiously with his sword at another hides and pole shelter, smaller than the first, its skins extending all the way down to the ground.

'I'm sure there's someone in there, Primicerius. I think I heard him, and I definitely saw the side move, though he's quiet as a mouse now.'

Saturninus circles the shelter warily, conscious that at any moment Caelofernus might bolt out, ferocious as a cornered boar. By now Magnillus has joined them, and Saturninus motions him and Vernatius aside and hurriedly whispers what he wants them to do. They nod their understanding and take up position, one on either side of the shelter, their swords raised aloft in both hands like executioners. Saturninus stands one pace in front of the entrance flap, the point of his sword angled downwards. He gives a quick glance to make sure that the other two are ready, then calls, 'Now!'

CHAPTER THIRTY

The two Vadumleucara men scythe their swords downwards, the sharp tips slicing long gashes through the supple leather. To their astonishment, from inside comes a high-pitched squeal of terror.

Pascentia!?

For a moment Saturninus is paralysed, torn between hope and fear.

'By all the gods, there's a woman in there!' Magnillus declares as he grabs a cut edge of the leather with one hand and gives it a hard tug, ripping a whole section away from the barrel-shaped framework of hazel wands that support it. Vernatius on the other side does the same, exposing most of the interior of the shelter.

Lying huddled under a woollen blanket, on a bed of furs, is a young woman. Only her head and the hands that clutch the blanket up around her chin are visible. But she is not Pascentia. Saturninus breathes a quiet sigh of relief.

A pair of dark eyes in a tangle of hair, black and glossy as a rook, dart from side to side, as if trying to read the grim faces of the three men staring down at her.

'Please don't hurt me – please. I haven't done anything wrong. I'm their prisoner. They kidnapped me and made me go with them. I didn't want to, but they forced me. I – '

'Where's Carausius?' Saturninus interrupts.

The woman seems about to say something, then wavers.

Loyalty – or simply fear?

'I'll soon loosen her tongue,' Magnillus grunts, drawing back his foot to kick her.

She yelps, her feet scrabbling under the blanket as she tries to push herself out of range.

'No!' Saturninus flashes an angry glance at Magnillus. 'Melania – it is Melania, isn't it?'

The woman nods, her eyes still on Magnillus's heavy boots.

Saturninus's keeps his voice low and urgent. 'Melania, if you tell us where Carausius is, then it'll count in your favour at the trial. But if you don't, then you can expect no mercy from my Prefect. He's a hard man, and if I can't tell him that you helped us, do you know what he'll say? … He'll say, "She's just as guilty as the men." And that might mean the hunting dogs, with their cruel, tearing teeth. It's a terrible enough death for a man, but for a woman … '

'He ran away. When he heard Honorata scream he grabbed his sword and ran – I don't think he realised there were only three of you. He must be out there somewhere in the wood,' Melania adds, stating the obvious.

'So he *was* here!' And now he's …' Saturninus's clenches a fist in frustration.

'Shall we go after him, Primicerius?' Vernatius asks.

Magnillus gives him a contemptuous stare. 'Don't be stupid – he could be anywhere by now.'

Saturninus gazes intently into the dark wood, listening for any sound of a man moving. He hears nothing. If only he had seen Carausius bolt, then he could have raced after him, but now …? Bitterly, he realises the futility of even attempting to search for Carausius in that wilderness.

'No, Magnillus is right. He's had too great a start. We'd never find him in there now.'

'What's happening over there?' comes Canio's voice from the other side of the fallen oak.

'Carausius has got away,' Saturninus shouts back.

There is a cackle of injudicious laughter from Igillus, which stops abruptly and, Saturninus guesses, somewhat painfully.

Shortly afterwards, Canio joins them, still holding a length of the rope with which he had been trussing their captives. Melania twists her head around to look at him. Saturninus looks at the rope, then at Melania. He doesn't say a word, but she understands.

'If you promise to let me go, I'll show you where that pig Carausius hid all the money he stole.'

Saturninus shakes his head and replies quietly, 'I'm not going to horse-trade, Melania. But if you tell us where it is, then I'll make sure the Prefect gets to hear of it. I might even tell him that I believe your kidnapping story too – if you're co-operative and give us a list of all the other crimes that your alleged kidnappers have committed since they came north. Otherwise, I'll find the money anyway: it can't be far away.'

Melania purses her lips, as if about to challenge him to find Carausius's hoard unaided. One look at Magnillus's face, and the anticipation so clearly written on it, is enough to dissuade her. 'All right, I'll show you where it is,' she mutters sulkily. 'But at least let me get dressed first.'

Following her eyes down among the litter of the shelter, Saturninus notices a dress of rich red cloth lying crumpled in one corner. Canio spots it too, hooks it up with the tip of his sword and holds it out to her, about a foot beyond her reach. Clutching the blanket to her throat with one hand, Melania half rises and with her other hand attempts to grasp the dress. As she does so, Canio grins and moves back a pace. She wriggles forwards and tries to snatch it, but Canio retreats another step.

Saturninus sees a flash of anger in her dark eyes, anger that makes her throw aside the blanket as she stands up and picks her way between the hazel wands out of the remains of the shelter, letting them all see. Only Vernatius averts his eyes, and even he not immediately.

She has a firm, strong body. Not that of a marble goddess perhaps, but still retaining the promise of an exciting, animal sensuality. Then Saturninus notices the stretch marks on her belly.

So once you bore a child – perhaps more than one. Is it still alive somewhere? Did you love it, weep at your parting? Was it a baby girl, snatched away and smothered at birth? Or did you smother it yourself and bury it in a shallow grave, among all the other little unmarked graves behind some slave barracks on an estate where they forced you to toil like an animal?

He cannot know; tells himself he shouldn't care – but does anyway. Her hands are rough and stained, the nails cracked and blackened.

Grabbing the dress he tosses it across to her. With a faint, ironic bow towards him she deftly turns the dress the right way round and pulls it over her head, wriggling and smoothing it down over her hips. Picking up a wide belt of blue-dyed leather she buckles it around her waist, then hunts among the furs and blankets for her sandals. Squatting down, she laces them criss-cross around her ankles. Using fingers as combs to untangle her cascading black hair she smiles up at them all, confident now in the power and promise of her sexuality.

And Saturninus suspects that she has wit or instinct enough to know that promise is her best chance of escaping the fate of her former companions.

'We're waiting, Melania,' he reminds her.

Still smiling, she strolls up to the great trunk of the fallen tree, scans it for a few moments, and then with her strong nails prises out a plug of bark from what appears to be the hole left by the rotting of a light-starved branch. Feeling inside, she draws out a stout leather bag and hands it to Saturninus.

Although not particularly large, it is surprisingly heavy. Loosening the drawstring, Saturninus joggles out a clinking flow of bright coins – gold solidi, silver miliarenses and small silver siliquae – into the palm of his hand. He grunts appreciatively. 'Not bad. Not bad at all. We're clearly following the wrong trade, gentlemen. By the way, Melania,' he murmurs casually as he pours the coins back into the bag, 'I'll have the rest as well … It'll save you the anxiety of wondering whether your friend Honorata has run off with it while you're visiting Corinium.'

'There's nothing else in here, Primicerius.' Canio has evidently been thinking along the same track, and now has his arm in the hole as far as it will go.

Melania opens her mouth as if about to say something, but meeting Saturninus's bleak smile her nerve falters. With a distinctly sullen air she walks back to the tree and, from another hidden hole, pulls out a second bag. 'I was going to tell you about this one as well, if only you'd given me the chance,' she complains.

'Of course you were.' Saturninus peers inside and whistles softly, then pours the contents onto the blanket which Melania had vacated. Dozens of gold finger rings lie scattered on the soft wool, some solid and heavy, some set with engraved intaglios of blood-red carnelian or jasper, and some fretted around their wide circumference to form the letters of the names of their sometime owners. There are gold brooches too, and, from the very bottom of the bag, five small silver ingots, each shaped like the flayed skin of an animal. 'Anything else, Melania? Anything else that your kidnapper squirrelled away and I haven't yet given you the chance to tell me about?'

'No, nothing else,' Melania says irritably. 'I've given you all there ever was – I'd take a solemn oath to that.'

'On the altar of any god I'd care to name,' Saturninus murmurs, recalling Bonosus's words. 'Vernatius, you'd better make a quick search of the rest of the trunk. And both shelters too – see what else you can find. Magnillus, you and Canio tie the prisoners together with a neck halter and stand guard over them until we're ready to leave.'

If Magnillus is tempted to ask Saturninus if he doesn't trust him to make the search himself, then he evidently thinks better of it, perhaps unwilling to risk a candid answer.

'What about her?' asks Canio.

Saturninus hesitates; he wants to be merciful, but ... 'Tie her up with the others – at least until we get back to the horses. If she makes a run for it in open country, then we'll never catch her on foot.'

Melania calls him a bastard, and worse. Much worse.

Shortly afterwards Saturninus is standing at the edge of the clearing, staring into the wood, wondering ...

'There were only these in the small shelter, sir ... apart from the clothing, that is. And Bonosus told the truth about that: Carausius certainly does have a taste for fine, colourful tunics.'

He turns to see Vernatius holding out a battered steel helmet with hinged cheek-pieces, a chain-mail jerkin, dull with incipient rust, and a tiny gilt-bronze statuette. He takes the statuette and examines it. It is Mercury, god of merchants, travellers and thieves, with his winged hat, a caduceus in his left hand and a purse of gold in his right. It is clearly old, much of the gilding having been worn away to expose the dark bronze beneath. He thinks of the lead curse tablet in his belt pouch.

'What do you want done with them all, sir?'

'What? – oh, take them back to Corinium – plus Carausius's clothes and all the weapons you can find.'

'Even that pagan idol, sir?' Vernatius asks uncertainly.

'No, perhaps not that. I'll keep it for the moment ... Somehow I can't see whoever it was that Carausius stole it from ever going up to Prefect Aemilianus and demanding it back. Can you?'

'No, sir.' Still looking slightly troubled, Vernatius hurries off to search the larger shelter.

'Vernatius looks very solemn. What's that you've got?' Canio asks.

Saturninus tosses the figurine over for his inspection.

'Ah, my old friend Mercury. What are you going to do with him?'

'He belonged to Caraus ... to Caelofernus.'

'Oh, did he now. And you're going to ... ?'

'Carry him with me until I find the man. Better go and see if our friend Bonosus is still sleeping soundly.'

'Mothers, I'd forgotten him! Shall I tie him up with the rest?'

'No, let him be: he's done what he promised. Are the others fit to travel yet?'

'As fit as they'll ever be.' Canio lobs the Mercury statuette back to Saturninus.

'Right, then let's get out of this damned wood. Then I can start looking for Caelofernus again.' Seeing Canio's sceptical look, Saturninus adds, 'Well he won't stay in here, that's for sure. He knows that if we were to bring back reinforcements and encircle the wood then he'd be trapped, so he's got to get out and move on.'

'Maybe. But one man on foot could hide anywhere. Surely it's pointless trying to find him now?'

'Is it? Last night, I was sure that something was leading me to him. I think it still is.'

'So how come he escaped?'

'Maybe because today won't see the full moon rise? Or maybe because the gods want more sport from us both? I don't know. All I do know is that I've got to keep searching … And following wherever the *Parcae* choose to lead me,' Saturninus breathes, remembering Bodicca's words. He shrugs and begins walking back towards the path, pushing the Mercury statuette into the pocket of his belt pouch that already holds the lead curse tablet, so that they nestle side by side. He runs a finger over the folded lead. And wonders.

CHAPTER THIRTY-ONE

With Saturninus leading, the ragged line of captors and captives emerges from the wood, under the now-deserted lookout tree. Behind him come Canio, supporting the still-unsteady Bonosus, then the four prisoners, roped together like sacrificial beasts and urged on by the point of Magnillus's sword. Vernatius, loaded down like a mule, trudges along at the rear. After so long in the gloom of the wood, the bright sunlight pains Saturninus's eyes. He squints, turned his head away and raises a blocking hand against the still-rising sun.

A few yards outside the wood he hesitates, sensing that something is wrong but unable to pinpoint what it is. Suddenly it comes to him: the silence – the absence of birdsong. Quickened, he stares around, detects movement in the gorse and hears the faint metallic creak of the scorpio swivelling on its iron bracket. His mind races as he shields his eyes and peers into the sun. Almost without thinking, he drops down into a crouch.

'Down! Get down! Get back into the wood!' he shouts. But even as he does so he hears the unmistakable thud of the scorpio's arms striking the wooden spring frame and, an instant later, the swish of an arrow as it speeds past within inches of his head.

There is a scream of pain from someone behind him and Saturninus twists round to see Vernatius writhing in agony under the trees. Then he hears the clatter of the ratchet pawl as the trigger block is winched back for another shot.

'Stay with the prisoners – and whatever happens, don't follow me!' Then Saturninus is up and racing towards the gorse and the half-hidden scorpio – and the man who is operating it, a big man, naked to the waist and with wild blond hair and beard. Even as he runs, Saturninus sees the man fit another arrow to the bowstring and begin squinting down the arrow-channel, his left hand already on the snake trigger.

By now he is close enough to see the man's face – Caelofernus's face, the same face he saw in his dream! – as the man swivels the scorpio's body to point it straight towards him. He glimpses Caelofernus's hand jerk convulsively as he pulls the snake, but in the fraction of a second before the twin prongs of the claw fly up, survival instinct conquers anger and Saturninus dives to the ground.

He has a blurred image of Caelofernus snatching the back end of the scorpio upwards to lower the trajectory, but not quickly enough and Saturninus hears the muted plop of the arrow burying itself into the ground somewhere just behind him. He scrambles to his feet, then winces as pain shoots through his left knee where it struck against a hidden stone or root as he dived. Despite the wrenching pain he reaches the scorpio moments later, but Caelofernus has disappeared. Listening intently, he detects the sound of the man moving rapidly away through the wilderness of gorse ahead. Furiously angry with himself, he slashes through the scorpio's drawrope to disable it, before starting after him.

Every so often Saturninus halts, trying to gauge where Caelofernus might be – and every time, to his increasing frustration, it seems that the man is drawing further and further away. Then a time comes when he can no longer hear him. Grimly he pushes on, and as he does so the pain in his knee subsides to a dull ache, allowing him to break into a limping run. Acutely conscious that Caelofernus could be anywhere by now, even circling around behind him, he stops to listen again. Almost at once he hears the distant high-pitched neighing of horses and realises, with a stab of despair, exactly where Caelofernus is.

Breaking out of the gorse, he starts hurrying downhill towards the spot, nearly half a mile away, where Nitalis had been left to guard the horses. When he reaches the valley bottom he finds the ostler attempting to capture the nearest of several which are still milling wildly around. Together they manage to secure Antares, and as they do so Nitalis gasps out what had happened.

'On my life, Primicerius, I couldn't stop him! He was a huge man with a sword, and I saw my death in his eyes.'

'I know, I saw him myself … and I wouldn't have expected you to tackle him.' His anger gone, Saturninus feels only a stoic calm now. 'Just tell me which way he went.'

'Towards the Fosse Way.' Nitalis points eastwards. 'Riding as if all the Furies themselves were after him.'

'I hope they are,' Saturninus replies softly. He looks quickly around at the remaining horses. 'It was Magnillus's he took then?'

Nitalis mumbles apologetic confirmation. 'I think he would have killed the other horses if they'd been tethered, but I was holding them all on the same rope through their bridles, and him taking Magnillus's set the rest free. I suppose it were all those shiny *phalerae* medallions on the harness that made him choose the Centenarius's?'

'Could be.' Saturninus swings himself up into Antares' saddle, and as he does so Canio comes racing up to them.

'Damnation, Canio, don't you ever obey orders? … How's Vernatius?'

'He'll be all right, I think,' Canio pants. 'The arrow went straight through the muscles of his thigh, but I don't think it hit the bone or a big vein. It's just bloody and painful.'

'Well, at least that's something to be grateful for. No thanks to you though: if you'd disabled that damned scorpio like I told you to …' Saturninus reins in his tongue: now is not the time for recriminations. 'Anyway, now you're here you can help Nitalis round up the rest of the horses. But as soon as you've done that, then both of you ride them back up to the wood. Patch up Vernatius as best you can, then help Magnillus get him back to Vadumleucara and the prisoners to Corinium. I'm going after Caelofernus.'

'But why bother? He's no threat to you now. When the full

moon rises tomorrow he'll be forty miles away and still running.'

'And next month, and the month after – and on all the full moons in all the months after that? No, Canio, if I don't get him now, then he can pick his time and come back and kill me under any one of those moons. Wasn't that the message of the dream, stark and simple?'

And I must follow wherever the Parcae lead. First to Caelofernus … and then perhaps to you, Pascentia?

'But why go alone, surely – ?'

'Canio, I haven't got time to argue! Please, just for once, will you damned well obey orders?' And with that Saturninus whips Antares into a trot with the ends of his reins and starts off towards the Fosse Way.

'What about Bonosus?' Canio yells after him.

'Set him free,' Saturninus shouts back. 'He did what he promised – now let the winds blow him to wherever they will.'

When he reaches the Fosse Way there is no sign of Caelofernus. But among the wayfarers who, with the coming of daylight, seem to have emerged as mysteriously as butterflies in the spring, he finds several who saw a man answering to Caelofernus's description, heading north.

After a quarter of a mile he meets a couple of packmen, trudging southwards with long, measured strides. They too tell of a half-naked man on an army horse who had passed them some time before, riding furiously.

'And if you catch him, soldier, give him a good hard kick for me. The bastard tried to ride us down – and he'd have done it too, if we hadn't jumped out of his way in time!'

Sure now that he is heading in the right direction, Saturninus digs his heels into Antares' flanks and gallops off along the metalled road.

Three miles further on he notices, in the distance, a knot of people gathered at the roadside. Drawing nearer, he sees first a dead horse and then a dead man. The man is a stranger and near-naked, his head at an unnatural angle, half severed by a sword cut to the side of his neck. The horse is Magnillus's. The mingled blood of man and horse is still creeping slowly over the dusty stones of the highway.

Saturninus reins to a halt, staring down at the dead man. Even though he knows the answer, he has to ask. 'Who did this?'

There is silence for a moment, then a young woman clutching a baby pushes forward from the crowd, her eyes still wide with shock. 'I saw it, soldier – I saw it all! That poor man lying there had only just trotted past me, and there was I thinking how fine he looked, with his bright clothes and his great shining horse. And then, all of a sudden, I heard another horse behind me. Fast it was – its hooves sounded like thunder on the road. But before I could so much as turn around to see who it was a-coming, another man – half naked like a barbarian savage he was – shot past me and cut the fine man down with his sword. It was as if he really hated him. I saw the poor man's blood fly everywhere – look at it, all around you. And look, look here: some of it even hit me – I was that close!' And she points to several dark blotches on the pale brown cloth of her dress.

'The man who did it, he reined in so sharp that his horse skidded and stones flew up from its hooves. Then he jumped down, and even while that mortal body there was still twitching he pulled most of his clothes off and put them on himself, though they must have been messed with blood something terrible.'

'Took all his money too,' affirms a small, dark man who stands beside her. 'Leastwise, there's none on him now.' It seems that he has checked.

'But what possessed the demon to kill the horse as well?' Saturninus demands. In some way it seems even worse than the murder of the man, simply because it was so utterly pointless.

'Christus alone knows, soldier,' the woman sighs, comforting the baby who is beginning to cry. 'I certainly don't. All of a sudden he just stabbed it, then leapt up onto the dead man's horse and rode off again like the wind. But I do know this: before he went he glared straight at me, as if he wanted to kill me too … Oh,

dear Christus, I can still see those two evil eyes staring at us both!'
The recollection seems to paralyse her for a moment. Then,
hurriedly dragging over her head a pendant of black jet, she kisses
it, loops the cord around the baby's neck and presses the disc
tightly into its tiny palm. In an age of eclectic religious beliefs,
Saturninus feels no surprise to see this apparently Christian
woman wearing, as a protective talisman, a pendant carved with
the head of Medusa of the snaky locks.

He dismounts and looks closely at the dead man. He can be
no more than twenty-five years old, his newly-washed auburn
hair, curiously only slightly bloodied, ruffling in the warm breeze.
Such a short time ago he must have been full of life and energy,
with a fine, strong body that might have lived on for another
thirty or forty years. But now he is dead, and Saturninus finds
himself once again staring down at the utter, irreversible finality
of death. There comes to him then, unwanted, a sense of guilt: a
realisation that he too is a party to this man's murder.

*If I hadn't set out to save my own life by hunting down
Caelofernus, then this man would still be alive. At this very
moment he'd be riding along this road, a mile or two ahead, happy
and carefree in the sunshine.*

And then a strange thought ...

*Perhaps he is still riding along – on another road, in another
place. Riding into the light, as today he rode into the darkness.
Perhaps every man lives two lives, one in which he finds light, one
in which he finds darkness?*

But then he recalls a little of the Manichaean dualism that he
learned in the East: the story that, long ago, the dark invaded the
light, and in this world darkness and light are still inextricably
mixed in men.

*Only one world, only one life, and blind chance or the Parcae
decide where the darkness and the light shall fall.*

He shakes his head, pulls the regulation-issue army blanket
from the saddle-bag of Magnillus's dead horse and spreads it over
the dead man.

And I must continue chasing the darkness.

'There's a town a few miles ahead, isn't there?'

'Yes, soldier – Arcadolium,' the woman with the baby replies distractedly. 'It's about five miles further on.' The baby is still crying and she croons softly to it.

'I'll tell the civil guards there what's happened and get them to collect the body ... I suppose no one knows his name?'

The small crowd remains silent and several people shake their heads. Nobody knows. It is time to go: he has lost too much time here already. He remounts, eases Antares through the onlookers and rides away.

CHAPTER THIRTY-TWO

He passes lowland fields bright with growing crops of wheat and barley and Celtic beans. Great bumblebees burr past him, and peacock and brimstone butterflies flit among the white seas of tall cow parsley that grow thickly on the broad margins along both sides of the highway. But always in his mind's eye is the image of the dead man and the blood creeping over the stones.

Every mile or so he slows and asks some wagoner or pedestrian if he or she has seen Caelofernus, and always the answer is the same: that he rode past some time ago at a fast canter.

Just outside the small town of Arcadolium he catches up with a party of four horsemen, also travelling northwards. From the look of them, Saturninus guesses that they are a rich young man and three of his, or his father's, retainers; this latter three being dressed in identical tunics, vertically striped blue and yellow. He asks them if they have seen Caelofernus. None of them answers immediately, eyeing him with varying degrees of supercilious indifference.

'And who might you be?' demands the young man, who looks to be no more than eighteen.

Saturninus tells him. Tells him too that Caelofernus is a murderer and a highway robber.

'Corinium ... so you're outside your own territory then?' replies the young man, as though he has not really understood everything that Saturninus had said.

'He killed a man travelling on this very road, less than an hour ago. Have you seen him?' Saturninus asks again, conscious that the impatience is beginning to show in his voice.

'Yes, we saw him, Primicerius, he –' begins one of the retainers, older than the other two.

But before he can finish the young man cuts in, 'He went past us, barely a quarter of a mile back. I'm sure he went straight through the town ahead without stopping.'

'Riding fast?'

'No … not very fast at all, Primicerius,' responds the young man, apparently friendlier now. 'No more than cantering, I'd say. If you hurry you should catch him in a mile or two; three at the most … Isn't that so, boys?' he says, turning to his companions.

'That's right, master,' one of the younger retainers agrees. 'If you hurry you should overtake him a few miles the other side of Arcadolium.'

There is something about the way he says it, something that isn't quite right. 'Three miles at most, you reckon?' Saturninus asks the older man directly.

'That's what my master said,' the man replies neutrally.

Saturninus gets the fleeting impression that the man is avoiding looking him in the eye, but … He thanks them and rides quickly on into the town.

Arcadolium is a sleepy place, with one small *mansio* inn and posting station, and several shops lining both sides of the Fosse Way. There are few side streets, and none that appear to lead anywhere. Nowhere that Caelofernus could have gone but straight through. Saturninus finds the door of the civil guard post locked, and impatient hammering brings no response.

A wrinkled old man comes hobbling out of the doorway of a building on the other side of the street and calls across, 'Ecimus isn't there, soldier. He's gone after a runaway.'

'What about the other guards?'

The old man shakes his head. 'There are no other guards – not since Brumentius took sick and died back in the winter. The powers that be haven't got around to replacing him yet, or so

Ecimus says.' He chuckles. 'Myself, I don't think he's ever told them. That way he can keep drawing Brumentius's pay.'

Saturninus doesn't comment: time is too precious now. 'Will you give Ecimus a message when he returns? Tell him that Primicerius Saturninus, of the Corinium civil guard, says that there's a dead man lying at the side of the road five miles south of here, and that he should arrange for the body to be collected. I don't know the dead man's name, but perhaps someone here does. By the look of him he was rich, so there'll probably be a reward from his family for anyone who lets them know what's become of him. Have you got that?' he asks quickly, conscious that with every passing moment Caelofernus is getting further away.

'Yes, Primicerius Saturninus, I'm sure I can remember that,' the old man replies. 'A reward, you say? Well, that should interest our Ecimus, if nothing else does.'

'Oh, and there's a dead horse there too,' Saturninus adds. 'And a saddle, if nobody's stolen it yet, both of them the property of the Corinium civil guard. He can keep what he can get for the horsemeat, but tell him he's to store the saddle and harness safely here.'

'Horsemeat, you say?' For a moment Saturninus could swear he sees the old man's ears twitch. 'My son has an ox and cart, Primicerius – if we go and collect the body, can we have the dead horse?'

'Yes, if you like,' Saturninus replies, urging Antares into a trot. 'But you'd better be quick or they'll both be carrion before the day's out.'

Once clear of the town, Saturninus works Antares up into a steady gallop. As he rides he gazes intently ahead, hoping to glimpse Caelofernus before the man becomes aware of his presence. But first one mile passes, then two, then three, and still there is no sign of Caelofernus, and Saturninus's eyes start to ache with staring into the brightness ahead. He is riding fast, not at a wild gallop, but surely fast enough to catch a man who is only cantering. At last, four miles north of Arcadolium, he stops an oncoming cart loaded with bundles of brushwood and questions the driver.

'A big man in a bright tunic and riding a fine horse?' the man repeats slowly. 'No, soldier, I can't say that I've seen him. Mind you, I only turned onto the highway a mile or so back, so he might have already gone past by then.'

A gnawing suspicion is already forming in Saturninus's mind, but he has to continue, has to be utterly sure. He rides on, stopping every traveller he meets now. All tell the same story: Caelofernus is nowhere on the road ahead.

Perhaps he turned off the highway somewhere north of Arcadolium? But why would he? Saturninus slows, stops, hesitates, then wheels about and starts cantering quickly back towards the town. On the way, he asks all the other people he overtook since leaving Arcadolium if they have seen Caelofernus: and the answer is always the same.

He arrives back in the town the better part of a summer hour after leaving it. The old man is no longer in his doorway, but there are several other people about that he recognises, and none of them saw Caelofernus pass through the town, galloping, cantering or otherwise. Then he notices the four horses tied up outside the *mansio* – four horses with embroidered saddlecloths and tooled leather saddles. Breathing deeply and evenly, trying to control the anger and despair churning within him, he walks under the *mansio's* arched entrance, along a short corridor and into the reception area beyond. There is no sign of the four men. A florid man – probably the proprietor – sits at a small table, playing dice with a couple of flour-blotched characters who might be bakers or millers.

'Where are they?' he demands.

None of the three men asks who he means, but one points to a curtained-off back room from which, as he walks towards it, Saturninus can hear voices and laughter. Snatching aside the curtain he stands in the doorway staring at the four as they sit or lounge behind a long, narrow table littered with pewter goblets and several flagons of wine.

The young man, sitting in a heavy, high-backed chair, regards him with insolent amusement. 'Well, well – if it isn't our brave soldier. Tell me, did you enjoy your ride?' He glances sideways to his retainers, who laugh obediently. 'I always enjoy a good gallop myself – it aids the digestion.' More laughter.

With a deadly calm, Saturninus scoops up a near-full goblet and throws the contents into the young man's face, then lets the goblet fall. It teeters on the edge of the table before dropping off. 'Why did you do it?' he asks softly.

The laughter dies abruptly, and for a few moments there is absolute silence, broken only by the sound of the goblet rolling slowly backwards and forwards on the uneven stone-flagged floor.

'You saw him, didn't you? You saw where he went, and then you lied to me. Why? ... Was it just something to laugh about with your useless friends, or does it go deeper than that? Was it because your natural instinct is to cause mischief and pain whenever you get the chance? ... Well, answer me, damn you! Why don't you answer me?' Saturninus feels the strange sensation of being two men inside the same body – the one angry and vengeful; the other dispassionately observing the angry man, simply puzzled as to why the young man lied.

The young man, wine dripping down his face and onto his expensive tunic, turns scarlet with rage. 'How dare you ... how dare you!' he roars. 'Do you know ... have you any idea who my father is?'

'No – no idea at all. Didn't your mother ever tell you – or wasn't she sure herself? Had business been good that night?'

The young man seems to swell with anger and his mouth opens. But before a single word can emerge, Saturninus has drawn his sword, reached across the table and touched the point against the base of the youth's throat, forcing him as far back into the chair as he can go.

'Now I'll count to three.' He is faintly surprised by how far away his voice sounds. 'Just three, and then, if you haven't started telling me the truth, or if I don't happen to believe you, then I'll drive this sword right through your throat and watch the blood gush out like a fountain ... Have you ever seen a man with a deep throat wound – heard the terrible sucking sound as he tries desperately to breathe, as all the while he's drowning in his own blood?' He allows a few moments for the words to take effect, then begins, 'One ...'

There come scuffling sounds and movement to his right. Saturninus glances past the youth to see one of the younger retainers advancing hesitantly towards him with a drawn sword. He stares coldly at the man. 'Well, come on, my hero; don't be shy. You've nothing to lose ... except a hand perhaps, or an arm. But if that happens, your grateful master here will look after you for the rest of your life, won't he? And if I should kill you, then I'll probably do it fairly quickly. Twelve years in the army at least taught me how to kill efficiently. But come now, don't be discouraged – after all, you might be lucky and get me before I stab your master. Of course, if you don't, and I kill him, then you might have some trouble explaining to his heartbroken father how your recklessness got his precious son slaughtered like a hog.'

The man has already halted. Now his sword wavers and sinks slowly to his side.

'Good dog: now drop it on the floor.'

There is a flash of anger in the man's eyes.

'Now!' Saturninus hisses. He bangs the table with his free hand, making the goblets and flagons jump.

The sword clatters onto the stone flags and Saturninus looks down at the young man and smiles. 'Such loyalty. Now, where were we? I was counting, wasn't I – and I was about to say, "two." And after two comes ... Three.' He pulls the sword back slightly, as if to stab forwards.

'No!' the young man shrieks. 'I'll tell you, I'll tell you! The man you're after turned off the road onto a track leading west, not half a mile south of here.'

Saturninus reflects for moment. 'No … you're still lying. One of the other people I asked would have seen him if he had.' The tendons under his right wrist stand out as he jabs the sword point a quarter inch into the young man's throat.

The youth screams like a noosed hare with shock and the terror of death. 'It's true, it's true!' he gurgles. 'Oh sweet Christus, save me! Tell him it's true, Terentius, tell him, tell him!'

'The master *is* telling the truth,' comes the voice of the older retainer, ragged with suppressed emotion as he stares at the bright blood beginning to run down the blade and drip onto the table top, mingling with the spilt wine.

'We heard the sound of someone riding fast behind us. We turned, and saw the man you described stop, stare briefly at us, then branch off onto that side track. I beg you, be merciful to my master – he's scarcely more than a boy and has much to learn.'

Saturninus gazes at the young man; gazes into his fear-wide eyes. And the angry man and the dispassionate man both know that he will never change – that he cannot change, any more than a crow can metamorphose into a peacock.

If he doesn't die here today, then how many lives will he blight before some other death at last claims him?

The hand that holds the sword is no longer Saturninus's: it belongs to another man, a stranger, cold and cruel. He is only dimly aware that his grip on the sword hilt is tightening again, but the youth, desperately pushing himself as far back into the heavy chair as he can, senses it: his eyes close and his entire body flinches.

Perhaps it is that shrinking from coming pain, that reminder of a shared mortality, which cures Saturninus of his madness. Or perhaps it is her image that his brain conjures before him in those fateful moments, her gentle face horrified at what he seems about to do. He never knows for sure, only that, afterwards, he remembers whispering, 'Pascentia?'

And perhaps the youth hears him, for moments later his eyes flicker open again. But by then, Saturninus is standing in the doorway looking directly at him, sword sheathed and about to leave. 'No, I'll let the *Parcae* alone decide when to cut the thread of your miserable life. I suspect they'll enjoy it more than me.' He takes a sudden step back towards him, and the youth recoils so violently that he almost overturns the chair. 'But if you've lied to me for a second time … then I swear that none of you will live to see today's sunset.' And he turns abruptly and is gone.

CHAPTER THIRTY-THREE

Saturninus finds the trackway easily enough. Half a mile south of Arcadolium it leaves the Fosse Way and twists westwards, unmetalled and rutted, between fields and small woods. Some way along, out of sight of the highway, he comes across two *pagani* hoeing a field of young cabbages. They are moving steadily up the rows at a measured pace, side by side, appearing to exchange not a word, their hoes rhythmically rising and falling as they hack into the sun-and-wind-crusted soil. Their faces say they are father and son.

'Indeed we did, master, we saw him right enough. Fearsome looking man he was too, but on a fine horse … though that was quite some time ago, mind.'

'How long?'

The men look helplessly one to the other, as if puzzled how to express a time interval shorter than half a day. 'About five or six rows back,' one of them answers at last.

A long time. It had been too much to hope that Caelofernus would have stopped to rest after quitting the highway. 'And where does this track lead?'

'Nowhere much, master. The river's only four or five miles that way, and there's no ford across it for many a mile. Much too deep, you see.'

'River? What river would that be?'

'Why, the Avon of course, master.'

'Of course.'

'Don't forget he asked about the temple,' the younger *paganus* reminds his father.

'Ah, that's right, he did, didn't he? Said he'd heard there was a temple of Mercury somewhere in these parts, and did we know where it was? So I told him – I said you go no more than a mile further along this track, just past Widow Ingenua's farm, and then you branch off north. Another half mile or so, and you're there.'

Saturninus remembers again the little figurine of Mercury, protector of wandering men and thieves, that Vernatius had found in Caelofernus's tent and which now lies in his own belt pouch, beside the *defixio* curse tablet.

'Did the man say anything else?'

'No, not a word that I can recall.'

'He didn't even give us so much as a thank-you before he rode away,' the younger *paganus* remarks sadly.

Saturninus takes the hint and gives them each a couple of coppers before setting off again at a fast canter.

A mile further on, past a small farmstead, he arrives at a place where two vast pollard oaks stand on the right-hand side of the track, like natural gate pillars. Between them, just as the elder *paganus* said, a well-used path leads off to the north-west. He follows the path as it winds through a coppice of nut hazels, their near-vertical branches shaking in the warm wind and flickering the bright green tops and paler undersides of their broad, serrated leaves.

Light and dark: everywhere light and darkness mingled.

As he emerges from the coppice he notices, half hidden by trees on the rising ground in front of him, the unmistakable outlines of a temple. Like a thousand others scattered across the land, it is built as a square tower surrounded on all sides by an open cloister-like ambulatory.

Screened by the ground-sweeping branches of a great ash, he studies the temple intently, looking for Caelofernus, or his horse, or anything else that might indicate the man's presence there. There is nothing: no movement of any kind to disturb the apparent tranquillity of the place under the drowsy sun. Near the temple stand a cluster of stone-walled buildings. He is about to move off when a woman with long grey hair emerges from one of these buildings, carrying a wooden bucket. She peers cautiously around, then begins walking towards a tile-roofed well-head. Easing Antares forward, Saturninus rides slowly up to her. She returns his greeting, but appears nervous and ill at ease.

Guessing, he asks softly, 'Is he still here?'

She looks up at him curiously, as if wondering how he could possibly have known. 'No, not any more. He's gone now – and may the god forbid him ever to return! That terrible man frightened my poor husband half to death. Who is he?'

'His name is Caelofernus, but he calls himself Carausius. And he's a robber and a murderer … Did he harm your husband?'

'No – at least, nothing you can see. But he drove away a man and a woman who were worshipping here – drove them away with a drawn sword, then forced Quirinalis, my husband, to sacrifice a cockerel on the altar. And afterwards he drank its blood, and made Quirinalis drink it too, before asking the god to take vengeance upon his enemies.' The woman hesitates, then asks, 'Would you be one of those enemies?'

'I am,' Saturninus confirms. 'His last enemy in this world, I hope.'

'The Christians say that the last enemy is Death, *Thanatos*.'

'Then may the *Parcae* let me be the one who sends Caelofernus to him. Which way was he heading when he left here?'

'Westwards, towards the river.'

Saturninus thanks her, and is about to set off again when an unwished-for thought comes to him. He tries to ignore it: the rational part of his mind is telling him that now he should be pursuing Caelofernus as fast as Antares can carry him. But fatigue and the events of the last days have left him unable to ignore that same powerful superstitious instinct he felt at Fonscolnis – and that instinct is crying out that there is something that he must do here before he leaves. 'Where's your husband now?'

'In the temple, resting. He feels safer there.'

Saturninus finds the priest, a tall, thin man, a decade or so younger than his wife, sitting in a chair in front of the altar. Quickly he tells him who he is and why he's there. Then, 'Your wife tells me that Caelofernus sacrificed to Mercury here, and now I must do the same. Have you got another cockerel?'

At first the priest remains absolutely immobile, staring at the altar. But before Saturninus can repeat his request, the man murmurs, 'Caelofernus – was that his name? … There's a pen, a hundred paces east of here, behind the elder bushes. Take any bird you want.'

Saturninus hurries out and finds the pen behind a thicket of elders, whose tight-packed heads of blossom are already beginning to show cream. Catching one of the big, pure-white cockerels he grips the bird by its scaly legs and carries it, upside down, back to the temple. At first it shrieks and beats its wings furiously, as if it knows the fate that awaits it. Then it hangs silent, tense, its beak agape, its bright unblinking eyes missing nothing.

The priest is standing now, waiting, gripping a small, curved-bladed knife with a golden handle. Saturninus holds out the bird and the man takes it and walks over to the altar. Behind it, on a plinth, stands a seven-feet-tall statue of the curly-haired young god, carrying a caduceus in one hand and a bulging money purse in the other. There is a serene and enigmatic smile on his stone lips.

'May I ask your own name?'

'Saturninus.'

'And what is it that you wish of the god?'

'I wish to find this man, Caelofernus, who calls himself Carausius, and who was so recently here. And when I have found him, I beg the god to give me his own strength, that I may kill Caelofernus and end his evil forever.'

The priest nods gravely and holds the doomed cockerel upside down over the altar, in the top of which a small charcoal fire glows. As if sensing what is coming, the bird's demented shrieks fill the temple: but the priest, already halfway into another world, pays them no heed.

'Great Mercury, herald of the gods and guide of Persephone on her first journey out of the Lower World,' he intones softly, 'accept the life of this herald of the new day. And grant to Saturninus, your supplicant, that he may both find and slay his enemy, Caelofernus ... And, O Celestial Messenger, this is also my prayer, the prayer of your servant Quirinalis. For I believe that this Caelofernus is a profoundly wicked man, and the enemy of all mortals who do truly love you.'

While the priest is speaking, Saturninus takes from his belt pouch the lead *defixio* curse that Mercury's priest at Fonscolnis made. Carefully he unrolls it, remembering as he does so the words he dictated those two days, long as years, ago.

To the man whom I know as Caelofernus, let there never again come sleep, either by day or by night, until Death and I both find him and drive him into the eternal night from which there can be no return.

The priest looks to Saturninus, who, expressionless, nods his assent.

Another death on my road to Caelofernus.

With a swift, scything stroke of his golden knife, Quirinalis severs the cockerel's neck, its head dropping onto the fire in the *focus* of the altar. In the sudden silence the bird's wings beat with manic fury for several moments, flying into death as its blood pumps out into the uncaring air. Saturninus stretches out his hand and allows the warm blood to splatter onto the letters of the *defixio*. It runs down over his fingers and drips onto the *focus*, where it hisses on the charcoal fire.

When the last signs of life have vanished, Quirinalis lays the cockerel's body reverently onto the floor in front of the altar and bows low to the statue behind it. The air is tinged with a haze of bluish smoke and the acrid smell of burnt flesh.

Noticing the *defixio*, the priest says, 'If that is what I suppose it to be, do you wish to leave it here for the god to read?'

Saturninus considers for a moment, the cockerel's blood still slowly trickling from the lead. 'Perhaps the god read it some time ago,' he murmurs. 'But yes – set it up there, facing the altar. That demon Caelofernus will probably never pass this way again, but if he ever should ...'

Quirinalis shudders at the thought. 'I'll do it now.' He accepts the *defixio* from Saturninus and then, from a small chest in the far corner of the temple, fetches a hammer and a large iron nail. 'Here, perhaps?' He holds the *defixio* against the wall at head height.

Saturninus nods, and the priest, with three deft blows, drives the nail through the lead and into a mortar joint between the stone blocks of the wall.

Saturninus thanks him and offers him three siliquae for his services, but Quirinalis declines them, saying he wants nothing for hastening Caelofernus's end.

'Several times I thought he was going to kill me. He wanted to kill me – I saw it in his eyes. In the end, I believe it was only his fear of the god that stopped him from doing so.'

Acutely conscious now of time passing, Saturninus hurriedly remounts. But just before he rides off he asks the priest if Caelofernus had said anything that might indicate whether he had a particular destination in mind.

'No, nothing. But when he reaches the Avon he'll have to go either north or south, for there's no crossing it in these parts, except by coracle.'

CHAPTER THIRTY-FOUR

After three miles at a brisk canter, Saturninus himself reaches the Avon. It is slow and wide, the translucent greeny-brown water flowing south-west in great meandering loops, between banks dense with willow and rapidly-lengthening reeds. Finding no one there to tell him which way Caelofernus has gone, Saturninus has to decide whether to follow the river upstream or downstream. He is acutely aware that if he makes the wrong decision now then he will never catch the man. But surely it has to be upstream? After all, north was the direction in which Caelofernus had been heading before he branched off the Fosse Way.

Perhaps he intends to rejoin the highway somewhere on the other side of Arcadolium?

So he sets off upstream, cursing the sinuous course of the river and the dense vegetation which slows him and provides perfect cover for an ambush. After a mile or so he spots, some distance away from the river, an old man tending a group of straw beehives at the edge of a field of beans. The beans are just coming into flower, their sun-warmed, summery fragrance drifting on the breeze.

'Have you seen a rider pass this way?' Saturninus calls across to him. There is no response. Saturninus canters over and repeats the question.

Startled, the old man straightens up and stares around in confusion. 'What was that you said, soldier?'

'A big man on a horse – have you seen him pass this way?'

'Today, you mean?'

'Yes, of course today – since mid-morning or so?'

'No, that I haven't, soldier; I'm sure of it. Although, truth to tell, my hearing isn't what it was and I'll allow it's possible that even a man on horseback could have passed by without me noticing.'

Saturninus thanks him and rides on. Half a mile further upstream he comes across a girl-child, no more than eight years old. She is gathering the tips of young nettles for soup, deftly nipping them off between finger and thumb and dropping them into the large wicker trug that lies at her feet. He notices that the trug is almost full. 'Have you seen another man on a horse pass this way?' he asks.

She stares at him wide-eyed and shakes her head.

'Are you sure – absolutely sure?'

The girl nods.

'And you've picked all those nettles here?'

'No.' She shakes her head again and points to the wood behind her, which starts just above the river bank and runs back way into the distance. 'I found most of them around the edge of the wood – and some in the fields as well.'

'Did you?' he replies quietly. So north still remains the logical way to go. And yet, that nagging instinct is again whispering insistently … Impulsively, he reaches into his belt pouch and pulls out the largest coin he can find – a copper *centenionalis*, struck under Constantius some fifteen years before and bearing his diademed bust on the obverse. On the reverse, a tall soldier is in the act of stabbing a barbarian horseman as he tumbles from his falling mount: around them runs the legend *FEL TEMP REPARATIO*.

'Felicium temporum reparatio,' he quotes softly.

'What does that mean?'

'The return of happy times,' Saturninus replies.

'Oh,' says the girl solemnly.

'Heads for north, soldier for south,' he murmurs. The girl looks on curiously as, with a flick of his thumb, he sends the coin spinning high into the air where, for a moment, it flashes the fire of the sun. He catches it one-handed as it falls, slapping it onto the back of his left hand, then lifting his right palm to see Constantius's unsmiling face.

'So ... both logic and the gods agree that I should keep riding north,' he breathes. But then he recalls how Caelofernus had evaded him at Duboceto Wood, and again out on the Fosse Way.

So perhaps I can trust neither logic nor the gods? No one but myself.

The next moment he has decided. 'Here – catch,' he calls to the girl, lobbing the coin across to her in a slow arc. He watches her clap both hands together to capture it, then he turns and starts riding quickly back along the way he came.

And only two hundred yards downstream from the spot where he first reached the Avon he meets a man, brown as a ripe hazel nut, baiting eel lines among the reeds.

'Yes – I did see a man like that, soldier,' he answers in response to Saturninus's inevitable question. 'Heading downriver, he was. Reckon he must be miles away by now though.'

So he is heading south!

His words give Saturninus a certain grim satisfaction. He rides on, as quickly as he can, though his progress is slowed, as Caelofernus's must have been, by the little brooks and ditches that flow into the river.

At last he reaches a place where a larger brook enters from the east, and there the Avon itself turns and begins heading almost due west.

Which way now? Is Caelofernus still following the river, or ...?

And at that moment he realises that their circuitous route back from Arcadolium has brought them – himself and Caelofernus both – to this point which can be no more than half a dozen miles north of Duboceto Wood. Quickened, he wonders if it is just possible that Caelofernus might be making his way back to the wood, perhaps to retrieve any spoils not found by the raiding party that morning?

Because he can't know that Melania revealed their hiding

places. And besides, there may be others of which even she was unaware?

He realises only too well that, for him to return to Duboceto now, is definitely the final throw of the dice. But Antares is tiring, and if Caelofernus is still following the Avon westwards then he will almost certainly never catch him. Fatalistically, he realises that the choice has made itself. He fords the brook, Antares' hooves sinking deep into the grey-black silty ooze and releasing the trapped gasses of decay – the smell of lowland rivers. Then he squeezes his heels against the horse's flanks and begins cantering southwards, away from the Avon.

CHAPTER THIRTY-FIVE

It is early afternoon when, from the high ground to the north, Saturninus sees the tree tops of Duboceto Wood for the second time that day. Working his way around to the east, he tries to locate the path into the wood again. The tall lookout tree pinpoints it, but the wilderness of gorse hides the actual entrance, and he realises that he will have to go in blind. Cautiously he rides between the gorse, finding an easier route than had been visible in the pre-dawn darkness. But at the path entrance, where he had hoped to find it, there is no sign of Caelofernus's stolen horse.

I told myself not to hope. Told myself that the chances of finding him here were slim. But of course, I did hope. I willed him to be here, and now ...

The disappointment is crushing. He dismounts and is about to enter the wood when he realises that, if Caelofernus were to arrive while he is inside, then Antares' presence will betray his own. Hurriedly he canters around to the south side of the wood and tethers the horse there. He ties him loosely, so that if, by some cruel chance, Caelofernus were to approach from that direction, Antares can break free: he has not forgotten the fate of Magnillus's horse. Before he leaves Antares he unstraps the boar spear from the saddle. Carrying it over his shoulder he runs back to the lookout tree.

There is still no sign of Caelofernus. Saturninus hesitates, then steals down the path that leads to the fallen oak, listening intently as he goes for any sound of an oncoming footfall, but hearing none. The camp appears exactly as they had left it that morning, though eerily silent and still now. As he prowls dejectedly around the deserted shelters he wonders how many seasons will pass before the unrelenting agents of decay will have obliterated them completely.

And Caelofernus is not here, and will almost certainly never be here again.

For a moment ... but there is no point in going back to the Avon and trying to pick up his trail: that has long gone cold. Now he can only wait here in the wood and hope that Caelofernus will still come. Hope that the man has gone further along the big river, and then waited there to make absolutely sure that he is not being followed and that the soldiers have left the wood, before himself turning south. Saturninus is only too well aware that it is a faint hope, but it is now the only one he has. He settles down to wait behind the great dead tree.

In the oppressive silence of the clearing the furtive movements and scufflings of small, unseen creatures in the depths of the wildwood seem preternaturally loud. Once, from far away, come the harsh shrieks of a jay, and he tenses and waits for whatever disturbed the bird to move closer. But time passes and nothing comes, and he slowly relaxes. He cannot see the sun, and in the filtered light of the wood he rapidly loses all sense of the progress of time. Slowly and insidiously his lack of sleep over the past days creeps up on him and his eyelids become heavier and heavier. And time drifts by.

Suddenly he wakes with a convulsive start, certain that, in the borderland between sleeping and waking, he heard an alien sound. Straining his ears he catches the scuff of what could be a footstep, as if someone or something is coming down the hidden path in front of him. He grips the wooden haft of the boar spear tightly and crouches down behind the oak's deeply ridged trunk, peering through the branches to see who or what will emerge. There is another brief rustle from among the dead leaves which litter the edges of the path, much closer now.

And then a man emerges slowly and warily into the clearing, his head moving from side to side like a snake's, never still. It is

Bonosus. Saturninus feels a vague anger as he watches to see what the little man will do. It rapidly becomes apparent that he has only come to scavenge. He starts rooting through the debris of the large shelter, picking over items of clothing and other odds and ends that Vernatius had not thought worth taking. From the muttered obscenities and grunts of exasperation, Saturninus guesses that Vernatius did a good job in locating any small hoards of coins and valuables that the other members of the gang had hidden there.

When Bonosus has worked his way all through the large shelter, he begins moving towards the far side of the fallen tree and Caelofernus's own tent.

There is no point in hiding. Saturninus simply waits, still as the great trunk itself, until Bonosus spots him. Then he says quietly, 'Hullo again, Bonosus. I thought I'd seen the last of you, my little weasel.'

Bonosus's nerves must be taut as lyre strings. He utters a weird, high-pitched squeal, stares at the boar spear in Saturninus's hand, backs away a few paces, then turns and bolts back along the path. Saturninus makes no attempt to go after him. He just stands and listens as the sounds of Bonosus's running feet slowly fade into silence. Then he leans back dejectedly against the dead tree, convinced that the game is now finally over: that even the remotest possibility that Caelofernus might return has fled away with Bonosus.

And then he again becomes aware of the faint sound of distant footfalls. At first he thinks it is only Bonosus, still running away – for sounds can carry strangely in woods. Then he realises that the noises are getting louder, rapidly louder, and coming towards him down the path. He darts back behind the oak and stares intently through the tangle of roots and dried clay, the adrenaline once more pumping into his blood.

Moments later, Bonosus, now screaming in mortal terror, bursts back into the clearing. Scarcely a dozen paces behind runs Caelofernus, sword in hand and gaining on him with every stride.

Bonosus swerves wildly to his left and dashes towards the roots end of the fallen tree, the spot where he last saw Saturninus. Neither slowing nor breaking his stride, Caelofernus races after him, holding his sword in both hands now and beginning to swing it sideways for the terrible blow that will sever Bonosus's head from his body.

So fast is Caelofernus moving that, even if he had seen Saturninus, he could have done nothing to avoid him. Probably he only glimpses him in the instant when Saturninus rises up from beside the dead tree and stabs the cruel blade of the boar spear forwards and upwards into the centre of his chest, just below the breastbone. It is Caelofernus's own momentum as much as Saturninus's strength that drives the blade in so deep that only the curved stop-bars, ten inches behind the spear tip, prevent it from penetrating even further. The force of the collision almost knocks Saturninus backwards, but in that moment of impact he feels his muscles turn to steel. He stands immovable, watching the expressions on Caelofernus's face change with the rapidity of clouds flying before a March wind – change from fury to disbelief and then to hate, a look of stark hatred that freezes on his dying face like wax dripping down a snuffed candle.

A hate so strong is hard to kill: it possesses a life of its own. Caelofernus's hands still grip his sword, and with a despairing blood-choked scream he scythes it wildly through the air. Saturninus twists sideways, but the blade smashes into the side of his helmet with such force that it half-stuns him. But the shock of the blow sends a charge of superhuman strength surging through his body, and with an animal roar of fury he lifts Caelofernus completely off the ground and holds him there, impaled and twitching, as he gazes up into those terrible eyes – holds him there until he sees the light within them at last begin to fade. Only then does he relax his grip on the spear and let the dead man collapse onto the ground.

It is victory – total victory: but so bewilderingly sudden, and his head is ringing so from Caelofernus's sword that Saturninus can scarcely believe it has happened. He stands, physically and mentally utterly drained, staring down at the dead man's face.

Is this really happening – or is it just another dream?

He sinks down onto his knees and slowly runs his hands over Caelofernus's face and hair and beard, feeling real skin, real hair. He puddles his fingers in the blood that oozes from around the spear's stop-bars, then touches them to his lips, savouring the salt taste of the blood, the proof of reality. Certainty comes then – comes with a rush of fierce exultation.

I really have killed him, Pascentia! I've killed the man that the dream warned would kill me ... or perhaps kill us both. Somehow, I've played the Parcae with their own dice – and won!

Standing, he places one foot on the dead man and eases the blade of the boar spear out of his chest.

The exhausted mind can conjure strange fantasies. Saturninus knows this. Yet as he looks down at the sprawled body and the bloody spear, an unnerving thought comes to him.

What if Caelofernus isn't truly dead?

Certainly his body seems lifeless ...

But when night comes, who can say what wonders the powers of darkness may work on one who was surely their own creation?

He also knows – everyone knows – the superstition that, to prevent the ghost of an evil man or woman from walking, their head should be cut off and buried between their knees. Once he had chanced to see the ritual carried out. Then, he had thought it stupid and barbaric. But now ... he begins to draw his sword, then, uncertain, lets it slide back into its sheath.

The pain in his head is growing steadily worse as the adrenaline that had masked it ebbs away. Taking off his helmet he impassively studies the jagged gash where Caelofernus's blade has perforated the metal, and when he touches the side of his head his fingers come away sticky with blood. It comes to him then that, when Caelofernus inflicted the wound, his transfixed heart must have stopped beating: that he was already dead.

That decides him. He must destroy Caelofernus's body – destroy it utterly.

And only fire will do that.

Turning, he notices Bonosus sitting hunched at the edge of the clearing, staring blank-eyed at the ground. The little man seems to be in a state of shock. He doesn't look up as Saturninus calls hoarsely, 'Bonosus ... Bonosus! Can you hear me?'

Bonosus nods slowly in acknowledgement, his eyes still fixed on the ground.

As if terrified that, should he look up, he will see Caelofernus standing in front of him, still alive.

'We've got to burn Carausius's body – burn it to ashes. But first I've got to get him out of this wood.'

Bonosus doesn't stir.

Saturninus squats down in front of him. 'Bonosus!' he hisses, 'If Carausius is still unburnt when night comes, then he might come back to life. Think of that – Carausius alive and coming after you again! And then there would be nothing that I could do to save you – absolutely nothing!'

That works. Bonosus's eyes widen in horror and he gapes up at Saturninus. 'He couldn't come alive again, could he?'

'I don't know, not for sure. But don't they say that demons are immortal – and wasn't he the closest thing to a demon that you and I have ever seen? Now get up, and help me carry him out of here.'

With much effort – for the dead are curiously heavy – and with no real assistance from Bonosus, Saturninus half drags, half carries, Caelofernus's body along the path and leaves it lying under the lookout tree. After a brief rest, he walks with Bonosus back to the place where he left Antares. There is no sign of Caelofernus's stolen horse. He leads Antares back to the great beech and then, while Bonosus holds the horse's head to calm him, he manages to heave the body up and drape it across the saddle.

To the north of Duboceto Wood the land rises, and there the gorse thins and gives way to rough pasture, erratically studded with great spiky thistles. On this high spot Saturninus slides

Caelofernus's body down onto the grass. Away to the south-west he notices, no more than five miles distant over the tops of the trees, the north-eastern end of his own hills. They appear blue in the warm haze, each individual tree clearly visible and seeming much larger than those on the nearer flat lands.

High above him, silhouetted black against the almost cloudless sky, a buzzard soars noiselessly on the thermals, its broad wings ragged-tipped, carving out great double circles of air half a mile across. He hesitates, then takes his cloak from a saddlebag and spreads it over the dead man.

CHAPTER THIRTY-SIX

For hour after hour, throughout the remainder of that long, hot day, Saturninus – and Bonosus too, spurred on by his own terrors – toil to build a great funeral pyre next to the spot where Caelofernus's body lies. Duboceto is ancient woodland, scarcely disturbed for millennia by anything but the changing seasons, and their searching yields great quantities of dead wood. Using Caelofernus's sword, Saturninus hacks the shed branches and light-starved saplings into manageable logs, then he and Bonosus haul them up to the site of the pyre using lengths of wild clematis vine tied around one of Antares' saddle horns. Both men are soon exhausted, but slowly the pyre rises higher and higher until at last, not long before sunset, it stands some six feet above the trampled grass.

Using the projecting branch ends as steps, Saturninus climbs to the top of the pyre, then heaves Caelofernus's body up with a loop of vine under the dead man's arms. He drags the body over to the centre and lays it out. Gold and gemstone rings still adorn Caelofernus's lifeless fingers. Saturninus does not want them, and he has come to realise that no power on earth could induce Bonosus to touch that body, or anything it has worn. Before descending, he takes the tiny gilt-bronze Mercury from his belt pouch and forces it into the grip of the stiffened right hand. The act is instinctive, or if it isn't, then he is too tired to analyse his motives.

Totally drained now, the muscles in his arms twitching from overstrain, Saturninus clambers down and squats at the foot of the pyre, his knees drawn up, his head sunk onto his chest. He takes several deep, slow breaths and then, with an effort, he opens his eyes and calls Bonosus over to him. From his pouch he extracts three siliquae and holds them out to the little man on his open palm. Bonosus approaches warily, but before he can ask, Saturninus explains huskily, 'You're free now, Bonosus. Take these, and go wherever you choose – but never back into my country.' He points towards the sunlit and shadowed hills. 'There, you have a wolf's head on your shoulders ... do you understand me? If you're ever found there again ...' He draws a finger across his throat.

'Goodbye, Bonosus. And may Isis – or whatever goddess or god you imagine is your protector – go with you on your travels. But,' he adds softly – so softly that perhaps Bonosus does not even hear him – 'keep one of those to pay old Charon the ferryman. I fear you may be meeting him before long.'

Bonosus, his hand trembling, takes the coins. He takes them quickly, as if he fears that at any moment Saturninus may change his mind, then retreats a few paces, then halts. He must want to go, to be far away from this place and from Caelofernus's body. Yet it is as if he fears even more to be alone on this coming night.

'Thank you, Primicerius, thank you. And may ...'

But Saturninus, almost oblivious to his presence now, is gazing at something far away over the tree tops. Bonosus hesitates for a few moments more, then turns and hurries down the slope, dodging between the gorse bushes, moving as fast as his tired legs will carry him. Saturninus never sees him again.

The glowing cherry-red disc of the sun is already beginning to disappear down behind a line of clouds on the north-western horizon. Saturninus takes the leather water bottle from his saddlebag, removes the stopper and takes a long drink. The water tastes tepid and stale. Suddenly he freezes, the bottle inches from his lips, as he notices a figure standing half-hidden in the long shadows at the edge of Duboceto Wood. It appears to be a woman, absolutely still and looking directly up at him. For a moment a thrill of fear courses through his veins, before he remembers Honorata, the woman with the water skin whose screams had so effectively woken the sleeping robbers in the early morning. Wondering what she wants, he throws the remainder of the stale water onto the grass, replaces the bottle in his saddlebag and turns to call to her. But she has vanished, and at the scent of water Antares neighs loudly, reminding him that the poor beast has not drunk for half a day now.

It is only as he rides slowly through the dusk, down to the little stream they crossed on the approach to the wood on the previous night, that he recalls … *Honorata's dress was dark blue, but the shadow woman's seemed much paler. And there had been something at her side; a large shape, even blacker than the darkness of the wood.*

And he remembers again the woman who had stood at the place where the three trackways met; the woman who had pointed to the north.

The woman who was nothing more than my hallucination.

Full night is dangerously near by the time that Saturninus rides back up to the high ground, but there is just enough twilight left for him to gather several armfuls of last year's dead grasses. He packs them, dry and rustling, in between the wood at the base of the pyre on the windward side. Then, taking a flint from his pouch, he strikes it several glancing blows with his dagger blade, sending showers of sparks down onto the dry grass. Soon a thin spiral of smoke begins to curl upwards as a tiny heart of fire glows among the tinder. He blows it as gently as a lover, and moments later several bright tongues of flame are licking up through the criss-crossing branches.

Standing back, he watches as the pyre, fanned by the rising night wind, is rapidly transformed into a roaring, crackling inferno of great leaping flames and showers of incandescent sparks that shoot up into the night sky. Staring into the all-consuming fire, Saturninus feels a manic energy ignite and surge through his veins, wild and reckless as the flames themselves.

Suddenly he realises that Caelofernus's body, stark black amid the orange flames, is slowly rising up into a sitting position, where it remains for several heart-stopping moments before sinking down again and disappearing into the inferno.

Slightly delirious now with fatigue and lack of sleep, he shouts out to the gods of the Lower World, and to the *Parcae* too, that he has won. That he has killed Death, his Death, the Death which they had sent to claim him, and so nothing now can kill him – that now he is as immortal as the gods themselves. The idea exhilarates him, and he roars with crazy, cathartic laughter.

The pyre flares even more fiercely, the tongues of flame soaring up until they seem momentarily to touch the stars. And by their shimmering orange light Saturninus sees three cloaked and hooded figures standing, side by side, about a dozen yards away, silently watching him from out of the cover of the night. He stares at them, their deep-set eyes reflecting the firelight as they meet his own, until the flames die and the figures fade back into the darkness. And when, a few heartbeats later, the flames rise again, almost as high as before, the figures have vanished.

They are the spirits of the earth and of the deep, dark powers of the earth: of the cycle of the seasons, of birth, healing, death and rebirth.

The words remembered from long ago.

Have you been reborn somewhere, Caelofernus? Are you still out there in this darkness – still waiting for me?

For a few moments he contemplates running out into the night after the *Cucullati*, desperate to know if they were really there. But …

Sometimes uncertainty is preferable to certainty, and the uncertainty that certainty brings.

Smoke, paler than the dark sky, twists upwards, drifting across the myriad stars that shimmer in the heavens directly overhead. In the south-eastern sky Saturninus glimpses the almost-full moon emerge from a wrack of luminous cloud. Quite calm now, he reflects that tomorrow will be the night of the full moon itself, the night on which he was to have died.

But now I'll see that moon rise, and live to see it set as well. But where will you be in that dawn, Pascentia? Where will you be as I watch the golden disc paling and dissolving into the brightening sky?

Muffled explosions are coming from the pyre now. It spits red-hot embers, which glow for a few moments among the dark grasses. He feels the searing heat when the breeze momentarily changes direction towards him, and the smell of burning flesh drifts with it. Antares whinnies uneasily, snorting and tossing his head. Saturninus leads the horse down the slope, unsaddles, and tethers him to a small tree in a grassy clearing among the gorse. Then, overcome by crushing tiredness, he beds down nearby, using as a blanket the cloak that had covered Caelofernus. The smell of the dead man still lingers in its weave, but he is beyond caring now.

CHAPTER THIRTY-SEVEN

Even as the orange tongues of fire are surging through Caelofernus's funeral pyre and up into the starry night sky, in a dark corner of the Vadumleucara guard post two men are holding a furtive conversation. They stand lounging against adjacent walls, as far away as the confines of the building will allow from the prisoners locked in the cells. Away too from Vernatius, now dozing fitfully on his bed as exhaustion and the pain of his wound drive him alternately into and out of sleep.

'But he ... never ... will ... know.' Magnillus's forefinger jabs Canio's chest in time with his words. 'Look, we'll be leaving him here tomorrow, so how will he know if it never reaches Corinium?'

'But when he *does* go to Corinium then he's bound to mention it, isn't he? And what will we say then?' Canio is tempted but wary.

'Don't worry about that. I'll make sure he never goes to Corinium for months ... years even. Him and Nitalis both. And I'll give them a few siliquae – tell them it's their share of the money we couldn't find owners for.'

'No, don't do that – when they spend it they're bound to tell all and sundry how they came by it, and that might start all sorts of hares running.'

'Perhaps you're right,' Magnillus concedes. 'Still, all the more for us, eh?' He grins. 'And besides, aren't I entitled to it? It was my horse that bastard Carausius stole, don't forget that.'

'It was the civil guard's horse,' Canio corrects him. 'But your harness,' he adds, before Magnillus can. 'Still, we'd probably get away with it ... if it wasn't for Saturninus. When he gets back to Corinium he's sure to ask if Carausius's loot is safely locked away.'

'But *will* Saturninus be coming back? In that dream of his, didn't you say he saw Carausius kill him under a full moon? Well, the full moon's tomorrow, Canio. Less than a day away now. And besides, perhaps he's already dead.'

Canio hears the serpent in Magnillus's voice. 'What in Hades' name makes you say that?'

'Because the moon he saw in his dream might not have been full. It's never easy to tell a moon that's one day short of the full from the real thing – you know that as well as I do.'

'Full or not, just because he saw it happen in some damned dream doesn't mean it actually will.' Canio doesn't like the way this conversation is heading. But he makes no attempt to end it.

'But *he* must believe it will happen, and that's what counts. And if he catches up with Carausius still believing it, then he's as good as dead. In a fight, when a man starts believing he's going to be killed, then killed he is. Seen it happen several times myself – bet you have too.'

That tweaks a stretched nerve in Canio's usually relaxed conscience. 'I knew I should never have let him go after that bastard alone,' he mutters. 'I should have gone with him, whatever he said.'

'You obeyed orders, Canio. His orders. Like a good soldier should,' Magnillus replies soothingly.

But Canio's conscience still pricks. He raises another objection. 'What about Melania – she's another one who knows we've got it.'

'But Melania won't reach Corinium, will she?' Magnillus whispers impatiently. 'You said as much yourself. One way or another, she'll never tell.'

'No, I don't suppose she will.' Canio pauses, then sighs. 'The keeping of it's one thing. I'd feel no guilt about that, but ...'

'But what, Canio?'

'If I were to agree to keep it, then maybe a part of me would start willing Saturninus not to come back – do you understand what I'm saying?'

'What? You're not turning Christian on me, are you, Canio? Listen, the gods alone will decide whether or not Saturninus comes back. Not you. Not me.'

'And if he does come back?'

'We're soldiers, aren't we, Canio? And soldiers are supposed to have the courage to take risks.'

Canio gives Magnillus a sharp look. 'All right, damn you, I'll play with your dice – but we'd better have a good story ready, just in case Saturninus does make it back to Corinium alive.'

'Such as?'

'What about ... we simply forgot? We locked it away safely in the weapons store here. But in the morning, what with the prisoners attempting to escape like they did – remember? – and Vernatius's wound giving him a bad time, we forgot all about it. Gold and silver were the last things on our minds that morning – simple, honest soldiers that we are.'

Both men snigger. But then Magnillus asks doubtfully, 'Do you really think Saturninus will believe that?'

'He will if he wants to,' Canio replies cryptically. 'We'll just leave the money where it is, and if Saturninus does come back, then we'll remember all about it. And if he doesn't come back...'

'Then we'll console our grief by drinking to his memory.' Magnillus's teeth gleam faintly in the dimness as he smiles. 'But whatever we might tell Saturninus, shouldn't we carry those two bags with us when we leave in the morning?'

'No; best not take them to Corinium.'

'Why?'

'Because,' Canio explains, 'they'll be safer here. Even if Saturninus doesn't return, we'll have to wait months before spending any of that money or selling the jewellery – and there are far too many prying eyes in Corinium to hide them safely there.' What Canio doesn't say is that, should anyone start asking awkward questions, those bags will be found in Magnillus's possession, not in his.

'Remember to bring the key with you tomorrow,' he reminds Magnillus. 'We don't want anybody rooting around in the store while we're away – and maybe helping themselves to the gifts that a grateful empire has seen fit to bestow upon us.'

'Ah ... that might be a problem. You don't need a key to get into it. The lock's so old and worn that I've seen Himilico pick it with a big bent nail. He won't know that Carausius's loot is still inside, but if he chances to go in while we're away and sees it, then he's bound to tell Vernatius.'

'So we'll just have to hide it somewhere else.' Canio's conscience is sleeping peacefully again now, as he considers the practicalities of the matter.

'Where? This place is as bare as a tomb – you couldn't hide so much as a poppy seed in it.'

'Well, there are dozens of fields around here, aren't there? We'll bury it in one of them for a few months.'

'Aren't you afraid that someone might dig it up and make off with it?' Magnillus enquires sardonically.

Canio was waiting for that. 'Oh no, Magnillus my old friend. You're the only one who need be afraid. You see, if it were to disappear, then it would be my duty – my painful duty – to tell Aemilianus that it had been left in your safe keeping. In fact, that I'd seen you lock it in your weapons store, to which you have the one and only key.'

'Would you really do that, Canio, old friend?'

'Best not to find out the hard way.' Canio smiles, deliberately showing his own excellent teeth.

Magnillus just looks at him. At last he says, 'Well, if we are going to bury it, then we'd better do it now – before Himilico gets back. We'll tell that donkey Vernatius that we're going into town for a drink.' He turns away, yawns and stretches.

A little while later, each wearing a long *cucullus*, both men slip quietly out of the front door of the guard post and start down the Fosse Way towards the centre of Vadumleucara. Hidden under his *cucullus*, Magnillus carries a spade.

After some two hundred paces they leave the highway and begin walking along a maze of little paths that eventually brings them into an area of rough sheep pasture.

There, scattered half-hidden among the grasses, Canio notices several irregular lumps of weathered limestone, the debris left from quarrying years before. Searching for a hiding place, they come across a drystone sheepfold, its circular wall waist-high. The dried mud inside is almost bare of grass, pockmarked by the cloven hooves that trampled and retrampled it countless times while still soft in the early spring.

'What about in there?' whispers Magnillus.

Canio vaults the wall and stamps several times. 'No: the ground's as hard as rock. And what happens if it's full of sheep when we want to dig the stuff up again?'

'Well, have you got a better idea?'

Canio does not reply. He glances around the landscape and in the fitful moonlight makes out the shape of a particularly large lump of stone sticking up out of the grass about fifty paces away. 'Follow me, Centenarius.' He clambers out of the sheepfold and strides across to investigate.

Magnillus follows, taking several irritable swipes with his spade at the ubiquitous clumps of thistles as he goes.

The rock is so heavy that Canio can barely stir it. 'Just about the right weight,' he grunts. 'Come on, help me roll it over.'

With both men throwing their weight against it, they manage to roll the stone onto its side. As it goes over, Canio glimpses a small lizard scuttle out from underneath and vanish like quicksilver into the surrounding grass. The soil where the rock stood is moist and soft.

'Spread your *cucullus* on the ground just there,' Canio orders, taking the spade from Magnillus.

'What for?' Magnillus asks suspiciously.

'To put the earth on, of course. Otherwise it'll show on top of the grass afterwards.'

'Why mine?'

'Because I'm the ducenarius and you're the centenarius, remember?' Canio hisses.

He waits until Magnillus has, less than gracefully, complied, then drives the iron-shod wooden spade into the damp earth. It takes very little time for him to dig a small pit an arm's length deep, and even less for him to drop the two bags of coins and jewellery into it and backfill the crumbly soil.

Magnillus carefully raises one edge of his *cucullus* and slides the remaining earth over the filled hole while Canio treads it firmly down.

'Right, that's enough,' Canio breathes. 'All we have to do now is get this damned rock back the way we found it.'

'Wait!' Magnillus whispers. From his belt pouch he takes a large goose egg and holds it up for Canio's inspection.

Canio guesses what is coming: he has seen similar rituals performed, years before in Germania.

'You see this?' Canio thinks he can hardly avoid seeing it, being less than a foot from his nose. 'For us, tonight, this represents the great cosmic egg from which our Lord Mithras was born.' Magnillus sets the egg gently down on the bare earth. 'Now, place the palm of your right hand on top of it.'

Canio hesitates.

'Well, go on; it won't bite you,' Magnillus asserts impatiently.

Deciding that he might as well humour him, Canio gives an exaggerated sigh, then squats down and puts his hand on the egg.

Magnillus places his own right hand flat on the back of Canio's and recites softly, 'Great Mithras, god of soldiers, lord of fair dealing between comrades, keep watch, I beg you, over this place and let no one take back from the earth what we have given into its care this night. Not without the knowledge and consent of both myself – being one who has passed, by both ordeal and initiation, into your Third Order of Soldiers – and of Ducenarius Canio here.' With that, he presses his hand sharply downwards, smashing the egg below Canio's palm.

Canio utters a comparatively mild expletive. 'Happy now?' he enquires, as he wipes his sticky hand on the grass. Diplomatically, he does not voice his suspicion that, if Magnillus were ever tempted to dig up their hoard alone, then it will be the weight of the rock rather than fear of divine retribution that will deter him.

It takes even more effort to tip the rock back into its original position but, straining and sweating, they manage it. Then Canio kneels and with his fingers combs the grass back around the base of the stone, teasing it back upright where it was crushed and trampled.

'There, that should do it. Nobody will know we've ever been here,' he mutters. 'Now let's get into town – I could do with that drink.'

By a circuitous route they begin walking back towards the Fosse Way, but as they approach the edge of a copse they encounter another night walker.

'Hey! Who's there?' a voice booms out of the darkness. 'What are you doing prowling around here where you've no business to be?'

Both men instinctively crouch low and creep into the cover of the trees.

'Who in the House of Hades is that?' Canio whispers impatiently.

'Sounds like Faustinus.'

'Who?'

'Faustinus. Shepherd. Lives in a hovel over there a way – though what in the name of the Evil One he's doing out tonight I don't know, not now the lambing season's well over.'

'If you don't show yourselves, then I'll set the dog on you,' comes Faustinus's voice again. 'He'll tear your throats out, he will.'

'I know that dog: it's almost as old as he is, and's got even more fleas,' Magnillus mutters contemptuously. 'Don't worry – I'll soon sort the fool out.' He stands up, and Canio thinks he is about to go after Faustinus and give him a kicking, or worse.

'No!' he hisses. 'If he recognises you, then sure as death it'll get back to Nitalis – and Vernatius too. And then they just might guess what we've been up to. Keep down and let's get away. The trees will hide us.'

Magnillus pauses, then appears to see the sense of it and starts following Canio as he slinks along, ducking under the low leafy boughs.

'I think there's two of them!'

Canio hears this new voice, high and excited, suddenly call out from some way in front. Immediately they stop and squat down again. 'Not another of the bastards! – who is it now?' he snarls.

'I don't damned well know,' Magnillus grates through clenched teeth.

'Well, whoever it is, I've had enough. Watch me, and do what I do.' Canio pulls the hood of his *cucullus* over his head and stands up. He stretches his arms out wide, taking the loose cloth of the *cucullus* with them, then grasps the edges of the arm-slits. Magnillus does the same, and in the feeble light of the clouded moon they look, in silhouette, like demonic winged figures out of nightmare.

Taking a deep breath, Canio gives a blood-curdling howl and charges in the direction from which the second voice came. Magnillus follows a few paces behind, shrieking like a soul in torment.

Canio glimpses a dark shape looming in front of him. It momentarily becomes a pale-faced youth before, with a yelp of terror, it turns and flees into the night. Canio runs after him, still screeching, and a few dozen strides later hears a dull thump. Moments later he discovers its source: in his panic the youth has run full-tilt into the low branch of a tree and now lies sprawled beneath it. His blood up, Canio gives a banshee howl of triumph.

Then the clouds momentarily clear the moon and he sees that the youth's eyes are wide open, staring up at the stars. '*Merda*!' he curses.

'What is it?' pants Magnillus, who has just caught up.

'I think he might have broken his fool neck,' Canio mutters.

Magnillus considers this for a few moments. 'Well, if he has then he won't be telling any tales, will he?' he grunts. 'Come on, let's get into town before we meet any more night owls.'

They hide the spade and their *cuculli* in the long grass near the Fosse Way, and before the moon had emerged again from the clouds they are sitting in a corner of The Vine Leaf drinking undiluted red wine and reminiscing about the events of the earlier part of the day. When Saturninus's name is mentioned, or almost mentioned, the conversation falters; but only for a moment.

CHAPTER THIRTY-EIGHT

Asleep on the grass near Duboceto Wood, Saturninus dreams that he can see Pascentia coming slowly towards him, walking down from the high ground where a thin trail of smoke still rises from Caelofernus's funeral pyre. She pauses, studying him as he sleeps, then kneels and lies beside him and kisses him on the lips. He struggles awake and finds to his amazement that she is actually there, looking just as she did on that last day at Burdigala, three years before.

It is daylight now, sunny and dry, and they lie among the lengthening grasses and whisper together, as lovers do. She strokes his hair, and he feels no pain from the wound made by Caelofernus's sword. Then she kisses him again and says, 'It's time we were leaving – we've a long way to go.'

He stands, takes her offered hand and pivots her gracefully back onto her feet, and together they walk away from Duboceto Wood. Hand in hand they wander for miles across the undulating grasslands, watching the cloud-shadows glide silently across hillsides where the warm breeze makes wave-like ripples flow through the grasses.

'Where are we going?' Saturninus asks.

'Towards the future – our future. Be patient and you'll see.' She smiles, and squeezes his hand.

Eventually they crest a high ridge, and there before them is the lowland plain, its tiny trees, fields and hedges all nestling in a vast bowl of sunlight that stretches far away to the blue southern horizon.

'That's where we're going,' she murmurs, pointing across the plain.

'So far?' Saturninus hears himself reply, as he gazes at the plain and the high, white clouds sailing across it.

'It's not so far now … not for us. We'll soon be there, together again.'

Puzzled by that, he turns to ask … But to his bewilderment she has vanished. And standing there, staring numbly out over the plain in the direction she indicated, he notices, far away, something that might be one of the old circles of standing stones. But he cannot be certain, not with the distance and the shimmer of the heat haze.

CHAPTER THIRTY-NINE

When Saturninus wakes for the second time the new sun has long since started its transit of the heavens. He sits up and looks wildly around, uncertain now if he really is awake … and remembering. The memory of Pascentia's vanishing is too painful and he struggles awkwardly to his feet. A wave of nausea sweeps over him. It slowly passes, and he takes a long drink from the water bottle he refilled on the previous evening. A dozen yards away Antares is cropping the grass beside the tree to which he is tethered, driving away flies with long, lazy swishes of his tail. Saturninus leaves him there and wanders back up to the high ground.

All that remains of Caelofernus's pyre is a thick bed of light grey ash and a few black log ends, carbonised and radially cracked, that lie scattered around its edge. Even now, the radiated heat makes him turn his face away. As the swirling breeze strengthens for a moment it strips off a flurry of ash to reveal a still-glowing heart of fire below. Walking back down to the wood's edge he cuts a long hazel sapling, then returns to the site of the pyre, trimming the sapling as he goes. Shielding his face with one arm from the searing heat, he stirs through the ash: but the pole encounters no resistance.

'Even the bones are gone,' he whispers to the wind. Then the green stick itself ignites. He tosses it into the centre of the ash, where it instantly bursts into flame along its entire length, the sap bubbling and hissing.

As he saddles Antares he glances back up the slope and sees the freshening wind scatter a great cloud of ash, like snow in summer.

In two or three years all the ash will have long blown away, or been washed into the ground by the rain. And the grass will have grown back, and it will be as though none of this had ever happened.

He washes his hands and face in the little stream and then, lying on the bank, plunges his head below the surface. The cold water stings his wound and he pulls out, wincing, seeing the red stain of the dried blood lazily dispersing in the current. He repeats the action, rubbing the close-cropped hair with his fingertips until all the blood is gone.

Suddenly he remembers Armiger. He hesitates, then remounts and rides back to the side of the wood, where he hunts around in the wilderness of gorse. He cannot find the body. It occurs to him then that Canio, or perhaps Magnillus, might have taken it back to Corinium to claim any reward on offer. He canters back across the undulating countryside to the Fosse Way, turns south, and begins the twenty-mile journey back to Vadumleucara.

The road is busy now, at mid-morning. He meets pedlars laden with enormous packs, drovers herding sheep and cattle, ox-drawn wagons, their axles and iron-bound wheels creaking and groaning, their oxen urged on by the long, iron-tipped goads of the carters. Once, he overtakes a train of a dozen mules, each laden with a pair of large black clay jars, one slung on each flank on a frame of woven osiers.

Riders – solitary or in small groups, ambling, trotting or cantering – approach, pass, and disappear into the distance, as do the enclosed carriages of rich men, drawn by matched pairs of fine horses, their occupants protected from the world by several hard-eyed mounted bodyguards in identical tunics. Occasionally he comes upon small gangs of roadmenders – lean, ragged men who seem never to look up as people pass by. They continue on with their never-ending task of breaking up rocks from the little cairns at the roadside, basketing the results into the potholes and tamping them firm.

It is well past noon when he arrives back at the Vadumleucara guard post. One of Antares' shoes has worn loose, and while old Nitalis is attending to it, Saturninus goes inside to check on Vernatius.

The trooper returns his greeting solemnly and respectfully. Yes, he has had his wound washed with rosemary oil. No, it is not very painful now, except when he tries to walk. Canio, Magnillus and the prisoners? They left for Corinium at first light. Centenarius Magnillus had estimated they would arrive by noon at the latest, so they should be there by now. Yes, he has everything he needs – Ducenarius Canio brought him a flagon of wine back from The Vine Leaf last night.

'And Carausius ... did the Primicerius ...?'

'Yes, I caught up with him at last. The man's dead now: just ashes blowing away in the wind.'

'Christus be praised. I feared that you would never catch him. Or if you did ...'

Stopping off at The Wheel, a large inn beside the Fosse Way on the southern outskirts of town, Saturninus lingers reflectively over a bowl of mutton broth and several cups of cool, watered wine. On the journey back from Duboceto the memory of that last dream – the dream in which Pascentia came to him – had tormented him with its vividness and its images of a coming reunion ... And of her subsequent vanishing.

But you must be still alive. Surely that's what the dream was telling me? But where ... where in all this wide world are you?

Then he remembers the dream which came to him as he lay on Corvusida long barrow, and her words,

'Just follow wherever the roads may lead.'

He leans back in his chair. The window shutters of The Wheel stand open, and through them he can see the highway stretching uphill towards the southern horizon – almost as if it is beckoning to him.

Is that where you are? Were you there, in Corinium, all this time?

He downs the last cup at one swallow and sets off to ride the last fifteen miles back to the little city.

It is a beautiful day, sunny and warm, with the world all fresh and green, and as the remaining miles to Corinium slip past he studies every female traveller he meets or overtakes. But none is her.

And then, still some miles from the city, his searching eyes chance to notice a woman in a light blue dress, not on the highway but at the edge of a steep coombe some distance away. Scarcely before his eyes can focus on her she begins to descend into the coombe, and moments later she has all but disappeared. Wheeling off the Fosse Way he starts riding quickly towards the spot, scarcely daring to hope, fatalistically half-certain that when he reaches the coombe she will not be there. Feverishly he urges Antares forwards, cursing the bushes and trees that obstruct his vision. At the edge of the coombe he halts and scans the gorse-scattered slopes below, at first seeing nobody, then glimpsing movement between the bushes no more than two hundred yards away. He stares, and moments later is certain it is the same woman. Heart racing, he starts Antares down the coombe towards her, terrified that he will lose sight again.

Closer now, he realises that her dress is pale, almost white, which puzzles him: back on the Fosse Way he had been certain it was blue. When only fifty yards separate them, the woman turns. She has a face of severe, glacial beauty, abundant dark hair coiled tight on top of her head. It is not Pascentia's face. The disappointment is crushing. He reins Antares to a halt and for a long moment stares at the woman. As their eyes meet he is almost certain that she is the same woman he saw at that now-distant crossroads two days before. A large black hound lopes silently out from the cover of a bush and sits on its haunches beside her, and now he is sure. Before he can call out to her she raises one arm and points to the north.

North again. But why? Caelofernus is dead ... And at Duboceto, Pascentia pointed to the south as the direction where she'd be.

He nudges Antares' flanks, determined to question her. Antares does not move. He nudges again, harder this time, but still Antares remains immobile, and now the woman is turning and beginning to walk away. Saturninus tries once more to urge Antares towards her, but the horse stands as if turned to stone. Further down the coombe is the beginnings of a beech wood, and by now the woman and hound are almost there. Scrambling off Antares' back, Saturninus starts running towards her. He is no more than forty yards away by the time she disappears into the wood, but when he reaches it the trees seem to have swallowed her.

The margins of the wood are open, with rows of deep drifts of last year's faded bronzy leaves. He stops and listens, but there is no sound of moving feet rustling through those leaves. He strides deeper under the trees, into the natural basilica formed by the great, grey trunks, then listens again. The silence is almost unnatural; nothing stirs. She is gone.

As he walks slowly back to Antares he finds himself glancing uneasily from side to side at the narrow sheep paths which wind along the sides of the coombe, looking for a point where three meet, and feeling a slightly shamed sense of relief at seeing none. Antares is now unconcernedly nibbling the turf, but as Saturninus mounts and rides back to the highway he himself is tense and restless, the confidence he had felt at The Wheel gone, the doubts and uncertainties returned.

When at last he arrives at the top of the long, shallow descent to the Verulamium Gate there is, as near as he can judge, only about four hours of daylight remaining: four hours until nightfall and the rising of the full moon.

For the last quarter mile before he reaches the city he rides past the monumental tombs and great headstones that line the road on both sides. They are carved with the names and images of the honoured and forgotten dead. Roman law had forbidden their bodies, or even their ashes, to be buried within the city walls, and so their families or heirs had arranged for their funerary monuments to be erected along the main highways leading out of the city. And here they stand, a constant reminder to the living, if any reminder is needed, that rank and power and wealth and even love – perhaps especially love – are all alike powerless against death.

He wonders how many times he has passed by them: one hundred ... two hundred? Then they had simply been old tombstones, nothing more. Now, out of nowhere, comes the eerie apprehension that he has only to look and he will see, standing in front of each stone, the near-transparent ghost of the person it commemorates, silently watching him. He forces himself to look, but all he sees are the names and images of the dead, and their relationships to those who erected the stones. And the ages of the dead.

"... He lived twenty-eight years one month and seventeen days ..." Younger than Saturninus by almost two years.

Or again, *"To the gods of the spirits of the dead and to Simplicia, daughter of Gaius Alfidius Priscus. She lived for five years, ten months and two days; a most innocent child – Sit tibi terra levis – May the earth be light for thee."*
He feels a terrible pity for them all, each alone in the endless night of death.

CHAPTER FORTY

As he clops across the bridge spanning the little River Churn, Saturninus sees the sentry at the Verulamium Gate step out into the roadway. The man holds up one hand in combined salute and indication that he has something to say. Saturninus returns the salute and asks if Canio and the prisoners have arrived.

'Oh, they got back a long time ago, sir. I wasn't even on duty then, but when I was at the barracks I saw the prisoners being led down to the cells.'

'The woman too?'

'Woman, sir? I didn't see any woman.'

Saturninus exhales loudly. He had half-expected that, knowing Canio's susceptibilities. Magnillus though ...?

'There's a message from the Prefect, sir. He left word that you're to report to him the moment you arrive.'

'Did he now? Do you know why?' Saturninus thinks he ought to ask.

'No, sir, but there's smoke in the wind, as they say. Ducenarius Canio's already gone.'

'Gone where?'

'Glevum way, apparently. That's the road they say he took.'

'But you don't know why?'

'No, sir, I do not.' The man shakes his helmeted head slowly from side to side for emphasis.

'And Centenarius Magnillus?'

'Can't say, sir. I haven't seen him at all. Perhaps he's at the barracks?'

'Yes, perhaps he is.'

Saturninus rides on into the city and there turns Antares over to Bupitus, the head ostler at the barracks' stables.

In the barracks themselves there is no sign of Magnillus. Apparently he and Canio went off together as soon as they had handed over the prisoners, but no one can say where he is now. Saturninus asks the duty centenarius if the recovered money and jewellery are under lock and key in the strongroom.

The man looks puzzled. 'What money and jewellery, sir?'

Saturninus pauses, taking in the implications of his reply. 'Never mind. If you do see Magnillus, please let him know that I've arrived back safely. I'm sure he'd want to know.'

In the anteroom to Aemilianus's office, Vitalinus briskly assures him that, yes, he is now fully recovered from the unfortunate illness that afflicted him on the journey to Fonscolnis. He also informs Saturninus that the prefect is attending a dinner party being given by Quintus Polemius Niger, one of the wealthiest landowners in the province, and that Saturninus is to report to him there, at Niger's villa just outside the city walls. After, Vitalinus adds, casting a supercilious eye over his travel-stained uniform, he has dressed suitably for the occasion.

Less than amused, Saturninus is about to point out that these last days have been rough, that he hasn't slept in a bed for the last three nights. Also that if Aemilianus doesn't like the way he looks right now, he can go jump in the Churn ... Until he again remembers Pascentia's words that came out of the mist beside that unrecognised shore ...

'Just follow wherever the roads may lead.'
Is that where you'll be – at Niger's villa? So close?

Almost running back to the Verulamium Gate, Saturninus climbs up to his room in the bastion tower, unlocks the door and collects a change of clothes. Back at the barracks he finds that the baths there have been drained and not yet refilled, so he strides the few blocks to the public baths, only to discover that their double doors are locked. He hammers impatiently until a bolt is drawn back, one leaf is cautiously opened and out pops the shaven head of Felicio – bath attendant, reputed pimp and self-proclaimed eunuch.

'Oh, it's you, Primicerius.' Felicio smiles ingratiatingly. 'Of course – although I'm afraid it will have to be the main cold pool.' He sighs with exaggerated regret. 'There was a private function for the *collegium* of iron smiths here earlier this afternoon, and now there's not so much as a drop of hot water left in the whole building. Not a single drop ... although I could light a brazier in the caldarium, should you wish it.'

Saturninus declines. He has little time. And besides, Felicio is not a man he wants to feel indebted to. 'Just bring me a strigil, an oil jar and a towel, please.' He tosses a couple of coins, which Felicio catches.

'At once, Primicerius,' he responds smoothly.

He brings the requested items, and Saturninus waits until he has, somewhat reluctantly, retreated to his lair somewhere at the back of the building. After stripping beside the cold pool, Saturninus rubs himself vigorously all over with olive oil from the mottled blue and green glass oil jar, then scrapes it off again with the curved copper strigil. The water in the pool appears uninviting, a film of scum and oil covering the surface – but he dives in anyway, the coldness of the water taking his breath away. Quickly he washes off the remaining oil, climbs out, and dries himself with the towel. After dressing in his fresh uniform he makes a bundle of the dirty one and walks out into the street, feeling clean for the first time in days.

On his way back to the barracks, carrying his old uniform under one arm, he comes to a crossroads and instinctively glances around before crossing the street. Coming towards him, no more than fifty paces away, he spots Magnillus, head down like a man walking into a gale. As sometimes happens, Magnillus seems to sense that he is being observed and suddenly looks up. Both men halt abruptly, but before Saturninus can wave or shout, Magnillus has turned and darted back along the way he came, rapidly becoming lost among the crowds.

For a few moments Saturninus, more annoyed than puzzled – he hasn't forgotten the apparently missing loot – is on the point of going after him. But Pascentia may be waiting in that villa less than half a mile away. He mentally shrugs, turns, and continues quickly on to the barracks. Magnillus can wait. Forever, if necessary.

He leaves his damaged helmet with the armourer and his dirty uniform at the barracks laundry. From there he walks briskly along the broad thoroughfare of the Via Erminus, until he arrives at the north-west angle of the city walls and the semi-circular theatre, built many years before, that stands there. Pausing for a moment he remembers how, less than a month before, he had seen the old stones come alive as the brazen voices of a troupe of touring players, grotesquely masked, had bellowed out the words of Plautus and Terentius, while five hundred noisy and excited spectators cheered and catcalled. He smiles at the recollection, wondering if the next time that troupe come to Corinium she will be sitting beside him, her head against his shoulder, the perfume of her skin only inches away.

Emerging from beneath one of the archways of the massive Glevum Gate, he returns the sentry's salute and gazes up at the sky. There are now, at most, only three hours of daylight left. And then the sun will set and the full moon will rise.

CHAPTER FORTY-ONE

The great villa of Quintus Polemius Niger stands some five hundred paces beyond the city walls of Corinium, its leafy grounds screened by a high wall of its own. As Saturninus approaches he notices two liveried guards lounging in the doorway of the stone gatehouse. He exchanges cursory nods with them, then walks on along the broad gravelled drive towards the villa. Dwarf hedges of manicured box line both sides of the drive and border geometrically-shaped planting beds where bronze fauns dance among the bright flowers and fragrant herbs of late spring.

Are you really here – returning with the spring, like Persephone?

At the main entrance, a semi-circular terrace of steps leads up to a pair of great doors, their faces covered with panels of sheet copper intricately moulded in high relief with scenes from mythology. The doors stand open. As he trots up the steps, Saturninus hears the rumble of wheels and turns to see a cart stacked high with bramble-tied bundles of brushwood coming through the gateway. He guesses it is fuel for the hypocaust stokeholes. Guesses too that the dinner party will be carrying on far into the night.

At the threshold of the wide entrance hall Saturninus is greeted by an affable chamberlain, who says that Aemilianus mentioned he might be coming. The man claps his hands and a boy of about ten seems to materialise out of nowhere and scampers up to them across the broad expanse of mosaic floor. The chamberlain whispers an instruction and the boy nods and disappears again.

As he waits, Saturninus gazes around the hall, where the walls are decorated with frescos of wild beast hunts set between panels of exotic imported marble. 'How long has the party been going on?'

'Oh, just about long enough for ...' The chamberlain lowers his voice and glances quickly behind. 'For him to have forgotten just what it was he wanted to see you about.'

Saturninus smiles, but tactfully says nothing. It seems that Aemilianus's weakness for the fermented juice of the grape is more widely known than he had realised.

But when he arrives, Aemilianus appears only slightly flushed, and that with irritation. 'Damnation, man, wherever have you been? – I needed you here hours ago.'

Saturninus manages to stifle an angry reply. 'Didn't Canio tell you – sir?'

'He said you'd gone chasing off after some mad-dog robber calling himself Carausius. He didn't say you'd be gone this long though ... Did you catch him?' Aemilianus asks, almost as an afterthought.

'I killed him with a boar spear,' Saturninus replies starkly.

Aemilianus blinks. 'Well, that's something, I suppose. Nevertheless, you really should have – '

'If it's about that report from Fonscolnis, sir,' Saturninus interrupts, 'I think I can set your mind at rest.' He wants to end this interview quickly. Pascentia will not be with Aemilianus.

'Oh that. No ... Ducenarius Canio assured me that business was concluded most satisfactorily – and those damned lying rustics taught a lesson they'll never forget, eh?'

Saturninus wonders just what tale Canio has told him? Whatever it was, it seems that Aemilianus swallowed it whole and feels much better for it.

The Prefect lowers his voice and explains, 'No, there's another matter that I, or rather His Perfection Governor Laetinianus, want investigating. There is a rumour – ' He stops abruptly, and

Saturninus realises that the door chamberlain is standing close enough to innocently overhear every word. Aemilianus's voice drops to a terse whisper. 'We can't talk here. Follow me.'

With a curious mixture of impatience and indifference, Saturninus attempts to guess what Aemilianus wants. But his heart isn't in it, because Pascentia is ...

'Where?' The word bursts out before he can stop it.

Aemilianus half turns. 'What's that you say?'

But Saturninus, gazing about him, does not reply. Aemilianus hesitates, then walks on.

They arrive at a wide corridor. On its far side, Saturninus sees three curtained-off doorways – a large central one, flanked by two smaller. From behind the central curtain comes a babble of voices. One voice, a man's, rises to make itself heard above the rest, then a roar of laughter erupts. Aemilianus pulls aside the left-hand small curtain, motions Saturninus through, then tugs it closed behind them.

They are in an annex to the triclinium, the main dining room of the villa, and separated from it by a row of columns with heavy, richly embroidered curtains hung between. A young girl household slave, waiting there to attend upon the diners if summoned, looks up nervously as they enter. Aemilianus gestures impatiently at her and she scuttles out, her bare feet pattering softly on the tessellated floor.

He peers quickly around the curtain to make sure she is not eavesdropping, then clears his throat and whispers, 'The matter that requires investigation is this: shortly after noon today, His Perfection and I were travelling back from Glevum. We had been attending a further sitting of the commission of enquiry into the tax shortfall, but His Perfection had other matters to attend to, which prevented him from staying for the entire day. You would have been there with us, of course, but for –'

Saturninus hears a shuffling of feet and an apologetic cough from outside in the corridor. A moment later the curtain is slid aside and a domestic in a brightly coloured tunic enters the annex.

Before Aemilianus can give voice to the annoyance written on his face, the man says quickly, 'It's your sister, sir. She would like a word.'

'What, now? Where is she?

'At the *praetorium*, sir – with His Perfection. She seemed most insistent, sir,' the man adds with practised humility.

Aemilianus presses his right fist into the palm of his left hand. 'Oh, very well.' To Saturninus he mutters, 'Wait here; I won't be long,' before stalking out.

Left alone, Saturninus moves quickly towards the triclinium. The annex is in deep twilight but the triclinium is brightly lit, and by the vertical flicker of light where two curtains meet he realises that a narrow slice of the room and its occupants must be visible.

Are you in there, Pascentia – only a few feet away?

He edges close to the curtains and eases them further apart, aware that his hands are trembling slightly.

Fine upholstered couches and long tables inlaid with multicoloured fruitwoods line the long sides of the room. The diner nearest to Saturninus is indeed a woman. Not Pascentia, but quite young – and beautiful too, in a taut, brittle way, although he can only glimpse her face in profile as she turns to talk or laugh with her fellow guests on either side. She wears a simple but elegantly cut dress of fine white linen, her blond hair carefully arranged in an elaborate waved coiffure. Delicate ladder-like earrings of gold filigree, set with tiny red gemstones, quiver and wink softly at the slightest movement of her head. She lies on her left side, half-supported by one elbow, and sometimes, as she turns or reaches out to the table for a cup, the thin material of her dress slips off one shoulder. And there it remains for several moments, partially exposing the curve of a white breast, before she casually hooks it back into place with two beringed fingers. There is little physical resemblance, but Saturninus recognises in her a certain cool, passive sensuality that Pascentia too possessed.

And still possesses?

Impulsively, he inches the gap between the curtains wider and looks all the way up and down the triclinium. To his dismay, he still cannot see her. What he can see, in the open space between the first tables and the entrance – where they can be viewed and admired by the diners – are the concentric rings of an Orpheus mosaic. The saviour-hero sits in the central circle, wearing a Phrygian cap and billowing cloak. He is singing – the song inaudible to the diners – and accompanying himself on his lyre, while at his feet lies a fox, listening as if entranced. In the first ring around Orpheus circle peacocks, pheasants and other exotic birds. In the outer ring, lions, spotted leopards, tigers and winged gryphons – those envoys of death – all pad docilely around. Saturninus stares at the man in the cloak, as childhood memories of the old story of Orpheus and Eurydice begin to return: Eurydice, who died, and who even Orpheus could not bring back from death.

No!

Opposite the woman with the earrings lounges a man. He is old, probably well into his fifties, but still vigorous in spite of his receding hair and near-toothless gums. These he reveals on the frequent occasions when he opens his mouth to stuff it full of the good things with which the tables are laden, or to bellow with laughter at some witticism of one of the other guests. But his eyes, muddy-green and deepset behind hooded lids, never laugh. They flicker around the tables at his fellow diners like those of a reptile, passionless and calculating. Saturninus recognises him as Gaius Papirius Cerialis, a man who owns large estates down in the south of the hills. He recalls the rumours he heard when he first returned to Corinium – of how Cerialis prospered in the dangerous times that followed the crushing of the Magnentian rebellion, now fourteen years past, by informing on those who thought him their friend. Studying that face, Saturninus suspects those rumours are true.

Again he gazes up and down the room at the other guests, in case he somehow missed ... But still he cannot see Pascentia – or any woman who resembles her. Yet there remain the inner corners of the room that his eyes cannot reach, however wide the gap.

As he stands there, irresolute, gripping the edge of the curtain, he becomes aware of a woman looking directly at him, appraising him. Saturninus returns her gaze, almost angrily, and sees her blush slightly before turning her head away. He releases the curtain and starts listening intently, wondering if he can recognise Pascentia's voice among that sea of voices, where the waves rise and fall and are never still.

He hears someone – a woman – telling the story of how Procopius, the usurper emperor who seized power in Constantinopolis some two years before, had been executed almost a year ago to this very day. Of how he was said to have been torn apart, tied between two trees which had been bent over and lashed together, and then the connecting ropes slashed. The story produces another roar of laughter.

Suddenly someone claps their hands. Saturninus hears a swish as the great curtain at the end of the room is pulled aside, then watches as twenty or so domestic slaves, male and female, file quickly past, each carrying either a great silver dish or two flagons of wine. The dishes of the *gustatio* first course have all been eaten or discarded, and coming now are the first dishes of the main course, the *primae mensae*. Three salvers bear steaming roast suckling pigs, at least half a dozen more carry roast fowl, and two deep bowls rattle with oysters which, he guesses, have been brought up live from Glevum in barrels of brine only a few hours before.

He glimpses dormice and hares, plump with savoury stuffings, on glistening beds of spiced spring cabbages; also several broad platters of honey omelettes. The domestics deftly remove the remains of the *gustatio*, refill the various wine goblets – some of silver, some of pale green or amber Rhenish glass – replace the finger bowls and the napkins of fine white linen, and then withdraw as quickly and silently as they came. Several begin exiting through the annex, not realising that Saturninus is standing there. And as they push through the curtains, he at last glimpses the occupants of the couches in the corners of the triclinium. None is Pascentia. A rush of desolation sweeps over him, but with it also a curious feeling of relief that she is not there; not among those, to him, estranged and estranging people.

CHAPTER FORTY-TWO

Shortly afterwards Aemilianus returns, still looking irritable.

'Right – the Glevum commission … The fact is, that on our way back we came across the carriage of Decurion Orbissus. One of its axles had broken, and His Perfection stopped and invited him to accompany us for the rest of the journey. Orbissus was returning from Glevum too, from business of some kind down at the docks.'

'Probably seeing his fleeces safely loaded – he ships thousands from there at this time of year,' Saturninus reminds him distractedly, his churning thoughts elsewhere.

'Yes, that's right – I remember him saying now … The point is though, he also said that he was told by the captain of a grain ship which moored at the docks early this morning, that …' Aemilianus's voice drops to a conspiratorial whisper. 'That one of the crew had seen what he swore was a Hibernian curragh – that's what they call those barbarian long boats made of hides – skulking in a creek on the other side of the estuary.'

Aemilianus appears to have forgotten that it was Saturninus who first described a curragh to him. Saturninus does not remind him: he wants this interview over quickly.

'Where was this curragh?'

'I don't know exactly. From what Orbissus said, it could have been anywhere between fifteen and twenty miles downstream from Glevum. That's one of the things I sent Ducenarius Canio back to Glevum to find out … And he should have been back by now: I can't think what's keeping the man?'

Knowing Canio, Saturninus could hazard several guesses. But he says nothing.

'His Perfection was most anxious that you should have been the one to go to Glevum, but I had to explain that you were still unavoidably detained. He did, however, insist that I told you personally as soon as you returned.'

'So you're taking this information seriously then?' Saturninus is aware of several reports of curraghs seen on the estuary that have crossed his desk over the past few years, none of them confirmed by anyone that Aemilianus considered a reliable witness.

'Yes, of course I am. The point,' Aemilianus goes on confidingly, 'is that His Perfection was somewhat alarmed by it ... I'm sure you understand why.'

Saturninus does understand why. He has heard from several sources that *vir perfectissimus*, Marcus Antistius Laetinianus, *praeses* of the province of Britannia Prima, has in the last months developed an irrational foreboding of a barbarian invasion. He has also heard that it is something of a standing joke at dinner parties.

'Well, if there really is a curragh on the Sabrina, then that sailor can't be the only one who's seen it. Has anyone gone down and spoken to the local fishermen? Even a coracle couldn't slip upriver without one of them spotting it – the tide rules their lives and they're out on the estuary at all times of the day and night.'

Aemilianus frowns. 'But surely, if one of them had seen it, they'd have reported it to us – wouldn't they?'

Saturninus suspects that Aemilianus has never met any Sabrina fishermen. 'Not necessarily.' He thinks it would be unwise to point out that those wiry, elemental men have little love for a civil guard which enforces payment of taxes in hard-earned silver coin. Also, that they worship strange gods – gods whose altars are sometimes seen smoking on the foreshore and whose tiny wooden images they take with them as they fish out on the broad estuary.

Aemilianus grunts. 'Well, if a curragh has been seen on the Sabrina, then some word of it may have filtered through to our garrisons in the south-west of the hills by now ... Maybe Ovilregis would know?'

'That's possible,' Saturninus confirms, and waits, suddenly aware of ...

Another road to follow? Another road that might lead nowhere? And yet, it leads south, which was where ...

'And if you left now,' Aemilianus continues, 'you could be at Ovilregis by nightfall. You could find out if they've heard anything there, then perhaps at dawn travel on down to the estuary and make further enquiries ... And I could tell His Perfection that you'll be back by this time tomorrow.' Saturninus notices that the Prefect does not look directly at him as he speaks – as if he is anticipating dissent, perhaps aware that the journey may well turn out to be a fool's errand.

But Saturninus does not dissent. 'Is that where the road is leading?' he murmurs. 'To Ovilregis ... or perhaps to the estuary at dawn?' Vivid in his mind now is that image of Pascentia standing alone on an unknown shore.

Whatever Aemilianus hears, or imagines he hears, he appears to take it as acquiescence. 'You can take with you as many men as you want, of course.'

Saturninus thinks he sounds relieved.

'No, I'd prefer to go alone.' Aemilianus looks as if he is about to object, but before he can do so, Saturninus forestalls him. 'If necessary, I can always take a couple of troopers from Ovilregis with me to the estuary. They'll have a better knowledge of the people and the country down there.'

Aemilianus wavers, then says 'As you wish ... Well, that's settled then.'

But Saturninus is once more looking through the gap in the curtains, into the triclinium beyond, uneasily aware of what it is about the Orpheus mosaic that keeps drawing his eyes back to it. 'They say he went down into the Lower World to bring the woman he loved back from death.'

'What? Who did?'

'Orpheus,' Saturninus murmurs, gazing at the man in the billowing cloak. He glances back at Aemilianus.

The Prefect is looking at him blankly.

'Doesn't the old story say that he begged Hades to let Eurydice return with him from the land of the dead? And that Hades agreed – but only on condition that Orpheus should never once look back at her until they both stood in the light of this world? And that as soon as he emerged into the daylight he looked back to see her sweet face. But she was still in shadow, so Hades dragged her back down into the Lower World and never again let her return.'

At last Aemilianus understands. 'Oh, you mean the mosaic in the triclinium?' He joins Saturninus beside the curtain and whispers, 'But we no longer regard that man in the cloak as being the Orpheus of the old blasphemous myths. We see him as Our Saviour, the Good Shepherd, sitting at the centre of the world. See – how he guards his flock of winged souls destined for Paradise, protecting them from the ravening beasts that prowl all around us in this fearful world.'

But Saturninus barely hears him. 'Perhaps the dead – even the dead who are still loved by the living – can never come back from the Land of Darkness? Is that the real message of the Orpheus story?' He turns to Aemilianus, but the Prefect is frowning again, his face taking on the affronted look Saturninus recognises as signalling that further discussion would be futile.

But you're not dead, Pascentia. You're still in this world – maybe at Ovilregis, or maybe somewhere beside the estuary at dawn. But wherever you are, I'm now certain that I'll find you before this coming night is over.

He says quickly, 'If that's all then, sir, I'll get back to the city and be away.'

Aemilianus appears to relax. 'Yes, of course ... and even if you don't reach Ovilregis by nightfall, there should be a good moon to light your way.'

'To light my way to her?' Saturninus wonders aloud.

Aemilianus's mouth purses but, before he can ask, Saturninus salutes, slips through the curtain and is gone.

Another roar of laughter comes from the triclinium, and Aemilianus's thoughts turn back to the dinner party. With any luck they won't have finished the first of the *primae mensae* courses yet, with at least another four or five more still to come before the desserts, if Niger is on his customary form. He brushes imagined dust from the chest of his dress uniform, then eases aside a curtain and returns to a more comfortable world.

CHAPTER FORTY-THREE

Saturninus retraces his steps back to the Glevum Gate, then hurries through the still-bustling city to the barrack stables. Once there, he orders Bupitus to re-saddle Antares and waits with patient impatience for the job to be done. Almost without realising he is doing so, he begins whistling a jaunty marching tune from his army days.

Perhaps surprised to find him so cheerful, Bupitus ventures to ask where he is going.

'Wherever the roads may lead.' Seeing the puzzled look on the ostler's face, Saturninus adds, 'I'm running a little errand for Aemilianus – should be back late tomorrow.'

He starts whistling again and begins walking Antares through the streets towards the Aquae Sulis Gate, from where the Fosse Way continues on southwards to that city. Suddenly he remembers the lyre – the lyre whose music she had loved. Impulsively he turns back, leaves Antares with Bupitus, and dashes up to his high room beside the Verulamium Gate. There he collects the lyre from where he had left it, propped against the wall, nearly four days ago. He hesitates, then rummages deep in the oak chest that stands near his bed and extracts a small leather bag containing ten gold solidi and some twenty siliquae. He fully intends to return to Corinium, and yet …. Instinct is driving him now.

Descending the staircase he strums a few slow chords on the lyre, savouring the notes and the memories they recall. Under Bupitus's quizzical gaze he carefully stows it in one of Antares' saddlebags before starting off again.

When he reaches the Sulis Gate he mounts and starts riding away from the city, past the great amphitheatre, the elliptically curved mounds of which are bright with fresh green grass and starred with yellow buttercups and white daisies. It appears so peaceful now, in the early evening sunshine, with a gaggle of small, ragged children laughing and shouting as they chase each other up and down the outer slopes. He envies them for their innocence of the terrible things that men have done, and will yet do, in the broad, grassy bowl below.

Light and darkness mingled.

After a mile or so he halts and looks back at the city. He sees the limestone of its walls glowing falsely golden in the sunlight, and tiny black figures moving slowly near the Sulis Gate. Already it seems so small and far away, slipping into unreality like a dream. Shortly after the second milepost he branches off the Fosse Way and onto the broad trackway that winds westwards towards the town of Vicus Ovilregis, some fourteen miles further on.

He notices how warm and tranquil the world seems, and fresh-new as spring glides into summer like a girl into womanhood. How the iron-hard, deeply fissured bark of the ancient wayside oaks contrasts so mysteriously with their tender new leaves, the ancient magic of the re-birth of green life from where, in the depths of winter, it had seemed gone forever.

Above, in the blue, almost cloudless sky, swallows wheel and swoop in their pursuit of flying insects; and from far away drifts the call of a cuckoo, that herald of summer. At a stream he pauses to let Antares drink from the cool, clear water that rushes and gurgles over its bed of yellowish gravel.

Memories of Pascentia drift through his mind as he waits for Antares to finish drinking, and later too, as the horse trots briskly on towards Ovilregis, the low sun on his right shoulder. He is restlessly aware that soon the full moon will rise in the east.

But where will we be as we watch it set in tomorrow's dawn?

As he canters westwards he watches the progress of the sun as it sinks in the north-west sky. At first a fiery disc of pale gold, flooding the evening countryside with a pure, warm light – a light in which the fields, trees, grasses and flowers stand out with a softly startling beauty and clarity that he has never noticed so intensely before. Later, as it begins to dip below the horizon, glowing now like red-hot iron pulled from a blacksmith's forge, so the shadows grow ever longer. Single trees cast their dark ghosts across whole fields, and the faint breeze from the south-west freshens.

He makes good progress along the winding trackway, rutted and ridged though it is by the wheels of carts that trundled along it through the winter mud. Even so, by the time he rides into the outskirts of Ovilregis, the red sun has already disappeared below a thin band of cloud on the horizon.

The town occupies a broad peninsular of rolling plateau land, beyond which, to the west, the hills drop down to the plain of the great Sabrina estuary in a series of deep coombs and broken, time-softened spurs.

The Ovilregis he sees is a sprawling town of workshops and forges that grew up inside the boundaries of what was once a great imperial estate. Even so, it can boast some impressive villas: villas with stone walls, great expanses of diamond-shaped stone roof tiles, and frescoed wall paintings and floor mosaics which rival the best in Corinium.

The main streets are metalled and kept in good repair by those same men who own the villas, and it is down these streets that Saturninus trots Antares in this time of dying light, between the setting of the sun and the rising of the moon.

By the time he reaches the civil guard post, dusk has already drained the colours from the land. Vaulting out of the saddle, he ties Antares' reins to a rail, raps on the door, waits a few moments, then unlatches it and steps inside.

CHAPTER FORTY-FOUR

The full moon is rising.

Saturninus has no intention of staying long in the guard post. He mentions the reported sighting of the Hibernian curragh to all the men present, but none has heard the rumour themselves. He is not surprised: Ulpius Vassedo, the centenarius, confirms that such tales are not uncommon – says that he has heard at least one in every year of the four he's been stationed at Ovilregis. Also, that he's yet to meet anyone who can swear that they've actually seen one of the curraghs themselves. Saturninus shrugs, tells them that this particular rumour has chanced to come to the ears of Governor Laetinianus – which produces a few wry grins and shaking of heads – and asks them to make their own enquiries in the morning. Discreetly, of course.

He takes a swift drink of wine with them, and listens politely as they recount a few items of local gossip – the interesting things that rarely find their way into official reports. But he declines their offer of further hospitality, mindful that the last thing soldiers really want is the presence of their primicerius when they are trying to relax. Besides, he is on fire with the thought that Pascentia may be somewhere out there in the streets, perhaps only yards away. Hurriedly he takes off his cuirass and requests Vassedo to keep it safe, saying that he will collect it later. He hesitates, then also asks him to stable Antares for the night.

'If anyone does hear anything about that curragh, I'll be over at The Cockerel,' is the last thing he says before he swings the outer door closed behind him.

Now dusk has shaded into actual night, but at last the full moon is rising. His pulse quickening, Saturninus begins wandering through the streets until he comes to a crossroads. There he halts and stares up at that moon, huge and low and pale gold in the south-eastern sky, its seas greyish-blue. It shines down, lighting the streets half as bright as day and casting, sharp and black, the moving, criss-crossing shadows of the men and women who pass. He walks slowly on, heading in the general direction of The Golden Cockerel inn on the other side of the town. As he walks he studies each pale female face that goes by. None is hers. Several times in the eerie streets he stops and waits. Waits for her to come. Others come and go, but never her. Time passes, and insidiously there comes again the memory of the vision in Leucesca's spring – of Pascentia standing on what he had thought then was the shore of some unknown sea, but now believes was the Sabrina estuary. Torn, he wonders if he should return to the guard post. If he leaves now, he could arrive at the estuary at around midnight, then begin searching along the shoreline in the moonlight. Racked by indecision, he paces ever more slowly through the moonlit streets until he is no more than a hundred yards from The Cockerel. Then, impulsively, he turns and begins hurrying back towards the guard post, convinced now that she must be somewhere on the estuary shore.

But, as he approaches the guard post for the second time, the uncertainties return.

If I search the estuary shore and can't find her there … what then?

His hand is actually on the door latch when some instinct compels him to turn, to look once more at the great moon in the south-eastern sky. And as he does so he sees a face – her face – on the bright surface of the moon. Only for a moment, then it is gone. But it is enough. Like a man in a trance, he starts walking towards that moon, towards her. He walks through the maze of streets, slowly while he can see it, hurrying when roofs and trees block his view, until at last he stands on the southern edge of the town. And there he waits, oblivious to the passage of time, staring up at the moon, waiting for her to appear again.

Occasionally people come and go. He pays them no heed, until, directly below the moon, he hears soft footfalls on the stony track leading up from one of the narrow coombs. Looking down he sees the dark outline of a woman approaching. When she is no more than twenty yards away, before he can see her face clearly, she halts in the deep shadow cast by a distant tree.

He stares wildly towards her, almost certain, yet fearful that it might once again be the woman of the crossroads.

'Saturninus?'

It is her voice.

'Pascentia?' His heart is beating so violently in his throat that he can barely speak her name.

Time stops as that word hangs motionless in the air, and then the figure begins walking slowly out of the tree-shadow until she stands silently before him in a pool of moonlight.

'Is it really you?' he whispers. Trembling slightly, he reaches out and touches her hair, her forehead, then runs the tips of his fingers down one side of her face, over her cheek in a slow curve that halts beside her mouth.

Gently she takes his hand and moves his fingers over her lips. He feels something warm and moist touch the pads of his fingers, one by one, and suddenly he is back on board the *Zephyrus* as it sails out of the Rhine delta and into the great, shining sea beyond, the tang of the warm salt breeze mingling with the scent of her hair.

'Where have – ?'

She releases his hand. 'Hold me!' Her voice is low, husky, urgent.

He moves closer, one hand curving around the small of her back as he draws her against his body. She seems thinner than he remembers, but just as real, just as warm, just as yielding.

And suddenly she is sobbing uncontrollably, tremors shaking her whole body. Saturninus holds her, rocking her slightly from side to side like a child, until at last she calms and whispers, 'I thought I'd never find you ... I seem to have been journeying alone for ever.' Then she starts sobbing again.

Saturninus can still hardly believe she is here. 'Hush ... hush,' he murmurs gently. There are a thousand things he wants to say to her, but somehow, at this moment ...

They stand there in the moonlight, still as trees. Saturninus feels the growing warmth of her body against his own and the wild beating of her heart – or perhaps it is his own? At last he finds his voice again and whispers, 'Where have you been these three long years? I thought ... everyone I met said that no ship ever built could have come through that storm.'

'Nothing came through the storm. Except me, it seems.'

'So what happened? Tell me.'

She turns her head away. 'It's all so ... confused. I have a recurring memory of seeing barrels on the deck of the *Zephyrus* breaking loose and tumbling over and over into the sea. And those terrible screams ... I heard them even above the howling of the wind. And then I was under that sea and ...'

'And what?'

'I ... No, not here,' she whispers.

Saturninus looks up and sees that they are being watched. The man moves on as soon as he realises they are aware of his presence, but something of their intimacy departs with him.

'This way – I know where we can be alone.' He takes Pascentia's hand and begins leading her gently towards The Golden Cockerel, through the silent streams of light and darkness flowing across the streets. There are still a thousand things he wants to say to her, to ask her, but in these first ecstatic moments he is content with the touch of her warm fingers against the palm of his own hand.

His heart is singing like a bird. And then, out of nowhere, it comes to him that this must be how Orpheus felt as he led Eurydice up out of the darkness of Hades' kingdom. It is an unnerving thought. Instinctively he grips her hand tighter and starts walking faster, until she is almost running beside him as he hurries her along. But he does not dare turn his head to look at her face until they are both standing, breathless, below the large oil lamp that burns in a window above the front door of The Cockerel. There he swings around and draws her closely against his body, and only then, with her trapped safe in his arms, do his eyes seek her face again. She smiles up at him, her eyes shining in the lamplight, and he kisses her forehead. At any other time he might have cursed himself for a fool for giving way to such a superstitious fear. But not this night. In this time of magical reunion there has come, like the snake in the Christian Eden, the terror that Pascentia might vanish as suddenly and mysteriously as she appeared.

There are a dozen or so people already in The Cockerel, sitting at tables or lounging around the bar. Saturninus recognises a good number of them, and they him. He returns their greetings affably, noticing, but not satisfying, the curiosity which his arrival with Pascentia has aroused. He walks over to the bar and speaks quietly to Necalames, the little man with jet-black hair and olive skin who runs the inn. Necalames nods vigorously and replies, 'At once, Primicerius,' then disappears into one of the back rooms. Moments later he re-appears with a boy of about twelve, giving him whispered instructions which he concludes with a soft cuff around the ear. 'Huctius here will show you up, Primicerius.'

As if anxious to avoid another cuff, the boy begins scurrying towards the foot of the long timber staircase that leads up to the first floor.

'The taper, boy, don't forget the taper!' Necalames smiles apologetically to Saturninus as Huctius sulkily retraces his steps and takes the long waxed taper from the little man's outstretched hand.

At the top of the stairs, Huctius pauses to light the taper from the large lamp that burns there. The boy walks on to the end of the wide corridor, then halts and unlatches the door to one of the rooms. Saturninus and Pascentia follow, and as the door swings open a stream of moonlight flows out and over her. She looks so startlingly beautiful, standing there bathed in its unearthly light, that Saturninus, without conscious thought, stretches out a hand and lightly strokes her hair. He waits until the boy has lit the four lamps that hang from the ornamental bronze stand just inside the doorway, then ushers Pascentia inside.

Huctius hesitates in the doorway. 'Necalames says I'm to bring your meals up as soon as they're ready.'

'That will be fine, thank you.' Saturninus smiles and closes the door behind the boy.

Lifting the tall lamp stand one-handed, he sets it gently down beside the table in the centre of the room, unhooks two of the lamps and re-hangs them up as high as they will go. Two big wicker armchairs with high, curved backs have been placed on opposite sides of the table. He waves Pascentia towards the nearest. The brilliant moonlight floods through the windows, competing with the lamplight and casting across the floorboards the patterns, greatly elongated, of the star-shaped iron grilles that hold the window glass in place. A stray shaft of moonlight falls across the large bed in one corner of the room, picking out the edge of the sheets that have been turned back invitingly. He walks over and draws the curtains across both windows, hesitates, then tugs them open again, suddenly fearful of shutting out this moon that has brought her back to him.

When he turns back from the windows she is still standing beside the table. Silently, in the sparkling radiance of the oil lamps, they study each other. Her face is certainly a little thinner than he remembers, and paler too. But the way she catches and returns his gaze with one simultaneously both shy and self-possessed, serious yet always on the point of smiling, that has not changed. And yet he senses a nervousness about her ... or perhaps it is his own. He wants to say something – anything – to break the silence.

He moves towards her, but she turns her head away slightly,

and gracefully settles herself into one of the armchairs, smoothing her pale blue dress behind her with both hands as she sits. Three years, he reflects, is a long time apart. Perhaps too long? And yet, back there in the streets ... But in the streets the half-light had hidden as much as it revealed. Here, in the unsparing light, emotions are naked, cautious, unsure. He pulls out the other armchair and sits down, facing her.

She is the first to break the silence. 'So ... what have you been doing with yourself these last three years, soldier? Married, with three lusty infants? Or not married, but still with three lusty infants? – in different towns, of course.' The words are bantering, but he picks up the anxiety in her voice.

'There's no one else,' he replies quietly. 'And there never was – not from that first day we met beside the Moselle.' He reaches out and takes her right hand. He feels the need to touch her – both to reassure her, and to reassure himself of her physical reality. His thumb slowly strokes her palm; then he lifts it and kisses each finger in turn.

'You mean ... you knew I'd come back some day?' There is a challenge, almost a hardness in her voice.

He hesitates, wondering just how much these long three years have estranged her from him. 'No ... I thought ...' He still holds her hand.

'That I was dead?'

The directness of the question disconcerts him, but he cannot avoid answering. 'Yes ... Everybody did.' There is a long silence, then he says, 'If I'd thought it was even remotely possible that ... How *did* you manage to survive that storm?'

'Your story first,' she replies lightly. 'That's a civil guard uniform you're wearing, isn't it?'

He looks into her eyes, but she turns her head away: she will tell her own story in her own time. 'It is indeed. Madam, you have the honour to be addressing the primicerius of the Corinium troop of the corps of *beneficiarii*, commonly known as the civil guard.'

'My, I am impressed. Should I salute, or merely sigh and clasp both hands to my heart?'

'Most of the local maidens do one or the other. A few do both.'

Her lips part in the beginnings of a smile. 'How long ...?'

Perhaps, he thinks, it is only his conscience that makes him hear accusation in those two little words. 'Oh, quite a while now.' He pauses, then says, 'Contrary to what we were told, it took only two days and five solidi each to persuade those damned tax assessors to go away. And back in the harbour I found Julius Stertinus about to sail, so I begged a passage back to Londinium with him.'

'Did the storm hit you too?'

'Only its very edge, but that was bad enough. That's why ...' But he wants to talk, to let her hear his voice, to let her know that he is still the same man she kissed and embraced on the quay at Burdigala.

'We stopped at a small port on the western tip of Brittany, and the people there said it had been the worst summer storm in living memory – that no ship could have survived it. After that, we hugged the coast of Gaul all the way to Bononia, looking for the *Zephyrus*, or any trace of it. But we found nothing. So in the end we sailed back to Londinium. And there I waited and waited, until everyone said there was no hope of you ever coming back ...'

Who excuses himself accuses himself.

They won't go away, those feelings of guilt. Saturninus looks down and traces the wavy grain pattern on the elm table top with one fingertip. 'Afterwards, I went to Corinium, and ... here I am.' He shrugs. 'Your turn now.'

'Yes, my turn now,' she repeats. 'Except that ...'

'What?'

Before Pascentia can answer, there comes a soft tapping at the door. 'That must be our supper,' Saturninus murmurs. Turning towards the door he calls out, 'Come on in.'

The door opens and the boy, Huctius, enters carrying a large tray on which are arranged two bowls of steaming soup and two small loaves of bread. He sets the tray down on the table, then goes back into the corridor and returns with an elaborately embossed pewter flagon and two wine cups of the same metal.

Saturninus thanks him, then tosses him a siliqua. 'See that we're not disturbed. I'll bring the bowls and the rest down myself when we're finished.'

Huctius scuttles out, staring down at the little silver coin as if he can scarcely believe his luck.

After the door has closed, Saturninus waits for a few moments, then asks, 'Except that, what?'

'Oh, nothing.' She says it lightly enough, but Saturninus noticed that she frowned slightly as she spoke, as if something remembered, or not remembered, is troubling her. But before he can ask, she says quickly, 'How did you get that gash on your head?'

He had guessed she would ask that. 'Quelling a riot in a brothel – the girls had heard a rumour that I wasn't going to pay them all my usual visit last night ... Don't worry,' he adds, 'the rumour was completely untrue.'

She grins and shakes her head in mock disapproval. 'Liar. How *did* you get it?' She seems more relaxed now.

But I haven't forgotten that troubled look.

'I'll tell you later. Come on, it's still your turn.'

CHAPTER FORTY-FIVE

Now it is Pascentia who stares mutely down at the table top, and Saturninus begins to think that she really doesn't want to tell him. He wonders if he should say, as casually as he can, that it doesn't matter, that she can tell him whenever she chooses.

But then she says, in a voice little more than a whisper, 'That terrible storm ...We were somewhere off the northern coast of Brittany, making good time with a warm south-westerly wind behind us. At first the storm was just a line of darkness, far away out on the Western Ocean. I hardly noticed it, but the sailors knew what it was and they begged Metilius to run for the coast, which was only a mile away.

'But even then it was too late. The wind suddenly strengthened and veered to the west, and all we could do was run eastwards, as all the while the sky behind us turned black as night and the wind rose to a howl. It was nightmarish how fast it came – like a great ravening beast bounding across the ocean towards us.'

He notices that she seems to be staring through the windows, as if out there in the moonlit night she can picture the storm raging again. She shakes her head, as if to drive the vision away, and continues calmly.

'Then the howling darkness was all around us. And the sea, which had been so bright and sparkling such a short time before, became like surging hills and valleys of dark water – hills that rose up, higher and higher all around the ship, until they seemed to shut out the sky. I saw Metilius clinging to the ropes which held down a stack of barrels. He was screaming something to me, but the cruel wind broke up his words and scattered them away like ...'

Like those beech leaves on the road to Fonscolnis? Like our lives?

He wonders what memories her mind is conjuring now, but before he can decide how to tactfully ask, she murmurs, 'Moments afterwards there came a great mountain of a wave. For an eternal moment it hung motionless above us, then it crashed down on the ship with a roar like a thousand thunderbolts. The next thing I remember, I was under the sea, and there was salt water in my mouth and a strange singing in my ears.

'But slowly the singing and the pain in my chest faded, and I opened my eyes. It seemed so very peaceful there, far beneath those fearful waves, and I felt myself drifting away, light and free as a dandelion seed on the summer breeze. All that I remember clearly, but ...'

'But what?' Saturninus asks gently. Her face has that distant, puzzled look again.

'The things that happened after the storm,' she replies slowly, 'I remember them of course, but not so well as the storm itself. It's as though I'm seeing them through poor window glass ... all dark and blurred.'

Saturninus rationalises, trying to suppress a little voice of unfocussed unease inside him. 'That's not so surprising: you almost died in that storm. It must have been like it is in battle – when you sometimes remember every moment because each and every one might be your last. Memories of things that happen afterwards, even years afterwards, never seem so vivid.'

'Yes, that's what I tell myself. But it's a strange feeling, isn't it, when even the past seems uncertain?'

He catches the wistfulness in her voice and asks, 'What happened when you reached the surface again? Did you find yourself next to a floating barrel or ...?'

'No, I don't think so – or perhaps I might have done ... I just don't know. The next thing I really remember is feeling the hot sun warming me, and life flowing back into my body as I lay on the hard, wave-rippled sand of a beach, my dress all sodden and clinging to me. I lay there, while the sun shone down and dried me as I drifted in and out of sleep. Later, I heard the distant roar of waves and realised that the tide was coming in again. So I crawled further up the beach, then stood up, weak as a new-born baby.

'I saw the beach curving away in both directions. Deserted. No barrels, no timbers ... no bodies. Nothing at all. Only the beach and the sea and the great sky. And the dunes, tall, dotted with patches of spiky grass. They shut out sight of the land beyond. So I struggled up through the soft, dry sand to the top, and from there I could see for miles inland across the green countryside. Far away I saw two riders, so I waved to them. They spotted me, and I thought they'd help me. But they turned out to be bailiffs from the estate of the great man who owned all the land in those parts, and they took me there and made me a slave.'

'Even after you'd told them who you were and how you came to be there?'

Pascentia bites her lower lip and gives a little shake of her head. 'They just laughed. They said that, whatever I once had been, I was nothing now.'

'Vermin!' Saturninus mutters. Then he asks softly, 'How bad was it there?'

She doesn't answer immediately, then says, 'Let's not talk about it – not now. In any case, I can't recall much about my time there.'

'No.' Saturninus assumes she doesn't want to remember ... or perhaps tell. 'How did you get free?'

She pulls a fragment of bread from her loaf and dips it into the soup. 'I was out working in the fields, when a man I didn't recognise came riding up to the overseers. He gabbled something and waved his arms a lot, then he and the overseers went galloping off in the direction of the great villa. I was too far away to hear properly what he said, but someone who was closer told me that a war band of Saxons had landed and was marching towards the villa.'

'It was a long way west for Saxons.'

Pascentia shrugs. 'Yes, I suppose it was. Perhaps they weren't Saxons. Perhaps they were only *bacaudae* – wandering men. But whoever they were, they were my salvation. When the overseers were out of sight, I took my chance and ran. I didn't stop, even when night came ... I have a dreamlike memory of running through an endless night, always fearful that if I stopped, even for a moment, someone or something would seize me and drag me back to that awful place. But dawn did at last come, and when it came my pursuers faded away like the phantoms they were.

'By then, I was totally exhausted. I slept all that day in a great green forest, and when night came I started south again, the moon and the stars my only guides. As the days and miles passed I began travelling in daylight, and at last, weeks later, I walked into Burdigala. I found a couple of Metilius's old wine trade friends there, men who'd been looking after his vineyard, and they took me in.'

She makes it sound so simple: Saturninus knows it could not have been anything of the sort. 'But how did you live during those weeks?' he asks gently. 'Getting food and avoiding slave bailiffs ...?'

'I ... don't exactly recall. Does it matter?' She hesitates, then says, 'Metilius's friends begged me to stay, but after a couple of weeks I said I had to come back here to ...' She gives him a quick, wan smile. 'Do you remember our little villa there, in the vineyard? I know you only spent a few nights there, but ...'

'Did you really think I'd forget? I remember as if it were yesterday – especially your room, and the little bronze figurine of Aurora that stood on the window ledge ... and the first rays of the rising sun that lit it like a flame and cast its shadow across your bed like a sundial.'

She smiles again, a happier smile now. The old smile. 'That villa is so beautiful, nestling amongst the endless rows of vines. Especially in the spring, when the new leaves are all fresh and green ... and in the autumn too, when the leaves are colouring yellow and the vines are heavy with dark grapes. It's mine now, they said. That's why they couldn't understand why I wouldn't stay. We could go back there, Saturninus, you and I.'

'We could go anywhere in this wide world.' He thinks he understands what she is trying to say – that it is the future that matters, not the past. 'And while in Burdigala I suppose you asked around among the merchants and sailors who traded with Londinium, and eventually discovered that I'd gone back to these hills?'

I won't tell you that it was Viventia who told me – not yet. That just might lead to Caelofernus, and that story can wait for another day.

'That was a very good guess.' Her eyes narrow and she tilts her head to one side, as if about to ask if it is something more than guesswork. But then she says, 'And a merchant in Metilius's old guild had a ship sailing for Londinium that was going to drop off part of its cargo at Abona, so ...'

'Here you are.'

'Here I am.' She gives a conjurer's flourish with both hands spread wide.

'Pascentia ...'

'Yes?'

'When you were in Burdigala, did you hear anything of Metilius?'

She sips the wine. 'This is so like one he used to import ... No, nothing. Not from the locals, not from sailors and merchants who'd been back and forth to Londinium in these past three years. He's dead, Saturninus. Him and all the crew. They all drowned in that terrible storm. And he was so kind to me, even when I was young and he could have done whatever he wanted with me and nobody would have cared.'

Saturninus looks into her eyes and sees that they are moist with incipient tears. He reaches across and gently squeezes her hand.

She slides her free hand over his. 'We lost each other for three long years, Saturninus. Promise me that we'll never lose each other again?' He hears the urgency and, for a moment, something close to fear in her voice. But before he can reply she says, almost as if it were a confession, 'Once, on the long journey down to Burdigala, I stood on the top of a high hill and looked for miles and miles over all the land around – way, way into the distance. In all my life I never felt such intense loneliness as I did at that moment. I longed for you to be there, standing beside me with your arm around my shoulder, comforting me, giving me strength.

'But of course, you weren't there. Or anywhere, in all that great emptiness that stretched to the horizon so far away. Up there on that hill, where the tallest trees, and even whole towns, dwindled away to nothing in the distance, I realised how tiny we both were, and how immense the world. And then all the fears and jealousies that I'd managed to push away for so long came back to torment me. I thought you might have found a new love, with me quite forgotten. Or that you might be dead, or simply lost to me in the vastness of the world, so that I might wander alone for the rest of my days and never find you.'

He squeezes her hand tighter. 'But now we *have* found each other again. We can't change the past: it happened. But now it's gone – gone forever – and only this moment and the future matter – a future where not even Hades himself can ever part us again.' At the back of his mind there still lingers an image of that Orpheus mosaic.

'Hush, you mustn't say that!'

'Why not?'

'I ... don't know.' Saturninus glimpses that uncertain look again. She asks quickly, 'You never did say how you came to be here in Ovilregis tonight?'

So he tells her about the rumoured sighting of the Hibernian curragh on the Sabrina and how, in the morning, he had been planning to ride on down to the estuary to discover if anyone there had seen it.

And when he has finished she says, 'How strange, the way

these things happen ...' He looks at her questioningly and she explains, 'As I was walking up along the estuary from Abona, I met a fisherman called Trencorix. I knew him when I was a child, although I hadn't seen him for years. We got to talking, and I remember him saying that he'd seen what might have been a curragh drifting down the estuary, although he admitted that it was too far away for him to be really sure.'

'When was this – I mean, when did he see the curragh?'

'Why, last night, I think.'

'Yes, I suppose that would fit.' He sighs. 'So, come the dawn, I'll have to go and see your friend Trencorix. Where does he live?'

'He has a little house on the edge of a grove of trees, not far from the great red and grey cliffs at Aust ... But in the morning he'll probably be out on the estuary in his coracle, netting the fish that come upriver with the tide.'

'For how long?'

'It depends on his luck, I suppose. But even after he's caught all he can, he'll let the current carry him down to Abona. Most of the fishermen sell their catch there.'

Saturninus sees a look almost of pain flicker across her face.

She groans. 'Oh no, does that mean ...?'

'What choice do I have?' he replies quietly.

'But he wasn't even sure that it was a curragh – he said it could have been just a floating log.'

'But if it was a curragh ...?'

There is a long silence, then she says, 'All right – but I'll come with you.'

'No!'

'But it's a long way, and you'll never find Trencorix's house without me – not in the dark.'

'There'll be moonlight, and I'll take one of the troopers from the garrison here to guide me.'

'Do you think he'll know where it is? Anyway, you'll feel such a fool if it does turn out to have been only an old tree trunk that Trencorix saw.' Seeing him waver, she touches her hair and adds, 'Of course, if you'd prefer the company of some big hairy trooper, grumbling about missing his beauty sleep, as you ride through the romantic moonlight …'

She gives him an exaggerated grin. It is the same Pascentia who captivated him on the voyage back from the Moselle those three years ago. Even as he allows himself to be persuaded he knows that he would never – could never – leave her on this night. For the terror that she might vanish again, as suddenly and mysteriously as she appeared, has not wholly left him. 'Drink your soup before it gets cold,' he whispers, by way of conceding defeat.

They finish their meal in near-silence, but now it is the silence of intimacy, where no words are necessary. Afterwards, Saturninus stands and pours himself another cup of wine, then offers to refill her own.

'Please,' she replies. 'What shall we drink to?'

'To ourselves. To long life and happiness – perhaps somewhere far away.'

They bring their cups together with a soft clink and look into each other's eyes.

'Long life and happiness.' First he, then she, speak the words, then they drink.

'How long before Trencorix sets out to go fishing?' Saturninus asks softly.

'I don't exactly know – it'll depend on the tide.' He sees the understanding come into her eyes, and she adds, 'Probably not until nearly dawn.' She glances almost timidly towards the large bed, but then shakes her head and murmurs, 'It's so strange … I've longed for this moment through three endless, lonely years, and now … I can't explain why, not even to myself. I want you so badly, and yet tonight … tonight seems somehow …'

The anguish in her voice almost frightens him. 'Too soon? I understand,' he says gently, although in truth he is unsure if that really is what she means.

Or is it that vast, all-seeing moon that's making us both shy?

'But do you remember that night in Burdigala – that sultry July night when there was a bright half-moon in the sky ... and afterwards, when we lay naked side by side on your bed and whispered of the future?'

Her face lights up in a radiant smile. 'Of course I do. The memory of that night ... I don't think I could have endured these last three years without it.'

'So why don't we pretend that it's that night again? We'll lie in each other's arms and talk about the future – you and I, together against the world.'

He sets his cup down on the table and begins, very gently, to unlace the drawstring that closes the high neckline of her dress. He eases it off her shoulders, the shadows cast by the lamplight accentuating the dark cleft between her breasts.

'Kiss me!' That low, urgent voice again.

There is a muted scuffling from behind the door. They both hear it, and both tense. Saturninus raises a finger to his lips, then takes three long paces and snatches the door open a few inches. Nothing. He opens it wider. Outside there is nobody to be seen. He cocks his head to one side, listens, and detects a creak from the staircase at the other end of the corridor. Closing the door behind him he strides to the head of the stairs, just in time to see Huctius disappearing around the bottom step. He breathes an imprecation on the boy, then turns and retraces his steps.

Pascentia meets him in the doorway, her dress again laced neatly to her throat, carrying the tray with the two bowls, both cups and the flagon balanced on it. 'Shame on you, soldier, trying to seduce a poor country girl,' she scolds with affected primness. 'Let's go and see Trencorix, and then, afterwards, we'll have the night and the moon all to ourselves ...' Suddenly quiet and serious, she adds, 'And perhaps we'll find a place where there are no prying eyes, where we can dream ourselves back to that villa in Burdigala.'

Saturninus smiles ruefully, then makes as if to tickle her ribs.

'No you don't,' she giggles, swerving agilely past his outstretched arms before trotting off down the corridor.

He catches up with her at the foot of the stairs, and while she goes to seek out and hand the tray to Huctius, he settles his account with Necalames.

The little man appears worried by his guests' unexpectedly early departure, and enquires anxiously if the room had been to the Primicerius's entire satisfaction.

'It was fine, Necalames, just fine. And the meal too,' Saturninus adds, to save him asking. 'But I can't stay longer ... Civil guard business,' he whispers.

Outside, as they stroll back towards the guard post, Saturninus curls his arm around her waist and she snuggles her head against his shoulder.

While she waits, hidden in the shadows, he tells a sleepy Ulpius Vassedo what he has learnt at The Cockerel, and why he is going to investigate now, instead of waiting until morning. He declines Vassedo's offer of assistance, using Pascentia's excuse that what Trencorix saw may turn out to be nothing more than a floating log. Vassedo appears to have forgotten about the cuirass, and Saturninus doesn't remind him. He will collect it tomorrow, on their way back from the estuary.

One of the troopers brings Antares round from the stables. Saturninus checks the tightness of the saddle girth, then walks the horse through the streets, one hand holding the reins, the other gently caressing her wrist. At the edge of the town he halts.

'Come on, you've done enough walking.' He stoops down and interlaces his fingers.

'Why, thank you kindly, Primicerius,' she replies, carefully placing one foot into his cupped hand and letting him propel her gently upwards until she sits side-saddle, facing him. 'Aren't you going to climb up behind me?' she enquires innocently.

Saturninus pulls a face, aware she knows as well as he that the shape of the military saddle with its leather horns – two horizontal at the front, two vertical at the back, designed to cradle a cavalryman during a charge – does not permit such an arrangement.

They take the stoned track that leads westwards and soon begins to drop down to the plain of the Sabrina. The full moon is now high in the near-cloudless southern sky, turning the night into an eerie parody of day: sinister, even frightening to some, but not to them. Antares ambles along, while they whisper and laugh together like the carefree lovers they have become, the rest of that magical night and all their lives stretching out before them. They make good time, and not long after midnight they are less than a mile from the Sabrina, the faint tang of salt water carrying on the breeze. It conjures up memories of distant places where they once walked together, and one day soon might walk again.

CHAPTER FORTY-SIX

In the time of another full moon.

It is a little over a year later, in the long evening of a fine June day. A young woman and a tall, lean soldier have just met again at a place some miles to the west of Ovilregis, out on the plain that lies between the Long Limestone Hills and the wide estuary of the Flumen Sabrina.

The young woman is slim, with a pale face and hair the colour of new-tarnished copper. Sitting on a small mound amid a sea of flowering grasses, she waits as Canio dismounts and ties his reins to a nearby tree stump.

Determined to show no sign of nervousness, she smiles and asks, 'Are you fully recovered now?'

'Recovered from what, my pretty one?'

'From whatever it was you were suffering from when we met in Corinium.'

'Oh, that. It was just tiredness. The pressures of command, you understand?'

'Yes, of course. But happily the medicine you were drinking seems to have revived you. Tell me, where exactly did you find his horse? ... your horse, I should say. Necalames remembered you saying that it was somewhere around here, but he didn't know exactly where.' She is trying to imagine how the place must look in moonlight.

Canio sighs. 'Ah, poor old Necalames: he's not the man he used to be.'

'So I was told ... although I don't think that anyone who lived through the time of wolves will ever see the world quite as they did before. Saturninus's horse though, where – ?'

'Antares was just over there, about a hundred paces from where you're sitting now. The morning sun shining on his coat made it look as red as fire.'

'I suppose that's why Saturninus called him Antares,' she murmurs. Seeing a look she takes for uncertainty on Canio's face, she adds, 'It's the red star of summer – '

'In the constellation of The Scorpion. It was mentioned to me once.'

'By Saturninus?'

'No, Antares himself brought it up in conversation one day.'

She smiles tolerantly. 'Did he still have his saddle on?'

'Saddle? He did, yes – saddle, bridle, boar spear, saddlebags …'

'But nothing in the saddlebags?'

'There was his cloak and the usual odds and ends – that's all I can recall. Why do you ask?'

'Oh, it's just that someone in Corinium told me that he put something else in.'

'Something like a lyre?

'You knew?'

'Bupitus told me. But it wasn't there. It must have been lost when …' Canio gives an apologetic shrug.

'You don't still think the Hibernians from that first curragh killed them, do you?' she gently chides him.

Canio gives her a sardonic look. 'What else can I think?'

'Then why weren't their bodies ever found?'

'They reckoned the Hibernians must have thrown them into the estuary.'

She shakes her head. 'I heard that when that curragh was last sighted – on the night *before* the full moon – it was already coming down the Sabrina, probably on its way back to report to their main fleet. Didn't they reckon it had only come to find out whether there were any war galleys from the *Classis Britannica* stationed in the estuary?'

'Some thought so.'

'So by the following night – the night when Saturninus came to Ovilregis – it should have been long gone,' she continues patiently.

Canio appears unconvinced. 'Well, if it wasn't the Hibernians that got them, then what did?'

'Nothing got them.' Before Canio can object, she asks, 'It's not far from the estuary to here, is it? Not far for a horse to wander?'

'About half a mile, I suppose.'

'And at the estuary it would have been easy enough to board a ship coming down the Sabrina.'

'No – ships can't get close-in to the shore. Too shallow, like a seashore. Haven't you ever been there?'

'Not this far south,' she admits. 'But are you saying it's not even possible that they got away by sea?'

Canio blows out a long breath. 'I suppose they could have done, if they'd really been minded to. They could have used the old jetty that was built to load the grain ships. Ships do sometimes wait there for the tide to turn and the water level to drop far enough for the pilots to see the channels between the mudflats. But Saturninus wouldn't have just sailed away with his sweetheart, not if he thought the invasion was coming.'

'But why should he have thought it was coming? One solitary curragh – which nobody then was even sure existed – doesn't make an invasion.'

Canio still looks doubtful. 'But this supposed ship of yours – it was night, remember, and ships don't sail down the estuary at night for fear of running onto the mudflats.' He appears to reflect for a moment, then corrects himself. 'Not often they don't anyway.'

'But there was a full moon to see by, remember? And if they'd sailed on down the west coast of Gaul, then it would have been weeks before Saturninus even heard of the invasions.'

'Gaul? Now why would Saturninus want to go to Gaul? Did he or his sweetheart have kin there?'

She hesitates, fingering the large copper coin that hangs, medallion-like, from a thin cord around her neck. Looking down, first at Julian's bearded face and then at the great bull standing beneath its twin stars, she says, 'I heard that Pascentia spoke of a villa in ... in Gaul, somewhere. A place surrounded by endless rows of vines in a rolling countryside. Perhaps, after Saturninus had talked with Trencorix, they came across a ship taking on or setting ashore other passengers. And so they simply decided to go, there and then, while that magic full moon was still lighting their way, before the dawn could come and break its spell. Maybe, as they stood together on that jetty in the moonlight, the thought came to them that the ship had been guided there by some god ... or goddess. And that if they didn't go then, such a chance would never come again. Don't you think that's possible?' she asks. She is awkwardly aware that she has revealed more of her own thoughts and hopes than she had intended.

'Well, it could have happened that way – and perhaps it did,' Canio concedes. 'At least that would account for why no one ever found their bodies.'

She smiles, but Canio is looking eastwards. She thinks she understands that look. 'It won't take long to get back to Ovilregis, not on Antares. Plenty of time to finish telling me what happened that day.'

'Oh, I will, don't worry. But I promised someone that I'd be back there by nightfall.'

'Ah – do I know the lady?'

Canio gives her a sly look. 'Tell me, just why are you so interested in what became of Saturninus – were you a sweetheart of his too?'

She should have anticipated the question, but she hadn't. 'Oh no, nothing like that ... I only met him the once, shortly before he disappeared.' Her face feels suddenly hot, and she looks away from Canio. 'He told me about his dream of Caelofernus, and promised he'd come back when ... he told you about the dream, didn't he?'

'Yes, he told me.'

There is a slightly awkward silence, then she says quickly, 'What happened at Ovilregis when they heard that Saturninus's horse had been found wandering here?'

'There was something of a panic. Ulpius Vassedo – he was centenarius in charge of the garrison there – set off at the gallop, with four of his men. And me.'

'But why were you in Ovilregis – I heard you'd been sent to Glevum?'

'And so I had, but one thing leads to another: when I got back to Corinium –'

'The following morning, wasn't it – ?'

'I heard that Saturninus might have gone off to the Sabrina Estuary, all alone. So I came after him ... As it happens, there was something else that I wanted to see him about too.'

'And what was that?'

'Oh, nothing that matters now.'

'No: time changes our perception of what matters and what doesn't ... Necalames said that after searching around here you went to Aust Cliffs with some of the men from Ovilregis.'

'I did. And we waited there, me and a couple of troopers called Bassus and Maenalis, until late in the afternoon, when the other two turned up. They'd been searching along the shoreline, looking for Saturninus.'

'And they'd found nothing?'

'Not a trace. But it wasn't long after those two arrived that young Maenalis nudged me and said, "See over there – what do you make of that?" And we looked to the south, over towards Abona, and there was smoke – thick columns of it rising up from two places a mile or so apart. They wanted to go and investigate, but I said no: I knew trouble when I saw it. So we waited and watched, and by and by another fire started, further east than the other two. Just a small drift of whitish smoke it was at first, but it soon grew thicker and darker like the others. And then we saw them.'

'The Hibernians?'

Canio nods. 'The sun was about a foot above the horizon when Bassus suddenly shouted out, all excited, "Will you look at that!" and pointed down the estuary. And there they were: hundreds of those damned curraghs coming out of the sea haze, across almost the full width of the estuary – and it must be all of two miles wide downstream from the cliffs.

'By then the tide had turned and was sweeping them up the Sabrina. In the distance they put me in mind of those beetles that go skimming across the surface of a pool when a shadow falls on them. And as they came nearer I remember seeing the men in them, plain as anything, their dark heads like rows of coffin nails.'

'And that was late in the afternoon,' she muses aloud. 'So if Saturninus and Pascentia were on board a ship that had come down the estuary during the previous night, they would have been well out to sea long before the Hibernians arrived.'

'Yes, I suppose they would – if your goddess had been watching over them,' Canio adds drily.

'I believe she was.'

Canio just grunts. 'Anyway, I'm sure you know the rest. We warned everyone in Ovilregis – but what could we do against so many? And then there were the Saxons over to the east as well, although of course we didn't know about those bastards then ...' Canio stops and glances towards the north-west, where the sun is already beginning to sink below a line of distant Cambrian hills.

She too gazes at the setting sun, wondering if Saturninus and Pascentia are watching that same sunset in far-off Burdigala, the shared experience uniting them and her across the long, estranging miles. Then she smiles at Canio and slips down off the mound. 'I'm sorry – I've kept you too long from your appointment at Ovilregis.'

'Oh, it's not that important. Besides, I've a little business proposition that I'd like to put to you.'

This is unexpected. 'Now? Can't it wait until later? I'd rather like to be alone here, for a little while ... I can't explain exactly why,' she concludes apologetically.

Canio looks as though he is about to object, then appears to change his mind. He shrugs. 'All right, if that's what you want – but you will meet me at The Cockerel later tonight, like we agreed?'

'I'll be there, don't worry ... And you can put your little business proposition to me then.'

Vilbia waits until Canio has re-mounted Antares, waved farewell, and ridden out of sight. Then she strolls over to the old cemetery, which lies half-hidden in the lush greenery of midsummer, some two hundred yards from the spot where Antares was found wandering a little over a year before. Tall flowering grasses grow here, just as they grow all around, their feathery heads trembling in the cooling breeze. Catching a faint, delicate perfume she glances around and sees a tangle of dog roses trailing over the top of the nearest of the ancient tombstones. Impulsively she reaches up, picks one of the deep pink, five-petalled flowers and breathes in the rose's heady fragrance, intense after the heat of the day.

Still holding it, she begins wandering through that peaceful place, trying to picture Saturninus and Pascentia travelling past a year ago, imagining what they are murmuring to each other in the moonlight as they plan a new life together. Now and then she pauses and looks more closely at the time-blurred image of a long-forgotten man or woman, or at an inscription cut into the mellow, sun-warmed stone.

Then she notices, on the far side of the cemetery, one stone which stands slightly apart from the others. From where she is now, only its blank back is visible, and as she gazes at it there comes a vague curiosity to learn what is written on its other side. She walks over to the massive stone, as tall as a man, nearly three feet wide and a hand's span thick. At first she is unable to make out any words, most of the once-crisp lettering having been degraded by the frosts of countless winters, or obscured by great crusted blotches of yellow and orange lichens.

And then her searching eyes stop abruptly, as they find the

one legible part of the name of the long-dead man above whose ashes the stone was raised, the part over which the surrounding lichens seem unable to grow. She reads and re-reads the name, and as she does so the rose slips from her fingers and drops unnoticed to the ground. She reaches out and slowly traces, one by one, all eleven letters with her fingertips, unwilling to believe what her eyes tell her is true. But the name really is CAELOFERNUS.

In bewildered fascination she stares at the name, as one by one the questions without answers stumble into her mind. She stands there, still as the stone itself, while the light slowly fades and submerges the letters back into the blank anonymity of its face.

At last, long after the red sun has sunk completely below the far-away Cambrian hills, she whispers, 'And behind that mask ... Oh Saturninus, what was it that you said about your dream? ... That it might have been like a dog barking in the night at something hiding out there in the darkness – something that it hears but cannot see? ... Did you see something come out of the darkness, here on that night a year ago? Come back and tell me ... *please.*' She waits, almost as if expecting a reply, but of course none comes.

And now the night breeze is rising, and as it sighs mournfully through the grasses and the old stones she hears, mixed in with the wind, what sounds to her like laughter, mocking and cruel. Gazing warily around, in the deceptive twilight she imagines that she sees something move among the stones. A scream rises in her throat, yet from somewhere courage comes and she waits, silent and still, for whatever it is to come closer. But nothing appears, and then the breeze itself fades and vanishes. Her face set and taut, she begins edging backwards, then turns and starts walking quickly away from that place, back towards the dark line of the Long Limestone Hills from which she came.

And above those hills, in the south-eastern sky, she sees a huge full moon silently rising, its ancient all-seeing face lit glowing gold by the light of the vanished sun. It is a face familiar and loved since childhood, and now seemingly so close that she could stretch out an arm and touch it as it floats there between the earth and the stars. But her childhood is gone, and she knows it now for what it really is: an alien land, unknown and unknowable, its dark other face forever hidden. As if it were itself a dream.

HISTORICAL NOTES, GAZETTEER
AND MISCELLANEA

1. EMPERORS
Galerius: Caesar (junior emperor) AD 293-305, Augustus (senior emperor) 305-311. Campaigned successfully against the Persians in Mesopotamia 296-298 and made territorial gains. These gains were handed back after the emperor Julian's death in 363, in exchange for the Persians agreeing to allow the survivors of the invading Roman army to retreat relatively unmolested.

Constantine I (The Great): AD 307-337. The first emperor to convert to Christianity. He believed that his victory over his rival Maxentius at the Milvian Bridge in Rome in 312 was due to the intervention of the Christian god, and so, in 313, issued the Edict of Milan which abolished the penalties for practising Christianity. The public emergence of the Church during his reign mirrored the beginnings of the slow transformation of the ancient world into the medieval one. Most emperors after Constantine were at least nominally Christian.

Sons of **Constantine I:**
Constans: AD 337-350. Catholic Christian. Ruler of the western half of the empire. Murdered at instigation of Magnentius early in 350. Said to have been outspokenly contemptuous of his soldiers and consequently unpopular with them.

Constantius II: AD 337-361. Arian Christian. Ruler of the eastern half of the empire 337-350, then augustus of the entire empire following the death of Constans.

Magnentius: AD 350-353. Probably pagan (but sought the support of Catholic Christians against the Arian Constantius). An outstanding military commander of barbarian origin, he seized power in Gaul, but after initial successes which gave him control of much of the western half of the empire he was defeated at the terrible battle of Mursa in September 351 (see below). He retreated back into Gaul, but after further defeats committed suicide in August 353. He enjoyed considerable support in Britain, which resulted in reprisals against his followers after his fall.

Julian: AD 360-363. Pagan. Appointed Caesar by his cousin Constantius II in 355. Rebelled against him in 360, but Constantius died of fever before a battle could be fought. He invaded Persia, but was mortally wounded and died on 26th June 363.

Valentinian I: AD 364-375. Christian. Probably the last really competent emperor to rule the western half of the empire, but a harsh man with a violent temper which was to cause the stroke which killed him.

2. HISTORICAL EVENTS

AD 343: Invasion scare in Britannia. Details are scarce, but it seems that Constans crossed from the Continent in mid-winter in response to an incursion by tribes from north of Hadrian's wall.

AD 350: January. Magnentius proclaimed himself emperor in Gaul.

AD 351: September. Battle of Mursa Major (modern Osijek, 100 miles north-west of Belgrade). It was said to have been the bloodiest battle of the fourth century, with Magnentius losing 24,000 men and Constantius 30,000. Although Constantius was nominally the victor, his losses were so great that he did not pursue Magnentius but retreated back towards the East.

AD 353: August. After a final defeat at Mons Seleucus in Gaul, Magnentius committed suicide at Lugdunum (Lyons).

AD 353-5: Constantius II sent the imperial notary Paulus to Britain to track down supporters of the Magnentian rebellion. He became notorious for his zeal and acquired the nickname 'Catena' (Chain) due to his malignant skill in linking together facts and rumours to entrap suspects, whom he then sent in irons to Constantius. He was burnt alive following the treason trials under Julian at Chalcedon in late 361 or early 362.

AD 359: The Persians besieged, captured and sacked the city of Amida on the upper Tigris (then part of Roman territory) after a siege of some 73 days between late July and early October.

AD 363: Julian invaded Persia with the intention of ending the constant pressure on the eastern frontier. After initial successes he reached Ctesiphon, the Persian capital, but for reasons that are now unclear he did not attempt to capture the city and began a retreat northwards, only to be mortally wounded in battle soon after.

AD 367: The *Barbarica Conspiratio*, when Britain was invaded by waves of apparently co-ordinated barbarian tribes from beyond the frontiers – Picts from north of Hadrian's wall, Saxons and Franks from across the North Sea, and Scotti and Attacotti from Hibernia (Ireland) and the Western Isles.

Following the *Conspiratio* came a period of near-anarchy, with bands of army deserters roaming the countryside, the situation further complicated by a short-lived bid for power by a Pannonian exile called Valentinus.

3. FOURTH CENTURY ARMY RANKS, etc.

Comes: An officer either commanding one of the units of the prestigious mobile field army, or holding a special commission such as the defence of the city of Amida

Dux: An officer commanding a static frontier army. Although in medieval Latin texts *comes* is translated as count and *dux* as duke, in the late Roman army a *comes* outranked a *dux*.

While the old-established army units retained their ranks of *centurion*, *optio*, etc, in the new army units of the fourth century, the NCO ranks were (in descending order of seniority):
Primicerius
Ducenarius
Centenarius
Biarchus

The 'Civil Guard': in the absence of hard facts, I have made several assumptions, namely:

(a) That there must have been some form of policing organisation. I have called it the Civil Guard and assumed that it was a paramilitary organisation, largely staffed by ex-soldiers or men seconded from army units.

(b) That it was the successor to the corps of *beneficiarii consularis* of the earlier empire.

(c) That the titles of its ranks were *primicerius*, *ducenarius*, etc.

The *Classis Britannica*: A fleet of war galleys stationed at various points around the coast of Southern England and South Wales to intercept pirates and barbarian raiders.

4. GAZETTEER

(Names marked * are my fictional names for real places whose Roman names are now lost).

Abona: Bristol.
Alaunarraco*: Uley, Gloucestershire.
Amida: city on Upper Tigris, now in south-east Turkey (Diyarbakir).
Arcadolium*: small town near Chesterton-on-Fosse, Warwickshire.
Bononia: Boulogne.
Burdigala: Bordeaux.
Colonia Agrippina: Cologne, Germany.
Confluentes: Koblenz, Germany.
Corinium (Dobunnorum): Cirencester.
Corvusida*: Notgrove long barrow, Gloucestershire.
Cunetio: Mildenhall (Wiltshire).
Dornolana*: Dorn, near Moreton-in-Marsh, Gloucestershire.
Dubris: Dover.
Durnovaria: Dorchester (Dorset).
Fonscolnis*: Wycomb, near Andoversford, Gloucestershire.
(Flumen) Leucara*: River Windrush.
Glevum: Gloucester.
Londinium: London.
Lugdunum: Lyons.
Maglocrouco*: Belas Knap long barrow, above Winchcombe, Gloucestershire.
Moguntiacum: Mainz, Germany.
Mursa Major: a city in the province of Pannonia (Osijek, eastern Croatia, 100 miles north-west of Belgrade).
Ovilregis*: Kingscote, Gloucestershire.
(Flumen) Sabrina: River Severn.
(Flumen) Tamesis: River Thames.
Treveri: Trier, Germany.
Vadumleucara*: Bourton-on-the-Water, Gloucestershire.
Venta: Winchester.

5. THE PARCAE

The Roman name for the Fates, the three daughters of Night: Clotho, who spun the thread of a man's life; Lachesis, who decided the length of that life-thread; and Atropos, who cut the thread when it was time for that man to die.